THE BILLIONAIRES COLLECTION

High-powered negotiations, exotic locales and lavish parties…marriages of convenience, surprise pregnancies and undeniable passions. This 2-in-1 collection will take you into the luxurious world of the rich and powerful, where all that you could ever desire is at your fingertips.…

But for these irresistible tycoons, the thing they want the most is the thing they'll have to work the hardest to attain.… Because the stakes are never higher for these passionate, jet-setting men than when they're fighting for the affection of the women they love.

KATE HEWITT

has worked a variety of different jobs, from drama teacher to editorial assistant to church youth worker, but writing romance is the best one yet. She also writes short stories and serials for women's magazines, and all her stories celebrate the healing and redemptive power of love. Kate lives in a tiny village with her husband, four children and an overly affectionate golden retriever. Visit her online at her website, www.kate-hewitt.com.

KATE HEWITT

Wed in Greece

HARLEQUIN® THE BILLIONAIRES COLLECTION

Recycling programs
for this product may
not exist in your area.

ISBN-13: 978-0-373-60616-0

WED IN GREECE
Copyright © 2014 by Harlequin Books S.A.

The publisher acknowledges the copyright holder
of the individual works as follows:

THE GREEK TYCOON'S CONVENIENT BRIDE
Copyright © 2008 by Kate Hewitt
BOUND TO THE GREEK
Copyright © 2011 by Kate Hewitt

This edition published by arrangement with Harlequin Books S.A.

For questions and comments about the quality of this book,
please contact us at CustomerService@Harlequin.com.

Printed in U.S.A.

CONTENTS

THE GREEK TYCOON'S
CONVENIENT BRIDE

PROLOGUE

HE WATCHED HER from the shadows.

Lukas Petrakides stood behind the camouflaging fronds of a palm tree, his eyes tracking the young woman as she slipped from her hotel room onto the silky sand of the beach.

Dark, wild curls blew around her face and her slender arms crept around herself in a hug that was pitiably vulnerable.

He hadn't meant to stumble upon her—or anyone—here. He'd been consumed with a restless energy, his mind full of plans for the new resort that had just opened here in the Languedoc, minutes from a sleepy village, stretching out to a pristine beach.

He'd needed to escape the confines of his own suite, his own mind, even if just for a moment.

The wind and the waves shimmering beneath a diamond sky had soothed him, and he'd slipped off his shoes, rolled up the cuffs of his trousers, and strode down the smooth, white sand.

And had found her.

He didn't know what had drawn him to her, why that slender form seemed to hold so much grace, beauty, desire.

Sorrow.

Her head was bowed, her shoulders slightly slumped. The look of someone in grief or pain.

Still he felt a blaze of feeling deep within. A need. A connection.

He took one step towards her, an impulse, an instinct, before checking himself. He knew his presence here would cause questions, complications he couldn't afford.

He had to keep his reputation above the faintest reproach. He always had. So he stood in the shadows, watched her walk towards the waves, and wondered.

She stood on the shore, the waves lapping her bare feet, and gazed out at the calm waters of the Mediterranean. She threw one worried glance over her shoulder towards the sliding glass door of her hotel room, as if someone were there, waiting, watching, as he was.

Who waited for her in there? A boyfriend? Husband? A lover?

Whoever it was, it was none of his business.

If he were a different man—with a different life, different responsibilities—he might not check that impulse. He might walk up to her, say hello, make conversation.

Nothing sleazy or sordid; he didn't want that. Just honest conversation, a shared moment. Something real and warm and alive.

The desire for it shook him, vibrated deep in his being. He shook his head. It was never going to happen.

A bitter smile twisted his lips as he watched her. She dropped her arms, raised her face to the moon-bathed sky. The breeze off the sea moulded her cheap sundress to the slight contours of her body. Her curves were boyish at best, yet Lukas still felt a stirring of desire.

A desire he wouldn't act upon. Couldn't. As the only son of his father, the only heir to the Petrakides real estate fortune, he carried too many responsibilities to shrug them off lightly for a mere dalliance with a slip of a girl. For a moment's connection.

He would never let it be anything more.

His grey eyes hardened to pewter. He thought he heard her give a little shuddering sigh, but perhaps it was the wind. Perhaps it was his imagination.

Perhaps that sound had come from him.

She jerked her head around sharply, and he drew in a breath as he stepped back, deeper into the shadows. Had he made a sound—one that she'd heard?

Her gaze swept the beach, fastened on the sliding glass door to her hotel room. She hadn't seen him, he realised; something from inside the room—a person? A man?—had beckoned her.

Her body sagged slightly, her arms dropping to her sides, her head bowed as she turned to head back inside.

Lukas watched her go, wondered who—what—had called her. Why did she look so sorrowful, as if the weight of the world rested on those slight shoulders?

He knew how that felt. He understood about crippling weight.

The sliding glass door closed with a click, and, suppressing another wave of longing, Lukas turned to head back to his private suite.

CHAPTER ONE

RHIANNON DAVIES CHECKED her reflection one last time before nodding to the babysitter.

'Right...I should only be an hour or two.' She glanced uncertainly at the baby sitting on the floor, chewing on her house keys and looking at her with dark, soulful eyes. 'She might need a nap in a little while.'

The babysitter, a stout Frenchwoman with an impassive expression, nodded once before stooping to pick Annabel up in her arms.

Rhiannon watched, noticed how the older woman's arms went comfortably around Annabel's chubby middle and carried her with a confident ease she had yet to feel herself.

'I don't think she'll cry,' she ventured, and was answered with another brisk nod.

In the two weeks since Annabel had been in her care, the baby had hardly cried at all. Despite the whirl of events, the change of both home and mother, she simply regarded the world with big, blank eyes. Rhiannon suspected the poor mite was in shock.

That was why she was here, she told herself firmly, not for the first time, ignoring the pangs of guilt and longing stabbing her middle. Her heart.

She had come to France, to this exclusive resort, to

Lukas Petrakides, to give Annabel some stability. To give her love.

Annabel stuck a fist in her mouth and chewed while gazing in blank curiosity at the woman who'd come so abruptly into her life.

Rhiannon.

They hadn't bonded, Rhiannon acknowledged, hadn't really tried. It was too strange, too difficult, too sad.

She'd never even held a baby before Leanne, pale-faced, wide-eyed, had thrust a sleeping Annabel into her arms. *Take her.*

Rhiannon's arms had closed around the solid little form as a matter of instinct, but her arms had been at awkward angles and she hadn't been sure how to cuddle.

Annabel had woken up with a furious screech.

'Goodbye, sweetheart.' Hesitantly Rhiannon stroked one satiny cheek. Annabel simply blinked.

It was better this way, she knew. Better they didn't get attached. Then it would be so much easier to say goodbye.

A lump formed in her throat; she forced it down. She would do what she had to do to secure Annabel's future and, more importantly, her happiness.

No matter what the cost.

She stole one last look at her reflection: dark curls, mostly tamed behind her ears, a face pale but with a sprinkling of freckles in stark relief, a smart if inexpensive skirt, and a matching sleeveless top in aquamarine. Modest, businesslike. Appropriate.

Suppressing a sigh, she slipped out of the hotel room.

The sun was bright, the air fresh and clean as she walked along the outside corridor. The newest Petra Resort, situated in this remote, exclusive corner of the

Languedoc province of France, was simple, spare and elegant. Having arrived in darkness, she now took note of the bougainvillaea spilling from terracotta pots, the climbing vines, the clean colours.

It had cost her half a month's salary—far more than she could possibly afford—to book even the cheapest room at the resort on its opening weekend. If there hadn't been a last-minute cancellation she wouldn't have got in at all.

Taking a deep, cleansing breath that was meant to steady her jangling nerves, Rhiannon hoped this journey would be worth it. For Annabel.

She closed her eyes briefly. This was all so, so crazy.

Only a fortnight ago Leanne had exploded back into her life—and out again just as quickly. Leaving confusion and Annabel in her wake. And the name of Annabel's father.

Rhiannon bit her lip as fresh doubts assailed her, washed over her in a sickening wave. What if Lukas refused to talk to her? Or, worse, denied his responsibility? When she'd attempted to contact him by telephone she hadn't made it past the first hurdle.

We'll give Mr Petrakides your message.

Yeah, right. The disbelief and scorn had been obvious, shaming. They hadn't even taken her number or her name.

Then she'd read in the local newspaper that a new Petra resort was opening in France, seen that Lukas Petrakides would be there at a reception for the resort's first guests. She knew it was a chance—perhaps the only one—for Annabel to know her father. Her family.

Every child needed parents. Real ones, not strangers who took them out of duty, obligation.

She believed that with all her heart. She wanted more for Annabel. She wanted to give her a family. She didn't know where she herself would fit into that equation, if at all. The thought had first chilled her; now it merely numbed.

She understood about sacrifice. She was prepared.

Rhiannon walked down several corridors, looking for the lounge that the resort had advertised as the location for the 'Meet and Greet' reception.

Whenever a new Petra resort opened—and now there had to be half a dozen—Lukas Petrakides, the founder's son and CEO of the company, came to meet with his guests.

His fans, Rhiannon thought wryly. For since learning the name of Annabel's father, she'd researched the man and come up with some information. Although reclusive, Lukas Petrakides was adored by the Greek public and press alike—considered broodingly handsome, unfailingly polite, stunningly charismatic.

Rhiannon smiled at the thought. Surely the magazines had to be making some of that up?

They had to make something up, for Lukas Petrakides was notorious for not providing gossip for the rumour mill. Unlike other Mediterranean tycoons, he didn't appear in public with the latest model or starlet on his arm. His only escort was one of his three older sisters. Photographs were rare. He didn't party, didn't drink, didn't dance.

Didn't do much of anything, it seemed, except work.

Considering such a reputation, Rhiannon couldn't quite dismiss the faint sense of disbelief that Lukas Petrakides had, at least on one occasion, put aside his own responsibilities for a weekend of no-strings romance. Sex.

One person had cracked his armour and found if not his heart then his libido.

Leanne… And the result of that union was back in her hotel room.

Rhiannon dragged in a shuddering breath, needing the air, the courage. She hadn't been able to formulate a plan beyond the basic: book two nights' accommodation at the Petra Resort, attend the reception, find Lukas Petrakides.

And then…?

Her mind skittered frantically, in time with her rapid pulse, even as her heart provided the answer.

And then he'll want her. He'll love her, he'll take her into his home, his heart. They'll be a family, happy, loving, perfect. The End.

Rhiannon's mouth twisted in painful acknowledgement of this fairy tale. Life didn't work that way. It hadn't for her.

But surely it could for Annabel?

She knew Lukas was a man of responsibility; the tabloids held him up as a paragon. It was his shining reputation for integrity, honour, and an unfailing sense of duty that had made the decision for Rhiannon.

This was a man who could—and she prayed would—take on the mantle of fatherhood without a qualm or quiver. A man who would welcome his daughter with open arms.

She finally came to a pair of double doors, guarded by two impassive-looking security guards who asked for her room number.

One of them scanned a list. 'Name?'

'Rhiannon Davies.' Her heart pounded but at least her voice sounded calm.

The guard nodded brusquely, and Rhiannon was given entry. She slipped between the doors, taking in the diamond-spangled crowd with a sinking heart.

She didn't fit in here, and it was obvious. This was a party for the rich and famous, or at least the socially savvy. Not her. Never her.

She scanned the room, a blush rising to her cheeks as she caught the curious stares, the scornful looks. She knew her outfit was inexpensive, but it was hardly tawdry or inappropriate. Yet Rhiannon felt as if she was standing there naked by the way a few well-heeled, skimpily clad society she-devils were looking at her.

For heaven's sake, *they* were wearing fewer clothes than she was. She lifted her chin, stiffened her spine. She didn't care what anyone thought about her; all that mattered was getting to Lukas.

Telling him about Annabel.

She scanned the room again, took a few steps inside. And saw him.

Once her gaze fastened on his form, she wondered how she could have missed him for a moment. He was tall—taller than most men—dressed in an elegant grey suit, perfectly cut, moulding to his powerful shoulders and trim hips. He leaned against the bar, a drink in one hand, although Rhiannon saw it was virtually un-touched.

She saw his suave smile, imagined she could hear his dry chuckle across the room, watched his grace-ful movements. And still the thought sprang unbidden into her mind.

He's unhappy. He's lonely.

She shook her head slightly; the idea was ridiculous. Who could be either lonely or unhappy with the crème of society jostling for his attention, for one word from those sculpted lips?

She almost laughed at herself; Lukas Petrakides was every bit as handsome as the tabloids claimed he was. She had expected to be intimidated; she hadn't expected to be affected.

Squaring her shoulders, Rhiannon waded into the expensive fray. She walked towards the bar, stopping a few feet before the man himself.

Uncertainty washed over her with the scent of expensive, cloying perfume from the women jostling her, queuing for Lukas's attention. She hadn't considered the crowds, the difficulty in approaching him. She should have.

She nibbled at her lip as she considered her options. She wanted to speak in private, but she doubted a man like Lukas Petrakides would consider a request for a private conversation from a person like her—plain, poor, socially irrelevant.

Still, there wasn't much else she could do. This was why she had come. Phone calls and letters could be ignored, dismissed. Face to face it would be more difficult for him to ignore or deny...if she was able to speak to him at all.

She was just about to take a step forward when he turned. Saw her. Looked at her almost as if he recognised her...*knew* her. And she felt a sudden penetrating flash of awareness come over her like a shiver, a shock—as if *she* knew him. Impossible. Ridiculous.

Still, the expression in his eyes dried her mouth, her words. Her thoughts. His eyes had been described in the tabloids as grey, but Rhiannon decided that they were silver, the colour of a rain-washed river. A small, tender smile quirked his mouth upwards.

He raised an eyebrow, gestured to the space next to him at the bar even as a matron droned on in French at his other side.

Rhiannon's pulse kicked into gear and a strange new sensation flooded through her—pleasant, fizzy, limb-weakening.

Desire.

All it had taken was one smile, one look from those piercing eyes, one tiny glimmer of tenderness, and she was hooked. Caught.

Was she that desperate? That obvious?

Yet she couldn't deny the connection that seemed to pulse between them across the crowded room, as present and real as if a wire stretched between them, drawing her to him.

She walked towards him, towards the heat flaring in his gaze, as if it were a place she had always meant to go. To be.

He watched, a faint smile curving those exquisite lips, lighting his eyes.

Then she stumbled, caught herself on the bar. Her slick palms curled around cool marble. She heard the low titter of speculative, jealous voices from around her, a mocking wave of sound, and felt a humiliating blush crawl up her throat and colour her face.

Just as well, she told herself. Her clumsiness had broken the spell he'd cast over her, the magic he'd woven. This wasn't about her; it was about Annabel.

She turned to Lukas, and saw in his eyes an expression of gentle amusement.

'*Ça va?*' he asked, and Rhiannon tried to smile.

'Ummm...*ça va bien.*' Her rusty schoolgirl French to the rescue, she thought wryly.

But it obviously didn't impress him, for he smiled slightly and said, 'You're English.'

'Welsh, actually,' she admitted. 'I did a GCSE in French, but it's been a while.'

His smile deepened, his eyes lightened to the shimmering colour of dawn on the sea, and Rhiannon saw he had a dimple in his cheek.

'Can I get you a drink?' He was looking at her again in that assessing way, as if he were taking her in, deciding who she was. Considering his own reaction.

And she was considering hers—the way she leaned towards him, intuitively, a matter of instinct as well as desire. Every sense was humming, every nerve on high alert. When he looked at her in that warm, considering way, every thought in her mind seemed to vaporise. All she could do was feel.

'I'll have a white wine,' she said into the silence.

'Done.' He smiled, scattering her thoughts to the wind, and a glass of wine materialised before her. She took a grateful sip, letting the cool liquid zing pleasantly through her system. She put the glass down, turned to Lukas.

He was looking at her with expectation, yet also with something more. The languorous warmth of male appreciation, the treacherous heat of desire.

It thrilled her. It scared her.

It turned her mind to cotton, her bones to wax. Made her waver. Made her want.

Her mouth was dry, and she licked her lips. Tried to form a thought, a word. A sound.

'Are you here alone?' Lukas asked. His tone was one of polite interest, but his eyes were roaming her figure, stroking her as they flared with a heat Rhiannon felt flicker in her own core.

Could this actually be happening? Was Lukas Petrakides flirting with her? More than flirting; openly wanting. *Her.*

Her heart craved it, feared it. No, he couldn't be. Not him…not with a girl like her. A girl from nowhere, a girl with nothing.

Except a baby. His.

The reminder of Annabel's presence, her need, pulsed demandingly through Rhiannon's mind and heart.

That was why she was here…for Annabel. Only for Annabel.

'Yes, I'm alone,' she finally answered, her voice little more than a croak. She tried to gather her scattered wits and failed. She hadn't expected this reaction—treacherous, molten, overwhelming.

Real.

This was not part of her plan.

'You are?' He sounded surprised, and his gaze flicked over the crowd before coming to rest on her face with penetrating intensity. 'A holiday alone?' he clarified, and Rhiannon's blush deepened.

She really did sound pathetic. If he were flirting with her it had to be out of boredom or pity or both.

Except it didn't feel that way.

'Yes, although…' Now was the time to state her purpose. To mention Annabel.

Why was it the last thing she wanted to do?

'Although…?' he prompted. The matron on his right

had left with a loud sniff, and Rhiannon could feel the speculative stares from the people around them.

They were wondering how a bourgeois bit-piece like her had captured Lukas Petrakides's attention. She couldn't blame them—even if she didn't appreciate the contempt that was drawing like a palpable shroud around her. She was wondering the same thing herself.

'Nothing.' Coward.

'Ah.' There was a moment of silence, pregnant with possibility, heavy with intent. Rhiannon waited, too overwhelmed to speak, too affected to formulate more than a hazy thought…a need.

She didn't want him to go.

She wanted him.

It was ridiculous; it was real. Something pulsed to life between them—something Rhiannon couldn't even understand.

Lukas's mouth twisted in a smile, and he took a sip of wine. He looked undecided for a moment, vulnerably uncertain, and then resolve hardened his eyes, his face, his voice. 'It was nice chatting with you,' he said, and Rhiannon knew it was a dismissal.

For a moment she thought she saw regret shadow his eyes, but it was replaced with a formal cursory courtesy that she suspected was the expression with which he greeted everyone in the room.

If they'd shared a real moment, a connection, it was gone.

And so was her chance.

'Wait.' Lukas had already turned away, and Rhiannon was forced to scrabble at his sleeve. 'I need to say something to you.'

He turned. Hope lit his eyes for one wonderful moment. Rhiannon took a breath.

'I have something you need to hear.'

He stilled. The blank look returned, and suddenly it seemed dangerous.

'What would that be?'

Rhiannon took a breath. The desire she'd felt, the warmth, the connection, were distant memories. All she felt now was uncertainty. Fear. The cold, metallic tang was on her tongue. She was handling this wrong. She knew she was. But if Lukas would only listen to her, then he would understand.

He would accept, and he would be glad. She had to believe that.

'I think it would be better said in private.'

She spoke in a low voice, but still heard the shocked indrawn breaths from the gossipy vultures around her.

'You do?' His voice was soft, musing, but his eyes were as hard as steel.

She kept saying the wrong thing. She saw it in the way he looked at her now, with derision and dislike. What had happened? She didn't understand this world— its politics, its hidden agendas. She just wanted to tell him about his daughter.

'Yes…it is important, I promise. You need to know…' She trailed off uncertainly. She felt tension thrum in the air, in her body. In his.

There was a connection, but it wasn't a good one.

It felt very bad.

'I cannot imagine,' Lukas replied in a voice of lethal quiet, 'that you have anything to say to me that I need to know, Miss…?'

'Davies—Rhiannon Davies. And please believe

me—I do. I only need a moment of your time...' And then a lifetime. But there would—please, God—be other opportunities to discuss their future. Annabel's future.

'I'm afraid I don't have a moment...for you,' Lukas said, his tone chillingly soft.

'No... No... Just wait...' She flung one hand out in appeal; it was ignored. 'You don't understand. Someone else is involved. We have a mutual friend.' Her words came out stilted, strained. Awful. Why hadn't she thought of a better way to handle this?

'I don't think we've ever met,' Lukas said after a tiny pause. 'And I doubt we have any mutual friends.'

They were from different worlds; it was glaringly obvious. He was accustomed to wealth, privilege, power—light years away from her small suburban existence in Wales.

He had power; she had nothing.

Except Annabel. The realisation gave her a much-needed boost of courage.

'No, we haven't met,' she agreed, meeting his gaze unflinchingly. 'But there is someone we both know—both care about. A friend...' Although, according to Leanne, she and Lukas had been a lot more than friendly.

For a moment Rhiannon's mind dwelt on that strangely unwelcome possibility—Lukas and Leanne, bodies entwined, fused. Lips, hips, shoulders, thighs. Passion created, enjoyed, shared. They'd made a child together.

She shook her head. She didn't want to think about it. Hadn't even asked Leanne about the details. A weekend of passion, Leanne had said with a sigh, before naming the father.

Take care of her for me. Don't let her down.

Love her.

That was what this was about. That was why she had come.

Annabel needed love. Real love. The love of her father.

'Someone we both care about?' Lukas repeated, and this time Rhiannon heard more of the steel. The incredulity. Her heart rate sped up, doubled. She nodded.

'Yes... And if you'd just give me a moment in private, I could explain. It would be...worth your while.'

He froze, and Rhiannon felt as if her heart had frozen as well. For a moment everything seemed suspended, still, that terrible moment before the storm hit and the lightning struck.

'Worth my while?' he repeated. It was a simple statement, yet it held a wealth of unpleasant meaning. Alarm prickled along Rhiannon's spine, tingling up her nape as Lukas made eye contact with someone over her shoulder. Something was happening. Something bad.

He gave a brief, almost indiscernible nod, then his icy gaze snapped back to her—unyielding, unmerciful.

She suppressed a shiver.

Had she actually thought this was a gentle man?

'I'm just trying to be polite,' she explained. 'By requesting some privacy—'

'I can be polite,' he replied with silky, lethal intent. 'As a courtesy, I'm letting you know that you have five seconds before my security guards escort you from this room and this resort.'

Shock shot through her, followed by scathing disbelief and, worse, hurt. She should have expected this, but she hadn't. After that first moment she'd thought he might be kind.

Different.

She'd believed what the tabloids said—the image of the man they exalted.

She was a fool.

'You're making a mistake.'

'I don't think so.'

'Please...I don't want anything from you—at least nothing that you wouldn't be prepared to give—' She grabbed his hand; he removed it with distaste.

'Is that so? Because I'm prepared to give you nothing. Goodbye, Miss Davies.'

Before Rhiannon could form a reply, one last appeal, a hand clamped none too gently on her arm.

'This way, miss.'

He was kicking her out! Humiliated fury washed through her in sickening waves as the security guard tugged her firmly from her stool. She stumbled to her feet, threw a hand out to the bar to steady herself.

Lukas Petrakides watched impassively with cool grey eyes.

Rhiannon hated him then.

'You can't do this,' she said in a furious whisper, and he raised one eyebrow.

'Then you don't know me very well.'

'I don't want to know you! I want to *talk* to you!'

The guard was tugging her backwards, and Rhiannon was forced to follow him, stumbling, while a murmur of curious whispers and titters followed her, surrounded her in a mocking chorus.

Lukas watched, arms folded, eyes hard, expression flat.

This was her last chance. Her only hope.

'You have a baby!' she shouted, and was rewarded

with a ripple of shocked murmurs in the crowd and a look of stunned disbelief on Lukas's face before she was pulled through the doorway and out of sight.

CHAPTER TWO

You have a baby.

Lukas barely registered the din of speculative gossip that rang out around him. Someone spoke to him, an excited jabber. He merely shrugged before forcing himself to reply politely.

You have a baby.

Absurd. Impossible. The woman was a liar.

He knew that—knew she was just another common blackmailer, a petty thief looking for a handout.

He'd seen them, dealt with them before. He'd recognised the patter as soon as she'd started, the female flattery disguising the threat underneath.

Mutual friends. Something he needed to hear.

Hardly.

He just didn't understand why he felt so disappointed.

Last night, when he'd seen her on the beach, he'd felt a connection. And then when she'd shown up at the reception, met his gaze, walked towards him with a smile that was tender, uncertain and yet filled with promise, he'd felt it again. Deep, real, alive.

False. All he'd felt was cheap, easy desire. Lust masquerading as need.

His disappointment was no more than he deserved for giving in to desire for something—someone—for even a moment.

Wanting was weakness. Desire was dangerous. He'd seen the shameful results, lived with them every day.

He had responsibilities, duties, and those were what counted. What mattered.

Nothing else did.

Nothing else could.

He knew the drill: his guards would take her to a discreet office kept for just this purpose, make her sign a gagging order, and show her the door.

He'd never see her again.

Yet suddenly he wanted to know. Needed to know just what her game was—what information she pretended to have, what she hoped to get.

Then he'd forget her completely.

'Excuse me… *Pardon*...' He repeated the phrase in several languages as the crowd mingled and jostled for his attention, moving past everyone with firm decision.

He pushed through the double doors, strode down the corridor towards the lobby.

What had she expected? That he would believe her dirty little tale and cut her a cheque? He shook his head slowly, disbelief and fury pouring through him, scalding his soul.

Had she been planning her little manoeuvre last night, on the beach? Was there someone else involved? Some man waiting greedily back in their hotel room?

Or was she playing another game? Selling her story to a tabloid? The gossip rags had so little dirt to dish on him, it wouldn't surprise him if they were paying people to make it up.

He strode into the lobby, heard the flutter of greeting from an army of receptionists and ignored them, making for the small office, its door discreetly tucked behind a potted palm in one corner of the spacious room.

He paused outside the door, listening. Waiting to hear what ridiculous tale she would spin.

'I don't want money!' He heard her furious denial, shook his head. What was she playing for? A bigger bribe?

'Sign this statement, Miss Davies.' Tony, one of his two security guards, spoke with weary patience. 'By signing it you agree not to sell or disclose any information regarding Mr Petrakides, the Petrakides family, or Petrakides Properties. Then you will leave this resort. Petrakides Properties will pay for one night's accommodation in a local hotel as redress. Your belongings will be sent there this evening.'

Lukas heard the silence through the door, felt her incredulity, her fury, her fear. His hand rested on the knob.

'That's not possible.' Her voice was a whisper, with a thread of steel through its core.

'It is in every way possible,' Tony replied flatly. 'And as soon as you sign the statement, it will be put into effect.'

'I'll sign the statement,' Rhiannon replied with barely a waver. 'But you *cannot* throw me out of this resort. There is a baby in my hotel room, and that child belongs to Lukas Petrakides!'

Lukas's hand tightened on the knob as shock and outrage battled for precedence. Had the lying slut actually brought a baby as proof? Used an innocent child in her despicable scheme? It was vile. He should have her arrested, prosecuted…

The Petrakides family's policy, however, was to remove any instigators as quickly and quietly as possible. Prosecution, in this case, was not an option.

For a brief moment Lukas imagined his father's reaction when the tabloids printed the story about his so-
called child. He knew someone at the party would dish
the goods.

His mouth tightened; his heart hardened. She wasn't
worth the trouble she'd put him to.

'If that is so,' Lukas's security guard said after a tiny,
tense pause, 'then I will escort you to your hotel room
to collect this child. Then you will go.'

There was a silence. When her voice came out, however, it shocked him. It was small and sad and defeated.

'You have this all wrong,' Rhiannon said. 'I don't
want to blackmail anyone—least of all Lukas Petrakides. I simply have reason to believe his daughter
is in my care, and I thought he should know that…know
her.' This last came out in a sorry, aching whisper that
created an answering throb in Lukas's midsection. His
gut, not his heart.

She was sincere, even if she was mistaken. Or she
was a phenomenal actress. He forced himself not to
care. Then he shook his head slowly. She had to be acting, faking. How on earth she could possibly believe she
had his child when he had never seen her before—what
could she be playing at?

Still he paused. Wondered. Wanted to know.

And he realised with damning weakness—need—
that he wanted to see her again.

He turned the knob.

RHIANNON CHOKED BACK a scream of frustration and defeat. This had gone so horribly, horribly wrong. No one
believed her; no one even cared.

From Lukas Petrakides down, all she'd come up

against were blank walls of indifference, unconcern. They didn't care what she had to say, what truth there might be to her tale.

They wanted her gone.

'I don't want money,' she repeated, for what felt like the hundredth time. 'I just want a moment alone with Mr Petrakides to explain. That's *all*.'

'So you've said before, Miss Davies,' the guard told her in a bored voice, clearly unimpressed.

'Then why don't you believe me?' Rhiannon snapped, but the security guard had gone silent, his gaze on the door.

She turned, her breath coming out in a sudden, surprised rush when she saw Lukas Petrakides standing there. He leaned against the doorframe, one hand thrust into the pocket of his dark grey trousers, the other braced against the wall.

She hadn't heard him come in, yet how could she ever have been unaware of his presence? He filled the space, took the air. She sucked in a much needed breath, tried to gather her scattered wits and courage.

Lukas flicked her with a cool, impassive gaze even as he addressed the guards.

'I'll deal with this.'

The two men filed out of the room without a word.

Rhiannon watched, sickened by the blatant display of power. *Abuse* of power. Lukas was a man who expected obedience—total, absolute, unquestioning.

She was so out of her depth, over her head, and it scared her.

Yet this was Annabel's father.

They were alone in the small room, and she was conscious of her own ragged breathing, her pounding heart. His eyes flicked over her in cool and clearly un-impressed assessment.

'You have a child in your hotel room?' he asked in a detached voice, as if it were of little interest.

'Yes…yours.'

'I see.' His smile was cold, mocking, a parody. 'When did we conceive this child, I wonder?'

Shock drenched her in icy, humiliating waves as she realised the assumption he'd so easily—and obviously—made. He really did think she was a liar. 'Annabel's not mine!'

'Annabel. A girl?'

'Yes.'

'Whose child is she, then? Besides mine, of course.'

'Leanne Weston. You…you met her at a club in London, took her to Naxos.' She felt silly repeating information he must already know—but perhaps he needed clarification? Perhaps, despite his reputation, there had been women? Many women.

The thought made her stomach roil unpleasantly.

He raised his eyebrows in surprised interest. 'I did? Ah, yes. Naxos. Beautiful place. Did we have fun?'

Rhiannon gritted her teeth. 'I couldn't say, but from Leanne's description you were certainly busy!'

'And why is she not here herself?' Lukas questioned silkily. 'I'd recognise her, of course. Perhaps I'd even recall our dirty little weekend. Or would you prefer that I do not see the woman who supposedly bore my child? Maybe I wouldn't recognise her after all?' The derisive lilt to his voice made Rhiannon grit her teeth.

'If Leanne were able to be here, I hope she would be,' she said, her nerves taut, fraying, ready to split apart. 'Although after your weekend affair she was pragmatic

enough to realise it was over. You never gave her your
phone number, or attempted to contact her.' Frustration rose within her, clamoured into a silent howl in
her throat. 'But this is nonsense to talk like this. I don't
care about what you did with Leanne in Naxos. What
I care about is your daughter, and I should think that's
what you would care about too.'

'Ah, yes, my daughter. This Annabel.' He folded his
arms, smiled with the stealthy confidence of a predator. And Rhiannon was the prey. 'You brought her here?
To the hotel?'

'Yes…'

'I suppose you thought the added embarrassment of
an actual child on the premises would increase your
pay-off?'

'My what?' Rhiannon shook her head. Did he still
think she wanted to blackmail him? Was that what this
horrible little interrogation was about? 'I don't want
your money,' she said tightly. 'As I've said before. I just
wanted you to *know*.'

'How kind of you. So now that I know, we can say
goodbye. Correct?' His cool eyes suddenly blazed silver
with challenge; Rhiannon felt a hollow pit open inside
her—a pit to drown in.

She'd come to France to find not just Lukas Petrakides, but a man who would love Annabel openly,
wholly, unconditionally.

The way fathers did.

The way they were supposed to.

She should have realised what a fantasy that was.

'I thought you were a man of responsibility,' she said
in a choked whisper. 'A man of honour.'

Lukas stilled, his eyes darkening dangerously. 'I am.

That is precisely why I'm not going to pay you to keep silent about your little brat!'

'*Your* brat, if you choose to use such terms,' Rhiannon flashed, wounded to her core by his nasty words, his brutal assessment. He was talking about his own *child*. She shook her head. 'I don't understand how a man like you—a man like the papers claim you are—cannot care one iota for your own flesh and blood. I thought…' She shook her head slowly, realisation dawning with painful intensity and awareness.

'You thought what?' he demanded flatly, and she looked up at him with wide, guileless eyes.

'I thought it would be different because she was yours.' It came out as a wretched whisper, a confession. An aching realisation that a dream she'd cherished and clung to for so long was in fact false. Rhiannon didn't know what hurt more—the current reality or the faded memory. Annabel's past or her own. 'I thought you would care.'

He stared at her for a moment, his mouth tightening in impatience. 'But you *know*, Miss Davies, that this is a fabrication. I don't know who dreamed up your sordid little scheme—whether it was you or your suspiciously absent friend Leanne—but we both know I did not father the child that is in your hotel room.'

Rhiannon stared at him in disbelief. 'But you…you said you were in Naxos!'

'I may have visited my family's resort in Naxos,' he agreed with stinging clarity. 'But I did not take your friend—or any other woman there—and I certainly did not father a child.'

'But Leanne said—'

'She lied. As you are lying.'

'No.' Rhiannon shook her head. 'No. She didn't lie. And neither did I. She was so certain…she spoke of you so warmly…'

He made a sound of impatient disgust. 'I'm flattered.'

'But how do you know? How can you be sure?' She gulped down her own uncertainties, the fears clamouring within her, threatening to spill over in a scream of denial, of desperation. Everything had been turned upside down by this revelation.

Rhiannon had never doubted Leanne's word. Never. There had been no reason to—no reason for her friend to lie. Now she wondered if she should have questioned. Doubted. If Leanne, for some inexplicable reason, *had* lied. It would be a terrible deception. And for what purpose?

But, no… When Leanne had named Lukas Petrakides as the father of her child she'd been so certain, so…*appreciative.* Wistful. The memory, for Leanne, had been sweet. There had been nothing calculating or deceptive about her explanation—and why should there have been?

She'd been dying.

'How do I *know?*' Lukas raised one eyebrow, as if daring her to make him answer such a question.

'I mean…' Rhiannon felt humiliating colour flood her face. 'There must have been women…' She assumed, despite his unsullied reputation, that there still were women. There were always women. Attractive, wealthy, discreet, willing to give and receive pleasure—satisfy a need.

'Ah.' His smile was mocking, bittersweet. 'But there you're wrong, Miss Davies. There have been no women. Not for two years.'

His face remained impassive even as Rhiannon gaped in shock. She wasn't sure why she should find this so surprising; *she* hadn't slept with anyone in the last two years. Or, for that matter, ever.

Lukas Petrakides, however, exuded raw strength, powerful virility. The idea that he'd gone without women—without *sex*—for such a length of time seemed ludicrous. Impossible.

Men like him thrived on passion…needed it. Didn't they?

Was Lukas really different? Was he gay? The thought was absurd. Cold, then…? Although there seemed nothing cold about him.

Was he just incredibly restrained?

After her mind had stopped whirling she realised with cold, stark clarity just what this meant.

Annabel couldn't possibly be Lukas's child.

She'd come here for nothing.

'Are you…sure?' she asked, her voice a rusty croak. Yet she knew what an inane question it was—just as she knew he was telling the truth. In some bizarre, inexplicable way, she trusted him. Trusted his word.

'I don't forget such things. If there was any possibility of course I would have a paternity test taken. If the child were indeed mine I would care for it. Naturally.'

Rhiannon shook her head. She didn't want to believe it. Didn't want to consider the utter waste of her travelling to France, spending far more money than she ever should have on a hotel and, worse, losing any hope of a better life for Annabel.

Lukas Petrakides was not Annabel's father. Rhiannon stared, her mind forming one impossible denial after another. She wanted to cry. To cry for Annabel, for herself.

For lost dreams of the father-daughter reunion she'd been dreaming of for years.

It was never going to happen.

But she wasn't going to cry.

'I'm sorry your little charade didn't pay off,' Lukas said with a cold smile. 'But at least you can be thankful that I won't press charges. You and your...prop will vacate the premises within the next fifteen minutes.'

'My prop?' Rhiannon repeated blankly, before she realised he was talking about a person. A child. Annabel. 'You still think this is a blackmail attempt?' She shook her head, surprised at the rush of relief that Annabel would not be tied to a man who thought so little of her, of humanity. 'Why can't you believe I came here with your interests—Annabel's interests—at heart? I didn't come for money, Mr Petrakides. I came to find Annabel a father.'

'Charming.' Lukas's eyes were flat, cold and hard. 'Since you didn't, you can leave.'

Rhiannon knew he didn't believe her, and she forced herself not to care. She didn't need to impress Lukas Petrakides; she was out of his life, and so was Annabel.

Yet it still hurt.

She straightened her shoulders, lifted her chin. 'Fine. I'm sorry I wasted your time.'

Lukas jerked his head in the semblance of a nod. Rhiannon forced herself to continue, even though she didn't want to accept anything from this man...to need anything from him.

'You mentioned another hotel as redress? Could I have the details, please?' Colour scorched her cheeks.

If she'd had any money left she wouldn't have asked, but she was desperate, and they needed a place to stay until their flight tomorrow.

'The information will be at the front desk by the time you leave.'

'Thank you.' Stiff with dignity, her legs trembling, she walked out of the room. Lukas's eyes seemed to burn into her back.

She wouldn't cry. She wouldn't. She was stronger than that. Tougher. In all the years of loneliness, disappointment, and grief, her eyes had remained dry. They would remain so now.

LUKAS WATCHED HER go, his lips twisting in a mocking smile. She'd given up quite easily when she realised he wasn't playing ball. She was obviously an amateur at the blackmail game—as was this mysterious Leanne.

Had they honestly thought they could pin something on him—*him,* Lukas Petrakides? That he would bow to their outrageous demands?

Something pricked him, pricked his conscience, and he realised with a jolt of uncomfortable surprise what it was. Guilt.

Why should he feel guilty?

Because she so obviously didn't want your money. She hadn't actually asked for a single euro.

Had he assumed the worst?

He shook his head. The baby wasn't his, and the friend Leanne had to have been lying. She'd have to know she hadn't slept with him!

And yet…what if Rhiannon hadn't known?

What if she'd been duped?

Lukas hesitated; he didn't like uncertainty. He didn't like not knowing.

So, he decided grimly, he would find out.

RHIANNON'S MIND WAS numb as she paid off the babysitter and began packing her paltry possessions. Annabel was asleep in the travel cot, one arm flung above her head, her breath coming in soft little sighs.

Rhiannon gazed down at her sleeping form with a mixture of longing and desperation. What now? What future could they have? What future could she offer this child?

'I tried,' she whispered as she gently touched one chubby fist. 'I really tried.'

'Whose child is that really, Miss Davies?'

The harsh voice had her whirling around. Lukas stood in the doorway, his face composed, closed. Cold.

'How did you get in?' she demanded, and he shrugged.

'I own the hotel, Miss Davies. I can enter whichever room I please.'

'It's a violation of privacy—'

'If anyone is going to speak of violation, it should be me,' he replied. 'Whose child is that?'

'Not yours, apparently,' Rhiannon snapped. 'And you don't need to know anything else. You're not involved, Mr. Petrakides, as you were kind enough to remind me.' She turned away, stuffing her belongings into the cheap suitcase.

He watched, nonplussed. Rhiannon was conscious of the mess of the room: the spill of cosmetics by the bathroom sink, a bra hanging on the back of the chair.

She grabbed the garment and stuffed it in the bag, saw how Lukas's lips quirked in a rueful smile.

She glared at him. 'Why are you here?'

In response he moved closer to the cot and studied Annabel.

'This Leanne is the mother?' he asked after a moment.

'I told you she was!' Rhiannon replied in exasperation. What was he playing at? Why did he care now?

'And you really believed her?' Lukas continued slowly. 'That she had an affair...with me?'

Rhiannon paused. He sounded different—as if he might believe she actually wasn't in on the so-called scam. 'She had no reason to lie,' she said after a moment. In her mind she could picture Leanne's wasted body, hear the cough that had racked her thin frame.

'Didn't she?' There was a cynical edge to his voice that Rhiannon didn't like. 'Surely,' he continued, turning away from Annabel, 'you must realise that she was hoping for this exact situation? Even if I didn't acknowledge the child—which she no doubt expects—I might be willing to cut a generous cheque to keep this unfortunate episode from reaching the press. I guard my reputation very closely, Miss Davies, as you undoubtedly know. Where is this Leanne now? Waiting nearby? Or back in Wales?'

Rhiannon could only stare, her mind whirling at the bleak, base picture he'd painted.

'No, she's not waiting for anything,' she said finally, unable to meet his incredulous, derisive look. 'She's dead.'

The events of the last two weeks danced crazily before her eyes—Leanne's arrival on her doorstep, her

rapid descent to death, guardianship thrust upon Rhiannon without any warning. How could she explain
such a chain of fantastic events to Lukas Petrakides? To
anyone? It would sound made up; he wouldn't believe
her. He would think it was just part of some nefarious
blackmailing scheme.

She let out a wild hiccup of laughter, her arms wrapping around herself as a matter of self-protection. Self-
denial.

Lukas muttered something under his breath, then
moved towards her. 'Why don't you sit down?' Before
Rhiannon could protest, he pushed her onto the edge
of the bed. His hands burned her skin through the thin
fabric of her blouse. She felt their warmth and strength
like a brand.

'You're in shock,' he stated flatly, rummaging in the
room's minibar and coming up with a small plastic bottle filled with a clear liquid.

'I'm not in shock,' she protested, even as her insides wobbled and rebelled. 'I'm...I'm *sad*.' She knew
it sounded pathetic; she could tell Lukas thought so
too by the way he raked her with one uncomprehend-
ing glance.

He wouldn't understand, of course. He didn't care
about Annabel, and he probably wondered why she
seemed to. Rhiannon closed her eyes.

She'd only known the baby two weeks. She still
hadn't quite figured out how to hold her, and bottle
feedings were awkward. The nappies she put on fell
off half of the time. She wasn't used to infants, to their
noise and dribble. Yet she loved her. At least, she knew
she *would* love her, if she was given the chance.

If she let herself have the chance.

She'd known from the moment Leanne named Lukas Petrakides as the father that she would give Annabel up if she needed to. If he wanted her to.

And she'd hoped he would...for Annabel's sake. Annabel's happiness.

Lukas poured the liquid into a glass and put it into her hand. Her fingers closed around it and she opened her eyes.

'Drink.'

She squinted dubiously at the glass and drank. Only to promptly splutter it all over the carpet—and Lukas's shoes.

'What is that stuff?' she exclaimed, wiping her mouth with the back of her hand. Her throat burned all the way to her gut, which churned in rebellion.

'Brandy. You've never had it, I take it?'

'No.' Rhiannon gazed up at him resentfully. 'You could have warned me.'

Lukas took out a handkerchief and handed it to her. 'It was for the shock.'

'I told you I wasn't in shock!'

'No? You just looked as if you were about to faint.'

'Thanks very much!' Rhiannon's eyes blazed even as hectic, humiliated colour flushed her face. She lowered her voice for Annabel's sake, and it came out in a resentful hiss. 'I admit the last fortnight has been a bit crazy. I have every right to look pale.'

She struggled upwards, for control, only to have him place his hands on her shoulders and push her gently, firmly back down onto the bed.

'Sit down.'

His palms were flat against her breastbone, his fingers curling around her shoulders. Suddenly everything was different. The hostility in the room was replaced with a tension of a completely different kind.

Desire.

Rhiannon gasped at his sudden touch, at the rush of surprised feeling it caused within her.

Lukas's mouth flickered in a smile—a sardonic, knowing curve of his lips. His head was bent towards hers, his face inches from her own. Her eyes traced the hard line of his mouth, a mouth with lips as full and soft and kissable as an angel's.

Some angel. Lukas Petrakides, with his dark hair and countenance, looked more like a demon than a cherub. But he was a handsome devil at that. And dangerous.

Her whole body burned with awareness of this man—his body, his presence, his scent. He smelled of pine and soap, a simple fragrance that made her inhale. Ache. Want.

He looked down at her for a moment, regret and wonder chasing across his face, darkening his eyes to iron. His hands were still on her shoulders, tantalisingly close to her breasts, which seemed to ache and strain towards him, towards his touch.

What would it be like to kiss him? To feel those sculpted lips against hers, to caress that lean jaw? Rhiannon's face flamed. She was sure her thoughts and her desire were obvious. She could feel the hunger in her own eyes.

She tried to look away. And failed.

This was about Annabel.

Her mind screeched a halt to her careening heart, and she dragged in a desperate breath.

This wasn't about her—her need to be touched. Loved.

'No…' It came out as a shaky whisper, a word that begged to be disbelieved. 'Don't.'

Lukas stilled, then dropped his hands from her shoulders.

Rhiannon felt bereft, empty. Stupid. A moment of desire, intense as it was, was only that. A moment.

A connection. He stood up, raked a hand through his hair. The room was silent save for their breathing, uneven and ragged, and Annabel's little sighs.

She hiccupped in her sleep, and Lukas turned, startled. He'd forgotten the baby—as she had, for one damning moment.

'We don't want to wake her up,' he said after a moment. 'Come outside.' He opened the sliding glass door that led outside.

The beach in front of the hotel room was private, separate from the crowded public area and blissfully quiet.

Rhiannon kicked off her heels and dug her toes in the cool, white sand. The sun was starting to sink in an azure sky, a blazing trail of light shimmering on the surface of the water.

It was the late afternoon of a day that had gone on for ever.

'What has happened in the last fortnight?' Lukas finally asked, his face averted.

She shook her head, tried to focus. 'Leanne—Annabel's mother—was a childhood friend of mine,' she began stiltedly, words and phrases whirling through her mind. None seemed to fit, to explain the sheer impossibility and desperation of Leanne's situation. Of her own situation. Where to begin? How to explain?

Why would he care?

Why had he come back?

'And?' Lukas prompted, his voice edged with a bite of impatience. His hands were on his hips, his powerful shoulders thrown back, grey eyes assessing. Calculating.

Rhiannon looked up; her vision was blurred. She blinked quickly, almost wanting another sip of that terrible brandy to steady her nerves. Shock them into numbness, at least.

'She came to me after she'd been diagnosed with lung cancer and asked me to be Annabel's guardian. She only had a few weeks to live. She'd lived hard already, so she didn't seem that surprised. She told me she'd never expected to live long.'

'A waste of a life.' It was a brutal, if accurate, assessment.

'To be fair to Leanne,' Rhiannon said quietly, 'she didn't have much to live for. She was a foster child, shipped from one family to the next. She'd always been a bit wild, and when she came to live in our little town in Wales, well...' She shrugged. 'There wasn't much room for a girl like Leanne. People tried to reach out to her at first, but I don't...I don't think she understood how to accept love. She pushed everyone away, grew wilder and wilder, and eventually no one wanted her around any more.'

'Yet you were her friend?'

'Yes...but not a very good one.' Rhiannon felt a familiar pang of guilt deep inside. She could have done more, helped more. Yet the needs of her own family had taken precedence; they always had. 'We lost touch after school,' she admitted, after a moment when they had both seemed lost in their own separate thoughts. 'I never bothered to try and reconnect.'

'Yet she came to you when she was dying, to care for

her child?' Lukas raised an eyebrow in obvious scepticism.

'I was the only person she trusted enough to care for Annabel,' Rhiannon said simply. 'There was no one else. There never had been.' The realisation made her ache. It was also the leaden weight of responsibility that rested heavily on her shoulders, her heart.

She would not let Leanne down.

She would not let Annabel down.

She saw Lukas's eyes narrow, his mouth tighten, and realised with an uncomfortable twinge that she was wasting his time. He should be at the reception, meeting and greeting, drinking and laughing.

Flirting.

'But this has nothing to do with you,' she said. 'As you have already made abundantly clear.' She shook her head. 'Why are you here?'

Lukas was silent for a moment, his eyes, his face, his tone all hard. Dark. 'Because I'm afraid it may have something to do with me,' he said finally, 'after all.'

'What? Are you saying…you did…?'

'No, of course not.' Lukas waved a hand in impatient dismissal. 'I don't lie, Miss Davies.'

'Neither do I,' Rhiannon flashed, but he merely flung out one hand—an imperious command for her to still her words, her movements.

His fingers, she saw, were long, lean and brown, tapering to clean, square nails. It was a hand that radiated both strength and grace.

She gave herself a mental shake; it was just a *hand*.

Why did he affect her so much? Why did she let him?

Was she just so desperate for someone—anyone—to want her? To want Annabel.

'I'd like you to tell me how Leanne came to mention my name. After the little stunt you pulled at the reception, the tabloids will be filled with stories about my secret love-child.' His face twisted in a grimace, and Rhiannon flinched. 'I want to know all the facts.'

'I wouldn't have said anything if you'd listened,' Rhiannon snapped, unrepentant. 'Instead of assuming some sordid blackmail story—'

'Just tell me, Miss Davies.' He spoke coldly, and Rhiannon realised that even though he'd returned, even though he'd shown a moment of compassion, of understanding, he still didn't believe her. Didn't trust her.

She drew in a wavering breath. 'I told you. She said she met you at a club in London. You took her to Naxos. To be honest...' She looked up at him with frank eyes. 'The man she described was younger than you are—a bit more...debonair, I suppose.'

He raised his eyebrows, his mouth curving in mock outrage. 'You don't think I'm debonair?'

The humour in his voice, in his eyes, surprised her. Warmed her. Rhiannon found she was smiling back in wry apology. It felt good to smile. It eased the pain in her heart. 'It's not that...' She could hardly explain the difference between the man before her and the man Leanne had described.

Her friend's glowing phrases had been indications to Rhiannon of a player—a man who lived life full and hard, just as Leanne had. The descriptions of Lukas Petrakides in the press hadn't matched up, but Rhiannon had been prepared to believe that the man with the sterling reputation had enjoyed one moment—well, one weekend—of weakness. Of pleasure.

She hadn't blamed him for it. It had made him seem more human. More approachable.

'She discovered she was pregnant several weeks later,' she finished. 'By that time she'd lost contact with you. She realised it had only been a weekend fling.'

'Something she was used to, apparently?'

'Don't judge her!' Rhiannon's eyes flashed angry amber as she looked up at him. 'You never knew her, and you don't know what it's like to live a life where no one cares what happens to you. Leanne had no one. *No one,*' she emphasised. 'She was just looking for a little love.'

'And she found a *little,*' Lukas agreed tersely. 'Did she try to get in touch with the father?'

She shook her head. 'No, she didn't see the point. She was sad, of course, but pragmatic enough to realise that a man like—like you wouldn't be interested in supporting her or her illegitimate child.'

'Surely she could have used the money?'

Rhiannon shrugged. 'She was proud, in her own way. It had been clear from the outset that it was a weekend fling. I suppose,' she added slowly, 'she didn't want to be rejected by someone…again. At least this was on her own terms.'

Pity flickered across his face, shadowed his eyes. 'A sad life,' he said quietly, and Rhiannon nodded, her throat tight.

'Yes.'

'So Annabel's own mother didn't bother notifying the father of her child, but you did?'

Rhiannon met his gaze directly. 'Yes.'

'Why come all this way? Why not call?'

'I tried. Your receptionist led me to believe you wouldn't get my messages. And you didn't, did you?'

Lukas shrugged. 'I'm an important man, Miss Davies. I receive too many messages, solicitations.'

'No doubt.' She didn't bother to hide the contempt in her voice. 'Too important to consider your own daughter.'

'She's not mine.'

'Then why are you here?' Rhiannon demanded. 'Why did you come back? Did you suddenly conveniently remember that you *did* go to Naxos after all?'

His eyes blazed silver—an electric look that sizzled between them so that Rhiannon took an involuntary step back.

'I told you I did not lie.'

Rhiannon believed him. So why was he here? What did he want?

'You took the chance,' Lukas continued, 'that I would want to know this child, and no doubt support it.'

'I didn't come here for money,' Rhiannon snapped. 'As I believe I've said before.'

'Not blackmail money,' Lukas replied, unfazed by her anger. 'Maintenance. If this Annabel were indeed my child, you would certainly be within your rights to think that I would support her financially.'

Rhiannon was disconcerted by his flat, businesslike tone. Was it all about money to people like him? 'That's true,' she agreed carefully. 'But that isn't why I came. If I'd just wanted money I would have filed a court order. I came because I believe children should know their parents. If there was any chance you might love your daughter—that you might *want* her...' Her voice wavered dangerously and she gulped back the emotion that threatened to rise up in a tide of regret and sorrow. 'I had to take that chance.' She didn't want to reveal so much to Lukas, to a man who regarded her as if she were a problem to be resolved, an annoyance to be dealt with.

Lukas stared at her, his eyes narrowed, yet filled with the cold light of comprehension. He looked as though he'd finally figured it out, and he scorned the knowledge.

'You didn't come for money,' he said slowly, almost to himself. 'You came for freedom.'

'I told you—'

'To give this baby away,' he finished flatly, and every word was a condemnation, a judgement.

'I want to do what's best for Annabel!' Rhiannon protested, her voice turning shrill. '*Whatever* that is.'

'A convenient excuse,' he dismissed.

Rhiannon clenched her fists, fury boiling through her. Yet mixed with it was guilt. There was a shred of truth in Lukas's assessment. She had been prepared to give Annabel up…but only because it was the right thing to do.

It had to be.

'There's no need for this,' she said in a steely voice. 'So why don't you just go? And so will I.' She turned back to the sliding glass door.

'No one is going anywhere.'

The command was barked out so harshly that Rhiannon stopped, stiffened from shock. 'Excuse me?'

'You will not go,' Lukas told her shortly. 'This matter has not been resolved.'

'This matter,' Rhiannon retorted, 'has nothing to do with you!'

'It has everything to do with me,' he replied grimly,

'since you have involved me in such a public way. You won't leave until I've had some answers.' He paused, reining in his temper with obvious effort. 'Answers you've been looking for too, perhaps?'

Rhiannon glared at him, but she didn't move. He was right, she knew. He *was* involved now, and that was her fault. She owed him a few more minutes of her time at least.

'Why do you think your friend lied?' he asked abruptly.

Rhiannon shrugged. 'I don't know. That's why I didn't think she *had* lied—she'd no reason. She was dying. I thought she'd want me to know Annabel's father, even if she never intended for me to get in touch with him.'

'She told you not to?'

'No, she didn't say anything about that. She just…' She swallowed, forced herself to continue. 'She just asked me to care for her. Love her.' Her throat ached and she looked down.

'A mother's dying request?'

Rhiannon couldn't tell if he was being snide or not. She gulped. 'Yes.' She looked up at him. 'She had nothing to gain by lying. I honestly think she believed she was with Lukas Petrakides…with you.'

Lukas stiffened, his expression becoming like that of a predator that had scented danger. There was no fear, only awareness.

'But we both know it wasn't me.' His mouth twisted wryly, but there was a hard edge of bitter realisation in his eyes. 'So it had to have been someone else…someone who told her my name.'

Rhiannon shook her head in confusion. 'Who would do that?'

Lukas muttered an expletive in Greek under his breath. 'I should have considered it,' he said, his face hardening into resolve. 'He's done it before.'

Rhiannon felt as if she were teetering on the edge of a dangerous precipice. She didn't want to look down, didn't want to cross over. She just wanted to tiptoe quietly away.

'Who are you talking about?' she asked faintly, and when Lukas met her gaze his face was full of grim realisation.

'My nephew.'

CHAPTER THREE

'YOUR NEPHEW?' RHIANNON stared at him in blank incredulity. He looked angry, determined. Hard. 'But how…? I mean why…?'

She'd come here with the assumption—the *belief*—that Lukas Petrakides was Annabel's father. A man of integrity, honour, responsibility. A man who would love her.

She wasn't prepared for alternatives.

She didn't want them.

'Why would your nephew use your name?' she finally asked as Lukas continued to stare, arms folded, his expression implacable. 'Who is he, anyway?'

'My nephew, Christos Stefanos, has used my name before.' Lukas stared out at the shifting colours of the sea—blue, green, scarlet and orange in the setting sun. 'I think he might have used it again with your friend. He's twenty-two, wild, irresponsible, unscrupulous,' he continued in a flat tone. 'He often travels to London— his mother, my sister Antonia, lives there. He could very well have met your Leanne in some club there, flown her to Naxos on a whim, and discarded her after a weekend. It is,' he finished with scathing emphasis, 'entirely within his character to do so.'

Rhiannon's thoughts were flying, whirling round and round in frightened, desperate circles. Lukas Petrakides as Annabel's father was one thing. He was known to be steady, responsible. A good father figure. That was why she had come.

This Christos was something else entirely.

'But why?' she asked again, clutching at one seemingly improbable thread.

'To impress your friend?' Lukas shrugged. 'Or more likely to annoy me. He likes to give me bad press, although the tabloid journalists are wise to him by now. They usually ignore his little peccadilloes.'

'But surely people—the press—would know he wasn't you?'

Lukas's mouth twisted in harsh acknowledgement. 'I keep a low profile. There are few photographs of me, and Christos has a family resemblance. He only does it outside of Greece—he knows he can't get away with it there.' He sighed, raking a hand through his hair. 'It has been an annoyance in the past, but now it poses...'

'A major inconvenience?' Rhiannon finished, and he gave her a cool look.

'A challenge, certainly.'

Rhiannon was silent for a moment. Her thoughts chased themselves down dark tunnels that led to implications her heart shied away from. There was too much new information. Too much to think about...to wonder about. To be frightened about.

'From the sound of him, I don't think he would make a good father,' she finally said. 'Would he?'

Lukas was ominously silent. 'I cannot say he is particularly suited for the role.'

'Or interested in it?' Rhiannon surmised, feeling sick. She'd come to France to find Annabel's father...

but not this. Not some young, rakish sot who couldn't care less. Not someone who would openly reject her.

'No, probably not,' Lukas agreed after a tense moment.

'He won't want Annabel,' she said in a hollow voice. 'Will he?'

Lukas's expression was like steel. Flint. 'No,' he said flatly. 'He won't.'

Rhiannon shook her head. This was so far from what she'd hoped. Dreamed. She realised now that the happily-ever-after she'd been planning in her head was a fantasy, pathetic and unreal. Could she leave Annabel with a man who didn't want her?

Could she take her home?

Nothing made sense. Nothing felt right.

'What are you going to do?' Rhiannon asked. She didn't like giving control to Lukas, no matter how used to it he was. She just didn't know what to do next.

Lukas was studying her in an odd way, his mouth twisting in a grimace of acknowledgement. 'You really don't want her,' he stated flatly. 'That's why you came, isn't it? To give her up...to anyone willing to take her.'

'If that were true,' Rhiannon snapped, 'I would have left her with Social Services. Don't mistake me, Mr Petrakides. I have Annabel's best interests at heart.'

'Undoubtedly.' It came out as a sneer.

Rhiannon shook her head. If Lukas wanted to judge her for giving up a child she couldn't truly call her own—if he thought her attempt to find Annabel's father was suspect—then fine. She refused to exonerate herself. She didn't need to.

'If Annabel is indeed Christos's child,' Lukas stated with flat finality, 'then she is my great-niece. My relative.' In case she didn't yet get it, he added with steely determination, 'My responsibility.'

'I see.' Rhiannon thought of every article she'd read, every glowing word about Lukas Petrakides being a man of honour, of integrity.

Of responsibility.

When she'd made her decision to find him, those descriptions had seemed like promises.

Now they were threats.

She didn't want Annabel to be someone's loveless responsibility. A burden. Yet now she realised she didn't have much choice.

She'd given her choices away when she'd embarked on this reckless mission.

'You will stay here until the issue of Annabel's paternity is resolved,' Lukas continued in implacable tones.

She'd expected as much, but his autocratic dictate still rankled. How about saying please? 'What about my responsibilities back home?' she demanded. 'My job, my life?'

'You can't spare a few days?' He raised one eyebrow in contemptuous disbelief. 'Surely you've already arranged a leave of absence?'

'Yes, but only for a few days...' She'd had holiday coming to her, as she rarely took days off.

'Then arrange some more.'

'It's not that simple...'

'Actually,' Lukas replied coolly, 'it is. Annabel is your first responsibility now—as you have told me yourself. You are her legal guardian aren't you? For the moment.'

For the moment. Panic fluttered through her insides,

left her weak and afraid. 'Yes, I am. But I'm under no obligation…'

Lukas waved this empty threat aside with scathing contempt. 'Do not think to outmanoeuvre or outrank me, Miss Davies. I don't care what the law says. If Annabel is related to me, I will be the one deciding what place you may have in her life…if any. Is that understood?'

Rhiannon blinked in shock at the cold assessment. *If any?* 'I'm her guardian… You can't—'

'If you didn't want to start this,' Lukas informed her with soft menace, 'you shouldn't have come. No one would have been any the wiser.'

'I came,' Rhiannon replied jerkily, 'because it was my responsibility to find her true family—'

'So let me fulfil *my* responsibility,' Lukas interjected with cold finality. 'Until her future is decided, you will remain.'

And then she would be dismissed. The thought frightened her. It hurt, and she hadn't expected it to.

It wasn't supposed to be like this.

Rhiannon knew there was no point in arguing, no use in being angry. He had the power, the money, and the expensive legal team to enforce whatever he wished; she had nothing. She didn't even know what her rights were, hadn't even checked. After all, it wasn't supposed to have turned out like this.

'Fine. I'll stay…but on my terms. Annabel is still in my care, and nothing has been proved yet.'

'Indeed. In the meantime, you can move to a better room. A private suite.'

Rhiannon stared at him. It was a generous offer, but

it was also a way to control her. Imprison her. 'I'm not moving rooms.'

'You must. You would be more comfortable, and so would the child. Besides, there is more privacy. Here—' he motioned to the expanse of beach '—anyone could come along. Photographers included.'

'Photographers?' Rhiannon repeated blankly, only to have him stare at her in disbelief.

'Paparazzi. Since you have so publicly announced that I have a child, the tabloid press are no doubt starting to swarm, clamouring for a photo or statement. I'd prefer for you—and the child—to be removed from such things.'

Rhiannon nodded jerkily, her mind whirling, becoming numb. 'All right.'

A cry pierced the stillness of the late afternoon, and Lukas jerked in surprise at the sound. Rhiannon hurried inside.

Annabel was sitting up in her cot, her hair matted sweatily to her flushed face, arms held up in helpless appeal.

Rhiannon scooped her up, breathed in her baby scent. It was becoming familiar, she realised. It was becoming dear.

Annabel's arms crept around her neck, held on. She nestled her chubby face in the curve of Rhiannon's shoulder and something in her splintered, fell apart to reveal the raw, aching need underneath.

She wanted this child.

She wanted to love her…and to be loved back.

She'd tried to hold the tide of emotions back, but they came anyway.

And now it looked as if Lukas Petrakides wasn't going to let that happen.

She turned, aware of his presence in the doorway. The fading sunlight outlined him in bronze, touching his hair with gold.

There was a look of fierce longing in his eyes, something deep and primal, before he noted tonelessly, 'She likes you.'

'We're starting to bond,' Rhiannon admitted cautiously. 'It's only been two weeks.'

'Two weeks? When did Leanne die?'

'Tuesday.'

Lukas stared at her in surprise, a frown marring the perfection of his features, putting a crease in his forehead. 'Four days ago?'

Rhiannon's hands stroked Annabel's back, her arms curling protectively around her warm little body. 'Yes. She only showed up on my doorstep a little over two weeks ago, and she died ten days later. Annabel has been in my sole care since then.'

'So there's been no time to formally adopt her?' Lukas surmised.

Rhiannon's arms tightened so that Annabel let out a squeal of protest.

'No, but Leanne did make me Annabel's legal guardian. I have the papers to prove it. It satisfied the immigration authorities, so it should be enough for you.' She lifted her chin. 'Annabel is *mine*.'

'If you wanted her to be,' Lukas said quietly. 'Somehow I don't think you do.'

Hurt and fury rippled through her at his brutal assessment. 'You're making assumptions,' she replied through gritted teeth. 'Annabel needs her bottle. So you'll have to excuse me.'

She turned away, escaped to the bathroom, where she'd rinsed out Annabel's army of bottles. She set the baby in her car seat and with shaking fingers measured out the powdered formula.

'Quite a set-up you've got here,' Lukas remarked, one shoulder propped against the doorway.

Rhiannon nearly dropped the bottle.

'Could I please have some privacy?'

'No. Annabel's now as much of my concern as she is yours. I don't plan on letting either of you out of my sight.'

Rhiannon's mouth twisted. 'Do you think I'll make a run for it?'

'I don't know what you're capable of,' Lukas admitted coolly. 'Or what you want. I wonder what you're after from this deal, Rhiannon Davies. Is Annabel your bargaining chip?'

She whirled around, the bottle flying out of her hand and landing on the tiled floor with a clatter. Annabel began to wail.

'I don't know what type of people you consort with,' she hissed furiously, 'but they must be different from the kind I'm used to. Because I would never, never stoop so low. I'm not in this for myself, Mr Petrakides. I'm here for Annabel, and all I care about is her well-being. If that means being without me, then I'll let her go. If it means being with me, then I'll fight tooth and nail to keep her. But I'm not going to obey your every barked-out command, or cater to your controlling whims. If I do anything—*anything*—it will be in consideration of Annabel only. Not you. Understood?'

She stood, chest heaving, fists clenched, and Lukas stared at her long and hard, his mouth tightening into a thin line of resolve before he gave a slight, self-mocking bow of acknowledgement.

'Understood.'

'Good.' She still didn't know if he believed her, but she didn't care. She was shaking, trembling from head to foot, as she scooped up Annabel, pressed her downy cheek against her pounding heart. Annabel, sensing her fear and anger, kept crying.

'You're in no state to hold her right now,' Lukas admonished, and he eased the baby from her reluctant grasp.

Rhiannon watched as he cradled her carefully, awkwardly. He wasn't used to babies, she thought.

The smile he gave Annabel was tender, his eyes widening in surprise at his own reaction to her toothless grin.

Rhiannon scooped the bottle from the floor and dumped it in the sink. As Annabel began to grizzle again, from hunger, she set to making another one.

She didn't know what was going to happen now, and she wasn't looking forward to finding out.

All she knew was the next few days might determine the rest of Annabel's life…and hers.

SEVERAL HOURS LATER Annabel was finally asleep. Stars glittered in an inky sky, reflected back in diamond pinpoints on the water, and Rhiannon prowled restlessly around the suite Lukas had insisted she move into a few hours ago. She'd never seen such luxury, and if the circumstances had been different she might have enjoyed it.

She ran a hand over the silky duvet on the king-sized bed, glanced in mocking derision at the whirlpool bath for two. All the trappings for romance, and totally unnecessary.

There was a separate sitting area, as well as a kitchenette filled with gleaming appliances and crockery—admittedly handy for dealing with Annabel's bottles and food.

A wide balcony stretched the entire length of the suite, and after one last check to make sure Annabel was settled Rhiannon slipped out into the warm cover of darkness.

She sank into a chair, brought her knees up to her chest and rested her chin on top. It was a pose from childhood—a pose of protection.

She closed her eyes.

She could hear the sounds of a party from the resort's gardens—was Lukas there? She hadn't seen him since he'd had her moved up here. Out of sight.

For the last few hours she'd entertained Annabel, fed and bathed her, keeping the doubts, the fears at bay.

Now they hurtled back with startling force.

Lukas had the power to take custody of Annabel, she realised dejectedly. She knew she was Annabel's legal guardian but the courts could easily decide in Lukas's favour—he had the support of extended family, including the baby's biological father. He was wealthy, powerful, connected to all the right people…

Anyway, this was what she'd wanted, she told herself. She'd come to France for Annabel to meet her father, to have a family.

The family she'd never had herself.

She'd *wanted* Lukas to take custody of Annabel, *to*

love her. She'd convinced herself it was best for everyone.

She just hadn't expected it to hurt so much. She hadn't prepared herself for the surge of protectiveness she'd felt when Lukas had threatened paternity tests, custody suits.

She'd expected to offer Annabel, not to have her taken by force.

Taken as a matter of duty rather than of love.

Duty. The word rested heavily on her. Lukas was a man of responsibility. He would do the right thing by Annabel, but he wouldn't love her.

Would he?

Not like I do. Not like I could.

She shook her head, dashed her hand against her eyes and the tears that threatened to fall. One fell anyway. This was stupid; she was being ridiculous. *She didn't cry.*

She had known this would happen—even if she hadn't anticipated the exact unfolding of events. She would just have to steel herself against the repercussions in her own heart.

'I thought you might be hungry.'

Rhiannon looked up in surprise. She'd been so lost in her own unhappy thoughts that she hadn't heard the glass door slide open, hadn't seen Lukas step out onto the balcony.

Yet now she felt him—felt the way his presence seemed to suck the air right from her lungs.

He was looking down at her with a quiet thoughtfulness that reminded her of that first moment in the bar.

Then she'd believed he was a kind man.

Now she wasn't sure.

Responsibility, integrity... They were good things, but they weren't kindness. They didn't encompass love.

She knew that well. Too well.

He placed a plate of food on the glass-topped table in front of her, then took her chin between his forefinger and thumb.

'You've been crying.'

'No, I haven't.'

In response his thumb traced the track of the tear down her cheek, straight to her heart.

'No?' he queried gently, and another tear followed silently, dripped onto his thumb.

Rhiannon jerked her chin out of his hand, scrubbed angrily at her eyes. 'I don't cry.'

He watched her thoughtfully for a moment. 'Why don't you eat? The lack of food won't help things.'

'Thank you,' Rhiannon mumbled, and self-consciously drew the plate towards her.

'A Languedoc speciality,' Lukas informed her as she dug into the beef stew. 'Made with black olives and garlic, finished with red wine.'

'Delicious,' Rhiannon admitted after one bite. She'd never had such food before.

He sat across from her, watching her with fathomless eyes. 'How long had it been since you'd seen this Leanne?' he asked after a long moment, and Rhiannon looked up in surprise.

'I hadn't seen her for ten years before she showed up on my doorstep with Annabel, asking me to take her.' She paused, toying with her fork, lost in memory.

'It must have been quite an inconvenience,' Lukas commented, his voice neutral. Yet Rhiannon still heard the judgement. Felt it.

'All children are inconveniences,' she said. 'That doesn't mean they're not worth it.'

'Doesn't it?' There was a cynical note to Lukas's tone that Rhiannon didn't like.

'What are you proposing to do?' she forced herself to ask. 'If Christos is the father? If Annabel is such an inconvenience to you...?'

'You think I'd palm her off like you've been trying to do?' Lukas finished, and Rhiannon jerked back at the scorn in his voice. 'I do my duty, Rhiannon. I'll do it by Annabel.'

'I was not palming her off,' she protested, and Lukas shrugged, unconvinced. Unimpressed.

'Call it what you like.'

'I was prepared to give you custody,' she admitted painfully, driven to the truth. 'A child should be with her natural-born parent—if that parent *wants* her.' She gazed unseeingly before her, the star-spangled sky blurring into a haze of colour. 'The parameters have changed now, though.'

'Yes, they have.' Lukas's voice was quiet, but held the underlying steel Rhiannon was coming to recognise...and dread. 'But some things remain the same.'

'Your nephew might not even be Annabel's father,' she pointed out.

'Perhaps he is not,' Lukas agreed implacably. 'But until the matter is resolved you will stay here. With me. When his paternity is proved—'

'If—'

'If,' he agreed smoothly. 'We will have matters to discuss.'

Rhiannon swallowed. She didn't want to ask what matters those might be—didn't have the courage. *I will decide what place you have in her life...if any.* She had a feeling, a terrible suspicion, that Lukas would cut her out of Annabel's life as if wielding a pair of scissors.

And she'd started it all by coming here. By looking for Lukas.

Had she anticipated what might happen when she found him?

Yes, she had. She'd pictured Lukas cradling his daughter, his face suffused with tenderness. She'd anticipated shock, followed by gratitude and joy.

She'd anticipated, she acknowledged numbly, a ridiculous happily-ever-after that was never going to happen.

It hadn't happened before. Why should it happen now?

She'd been a naive, foolish *idiot* to think for one moment that it could.

Lukas placed his hand on her own. His voice was a condemnation. 'This is what you wanted.'

'No, it isn't.'

'You came here to give her away,' Lukas continued flatly, and Rhiannon shrugged helplessly.

'To someone who would love her. I wanted...' She stared down at their hands, his large brown one on top of her paler, more delicate fingers. 'I wanted her to have a family.'

Lukas was silent, his fingers heavy on hers. She felt his warmth, his heat, and it fanned quickly, alarmingly, into a more dangerous flame.

Desire.

Suddenly it was there, thrumming to life, palpable, heady, filled with possibility.

She wanted to jerk her hand away, but Lukas's hand was still on hers, still heavy, staying her own movements. And somehow Rhiannon knew she wouldn't move her hand even if it were free.

She watched as he turned her hand over, traced his thumb lightly down her palm. Rhiannon shivered. She was helplessly in thrall to him, to the barest of his touches.

She snuck a look at him from beneath her lowered lashes, saw he was staring at their hands too, watching his own thumb flick along her palm with an almost clinical interest, as if he too were captive to a greater need than either one of them had ever anticipated or experienced.

Then his eyes met hers, and Rhiannon was rocked to her core by the blatant need, the open hunger in them.

He reached out his other hand, slowly, deliberately, and tangled it in her hair. Rhiannon's mouth opened soundlessly, yet she didn't resist as he pulled her towards him, nearly out of her chair. He leaned forward, his lips a breath away from hers.

'I want to do this.' He spoke in a ragged whisper; it was a confession.

Rhiannon's head swum dizzily. *So do I.* Yet she couldn't quite say it.

Lukas must have sensed her unspoken permission, or perhaps he didn't require it, for he touched his lips to hers once—a brush, a flicker, a promise.

Then the promise deepened into a certainty as his tongue plundered her mouth, took possession of her soul. Rhiannon's fingers bunched on his shoulders, clawed for purchase, for sanity.

Somehow she had slipped out of her chair, was kneeling on the hard tiled floor between Lukas's powerful thighs. She could feel his arousal against her heart.

His mouth continued to cover hers, plunging, plundering. Taking everything. His hands fisted in her hair, drawing her closer, binding her to him.

The kiss went on endlessly. She'd never felt so treasured, so desired, so needed.

So loved.

The thought was a cold slap of reality, a mocking laugh in the stillness of their entwined bodies.

There was no love involved here. She barely knew this man. All he felt for her was contempt, suspicion. She wanted him—oh, yes—and he wanted her.

But that was all.

Sex.

She pulled away, wincing as her hair tangled around Lukas's fingers. He was completely still, his hand still snarled in her hair, staring at her as if she were a stranger—as if he were a stranger to himself.

His breathing was ragged, uneven, and so was hers.

'I'm sorry.' He looked appalled, angry. Yet Rhiannon had a feeling that anger was not directed at her. Carefully he unwound the strands of hair from his fingers, smoothed the curls back from her fevered brow. 'That shouldn't have happened.'

'No,' Rhiannon agreed shakily, although the sense of loss she felt would have sent her to her knees if she hadn't already been there.

Lukas helped her back into her chair. 'Clearly I've been without a woman for too long,' he said with a cool smile, and Rhiannon's own mouth twisted in bitterness.

'That's what that was about? Sex?' Of course it was. She was such a pathetic fool, thinking for one second it could ever be anything more.

Lukas sat back, looking surprised. 'Obviously I desire you. I desired you when I first saw you.'

'In the bar.'

He looked discomfited for the barest of moments before he gave a quick, sharp nod. 'Yes. Before any of this happened with the child the desire was there. It was real.'

Real and warm and alive. Yet it was just desire—cheap and easy.

Even desire could be a burden.

It wasn't love, and Rhiannon knew that was what she needed. Wanted.

She'd just never had it.

'We should go to bed. Sleep,' she amended hastily, and Lukas acknowledged her slip of the tongue with a wry nod. 'It's been a long day.'

'Yes, it has.'

Rhiannon reached for her plate and he stilled her movement with one hand on her arm, his fingers curling around her wrist. 'Perhaps that was a moment of comfort we both needed,' he said. 'It won't happen again.'

He spoke in warning, as if he thought she might expect a replay. Did she seem so desperate?

Rhiannon's nerves were splintered, her emotions in tatters.

None of this was supposed to happen.

'Well, thank you,' she finally said, her voice strained and low, 'for that courtesy.' And without another word, not trusting herself to speak or meet his frowning gaze, she slipped through the door.

She heard him leave the suite from the safety of the locked bathroom. She sat on the edge of the bathtub, her fists in her hair, her lips still burning from his kisses.

Perhaps it was a moment of comfort we both needed.

Damned by compassion. Pity. No doubt his misguided sense of responsibility striking once again. He'd been trying to comfort her.

She didn't want comfort.

She wanted love.

She wanted it for herself, wanted it for Annabel.

She felt a terrible, hollow certainty that she wouldn't find it here.

CHAPTER FOUR

'WE NEED TO leave. Now.'

Rhiannon sat up in bed, blinking sleep from her eyes, clutching the covers to her chest. Annabel was still asleep, and Lukas stood in the doorway of her suite, fully dressed, his lithe body coiled and tense.

'What are you talking about?'

'What I'm talking about,' he bit out, 'is the press in front of this resort—thanks to the little stunt you pulled yesterday at the reception.' He pulled a rolled-up newspaper from his pocket and threw it on the bed.

Rhiannon unfurled it with shaking fingers and a leaden heart.

Secret Playboy? Lukas Petrakides Discovers his Love-child. Furious Mother Booted Out of Newest Resort! the headline screamed. There was even a picture— a grainy shot from a telephoto lens—of the two of them on the beach. The paparazzi photographer had clearly waited for his moment, Rhiannon realised with a sinking feeling. It was towards the end of their conversation yesterday afternoon, when they had clearly been in an argument.

Thank God they hadn't got a photo of their kiss last night. Just the memory caused a flush to crawl up her throat.

She looked up, met Lukas's blazing eyes. 'I'm sorry.'

'We can discuss this later,' he informed her tersely. 'Right now we need to leave. I have a private jet departing in twenty minutes for Greece. You and Annabel will be on it.'

'Greece?' Rhiannon repeated stupidly, and he slashed a hand through the air.

'Yes—to safety! You can't stay here now the press have wind of this story. Once they know we've gone, they'll give up the chase. For the moment. I don't want the press hounding the resort's guests, and I don't want them finding you or Annabel. The last thing I need is more sordid details.'

That was what she was, Rhiannon thought. A sordid detail. She opened her mouth to reply, but Lukas cut her off before she could frame a syllable.

'Get dressed. I'll wait outside the door.'

He flung open the door just as Annabel let out her good-morning howl of hunger.

Rhiannon scooped her up, prepared a bottle with clumsy fingers and a whirling mind. She dressed herself quickly, then found something for Annabel to wear, threw some nappies and the prepared bottle in a bag, and stepped outside.

'I'm ready.'

'Good.' Lukas had been leaning against the wall, arms folded, but now he pushed off and stood back to sweep her with an assessing gaze.

Rhiannon was conscious of her faded jeans and worn tee-shirt. Annabel had already dribbled on her shoulder. Lukas's mouth tightened as he looked at her, whether in disapproval or displeasure Rhiannon didn't know, but she forced herself not to care.

'Someone will bring your bags to the jet. Let's go,' he said, and as he strode quickly down the corridor she had no choice but to follow, Annabel screeching in protest.

LUKAS SAT BACK in the plane seat and rolled his shoulders, trying to relieve the stabbing tension which had lodged there since he'd seen those damn newspapers this morning.

He knew the news would be all over France, all over Greece, all over the world. His father would have seen it this morning. He would be furious.

Lukas had failed him, failed the family, by allowing such lies to be smeared across papers and television screens.

Yet Lukas dismissed the thought of his father in contemplation of the woman shrouded in misery opposite him. Rhiannon sat with Annabel on her lap, her face averted towards the window.

Lukas felt an unwelcome twinge of unease. He no longer believed Rhiannon was a blackmailer, yet he still didn't trust her. He *couldn't* trust a woman who was willing to give up a child entrusted into her care, no matter what excuse she gave…or what she had convinced herself to believe.

He suspected she'd persuaded herself it was for the best, that she was acting nobly, yet he saw the truth in her hunched position, in the awkward way she held the baby.

She wasn't used to children, he thought. She probably lived in a chic little flat that wasn't equipped for infants. No doubt she was eager to get back to her life… her lover. The thought made his expression harden in distaste…and in remembrance.

It doesn't matter to me. Take him.

He shook his head, banishing the memory, the mocking voice.

This was a different situation, a different woman... even if some aspects seemed the same.

His thoughts shifted to the baby in Rhiannon's arms. Her dark, curly hair and soulful eyes reminded him of photographs of himself as a baby. She had the look of a Petrakides. If Annabel was indeed Christos's daughter, which to Lukas now seemed a near certainty, there could be no question of her future. It would be in Greece, with the Petrakides family.

And, he acknowledged with grim certainty, Rhiannon Davies would not fit into that picture at all.

The baby gave a little shuddering sigh, and Rhiannon stroked her downy hair, a tender smile lighting her face. Lukas watched, feeling a now-familiar tightening in his gut. In his heart.

She looked as if she cared for the child, but he couldn't believe it. Didn't want to. It would be much easier for everyone, he mused, if there was no emotional attachment between Rhiannon and Annabel. Still, even if there were, he was confident he could convince her to return to Wales, to relinquish through the courts her guardianship of the child. All it took was the right price.

He watched Rhiannon smooth an errant curl back from her forehead, and he was suddenly stabbingly reminded of his own hand in those tangled curls, drawing her to him, tasting her wine-sweetened lips, burrowing himself in the warmth of her.

The kiss last night had been a mistake. A mind-blowing, sense-scattering event, but an error nonetheless. He'd wanted her; he still did. He didn't completely understand his desire for such a slight, average-looking woman, but he acknowledged the truth of it. Perhaps he had been without a woman for too long; perhaps it was something more.

It didn't matter. He never gave in to desire, never catered to need.

What mattered was his family, the Petrakides name, and his duty towards it. That was all.

TWO HOURS LATER the jet landed on the airstrip of the Petrakides private island.

Rhiannon stared numbly out of the window at the sparkling blue-green of the Aegean Sea, at the rocky shore leading up to landscaped gardens and a long, low, rambling villa of whitewashed stone.

'Come,' Lukas said, taking her hand as he helped her out of the plane. 'My father will be waiting.'

Rhiannon transferred a sleeping Annabel to her other shoulder as she stepped out into the sunshine. The air was hot and dry, the sky a hard, bright blue.

She inhaled the dry, dusty scent of rosemary and olive trees, combined with the salty tang of the sea. Annabel stirred, rubbed her eyes with her fists, and then looked around in sleepy wonder.

'Wait here.' Lukas stayed her with one firm hand, his countenance darkening with suppressed tension by the second.

A man was striding stiffly towards them. Tall, spare and white haired. Rhiannon had no doubt this was Theo Petrakides, founder of the Petrakides real estate empire. And he looked furious.

She stepped backwards into the shadow of the plane as the two men squared off.

Theo said something in rapid Greek; Lukas replied. A muscle bunched in his jaw but his voice was flat and calm, his posture almost relaxed.

This was a man in control. A man who did not give in to emotions, whims. Desires.

What about last night? Rhiannon shook her head in denial of the question her heart asked but her mind wouldn't answer.

Last night had been a moment of weakness for both of them and, as Lukas had said, it wouldn't happen again.

They were still speaking in rapid but controlled tones. Then Annabel let out a squeal as a gull soared low overhead, and Theo Petrakides's sharp grey gaze swung to her.

Rhiannon froze, her arms tight around a now struggling Annabel. Her heart rate was erratic and fast as the older man walked slowly towards her. He stood in front of her, a flat look in his eyes.

'This is the child? Christos's child?' he said slowly in English.

'We don't know yet for certain,' Rhiannon managed carefully, her voice a cracked whisper.

'His bastard.'

She jerked back as if slapped, saw the frank condemnation in Theo's eyes. She glanced involuntarily at Lukas, saw him shake his head in silent warning. Still, fury bubbled up within her, gave her courage.

'Annabel Weston is in my care,' she told the man quietly. 'She is my responsibility, no matter who the father turns out to be.'

He glanced at her, reluctant admiration flickering briefly in his eyes before he shrugged. 'We shall see.'

Panic rose in her throat, and she tasted bile. Was Theo implying that they would take Annabel away from her if Christos was the father? Lukas had said something similar.

Why had she not considered how this might happen? *Because you wanted the fairy tale.*

Theo strode away, and Lukas put his arm around Rhiannon's shoulders, guiding her towards the rocky path that led to the villa.

'None of you want her,' she choked out in a whisper, and Lukas simply shrugged.

'It's not a question of want.'

'But of responsibility, right?' She shook her head. 'I wanted more for Annabel.'

'I'm afraid,' Lukas said quietly, 'that what you want is not my primary consideration.'

She glanced at him, saw the grim determination hardening his eyes, his mouth, his words, and felt a stab of fear. She was not his primary consideration...or any consideration at all, she finished bleakly.

AN HOUR LATER Rhiannon prowled restlessly around her bedroom. It was large and spacious, with a wide balcony overlooking the sea. Annabel sat on the floor, playing happily with some seashells Rhiannon had found in a decorative bowl.

There was a light knock on the door, and with her heart rising straight into her throat she called out, 'Come in.'

Lukas opened the door. He'd changed from his business attire, was now dressed in jeans and a white cotton shirt open at the throat. Those few undone buttons revealed a tanned column of skin that Rhiannon couldn't seem to tear her gaze from.

'Have you found everything to your satisfaction?' he asked, and she jerked her eyes upwards towards his face.

His hair was damp, brushed back from his face, his eyes sparkling silver as he smiled with a wry amusement that caused her face to burn with humiliated realisation.

He knew how he affected her, and he thought it was amusing. No doubt he had women falling for him all the time, and he obviously had no problem putting them in their place. Rejecting them.

'Yes, fine,' she said shortly.

He glanced at her still unopened suitcase by the bed. 'You haven't unpacked.'

'We're not going to be here for long.'

'Perhaps not,' Lukas agreed. 'But it would be more comfortable, certainly, to enjoy a short stay.'

'Before I'm booted out?' Rhiannon interjected. 'Sorry, I don't feel like complying.'

Lukas shrugged, ran a hand through his hair. Rhiannon watched as it flopped boyishly across his forehead; she resisted the urge to brush it back with itching fingers.

'Suit yourself,' he said. 'I only thought you might want to be comfortable.'

'I don't want to be comfortable,' she snapped, even though she knew she was being childish.

Lukas's eyes flashed. 'You should—at least for Annabel's sake. Surely it is in her best interests for both of you to be relaxed and comfortable during your stay here? It is, in fact, your responsibility,' he continued in a harder voice, 'to be so.'

Rhiannon's mouth pursed in annoyance. 'It's all about responsibility, isn't it?'

For a half-second Lukas looked nonplussed. 'Of course it is.'

'Not love.'

His eyebrows rose. 'Who am I supposed to love?'

'Annabel!' Rhiannon cried, too angry and despairing to be embarrassed that he might have actually thought she meant *herself*. 'I came here so she could find her father...a father who would love her!'

'But I am not her father,' he reminded her. 'And I cannot love a child I've never even seen before. Not right away.'

'Especially one that is not yours, I suppose?' Rhiannon finished, and he shook his head, dismissing her jibe.

'If Annabel is Christos's child—which I believe she is—then I will make sure she is cared for. Absolutely.'

Rhiannon's mouth dried. *Absolutely*. It was a word that didn't allow for difficulties, differences. Flexibility. It was a cold, hard, unyielding word, and she didn't like it. 'I didn't want it to be like this,' she finally said after a moment, her eyes averted.

'I understand. But this is now how it is. How it will be remains for me to decide.'

'You,' Rhiannon said, 'and not me, I suppose?'

Lukas shook his head. 'I don't know what you want from me. If you came to the Petra resort to find Annabel's father, you succeeded. You did your duty. Now you will leave the rest to us.'

'I'm not going to leave it up to you,' Rhiannon protested. 'Annabel is my ward, not yours. Any decisions that are made will involve me.' Her voice came out more strident than she intended, and Annabel looked up anxiously. Rhiannon bent down, soothed her with a few hushing motions.

'The only decision that has been made so far,' Lukas said, with a deliberate patience that warned Rhiannon he was close to losing his temper, 'is for you to remain here until the question of paternity is resolved. All I'm asking now is that you stay here, in comfort, not snapping and biting like a fish on a line, and enjoy a few days in what most people consider to be paradise.'

Rhiannon watched Annabel bang two shells together, her eyes wide and round. Lukas's analogy was dead on, she realised grimly. She did feel like a fish on a line, dangling desperately—and, worse yet, she'd willingly put the hook in her own mouth.

'A few days—and then what?'

'That remains to be seen.' His mouth was a thin line, his eyes dangerously blank, and Rhiannon knew better than to press him now. She wasn't going to ask questions she didn't want answers to.

'Fine,' she said heavily. 'Have you spoken to Christos?'

'No. He is on a friend's yacht at the moment. I've left a message on his mobile, but he probably won't answer it until he is on shore.' His mouth twisted, tightened in derision. 'He doesn't like his holidays disturbed.'

'And this is the man you want for Annabel's father?' Rhiannon said with a shake of her head.

'No, this is the man who *is* Annabel's father. We cannot change that…if it is proved.'

He glanced down at the baby, frowning as he saw her suck the edge of a shell. 'Do you think this is an appropriate toy for the child?' he asked, taking the offending item from a reluctant Annabel, who immediately howled in outrage.

Rhiannon scooped her up, pressed the baby to her body in a defensive gesture. 'It's the best I could do. Leanne had few toys for Annabel, and there hasn't been time…'

'I will make sure that you are both adequately supplied while you're here,' Lukas said, although there was still a frowning furrow on his forehead.

'We don't need anything from you,' Rhiannon protested, as Annabel began to tug rather painfully on her earring.

The look Lukas gave her was swift, searching. Knowing. 'On the contrary,' he corrected quietly, 'there are many things you need from me. That is why you came, is it not?'

Before she could answer, he sketched a brief bow of farewell and left her alone.

'Ouch!' Rhiannon disengaged Annabel's chubby fingers from her earring. 'Not so hard, sweetheart.' She set the baby back on the floor, prowled the room once more.

Her heart was racing in time with her thoughts, whirling helplessly, out of reach, out of answers.

After a moment she flung open the doors to the balcony, went outside and breathed in the clean sea air. She needed it to steady her, for her senses were still reeling from Lukas's presence, his power.

He seemed determined to take responsibility for Annabel. To care for her.

This was what she had wanted—yet not like this. Never like this. With Annabel as discarded goods, unwanted, thrust on someone who believed he needed to do his duty.

Her life would be loveless; she would grow up with the cold knowledge that she'd only been taken in because there had been no other place for her, because no one had wanted her.

As Rhiannon had grown up.

I want her. The words burned in her brain and lit her soul. *I want her.* She would not give Annabel up so easily. When she'd envisaged giving her up, it had been to a loving home, to a father who wanted her. Who loved her.

A fantasy, she acknowledged now, and perhaps she realised that from the moment she'd spoken to Lukas Petrakides. A fantasy based on what she'd always wanted—always dreamed of—for herself.

But this was not about her, or her lost dreams. It was about Annabel. And she would not condemn the infant to a childhood like she'd had. She'd come to France, to Lukas, to keep that from happening. Now that things had changed she would do what was necessary to keep Annabel from being the burden she herself had been.

She'd thought that meant walking away. Now it meant staying.

'THE GIRL MUST go.'

Lukas jerked his contemplative gaze away from the study window and turned to see his father standing still and erect in the doorway. Though his hair was snow white, his face lined, Theo Petrakides was still a handsome and imposing man.

He was also dying.

The doctors had told Lukas that Theo had a few good months left in him—but it would go downhill from there. Theo knew; he accepted it with the grim stoicism with which he'd accepted all the tragedies in his life.

'I'll die well,' he'd said with cold detachment. 'I'll do my duty.'

Yes, Lukas knew Theo would do his duty in death—as he had in life.

Just as he would do his. His promise to care for Annabel had not been rash. As soon as the possibility had arisen that Christos might be the father Lukas had known what it would mean. The sacrifice he would have to make.

Caring for a child, he told himself, was hardly difficult. He'd hire a nanny, enlist the best help. It might mean travelling a bit less to be more available to her as a father. That thought, that *word,* shook him more than he cared to admit.

Still, he would do what needed to be done to provide for the child and, more importantly, to keep the Petrakides name free from scandal or shame. He would do his duty.

'What girl?' he asked now, forcing his mind back to the present, to the frowning countenance of his father.

'That English girl. She has no place in our lives, Lukas.'

Lukas's palm curled into a fist on the smooth, mahogany-topped desk. Slowly, deliberately, he flattened it out again. 'She's Welsh, and her name is Rhiannon. She does have a place in our lives, Papa—she's Annabel's guardian.'

Theo's eyebrows rose at hearing the casual, almost intimate way Lukas referred to both Rhiannon and Annabel.

Lukas realised he'd spoken about Rhiannon as if he knew her, liked her. He shrugged. What he said was still true.

'For now,' the older man agreed flatly. 'But when Christos—damn him!—is shown to be the father, she will have no place at all. You told me she's not related, just a friend of the mother. We are blood relations, and we will do our duty—even for Christos's English bastard.'

'Is that what you plan on telling the child, when she is old enough to hear?'

'I won't be around then,' Theo replied with brutal frankness, 'so you can do the honours. She can hardly complain if she has been well provided for. No one can accuse us of being ungenerous.'

'No, indeed,' Lukas agreed dryly, and Theo frowned. 'Don't tell me you've a fondness for that English piece?'

'She's *Welsh,* and, no, I have not. But I prefer to speak about any woman with respect.'

'She will only complicate matters,' Theo continued, ignoring his son. He strode to the window, watched the waves crash onto the rocky shore. 'If she isn't already attached to the child, she will become so, and we cannot have the bad press of a messy custody case. The tabloids would make a meal of this, Lukas. You've already seen what they've done with these rumours of your mistress and your love-child.'

'I have,' he replied tightly. 'But I believe Rhiannon is willing to be reasonable if we approach her with sensitivity. I don't want to take her from the child now. Annabel has had a great deal of upheaval in her life, and it would do none of us any favours to send Rhiannon away before she is settled.'

Theo glanced shrewdly at his son. 'None of us?' he repeated, and gave a dry chuckle. 'Oh, very well. If you must have her, have her. You've been without a woman too long, haven't you? You never learned how to be discreet in such matters.'

'I prefer to be restrained.' Lukas's head was throbbing with fury. He knew he should be used to his father's frank, crass ways—and he knew his father believed duty was a public matter, rather than a private one. As long as people saw what you did was right, it hardly mattered what you thought.

He felt differently.

'This would be solved,' Theo continued in a harder voice, 'if you did your duty to provide me with an heir and marry.'

'You know I never plan to marry.'

'Your duty—'

'I refuse to marry a woman I love,' Lukas intervened flatly, 'and I refuse to marry without love. It would not be fair to the woman.'

'There are plenty of women who would marry without love,' Theo scoffed.

Lukas suppressed a sigh. They'd had this conversation many times.

'Scheming gold-diggers or materialistic snobs,' he dismissed. 'Hardly suitable material.' The thought of not providing an heir for the Petrakides empire was an uncomfortable one, but he knew his limits. Marriage was outside of them. As was love.

'Fine,' Theo said, willing to let go of this thorny subject for a moment. 'Still, the English bit goes.' He stared his son down. 'And soon.'

Lukas gazed at his father. 'There is no question that she will leave when the child's paternity is determined,' he agreed coolly. 'There can be no place for her in our lives. But until then it would benefit us all to keep her sweet.' He busied himself with some papers on his desk. 'Now, I have work to do, Papa. I will see you at dinner.'

Theo glanced sharply at his son, but with a jerky nod he left the room.

Lukas swivelled to stare out of the window. The aquamarine sea stretched flatly to an endless horizon— yet he knew that only a few miles out there would be boats. Boats disguised as fishing vessels, but filled with photographers and journalists clamouring for an exclusive shot of Lukas with his illicit family. Photographs which would then be sold to tabloids around the world, to make the Petrakides name raked through the mud and the dirt once again.

He sighed, thrusting a hand through his hair. He understood the need to avoid bad press—God knew, the Petrakides family had had enough of it.

He also understood that Rhiannon Davies would have to go. As his father had said, her presence could only complicate matters, and he didn't want a Petrakides child—*any* child—attached to a woman whose motives in staying were at best uncertain, at worst suspect.

What did she want? he wondered, not for the first time. She didn't want to leave the child; she didn't want to stay. Lukas still wasn't sure if she was playing a high-stakes game, or if she simply didn't *know* what she wanted.

Hardly a woman to trust with a child, he thought in derisive dismissal. With a child's love.

Still, he had use of her, as did the child. He wasn't ready to release her just yet.

THAT NIGHT FOR dinner Rhiannon dressed in the outfit she'd worn yesterday to the reception—now slightly crumpled, but still clean at least.

She'd fed Annabel in the kitchen, under the eye of Adeia, the kindly housekeeper and cook. After giving the baby a bath in the huge tub in her adjoining bathroom, she'd put Annabel to sleep in the middle of the wide bed in her room. There were no travel cots, but Lukas had assured her one would be found by the next day.

Dinner, she'd been informed, was in the villa's dining room, and she was expected there at half past seven.

Rhiannon drew in a shaky breath and examined her reflection.

Her hair had turned wild and curly due to the moisture in the sea air, and no amount of brushing or spray would tame it. She'd abandoned any pretence at styling it, and settled for a slick of lipstick, a dab of perfume, and her old outfit.

It wasn't as if she were trying to impress either Theo or Lukas. Though she dreaded seeing the older man again. His words rang in her ears.

Bastard.

That was all he saw Annabel as. What would he think, she wondered with wry bitterness, if he knew *she* was illegitimate too?

What would Lukas think? Would he judge her an unfit mother? Damn her for the circumstances of her birth, as Theo seemed willing to do?

Rhiannon threw back her shoulders, her mouth hardening into a grim line. That wasn't going to happen. Because she was going to stick around. No matter what they said. No matter what they did.

After checking that Annabel was deeply asleep—exhausted, no doubt, by the upheavals of the day—Rhiannon headed downstairs. The wide, sweeping staircase led to a tiled foyer flanked with mahogany double doors that led to the villa's reception rooms.

Lukas came into the foyer from one of the rooms at the sound of her heels clicking on the tiles. He wore a light grey button-down shirt, expensive and well made, and charcoal trousers cinched with a leather belt. He looked comfortable, walking with the innate arrogant grace of someone who was used to being watched, admired, obeyed.

He swept her with a cool gaze that made Rhiannon uncomfortably aware of her unruly hair, her crumpled outfit. Her position weak, helpless.

Hopeless.

Who was she kidding? She might put on a face of bravado, but that was all it was. False courage. If Lukas didn't want her here, there was nothing she could do to convince him to let her stay.

She swallowed, realising afresh how out of her depth she truly was.

Out of her mind.

Lukas said nothing, merely took her arm to lead her into the dining room.

The table was set, and Theo stood by the wide windows that overlooked the shoreline. The stars were just visible in a lavender sky, and a few lights twinkled on the water.

'Are there boats out there?' Rhiannon asked, moving closer to the window to look.

'Journalists,' Theo replied flatly. 'Hoping to get a good photo. They know if they come too close we can prosecute.' He spoke slowly, deliberately, as if she were stupid. Rhiannon bit her lip, bit down the annoyance at the man's condescension, and turned to Lukas.

'Have they followed you out here already?'

'They've followed you,' Theo interjected. He smiled, but his eyes were hard. 'Something to do with what you said, I should think. My son's baby.'

Rhiannon flushed at the condemnation in his tone. 'I'm sorry. I was desperate, and I didn't realise the tabloids would make such a fuss.'

Theo looked unconvinced. 'Didn't you? Haven't you read the papers before? The Petrakides family has, alas, been mentioned many times before.'

'Have they?' Rhiannon lifted her chin, her eyes shooting amber sparks. 'I do not read those kinds of papers, Mr Petrakides.'

Theo's mouth hardened, and he jerked a shoulder towards the table. 'Shall we?'

He was gentleman enough to wait to sit until she was seated, but Rhiannon didn't like the way he so quickly and coldly assessed her. Dismissed her. Lukas, she feared, felt the same way. He was simply better at hiding his feelings.

It didn't matter anyway. She couldn't let it matter.

Adeia brought in the first course—vine leaves stuffed with rice and herbs, and a separate dish of olives and feta marinated in olive oil.

It looked excellent, and with an audible growl of her stomach Rhiannon realised how hungry she was.

The first course was followed by moussaka, and a rack of lamb with herbs and served with rice.

It was delicious, and by the time dessert arrived—a nut cake flavoured with cloves and cinnamon—she was so full she felt the waistband of her skirt pinch uncomfortably.

She was also aware of Theo's disapproval of his son. He never said anything outright; in fact he spoke slowly, as if he wanted to use as few words as possible, and even chose those with care.

Still, she saw the disapproval in the tightening of his mouth, the flatness in his eyes, the biting edge of his tone.

Lukas, to his credit, remained mild and relaxed throughout the whole meal, although Rhiannon noticed how his eyes darkened, blanked. His fist bunched on the tablecloth before he forced himself to shrug, nod, smile. Dismiss.

She wondered at the tension in the relationship, what secrets the Petrakides family harboured. What secrets Lukas hid behind the neutral expression, the cold eyes.

This was Annabel's family. Fear and uncertainty churned in Rhiannon's stomach as she thought of giving up her ward to these people.

She couldn't. And she didn't have to, she reminded herself. Not yet. Maybe never.

After cups of strong Greek coffee, Theo jerkily excused himself to bed. He walked stiffly from the room, leaving Rhiannon and Lukas alone amidst the flickering candles and the remnants of a fantastic meal.

'That was wonderful…thank you.' She dabbed at her lips with her napkin, suddenly aware of a palpable tension.

Lukas was rotating his coffee cup slowly between strong, brown fingers, his expression shuttered.

He looked up when she spoke, smiled easily, the darkness of his eyes clearing like the sun coming from behind storm clouds. 'You're not going to end the evening so soon?'

'It's late... I'm tired...' She should be tired, but right now her senses were humming in a way that made her feel gloriously awake and alive. She knew to stay, to linger in the dim, intimate atmosphere of the room, would be dangerous for both of them.

For some reason this attraction had sprung up between them—a powerful force that they both had to avoid...for Annabel's sake.

And for her own.

'Will you walk with me on the beach?' Lukas asked. 'There need not be enmity between us, Rhiannon.'

'Is that so?' Rhiannon tried to laugh; it came out brittle. 'It's easy for you to say that, Lukas. You're holding all the cards.'

'I think,' Lukas said carefully, 'we both want what's best for Annabel.'

'We might disagree about what that is.'

He nodded in acknowledgement, then shrugged. 'It's a beautiful moonlit night. The photographers can't see us in the dark. A few moments... You haven't had any fresh air since you've been here, and the island is beautiful.'

'I can't leave Annabel. If she wakes...'

'Adeia will listen for her,' Lukas said. 'She'd love to.'

Rhiannon hesitated. Perhaps getting to know Lukas would help. It might soften him to her case, to her hopes for Annabel. 'All right,' she agreed, not nearly as reluctantly as she knew she should. 'A few moments.'

Outside the sound of the surf was a muted roar in the distance, and the air was cool and soft. Lukas led her down a paved path to the beach, a stretch of smooth sand that curved around tumbled rocks into the unknown.

He kicked off his shoes, and Rhiannon did the same, enjoying the silky softness between her toes.

They walked quietly down the shoreline for a few minutes, the only sound the lapping of waves.

'Has this island been in your family long?' she finally asked, unnerved by the silence that had stretched between them.

Lukas gave a short, abrupt laugh before shaking his head. 'No, indeed not. Only about twenty-five years or so; the Petrakides fortune is very new.'

'Is it?' Rhiannon had not read that in the papers, but then she'd only been looking for salient details regarding the man she'd believed to be Annabel's father. 'I didn't realise.'

'My father started life as a street-sweeper,' Lukas stated with matter-of-fact flatness. 'He worked his way up to becoming landlord of a tenement in Athens, before banding together with a few partners and buying a block of derelict apartment buildings. They renovated them, turned them into modest, affordable housing units. And he moved up from there. Eventually he didn't need partners.'

'A real success story,' Rhiannon murmured, and Lukas acknowledged this with a brusque nod.

'Yes.'

They walked quietly for a moment, Lukas seeming lost in unhappy thoughts.

Success wasn't everything, Rhiannon supposed. It couldn't buy happiness. It couldn't buy love.

'Your father doesn't seem like a happy man,' she

ventured, surprised by her own candour as well as by Lukas's swift, acknowledging glance.

'No, he isn't,' he agreed after a pause. 'If he seems in a bad temper, it is in part because he is upset over the press. My father has wanted to prove to everyone that he deserves the wealth and success he has earned. He feels any stain on his reputation is a reflection of where he came from—the street. Although...' Lukas's face was obscured in shadow, but there was suddenly a different darkness to his tone. 'Things have not been easy for him lately.'

Rhiannon's steps slowed as memories clicked into place. 'He's dying, isn't he?' she said quietly.

He stiffened, turned in surprise. 'How did you know?'

'I should have realised sooner,' she admitted. 'I'm a palliative nurse—I work in hospices. I've been around a lot of people in his situation.' She shook her head. 'I assumed he was speaking so slowly because he thought I was stupid, but it's because he's losing his words, isn't he? What does he have? A brain tumour?'

Lukas nodded stiffly. 'The doctors have given him at most a few more months. It hasn't, by the grace of God, affected him too much yet, although he occasionally forgets things. Sometimes it is just a word, other times a whole event.' He shook his head. 'It is frustrating, because he knows he is forgetting.'

'I'm sorry,' Rhiannon whispered. 'I know how difficult a dying parent can be.'

'Do you?' Lukas's glance was swift, sharp, assessing, yet there was a flicker of compassion in those silver eyes. 'Tell me about yourself, Rhiannon.'

She shrugged, discomfited by the turn in the conversation he'd so quickly and effortlessly made. 'My parents died three years ago,' she said, as if it were of no consequence. 'I cared for them until their deaths. It is a difficult thing to do.'

'Yes…I suppose it is. And in the time since then?'

'I studied nursing, went into hospice care. It made the most sense after my experience with my parents.'

'A rather lonely-sounding life,' Lukas remarked, his tone expressionless, his face in shadow.

'No more than anyone else's.' Irritation prickled at his judgement. 'I like to think I make a difference. Help people in a time of need that most of us would prefer to ignore.'

'Indeed, that's too true. I only meant that spending time with people twice your age no doubt makes it difficult to find friends with whom you can socialise.'

Rhiannon shrugged. She could hardly argue with that. She didn't *have* a social life—had never had one. She gazed unseeingly at the dark stretch of water, at the stars strung above in an inky sky like diamonds pricked through cloth.

'Why did you come here, Rhiannon?' Lukas asked after a long moment, his voice musing. 'Most women in your position I believe would not have made such an effort. They would have sent a letter, or gone through a solicitor. But to come to the resort, to the reception, and think you could convince me I was a child's father—!' He shook his head, smiling slightly in disbelief, but Rhiannon was only conscious of her own prickling, humiliated response.

'I admit it was foolhardy,' she said in a tight voice that bordered on strangled. She was glad the darkness hid her flushed face. 'I thought a face-to-face confrontation would be the…strongest way to present Annabel to you.'

'To get rid of her, you mean?'

'You have a strange way of looking at things,' she retorted. She stopped to turn and face him. 'I wanted to give her to her father—her family. I would have been ignoring my responsibility if I hadn't attempted to find you. Wouldn't I? To keep her to myself, to make no effort to find a family who might want her, love her…' She trailed off, shaking her head. 'That would have been selfish.'

Lukas was silent for a moment. 'You wanted to keep her?' he asked in a different voice.

'Of course I did—do! She's a baby.'

'An inconvenience, as you said.'

She glanced sharply at him, unsure if he thought that, or if he simply thought *she* did. 'All children are inconveniences,' she said flatly. 'If you remember, I said that didn't mean they weren't worth it.'

'So you want her, but you're prepared to give her up?' Lukas said musingly.

'I *was*,' Rhiannon emphasised. 'Now things are different.' She turned to face him. 'You should know that I won't give Annabel up now. I may have been willing to earlier, when I believed you were the father, when I thought you would love her. But I realise now the situation is completely different. I don't know how I can fit into the family you envisage for her—your family—but I *will* have some part. I'm not walking out of her life now.'

Lukas regarded her silently for a long moment. Rhiannon's heart raced and her face flamed, but she met his gaze, stony-faced and determined, her fists clenched at her sides.

'What about your own life?' he asked in a mild voice. 'Your flat, your job, your friends? If Annabel is Christos's child, her life will be in Greece. Are you prepared to move here?' He quirked one eyebrow in cynical bemusement. 'To give up everything for a child that isn't even yours…for the child of a friend you hadn't seen in ten years? A child,' he continued, his voice turning hard, unyielding, *damning,* 'that you didn't really want? A child with a family in place—a family with far more resources than you could ever possibly have?'

Rhiannon's mouth was dry, her heart like lead. When he framed it in such stark terms her situation seemed bleak indeed. 'It's not about resources,' she said stiffly. 'It's about love.'

'Can you really see yourself in Annabel's life long-term?' Lukas persisted. He kept his voice mild. 'In Greece? Are you prepared to give up your life in Wales to care for a child that is no relation to you?'

His words wound around her heart, whispered their treacherous enticements in her mind. He was trying to dissuade her from staying, she knew. From complicating his life. And yet he made sense.

If she stayed in Greece she would have a half-life at best—the life of someone who lived on the fringes of a family. Again. Yet surely it was no less of a life than she had now.

'You've done your duty,' he continued. 'You've brought her to her family. When the paternity issue is resolved, you can return to your home, your life, with a clear conscience. Isn't that what you really want? Wasn't that what you planned all along?'

His voice was so smooth, so persuasive, and it made Rhiannon realise how impossible a situation this truly was. Could she really move to Greece, ingratiate herself into the Petrakides family...if they would let her?

Yet she couldn't leave Annabel. Not like this. 'I don't...' Her mind swam, diving for words, and came up empty. 'I don't know,' she admitted. 'It's a lot to think about.'

'Indeed.' She heard the satisfaction in his voice and realised he thought he'd chipped away at her resolve. And perhaps he had. She wanted to be in Annabel's life—she wanted Annabel to be loved.

Yet how could it happen? When Lukas had all the power and she had none? When this world—his world—was so foreign to her? So *above* her?

Could she ever even remotely fit in?

Lukas kept walking, and Rhiannon followed him. The waves lapped gently at their feet.

'You said all children are inconveniences,' he remarked after a moment. 'Is that how you were viewed?'

Rhiannon's breath came in a hitched gasp. She was surprised at his perceptiveness. She stared blindly out at the ocean, dark and fathomless, a stretch of blackness, a rush of sound.

'I was adopted,' she said after a long moment. 'My parents never quite got over my arrival into their orderly lives.'

'Many adopted children have loving homes, caring parents. Was that not the case with you?'

She closed her eyes, opened them. 'My parents cared for me,' she said, choosing her words carefully. She would not tarnish their memory. 'In their own way. But I often wondered about my natural parents, and I didn't want Annabel to be the same—especially if she discovered when she was older that she could have known her father and I never gave her the chance. I wanted to spare her that pain.'

Lukas was silent for a long moment. 'I see,' he finally said.

They continued to walk, Rhiannon with sudden, quick steps as if she wanted to escape the confines of the beach, the island, the reach of this man.

He saw too much, understood too much. And yet understood nothing at all.

Lukas grabbed her arm, causing her to stumble before he steadied her, turned her to face him. 'Who are you trying to escape?' His voice was soft, almost gentle, but his hands were firm on her arms and they burned.

'I want to go back to the villa,' Rhiannon said jerkily.

'I didn't mean to upset you.' His arms moved up to her shoulders, drawing her closer. 'I was trying to understand.'

'You don't understand anything,' Rhiannon spat. 'First you judge me as a blackmailer, then as a woman who is willing to give up a child like so much rubbish.'

'I may have been mistaken in those beliefs,' Lukas said quietly. There was no apology in his voice, merely statement of fact. 'I realise now, Rhiannon, that you want what is best for Annabel. You believed that was entrusting her to her family; I think you're right.'

'I've changed my mind,' Rhiannon choked, and his hands tightened briefly on her arms.

'You must trust that I will do my duty by Annabel,' he said calmly, and Rhiannon let out a wild, contemptuous peal of laughter.

'That's the last thing I want,' she cried. 'I don't want

Annabel to be bound to someone by *duty*.' It came out in a sneer, and Lukas looked at her in surprise.

'Why on earth not?'

Rhiannon drew in a shuddering breath. He was close. Far too close. So close that in the pale moonlight bathing his face she could see the gold flecks in his eyes, the stubble on his chin.

'You couldn't understand.'

'Not unless you explain,' he agreed, his voice soft yet firm in the darkness.

'I want you to let me go,' she whispered, but it didn't sound very convincing.

'I will…' Yet he was drawing her closer, and closer still, his lips a breath away from hers. Rhiannon let him hold her, let his breath fan her face, let her lips part open.

There was determination in his eyes, a fierce resolve, and Rhiannon knew that, like her, he was fighting against the tide of desire that washed over both of them, threatening to drag them under.

She knew by the light in his eyes, by the way his fingers bit into her shoulders.

And by the way he released her, suddenly, as if she'd scorched him, so she stumbled back in the sand.

'I'm sorry.' His voice was low. 'I didn't mean to start something here.'

'To kiss me?' Rhiannon challenged, irritated at how bereft she felt.

'I know nothing can happen between us,' Lukas said flatly. 'We cannot complicate matters more with a meaningless affair.'

His assessment stung. A meaningless affair? Of course he would never consider her as a worthy candidate for girlfriend, bride, wife.

She was so far below him, his world. All she was worth was an affair. Dirty, cheap. Meaningless.

'Nothing *will* happen between us,' she restated stonily. 'Because you need to do your damn duty.'

Lukas stared at her for a long moment. 'I've never had someone think so little of me for doing what is right.'

Rhiannon swallowed the guilt that rose up at his quiet words. 'I want you to *want* to do what is right,' she said. 'Not just do it out of some burdensome sense of *responsibility.*'

'You say that as if it's a dirty word.'

'It is!' Rhiannon couldn't hold back the emotion which caused her voice to tremble, her throat to ache. 'It *is.*'

They were standing only a few feet apart, tension binding them together like an invisible wire. Lukas reached out his hands, grabbed her shoulders, and pulled her towards him.

'*This* is not about duty,' he said in a savage whisper before kissing her. It was a hard, punishing kiss—a brand, a seal. When he released her they both were breathing in ragged gasps.

'But you didn't *want* that either, did you?' Rhiannon said when she finally found her voice.

'Yes,' Lukas disagreed flatly. 'The problem is, I want it too much. But I will not have it.'

He turned away, began striding down the beach. Alone in the darkness, Rhiannon had no choice but to follow him back to the distant lights of the villa.

CHAPTER FIVE

THE NEXT MORNING Rhiannon avoided the dining room in exchange for some rolls, yoghurt and honey in the kitchen with Adeia.

She wanted to steer clear of Lukas after their argument last night, and so, with Annabel on her hip and a pair of towels under her arm, she headed for a secluded part of the beach. She slathered them both in suncream and then set up Annabel in a patch of sand. The baby was happy, digging busily, letting the sand trickle through her fingers, chortling with glee at the feel of it on her toes.

Rhiannon watched her, trying to ignore the ache of longing within her, the churning fear at the thought of the future. She wanted simply to enjoy the sun-kissed moment.

Lukas had been completely wrong in thinking she wanted to give Annabel away; it hurt to think he'd judged her so readily, thought so little of her.

It was the last thing she wanted. She'd fought desperately with her conscience over the matter; her heart had wanted to keep the baby, but her mind had told her the father had a right to know. A right to love.

And, her conscience had argued, wasn't it selfish for a single woman in Rhiannon's precarious financial position to keep a child she had no real right to simply because she wanted someone to love? To be loved by someone?

Wasn't it selfish and pathetic?

Yet now, she thought grimly, she might not have the opportunity. Paternity suits, custody battles...

She should have considered this sooner, she supposed. She should have thought of all the possible outcomes to confronting Lukas Petrakides. If only her heart hadn't deceived her with promises of fairy tale endings and happily-ever-afters.

She really was pathetic.

Annabel looked up, gurgled and pointed, and Rhiannon froze. She knew. She could feel him behind her, picture his easy, long-limbed stride.

'Good morning.' Lukas approached them and crouched down next to Annabel. He wore a short-sleeved white shirt and olive-green shorts. He looked clean and strong and wonderful.

Rhiannon tore her gaze away. 'Good morning.'

'Sleep well?' He gave her a questioning glance even as he held Annabel's chubby fist, poured sand into her waiting palm. She giggled in delight.

'No,' Rhiannon confessed irritably. 'Did you?'

His smile was rueful, honest. 'No.'

She was gratified by the admission, although she remained silent.

'She's a cheerful little thing, isn't she?' Lukas said after a moment, as Annabel grabbed his hands and attempted to bring one lean finger towards her open mouth. 'And teething too, I suppose?'

'Watch out—she has two front teeth, and they're sharp.'

Gently Lukas disengaged his finger from Annabel's grasp. 'Thank you.'

'If Christos *is* Annabel's father, who will look after her?' Rhiannon asked suddenly. She needed to know. An idea had begun to form in her mind—hopeless, impractical, her only chance. 'She'll need a nanny, won't she?' she continued, and Lukas regarded her shrewdly.

'Undoubtedly.'

'Better for it to be someone she knows,' Rhiannon continued, and Lukas's mouth tightened.

'Infants form attachments easily. In any case, if she is Christos's child, *I* will adopt her.'

The thought weighed as heavily as a stone on her heart. She swallowed, looked away.

Lukas laid a steadying hand on her arm. 'I realise your own adoptive parents might not have been ideal, but this will be different.'

'Oh?' Rhiannon forced herself to look at him. 'How?'

'I will care for her—' Lukas began, looking slightly, strangely discomfited.

'My parents cared for me too.' Rhiannon cut him off. 'But let me tell you, Lukas, duty is a hard parent. It doesn't kiss your scrapes better, or cuddle you at night, or check for monsters under the bed. It doesn't make you feel loved, make you believe that no matter what happens, what you do, there'll be a place to come home to, arms to put around you. Duty,' she finished flatly, 'is a cold father.' She stared blindly down at the sand, trying to rein her emotions, her memories, back under control.

Lukas's fingers grasped her chin, tilted it so she was looking at him, and she knew he could see the hurt, the pain shadowing her eyes.

'Is that how your father was?' he asked quietly. 'Your mother?'

Rhiannon shrugged. 'I don't blame them. They did the best they could.'

'But it wasn't enough, was it? And you're afraid that Annabel will suffer as you did?'

'Yes, I am,' she admitted. 'And shouldn't I be? You've already shown me what a cold, restrained person you are.'

The look he gave her was full of hidden heat. 'Have I?' he murmured, his tone so languorous that Rhiannon jerked her chin from his hand, scooted a few feet away.

'Yes. In terms of how you see your responsibility towards Annabel.'

He shrugged, spread his hands. 'I can only promise to do what is right. To give her every opportunity, every comfort.'

'That's not enough.'

'It will have to be.'

She knew it was more than most men would give— more than she had any right to expect. But it wasn't enough. She wouldn't let it be enough.

Because she knew how duty without love became a burden, a weight. A resentment. As it had become with her. Lukas couldn't see that, couldn't understand.

A loud whirring filled the air, and Rhiannon blinked up in surprise as a helicopter came into sight.

'That's not the press, is it?' she asked, one hand shading her eyes, and Lukas shook his head.

'No, it is a Petrakides helicopter.' He pointed to the side of the craft. 'See the entwined Ps? That is our emblem.'

Rhiannon saw the entwined letters, first in the

Roman alphabet, then in Greek. 'What is a Petrakides helicopter doing here?' she asked.

Lukas took her hand in his, tugged. 'Come and see.' There was a surprising smile on his face, like that of a little boy, and, scooping up Annabel, Rhiannon followed him to the landing pad.

A young Greek man emerged from the helicopter as they approached, and Lukas called a greeting. The man called back, and began unloading boxes and parcels from the body of the chopper.

Rhiannon stood back uncertainly, until Lukas beckoned her. 'Come. These things are for you.'

'For me?' she repeated blankly.

'Yes…for you and Annabel.'

He took Annabel from her, jiggling the baby on his hip, so she could inspect the parcels. Hesitantly Rhiannon opened one box to find it full of baby toys, brightly coloured, soft and enticing.

'You shouldn't have…' she began, and he shrugged her protestation aside.

'Of course I should.'

More boxes revealed clothes—play clothes for Annabel, sensible, sturdy, and well made.

'Open that one.' A faint smile curved his mouth upwards, softened his face, his eyes.

Raising her eyebrows, too curious not to obey, Rhiannon opened the box he'd indicated.

'More clothes…' Not for Annabel, though. For her. She held up a white cotton blouse—simple, flowing, with scalloped lace along its scooped neckline. She found trousers, loose and comfortable, in turquoise silk. A sundress, lemon-yellow, with skinny, flirty straps.

She lowered the dress, her hands bunching in the filmy material.

'You really shouldn't have.'

'Perhaps not,' Lukas agreed quietly, his teasing little smile still flickering along her nerve endings, 'but I wanted to.'

It came out almost unwillingly, and Rhiannon found herself saying, 'You don't like to want things?'

'No, I don't,' he admitted, and there was a hardness to his tone that caused the light, happy atmosphere to evaporate. Even Annabel noticed, and squirmed in Lukas's arms.

'Why not?' Rhiannon asked, uncertainty causing her voice to waver just a little bit.

'Because wanting—giving in to your desires—causes misery and ruin. Not only for yourself, but for everyone around you.' Lukas spoke flatly. His face was hard, his eyes as flat and cold as steel. 'I've spent my life cleaning up other people's messes, paying for their mistakes. Mistakes that could have been avoided if they hadn't given in to selfish whims, desires. If they'd only done their duty—as I have done and you seem to think so lightly of.' With a curt nod, he handed Annabel back to her. 'I'll have these boxes delivered to your room. Dinner is at half past seven.'

Rhiannon pressed Annabel to her, inhaled her clean, innocent scent. She felt as if she'd just received an unexpected glimpse into Lukas's mind, perhaps even into his heart.

Who were the people he was talking about? Whose messes had he cleaned up? She could hardly ask, and she doubted Lukas would volunteer answers anyway. Yet it provided a flickering of understanding, even compassion, of why he rated responsibility so highly.

Annabel grizzled, and Rhiannon knew she needed a bottle and a nap. She headed upstairs, mind and heart still whirling.

SEVERAL HOURS LATER Annabel was fed and bathed, having spent an exhausting and enjoyable afternoon playing with her new toys. Rhiannon gave her a bottle before settling her in the new cot—not a lightweight travel one, but a sturdy pine frame bed, with soft pink blankets.

Rhiannon knew some assistant must have picked out the clothes and toys for them. All Lukas had had to do was issue a terse order over the phone. It had been a responsibility to him, a duty fulfilled.

Yet he'd *wanted* to…

She slipped on the white blouse and turquoise trousers, admiring the silkiness of the material, the way the clothes skimmed her figure, highlighted what slight curves she had without clinging or revealing.

Her hair fell in its usual curls around her face, wild and untamed, but her eyes sparkled and her cheeks were flushed with…what? Nervousness? Expectation?

Excitement.

Lukas was waiting for her at the bottom of the stairs. He smiled when he saw how she was dressed—a smile that for one soul-splitting second lit his eyes with feral possession and made both Rhiannon's heart and her step stumble.

She grasped the wrought-iron banister, her fingers curling around it for balance.

His smile turned polite, a courtesy, and he murmured, 'I like that outfit on you.'

'Someone who works for you has good taste,' Rhiannon quipped, to give herself time to recover from that one brief, scorching look.

Lukas raised his eyebrows. 'Why do you think I hired someone to buy you clothes?'

Rhiannon checked herself. 'Didn't you?'

He shrugged. 'Maybe I chose all the things myself, on the internet, and had them flown over.'

Was he teasing? A faint blush stole across her cheeks, rendered her speechless. The idea that Lukas himself had picked out the clothes, decided what she would like, what she would look good in, *knew her size*—it was so personal, so intimate... The thought burned her as much as his touches had.

He watched her with dark, knowing eyes—eyes that knew how discomfited she was, and perhaps enjoyed it.

He said nothing, merely took her firmly by the elbow, his hand dry and warm, and led her into the dining room.

Theo stood by his chair as they entered, stiff and straight, his shoulders thrown back, a haughty look hardening his features.

Rhiannon didn't take it to heart. She knew it was not directed towards her, but was rather a defence against compassion or, worse, pity.

She smiled at the older man. He looked away.

The meal Adeia served was again delicious, and Rhiannon found she could almost relax. Theo said little, but Lukas kept up a flow of conversation about the islands, Athens, business. All fairly innocent, innocuous topics that made Rhiannon drop her guard for one treacherous moment.

Then a phone rang, trilled against Lukas's chest, and

he slipped a mobile from his breast pocket. 'Excuse me... Hello?' His face darkened and he stood, turning away from Rhiannon. He spoke in rapid Greek before covering the mouthpiece of the little phone and saying, 'I need to take this privately. I beg your pardon.'

Rhiannon watched him go, her heart starting a slow, heavy thud.

Theo spoke what was already screaming through her own mind.

'That will be Christos.'

'Perhaps now,' Rhiannon said, as steadily as she could, 'we will get to the bottom of this.'

Theo's eyes glittered, and he said the one word with effort. 'Perhaps.'

The room was silent, heavy with tense expectation. Rhiannon couldn't eat, couldn't even pretend to pick at her food. Adeia cleared the plates and brought in the little cups of thick black coffee that burned down Rhiannon's throat like acid.

Still Lukas did not come.

What was going on? What was being said?

And, most importantly, what was going to happen?

Theo watched her, his eyes bright. Rhiannon tried not to let his stare unnerve her, even though her throat was dry, and she felt as if she would choke on her own words.

Finally Lukas returned, his face blank. 'Rhiannon, may I speak with you? In the study.'

'You can say it here,' Theo protested, his tone angry even though his words were halting. 'Is Christos the father?'

'I will speak to Rhiannon first. Excuse us, Papa.'

Woodenly Rhiannon followed him to a dark, wood-panelled room, with bookshelves lining all the walls except for a picture window that looked out directly onto a rocky outcropping, an unforgiving line of shore.

'That was Christos on your phone, wasn't it?' she said into the silence. 'Did he say…?'

'Yes, he did.' Lukas thrust his hands deep in his trouser pockets. 'He admitted everything. Meeting Leanne, using my name, taking her to Naxos. He repeated the story you told me almost exactly, and I hadn't even told him what you'd said.'

'It's not as if he would make it up,' Rhiannon said, her voice sounding stilted, unnatural. Why did this hurt? she wondered. It was no more than either of them had expected.

'I wouldn't put anything past Christos. He was adamant, in fact, that he had used protection, but mistakes can happen.'

'Annabel is not a mistake!' Rhiannon looked up, a fierce golden light in her eyes. She realised she was trembling.

'Not to you, perhaps,' Lukas agreed. 'But to Christos she is nothing more than that. As soon as possible I will begin adoption proceedings. Christos is delighted with the solution.' His mouth tightened briefly, and Rhiannon had a flickering of perception that Christos was not the kind of person who expressed his delight. No doubt he'd *expected* Lukas to take care of his child… his bastard. Thought it was Lukas's responsibility, as Lukas himself did.

'Obviously such action will require help on your part. As Annabel's current legal guardian, you will have to go through court to sign such rights over to me.'

Rhiannon stiffened. 'I told you, I'm staying in her life. I'm not signing anything over.'

Lukas sighed. 'Rhiannon, the last thing I want is a custody case. But Annabel is my great-niece—my blood relation.'

'Blood is so important to you?'

'Of course it is!'

Rhiannon shook her head, refusing to admit just how backed into a corner she was. 'Christos hasn't taken a paternity test yet—'

'No, but it is a mere formality now. He will take one when he returns to Athens.'

'Then we have a little time to work something out,' Rhiannon said. She drew herself up, met his gaze full-on. 'Because I don't want a court case either, Lukas, but I'm not bowing out simply because you feel you have more rights. Leanne didn't come to you when she thought you were the father. She came to me. That says something.'

'Oh?' Lukas was still—dangerously so. Rhiannon already knew what ran deep beneath those still waters. His eyes were a lethal silver, his expression like that of a predator right before it snapped open its jaws, devoured its prey. 'What does it say to you?'

'That Leanne trusted me to love Annabel.'

'Yet you were going to give her away.'

She refused to be drawn. 'I've already explained why I was prepared to do that—and, as I've said, things are different now. I'm staying.'

Lukas raised his eyebrows. 'For ever?'

Rhiannon swallowed. For ever was a long time. Yet she could hardly walk away when Annabel was older and more attached to her. She could hardly walk away at all.

'You haven't thought this through, have you, Rhiannon?' Lukas jeered softly. 'You're full of big ideas about loving Annabel, but you're not quite sure how it works out in the details. The *duties*.'

'I...'

'Because if you want to be her mother, if you want to love her, then you have to stay. You'll have to make your home in Greece. You'll have to live in the Petrakides pocket. You'll have to—' he finished with heavy emphasis '—become my responsibility...*if* I'm prepared to accept it.'

Rhiannon's mouth opened, and after a moment of silent struggling she finally choked out, 'I will never, ever, be someone's responsibility again.'

'It's not your choice.'

'It *is* my choice,' she countered fiercely. 'And just because you have an overdeveloped sense of what you're required to do in life it doesn't mean I have to fall neatly in with those plans! I'll stay in Annabel's life, but on my own terms, and not in "the Petrakides pocket", as you so snidely put it! I will provide for myself, live by myself, be completely independent...' She trailed off, running out of self-righteous steam at his look of blatant disbelief.

'That,' he said with quiet, final derision, 'is not going to happen. Do you actually think for one second that you can set up house somewhere and have me visit at weekends? My dreaded sense of duty requires a bit more action than that.'

Rhiannon pushed her hands through her hair. She wanted to slow down her whirling mind—knew she couldn't think through real solutions when her head felt as if it was spinning and her heart burned within her. 'I could be her nanny...'

'That is not your decision to make.'

'You can't cut me out of her life like this!' Rhiannon cried, her voice jagged, desperate.

'I can do whatever I want,' Lukas said bluntly. 'If you want to drag this through court, you can. But you will be bankrupted and vilified in the process. I will win any case, Rhiannon. Be assured.'

'Would you be so cruel?' she whispered, and he shrugged.

'I have Annabel's best interests at heart. I want to provide her with a secure, stable environment, and frankly I'm not sure you fit into that picture.'

Rhiannon shook her head. 'I'm not leaving until Christos takes the paternity test. We have some time to think of a plan that is beneficial to everyone.'

Lukas nodded brusquely, his face tight. 'Very well. We can speak about this later.'

Rhiannon nodded. She would have to think of a better game plan—a clearer idea of just how she could remain in Annabel's life without being beholden to Lukas Petrakides. How he would let her.

Right now, it seemed impossible.

She opened the study door, saw Theo outside, and realised he'd probably heard every word. She couldn't summon enough emotional energy to care. Jerking her head in a nod of goodnight, she walked stiffly out of the study and up the stairs.

In her room Annabel was sleeping soundly, and Rhiannon slipped out of the silky clothes and into her old pyjamas—a tee-shirt and pair of boxer shorts. A silky nightgown, modest and yet achingly sensual, had been included in the box of clothes, but she couldn't wear something so intimate. Not if Lukas had had anything to do with the choosing.

Lukas. She couldn't escape him, couldn't run from the way he affected her. Angered her. And yet he made her ache, need. Wonder, want.

Want. Why couldn't Lukas let himself want anything? What a cold existence—to deny yourself any pleasure simply because it was pleasing to you…made you happy. Was that why he hadn't slept with a woman for two years?

There had to be a lot of sexual repression going on there. Rhiannon smothered a rueful smile. If anyone was sexually repressed, it was her. One burning look from Lukas and she was on fire. He moved towards her and she melted. She'd never reacted to any man like that. She'd never had the chance.

Like Lukas, she acknowledged, she hadn't given in to desire. Hadn't allowed herself to want. There had been no time, no opportunity. And duty to her parents had bound her with loveless cords.

Unlike Lukas, she wanted love…not duty. She wanted *more.*

Rhiannon watched the moon sift silver patterns over the floor, listened to Annabel's soft breathy sighs of sleep, and felt miles from such relaxation herself.

Her stomach growled, and she realised that she'd eaten hardly anything at dinner.

She was hungry.

She slipped out of bed, opened her door as quietly as possible. It had to be past midnight. The house was quiet and still. Surely no one would notice—no one would mind—if she slipped down to the kitchen and grabbed a roll?

She tiptoed down the hallway, feeling strangely guilty. She stopped when she heard music.

It was coming from downstairs, floating from behind the closed door of the lounge, and it was haunting. Sad, melodious, beautiful.

Rhiannon walked downstairs, stood in front of the door, and listened. The music spoke to her soul and made her ache. Who was playing?

Stealthily, she pushed the door with the tips of her fingers and peeked in.

Lukas was at the piano, absorbed in his playing. His long, lean fingers moved gracefully over the keys, evoking that sound, that glorious emotion.

Rhiannon didn't know if she'd made a noise, or if the door had creaked, or if perhaps Lukas had just sensed her, but he looked up, his face freezing into a blank mask, his hands stilling on the keys.

'No...don't stop. It's beautiful.'

'Thank you.'

She knew that polite, impersonal tone. Knew it and hated it. She took a step into the room. 'I didn't realise you played the piano.'

'Not many people do.'

Rhiannon bit her lip. Something about that music, that soulful melody, made her want to breach his defences, to break that blank mask and find the man living, breathing, *wanting* underneath. 'Did you take lessons when you were a child?'

'No.' Lukas eased the cover over the keys. 'I taught myself.'

Rhiannon gasped in surprise; she couldn't help it. Anyone who played like that had to have natural talent, but to teach himself...? He must have been a prodigy.

'You're surprised,' Lukas remarked with a sharp little laugh. 'No doubt you think such a cold, *restrained* man shouldn't be able to play beautiful music.'

'Lukas…' Rhiannon didn't know what to say—hadn't expected him to remember her words from earlier. Hadn't thought they might hurt him. 'I always wanted to learn to play the piano,' she admitted.

'Did you have lessons?'

She shook her head, a sudden lump in her throat. She thought of the dusty piano in the front room of her parents' house, never touched, never played. It had been strictly off limits to her.

Lukas watched her for a moment, his eyes dark, fathomless, then he slid over on the piano bench and lifted the cover up again. 'Come here.'

'Wh…what?'

He patted the seat next to him. 'Your first lesson.'

Surprised, touched, Rhiannon moved forward. She sat next to him, thigh to thigh, creating a spark of awareness deep within her.

'Here.' He placed her hands on the keys, then laid his own hands gently on top. 'This is an E.' He plucked one note, moving her own fingers. 'And this is a D.' He continued playing notes, moving her fingers, until Rhiannon recognised the tune.

'"Mary Had A Little Lamb"!'

He smiled, a flash of whiteness. 'You need to start somewhere.'

'Yes…' She was suddenly achingly conscious of his hands on hers, the closeness of their bodies, the intimacy of the moment. Her heart began to thud, desire pooled in her middle, and she could only sit there helpless. Shameless.

'Why did you come down here?' Lukas asked, breaking the moment.

'I was hungry,' Rhiannon admitted. 'I didn't eat much at dinner, and then I heard...'

'Then you should go to the kitchen.' He rose from the piano bench. 'I'll show you the way.'

She followed him into the wide, friendly room at the back of the villa, its stainless steel counter-tops and appliances softened by the colourful prints on the wall and the scrubbed pine table.

Lukas opened the refrigerator. 'What would you like?' he asked over his shoulder. 'Bread, salad, or...?' His smile glinted with sudden mischief as he brought out a plate. 'The nectar of the gods?'

He proffered a tray holding a large slice of baklava, the traditional Greek dessert, dripping with nuts and honey. Rhiannon's mouth watered.

'Definitely the nectar,' she said, and, smiling as if he had expected no less, Lukas cut her a generous slice.

She'd thought he would give it to her on a plate, with a fork. Instead he offered it to her from his own hand, lifting the filo pastry to her lips for her to take a bite.

There was a challenge in his eyes, heady, seductive, and the atmosphere changed. Just as it had before, the simple exchange turned into something potent, filled with possibilities both wonderful and terrifying.

No. This time she would not play his game. He wanted her to literally eat from his hand, and she would not do it. She knew how this ended—had experienced it before—with him thrusting her away.

She wasn't going to give herself the chance to be rejected. Again.

'Thank you.' She took the baklava from his hand and took a bite.

Lukas watched, one hip braced against the countertop, his eyes following her movements as she self-consciously tried to eat the dessert.

Baklava was not an easy thing to eat at the best of times, and it was incredibly difficult when you had a spectator. Rhiannon was conscious of the flakes of pastry on her lips, the drip of honey on her chin.

Lukas reached out, touched the drip on her chin and licked his thumb. 'Sweet.'

'Don't.'

He raised his eyebrows, his gaze still heavy lidded, and waited.

'Don't,' she repeated, her voice a raw whisper. She set the baklava on the counter, wiped the honey from her mouth. 'You don't even *want* to. You don't even like me…'

Lukas's eyes flared with startled awareness. 'Why do you think I don't like you?' he murmured, and before Rhiannon could protest he was drawing her to him, his hands cupping her face, her head tilted back to meet his own regretful gaze. 'I fight with myself every day,' he said. 'I don't want to want you because of *me,* not because of you. Never because of you.' His lips were inches from hers. 'You drive me wild, Rhiannon. When I'm near you I can't think. I can only…' his voice came out in a jagged rasping of sound '…want.'

Rhiannon swayed towards him. She could feel the heat from his body, the desire pulsing through him, drawing her dangerously nearer.

No one had ever wanted her because of who she was, and yet here was Lukas wanting her. Wanting *her*.

Even if he didn't want to. Suddenly that didn't matter. All that she could get her head—her heart—around was that Lukas wanted her. And for that moment, with their bodies so close, yet not touching, his hands gentle on her face, it was enough.

She closed that last tempting inch, brushed her lips against his. His hands slipped up to tangle in her hair, to bring her even closer. Her arms went around him, revelling in the hardness of his chest, his shoulders, as he moulded her to him.

'Rhiannon...' he breathed against her lips. 'Rhiannon...I want you...'

She smiled against his mouth. 'You don't want anything.'

'I want *you*,' he repeated, almost savagely, and deepened the kiss. Rhiannon knew there was regret in his voice, and there was self-condemnation, but she didn't care. It was all too sweet, too wonderful, too consuming.

Her head fell back as she surrendered to the ministrations of his mouth, his tongue, his hands.

'You taste sweet,' he murmured against her skin, and she smiled.

'I was eating honey.'

'No, sweeter.' He was trailing kisses down her throat, his hands reaching under her tee-shirt to skim over her breasts, his thumbs teasing the sensitive nipples to aching peaks.

Rhiannon arched, moaned. She couldn't help it. She'd never felt so alive—every sense, every nerve ending humming, throbbing to life.

Lukas took her buttocks in his hands and hoisted her easily onto the countertop. Her legs wrapped around him as a matter of instinct, pulled him closer, felt his hardness at the joining of her legs, and gasped at the contact. Gasped with pleasure.

Somehow they were on top of the counter, tangled legs, bodies pressed together, his hand creeping up her thigh, nudging her old pyjama shorts aside to tease the damp curls at her femininity.

Rhiannon gasped at the intimate intrusion, the novel feeling of someone touching her where she'd never been touched before.

'All right?' Lukas murmured, looking down at her, his pupils dilated with desire, his face flushed with heat, his finger still teasing, nudging her knowingly, turning her to liquid heat.

Rhiannon opened her mouth to reply. She was about to say yes, of course she was all right. She was more than all right. Then, quite suddenly, she wasn't.

Suddenly she was aware of her rucked-up clothes, of the metal counter pressing coldly into her back, of the fact that she was lying splayed out on a chopping block like a piece of meat… And, really, wasn't she being treated like one?

Wasn't she letting herself be treated like one?

Lukas didn't love her. He didn't even *want* to be here with her. She was like a craving he had to satisfy, an itch he had to scratch, and he didn't even want to.

She closed her eyes briefly, unwilling to continue, unable to stop. She'd brought herself to this humiliating moment. She'd allowed herself to fall so far, stoop so low, simply because she wanted a little—*a little*—love.

And yet love had nothing to do with this.

Her eyes still closed, she felt Lukas pulling her shirt down. He kissed her navel, making her shiver. He tugged gently on her hand and Rhiannon slipped from the hard metal surface, her eyes open but averted.

'Look what giving in to desire does,' Lukas said, and Rhiannon heard the derision. 'Rutting like animals in the kitchen,' he continued flatly. 'No self-control at all.'

'I'll go,' Rhiannon whispered, her throat raw and tight.

Lukas had turned away from her, one hand fisted in his hair. Could he not even bear to look at her? Was he that disgusted?

'Perhaps it's best,' he said quietly, and Rhiannon fled.

LUKAS WAITED TILL he'd heard Rhiannon's soft, scared footsteps on the stairs, heard the relieved click of her door. Then he swore.

He strode from the kitchen, found the lounge, and sat down at the piano—his usual source of comfort. His refuge.

Except tonight there was no escape from the torment. His body throbbed with unfulfilled desire even as his mind ached with the knowledge of what he'd stooped to…what he'd almost done.

All because of desire.

He shook his head, his fingers splaying over the piano keys without making a sound.

Desire. He'd seen it ruin lives—his mother's, his three sisters', his nephew's. All of them had given away their self-respect, their dignity, for a few moments of grasped pleasure, a mistaken belief in love.

He'd spent his life witnessing their mistakes…paying for them. He'd promised his father, and more importantly himself, that he would never give in to base cravings, no matter how strong or urgent, and watch need wreck his life.

For a brief moment he remembered his own need—a boy begging for love. Clinging, grasping, pleading…a weak, pathetic fool.

Never again.

Of course he'd had women. He was neither a monk nor a saint. But the affairs had been brief, a matter of expediency on both sides, and each time the woman he'd used—he couldn't give it a better word—had understood what she was getting.

And what she wasn't.

But Rhiannon…*Rhiannon* was off limits. He knew that. She was innocent, vulnerable. Dangerous. An affair with her would lead to complications he didn't need, couldn't afford. He closed his eyes, imagining the tabloid headlines, the smearing of the Petrakides name.

And Rhiannon would be hurt.

He knew that—knew she was too innocent to keep herself from falling in love. Love was something he would never give. Something he would never want.

Because, as she'd reminded him, he didn't want anything. Refused to allow himself to want, to be weak.

Yet he wanted her.

Lukas swore again. Why did that slip of a woman, with too much curly hair and eyes like sunlit puddles, make him go crazy? Lose control? *Want* to lose control?

That was what chilled him the most.

Nobody made Lukas Petrakides lose control.

Nobody.

Except this one woman who had come closer than anyone else.

He stood up from the piano, strode to the window.

Outside the sky was black, pricked with stars reflecting blurrily on the sea below.

He could hear the gentle lapping of the waves, the timeless sound of surf and wind, and felt soothed by the power, the effortless control of the ocean around him.

Things had to change. Rhiannon had to go. He'd wanted to give her time, to sow the seeds of doubt that would have her leaving for Wales in good conscience, thinking it was *her* idea.

Now he realised there was no time. The desire was too strong, the danger too real. Tomorrow *he* would leave...and soon so would she.

The thought of never seeing her again made Lukas's gut twist. He didn't want her to go.

The realisation shamed him. Already she was making him want, making him weak. It had to stop.

Even if it hurt. Especially if it did.

CHAPTER SIX

'YOU'RE LEAVING?' RHIANNON clutched the back of the chair as she watched Lukas riffle through some papers. This was the Lukas from the resort—the business Lukas, the professional man.

He wore a grey silk suit, tailored and immaculate, and he didn't even look at her as he said, 'Yes. I have business in Athens.'

'You're just going to leave me here? Like...' Her mind struggled to remember the Greek myths from his school-days. 'Like Ariadne?'

Lukas looked up, eyes glinting briefly with admiring humour. 'Ah, yes. Poor Ariadne. Theseus just left her on that island—Naxos, in fact—after she helped him slay the minotaur. A fitting comparison. Remember, though, she was rescued by Dionysus.'

'I don't want to be rescued,' Rhiannon flashed, and Lukas smiled coolly.

'No one's offering. Christos will be arriving in Athens within the week, and I need to be there.'

'I should be too...'

'No, Rhiannon,' he corrected her gently, but with ominous finality. 'That is not your place.'

'Annabel...'

'Is my responsibility.'

'Not yet!' Rhiannon retorted, eyes flashing fire, and Lukas sighed.

'Rhiannon, after all we've discussed, haven't you yet realised how impossible this situation is? I know you feel an obligation towards Annabel, an admirable desire to see her well settled, but—'

'Well *loved*,' Rhiannon corrected fiercely, and Lukas acknowledged this with a brief, brusque nod.

'You cannot possibly mean to sacrifice your career, your life, to be near her in Greece. No one requires that of you.'

No one wants that of you. That was what he was really saying. Rhiannon looked down. It had been a long, sleepless night, reliving those shaming moments in the kitchen with Lukas, her own flooding desire.

She'd also tried to think of solutions, possibilities that would keep her with Annabel.

Nothing had come to mind.

'What if I want to?' she finally whispered, and Lukas stilled.

'Don't presume,' he warned softly, 'that what happened between us last night meant...*anything*.'

'Don't flatter yourself,' Rhiannon replied, blushing painfully. 'If I choose to stay in Greece it will be because of Annabel only, not you. Last night—'

'Was a mistake.' His tone was so final, so brutal, that Rhiannon flinched.

'One you seem to keep repeating,' she finally said through numb lips.

The look he gave her from under frowning brows was dark, quelling. 'You don't need to remind me. I'm well aware of the situation—which is, in part, why I'm leaving.'

'Because of me?'

He picked up his briefcase, slid his mobile phone into his jacket pocket and stood before her, glancing down at her with something close to compassion.

'You need to let go, Rhiannon,' he said quietly, adding so she barely heard, 'And so do I.' He handed her a mobile that matched his. 'Keep this with you. I've programmed my own mobile number on speed dial. You can ring me if you run into any trouble.'

And then, with a faint whiff of his pine-scented cologne, he was gone. Rhiannon slipped the phone into her pocket, then sagged against the study chair, her hands slick on the smooth leather.

She knew she should be relieved that Lukas was gone. At least now they wouldn't be clashing. There could be no confrontations. She had a week's reprieve— a week to decide how she could stay in Annabel's life... *if* she could.

Rhiannon realised the impossibility, the sacrifice. Was it worth it? Was she willing?

She had no answers.

From upstairs Rhiannon heard Annabel's faint cries as she woke from her morning nap. She hurried up, smiled involuntarily at the sight of Annabel's dark fleecy curls and wide brown eyes peering over the edge of the cot.

'Hello, sweetheart. Shall we go to the beach this morning? Try out all your new sand toys?'

As she picked the baby up, cuddled her close, she heard the sound of a helicopter's engine throbbing to life.

Rhiannon moved to the window, Annabel on her hip,

and watched the helicopter disappear into the horizon like an angry black insect.

The house suddenly seemed ridiculously silent and still.

'Come on,' Rhiannon said as cheerfully as she could, 'let's find your swimming costume.'

The morning passed pleasantly enough, and, after lunch in the kitchen with Adeia, Rhiannon put Annabel down for a nap and read one of the paperbacks Lukas had included in his box of provisions.

When Annabel woke again, she changed her and took her down to the kitchen. Adeia was busy at the stove, but had a ready smile for the baby.

'May we eat with you again?' Rhiannon asked, only to have her spirits sink when Adeia gave a vigorous shake of her head.

'Oh, no, miss,' she said in halting English. 'The master...Mr Petrakides...expects you to dine with him tonight.'

For one brief, hope-filled second Rhiannon thought the housekeeper meant Lukas. Perhaps he'd returned while she was upstairs, was waiting for her...?

The realisation of her own happiness at such a thought made her flush in shame. Of course Adeia meant Theo. And the prospect of dining alone with the sour old man made Rhiannon's spirits sink further.

She could hardly argue with the housekeeper, however, and to refuse Theo would be outright rude. With a sigh, Rhiannon set to feeding Annabel.

After giving the baby a bath and settling her for the night, she considered her own choice of clothing.

She finally settled on a pair of plain black trousers

she'd brought with her, paired with the scalloped lace blouse she'd worn before.

Theo was waiting for her in the dining room. His face cracked into a rare and reluctant smile as she entered.

'I didn't think you would come.'

'That would have been rude,' Rhiannon replied with a small smile, and he acknowledged this with an inclination of his head.

'Yes…but what is a little rudeness? After all, I have been rude to you.' He spoke slowly, but there was precision to his words. Rhiannon blinked in surprise.

'I'm surprised you admit as much,' she said after a moment.

Theo shrugged, and indicated for Rhiannon to take her seat. She did so, placing the heavy linen napkin across her lap. Theo poured them both wine and sat.

'I have come to realise,' he began carefully, 'that you will be around for some time to come.'

'Oh? Has Lukas told you as much?' Rhiannon could feel her heart starting to beat faster, the adrenalin racing like molten silver through her veins. It was fuelled by hope. She forced herself to remain calm, took a sip of wine and let the velvety liquid slide down her throat.

'He has said little,' Theo admitted with a faint frown. 'But that hardly matters. I am right, am I not? You intend to stay?'

'Yes, I do.' Rhiannon met his gaze directly. Adeia entered with the first course—a traditional Greek salad of tomatoes, cucumbers, feta cheese and black olives.

'You want to be this child's mother?' Theo asked musingly, and Rhiannon felt the word reverberate through her soul. Her heart.

Mother. A real mother. Mummy.

'Legal guardian' sounded terribly cold in comparison.

'Yes,' she said, and her determination—her desire—were evident in the stridency of her tone.

Theo nodded, and Rhiannon was surprised to see a gleam of satisfaction in his eyes. What game was he playing? She'd sensed from the moment he'd rested contemptuous eyes on her that he'd wanted her gone. She was a nuisance, a nonentity.

Yet now he seemed pleased that she intended to stick around.

Why? She should be suspicious, even afraid, but the hope was too strong.

'I don't know quite how it will work out,' she began carefully, after the first course was cleared. 'Lukas doesn't seem to think there can be a place for me. But...I'm hoping to convince him when he returns from Athens.'

'He doesn't?' Theo repeated, and he almost sounded amused.

'Yes. I intend to live my own life, Mr Petrakides, as best as I can. Back in Cardiff I was a nurse, and I imagine that my credentials could in some way be transferred to Greece.' The idea had come to her that afternoon, and though she knew it was half-thought and hazy, it still gave her hope.

He raised one sceptical eyebrow. 'And the language barrier?'

'I will have to learn Greek, naturally,' Rhiannon replied with some dignity. 'I intend to anyway, for Annabel's sake. She is, after all, half-Greek.'

'Indeed.' Theo swirled the wine in his glass thoughtfully. 'And how do you suppose my son will react to such plans? You living your own life—with Annabel in your care, I presume?'

'Not necessarily,' Rhiannon said quickly. 'Annabel could remain with you—with Lukas—as long as I have visitation rights.'

It was a compromise, and one she thought Lukas might accept. She could not become someone's responsibility... Lukas's burden...even if he wanted her to. She couldn't bear to see duty turn to dread, responsibility to resentment. And she couldn't let that happen to Annabel, either.

Theo merely laughed dryly.

'We shall see what happens,' he said, his eyes glinting with humour.

Rhiannon found herself feeling both uneasy and strangely comforted by his cryptic remark.

Theo excused himself to go to bed soon after dinner.

Rhiannon noticed his pale, strained face, the way he walked slowly and stiffly out of the room. She had not broached the subject of his illness, wanting to respect his privacy, yet now it tugged at her conscience, her compassion.

With a little sigh, and realising she was lonely, she went slowly upstairs.

The mobile phone Lukas had given her was trilling insistently when she entered the room. Rhiannon hurried to it before Annabel stirred, and pushed the talk button.

'Hello?'

'I've been trying to call you for over an hour,' Lukas said, annoyance edging his voice. 'You do realise what this phone is for?'

'Yes,' Rhiannon replied. 'For me to get in contact

with you. I had no idea you intended to use it the other way round.'

There was a brief pause, and then Lukas said gruffly, 'I wanted to make sure you and Annabel were all right.'

A ridiculous bubble of delight filled Rhiannon. Lukas almost sounded as if he cared. She didn't know why that should please her so much, why it made her face split into a wide smile, but it did.

Oh, it did.

'We're fine,' she said. She sat on the edge of the bed, the phone cradled to her ear. 'I had dinner with your father tonight.'

'You did?' Lukas sounded surprised. 'And you weren't on the menu?'

Rhiannon giggled; Lukas's answering chuckle made shivers of delight race along her arms, down her spine, straight to her soul. 'No, actually, I wasn't. We were both civil...more than civil. Although...' She paused, going over the dinner conversation in her mind. 'He almost sounded like he had some kind of plan.'

'Plan?'

'For me. Us.'

'Us?' Lukas repeated thoughtfully, and Rhiannon was conscious of the intimacy, the presumption of the word. There was no 'us'.

Except right now it felt as if there was.

'I don't know. Perhaps I was reading too much into a few comments,' she said hastily.

'You don't know my father,' Lukas replied. 'He always has a plan.'

They were both silent for a moment; Rhiannon could hear Lukas breathing. There was something so intimate about a telephone conversation, she thought. A conversation just to hear voices, to connect.

A connection.

'As long as you're all right,' Lukas finally said a bit brusquely, 'I should go. It's been a long day.'

'Yes, of course.' So much for the connection. 'Goodbye,' she said awkwardly.

Lukas's voice was rough as he replied, 'Goodnight, Rhiannon.'

Rhiannon listened to the click in her ear before disconnecting herself. She laid the mobile phone on her bedside table, closed her eyes.

The maelstrom of emotions within her was confusing, potent. She shouldn't be affected by one little phone conversation—yet she was.

She was.

She wanted him. She missed him.

Rhiannon pushed herself off the bed, grabbed her pyjamas.

She would not think about Lukas. There was no point. There was no future. In a few days, weeks, everything could change. Lukas could demand she leave.

Or he could ask her to stay.

Hadn't she learned there were no fairy tale endings? Rhiannon reminded herself. Surely she wasn't dreaming…again?

SHE WAS SHAKEN awake several hours later.

'Miss! Miss Rhiannon!' Adeia crouched next to her bed, her worn face tense and pale with anxiety. 'It's the master.'

'The master?' Rhiannon sat up, pushing her hair out of her face.

'Master Theo,' Adeia said in a high, strained voice. 'He came down to the kitchen for something to eat and he started…' She paused, baffled, searching for the word in English. 'Shaking.'

'Shaking?' Rhiannon was already slipping out of bed, throwing a dressing gown over her pyjamas. 'Where is he now? Has a doctor been called?'

'My husband Athos helped him back upstairs,' Adeia said. 'I called the doctor…he comes from the next island. He'll be here by boat as soon as he can. You said you were a nurse…?'

'Yes, I am. I'll have a look.' Rhiannon tossed a glance over her shoulder; Annabel was still asleep.

Adeia led her down the tiled hallway to Theo's bedroom, right at the end.

The room was surprisingly small and Spartan—the room of a man who had never grown accustomed to luxury. Theo lay in bed, still and silent.

Rhiannon approached the bed. He looked even more care-worn than he had this evening—smaller, somehow, more fragile. Rhiannon's heart gave a strange little twist and she laid her hand on the old man's brow.

His eyes flickered, then opened. 'What…what are you…?' he said in a weak, halting voice.

'You had a seizure,' Rhiannon informed him quietly. 'Adeia called me. I'm a nurse.'

'I want…' He swallowed, started again. 'I want a doctor.'

'The doctor's been called. He'll be here shortly. In the meantime, I'm just going to check your vitals.'

Theo glared at her, too weak to resist, and Rhiannon gave him a small encouraging smile as she quickly checked him over. He seemed all right, she decided, while at the same time acknowledging to herself the seriousness of a man Theo's age having a seizure.

DAWN WAS EDGING the sky when the doctor's boat scraped against the island's dock, and Rhiannon's eyes were gritty with fatigue.

She'd kept watch by Theo's bed, in case there was anything to report to the doctor. She'd watched him drift in and out of sleep, his eyes glazed, and knew she would have to ring Lukas.

'He's stable for now,' the doctor told her in a low voice after he'd seen Theo. 'As the tumour affects more parts of his brain, more aspects of his life will be affected.' He paused, his expression sober. 'He knows this…knows it will continue to get more difficult.'

Rhiannon nodded. It was no more than she'd expected, and yet it still hurt. It always hurt to hear of someone's pain, the suffering of watching a life slip slowly—or not so slowly—away.

'What should we expect now?' she asked.

The doctor shrugged. 'More seizures, some lessened mobility, increased difficulty in talking. You are his nurse?'

'Not…not exactly,' Rhiannon replied, surprised. 'I mean, I am a nurse, but not…'

The doctor looked nonplussed. 'You're here; you're a nurse. I don't see many others around. If you have questions, you may ring me. All you can really do is make him comfortable. We are managing his decline.'

Rhiannon nodded and thanked him, before heading upstairs with a heavy heart. She waited until Annabel was fed and dressed and busy with Adeia before ringing Lukas.

He answered on the first ring. 'Rhiannon? Is something wrong?'

'Lukas…' Her voice came out thready. She stopped, started again. 'Lukas, your father had a seizure last night.'

There was a moment of silence, frozen, tense, and then Lukas repeated blankly, 'A seizure?'

'The doctor came. He said your father's stable for now, but…'

'But?' Lukas repeated softly.

'But,' Rhiannon admitted, 'his condition is likely to deteriorate more rapidly from now on.'

There was another silence; Rhiannon's heart ached. She longed to comfort him, to put her arms around him. The realisation surprised her with its sorrowful power.

'I'll come back,' Lukas said finally. 'I should have been there.'

'There was nothing—'

'I should have been there.' His voice was flat, dead. 'Goodbye, Rhiannon. Thank you for telling me.'

Yet another responsibility Lukas had put on himself, she thought as she put down the mobile. Another burden weighing him down.

No man deserved so much heaped on his shoulders.

Lukas arrived by helicopter just a few hours later. Rhiannon watched from her window, Annabel playing at her feet. He went straight to his father; she heard his quick footsteps on the stairs. She wondered when—if— he would come to see her.

He'd left the island to escape her. She doubted he was in any hurry to see her again now.

'YOU SHOULDN'T HAVE come back.'

Theo's voice was thready, weak, and Lukas tried not

to let his shock show on his face. His father looked
half the man he had been only a day ago as he lay in
bed, his usually thick shock of white hair thin and flat
against his head.

'Of course I should have,' he replied evenly. 'You're
my father.'

'I'm fine.' Theo spoke in fits and starts, his voice
slightly wheezy. At times he struggled for over a minute for a certain word or phrase.

It made Lukas ache to hear his father like this—to
see a man who held the deeds to the most desirable real
estate in all of Greece in one triumphant fist reduced to
such weakness and misery.

'There was business to attend to,' Theo continued
with effort.

'I've seen to it.' Lukas stared blindly out of the window. 'Is the doctor acceptable? We can hire a nurse, of
course. One of the best from Athens.'

Theo shook his head.

Lukas heard the movement, the rustling of covers,
and turned. 'What?'

'I have a nurse.'

It took a moment for him to realise, and then he
stared at his father in surprise. 'You mean Rhiannon?'

Theo nodded. 'She suits me.'

It was the last thing he'd expected his father to say.
To admit.

'And,' Theo continued in a stronger voice, 'she suits
you too.'

This shocked Lukas all the more. His face went blank
and he turned back to the window. 'I don't know what
you mean.'

'You do.' It was all Theo could afford to say, yet somehow it was enough.

Lukas was silent, but a familiar restless energy was now pulsing through him. *She suits me.* Yes, she did. All too well. Yet he could not give in to the desire, the need. He knew where that led, had seen the destruction.

The weakness.

'Marry her, Lukas.'

He swivelled, stared in shock. 'What? You are joking.'

Theo shook his head. 'No.'

'You know I've said I'll never marry.'

'I know. But now…Annabel…she needs a family.'

'She'll have one—'

'Not some patched affair!' Colour rose in Theo's gaunt face. 'A real family. I'd rather pass this company on to a girl who grew up in a loving home than to a drunken lout like Christos. Marry her, Lukas.'

Lukas shook his head. 'But it would not be a *loving* home.'

Theo's eyes brightened shrewdly. 'Wouldn't it?'

He stiffened, turned back to the window. 'I can't.'

'Why not?'

The room was silent save for Theo's laboured breathing. 'I can't allow…' Lukas stopped, shook his head. He wouldn't go there. Wouldn't admit the truth. 'Because she wouldn't have me,' he finally said, shrugging carelessly.

'What?' Theo was so surprised he laughed. 'What— what woman wouldn't have you? You, the most desirable bachelor in all of Greece? Pah. Of course she'll have you.'

'You don't know her.'

'I don't need to. If not for you, then for Annabel. She'll do it for the child.'

The child. Would she? Instinctively Lukas knew she would…if she were given the right incentives, the right words.

He could have her.

It was too tempting, too dangerous. Too possible.

And yet…he wouldn't love her. Wouldn't allow himself that luxury, that weakness. But he could have her, enjoy her, and make her life better than whatever pathetic existence she'd had in Wales.

It could happen. He could make it happen. He saw his father watching him with bright, shrewd eyes and he jerked his head in the semblance of a nod.

'We won't talk about this again.'

'As you wish.'

RHIANNON SCRAMBLED UP from the sand as Lukas approached. Annabel was playing happily next to her with some new toys, but she clapped her hands in delight when she saw Lukas's long-legged stride down the beach.

'You saw Theo?' Rhiannon asked, and Lukas nodded.

'Yes.' He paused, his mouth a hard, unwilling line. 'He's not well.'

'No, he isn't.'

'I didn't expect…' He shrugged. 'Thank you for your care of him.'

'I was glad to do it.'

'My father has taken a liking to you,' Lukas said. 'He would like you to continue as his nurse, as time allows.'

'I would be happy to,' Rhiannon replied, and realised

she spoke the truth. Caring for Theo would give her a purpose on this island besides waiting for results. Answers. Perhaps it would extend her stay?

'This…changes things,' Lukas said slowly. 'As long as my father has need of you I would like you to stay.'

'Of course.'

'Perhaps…' He spoke carefully, choosing his words. 'Perhaps it will give us time to think of alternative solutions.'

'I have thought of something—'

Lukas held up one hand. 'We will discuss this later. The doctor is coming back tomorrow. I've arranged for him to take a sample of Annabel's blood for the paternity test. I know it's only a matter of form now, but it's still necessary.'

Rhiannon nodded. 'Fine.'

Lukas dug his hands in his pockets. 'When does Annabel nap?'

'After lunch. Why…?'

'We'll talk then.'

After Annabel had been settled in, Rhiannon found Lukas in his study, half buried in papers. He looked up as she peeked cautiously around the door.

'Rhiannon!' His smile was, quite simply, devastating. Rhiannon wasn't used to such a fully-fledged grin, showing his strong white teeth and the dimple in his cheek. For a moment he looked happy, light, without care.

Then the frown settled back on his mouth, his brows, and on every stern line of his face. It was the look she was used to—the look she expected. Yet for one moment she hadn't seen it, and now she wanted it banished for ever.

The thought—the *longing*—scared her with its force.

'I have asked Adeia to watch Annabel,' he said, and Rhiannon blinked in surprise.

'Are we going somewhere?'

'Yes. You'll need a hat…and a swimming costume.'

Rhiannon's brows rose. 'I thought we were going to talk!'

'We are, but I'd much prefer to do it in pleasant surroundings, enjoying ourselves,' Lukas said. 'Wouldn't you?'

Yes, she would. Even if it was a mistake. A temptation. 'All right. I'll get my things.'

Her heart was fluttering with a whole new kind of fizzy anticipation as she slipped on a bikini and topped it with the yellow sundress Lukas had bought her. There was a wide straw hat to match the dress, with a yellow ribbon around its crown, and strappy sandals that were practical enough to manage the beach.

Rhiannon didn't know where they were going, what they would do—what would happen—but she liked feeling excited. The prospect of an afternoon with Lukas seemed thrilling, even if they were going to have that dreaded 'talk'.

'You look lovely,' Lukas said when Rhiannon returned downstairs. He gestured to the picnic basket on one arm. 'I had Adeia pack us a hamper.'

'All…all right,' Rhiannon stammered, suddenly unnerved by what looked like all the trappings of a romantic date.

He led her not to the beach, as she'd anticipated, but to the dock.

Along with a speedboat for travelling to the nearest

island, an elegant sailboat rested there. It was this craft that Lukas indicated they should board.

'We're going to sail?' Rhiannon said dubiously. 'I've never...'

'Don't worry.' Lukas's smile gleamed as he stretched out one hand to help her on deck. 'I have. And we'll stay away from the press.'

He certainly had sailed before, Rhiannon thought, when she was perched on a seat in the stern of the boat, watching with blatant admiration as Lukas prepared the sails and hoisted the jib. Every time he raised his arms she saw a long, lean line of rippling muscle that took her breath away.

This felt like a date, she thought, as Lukas smiled at her over his shoulder. Lukas was relaxed, carefree, a different man.

Why? Was she paranoid to be suspicious? To doubt this change in events, in mood?

She didn't want to doubt. She wanted to enjoy the sun, the afternoon. Lukas.

'What are you thinking?' Lukas asked as he came to sit next to her once the boat was cutting a clear path across the blue-green sea.

'How we both need this,' Rhiannon admitted. 'A day away from the stresses and troubles back home.'

'Home, is it?' he murmured, without spite, and she flushed.

'For now, I suppose.'

'What was your home like growing up?' As always he'd switched topics—and tactics—so quickly Rhiannon could only blink in surprise. 'I know you were adopted, and it wasn't very happy, but...' He trailed off, spreading his hand, one eyebrow raised. 'Tell me about it.'

'There isn't much to tell,' Rhiannon replied, careful to keep any bitterness from her voice. 'I was abandoned when I was three weeks old. Left on a church doorstep, actually. My mother—my adoptive mother, I mean— arranged flowers for the church and she found me. I'd only been left a little while, she said, or she would have been afraid of what the squirrels might've done to me.'

Lukas's lips pursed briefly in distaste before he continued, 'Did she make any effort to find your mother or father?'

'No. Mum always said anyone who would leave a baby like that didn't deserve to have one. I used to dream...' She hesitated. 'I used to imagine them coming to look for me. I had all sorts of reasons why they might have abandoned me.' She smiled ruefully; it hurt, so she shrugged. 'Anyway, she and Dad adopted me— Social Services were happy to comply. Mum and Dad were upstanding members of the community, so everything was in order.'

'But you never really felt they wanted you?' Lukas finished, and Rhiannon flinched.

'I've never said that!'

His tone was gentle, his eyes soft and silver with compassion. 'You've never needed to.'

Rhiannon looked away, across the flat surface of the sea, glittering as if a thousand diamonds had been cast upon its waters. She hunched one shoulder. 'They were older when they adopted me. Late forties. They'd never expected to have children. Mum couldn't.'

'All the more reason to be overjoyed when they were given a chance with you, I would have thought.'

She shrugged. 'I suppose by the time I came along they were well set in their ways. A little toddler can be a burden, I know.'

'And you felt like one?'

'They never said it,' Rhiannon protested, almost desperate to exonerate their memory. 'It was just…there.' She paused, remembering all the moments, the pursed lips, the disapproving looks. The feeling that if she could just act as if she wasn't there, perhaps they'd love her.

Silly to think that way now, she knew. Yet that was how she'd thought when she was six, twelve, twenty-two.

'I remember one time,' she began, the memory rushing back with aching sorrow, 'I was hungry. Mum strictly forbade snacking between meals, but I'd missed lunch at school for some reason—I can't remember now. She was out at a flower guild meeting, and I made myself a sandwich. I cleaned up afterwards, so she wouldn't even know, but there was a drip of brown sauce on the worktop, and she was…furious.' Rhiannon managed a rueful smile. 'No dinner for me that night.'

She was surprised to feel Lukas's hand on her shoulder, slipping up to cup her cheek. 'I'm sorry.'

'Don't be.' She leaned against his hand; she couldn't help it. The strength, the security radiating from him, from that simple gesture, were overwhelming. 'It was a long time ago.'

'But the scars are still there?'

'Yes, I suppose they are.' She thought of her mother's pain-worn face on her sickbed, of how she'd cared for her endless day after endless day. Her mother had accepted those ministrations with pursed lips and hard eyes, glaring resentfully at the daughter whom she somehow blamed for her reduced circumstances.

She'd asked her mother once, right before she had died, if she'd loved her.

Her mother's mouth had tightened as she'd admitted unwillingly, 'I tried.'

Tears stung Rhiannon's eyes, surprising her. She was past tears. These were old memories, and she didn't like Lukas bringing them up.

She moved away; Lukas dropped his hand. 'Tell me about yourself, Lukas. You mentioned that you clean up after other people's messes. What's that about?'

His face blanked for a second, and she was afraid he wasn't going to tell her, that this wonderful moment of intimacy—an intimacy she'd never expected to share with him—was over. Then he shrugged.

'My mother left my father when I was five. She fell in love with another man—someone totally unsuitable. A racing car driver. And he lived life like he raced cars. Fast.'

'And?' Rhiannon prompted softly.

'They were killed in a car crash when I was nine. It taught me a lesson.' He could still hear his father's hard voice. *See where giving in to desire leads you. See what happens when you believe in love rather than duty.*

And he could hear his mother—her careless, mocking voice. He could hear his own pleas and they shamed him.

'What lesson was that?'

'She followed her own selfish desires—didn't think about what her responsibilities were to her husband, her children. Look where it led her.' He held up a hand to stop Rhiannon's comment. 'And my three older sisters have followed her path. Antonia, Christos's mother, is divorced, she's been in rehab half a dozen times, and is a wreck. Daphne is single, miserable, parties too much and is constantly getting in trouble with the press. And Evanthe, the youngest, is anorexic and has been suicidal in the past. All because of giving in to desire. Lust. What they call love. It made them weak, pathetic.' As he had once been, and would never be again. He shook his head in disgust before glancing at Rhiannon. 'Now do you see?'

'I see,' Rhiannon answered quietly. What she saw was three women desperate for love, who'd looked for it in all the wrong places. If she'd been given the chance, if her life had gone differently, perhaps she would have been the same.

Was that what she was doing here?

The question came so suddenly that Rhiannon jerked back in surprise.

No, surely not? Surely she wasn't falling in love with Lukas? Surely she wasn't so pathetic, so foolish, so naïve?

So desperate.

Yet she realised she *was* desperate. Desperate for love, for affection, for touch. All the things she'd never had from her parents. All the things she'd known she wanted somehow, some way. With someone.

Just not Lukas. Not from a man who prided himself on being emotionally unavailable, who saw love as a needless, harmful emotion—a selfish whim! Lukas only saw in terms of black or white, duty or desire.

There was no in-between, no room to negotiate, and certainly no room to fall in love.

'What?' Lukas raised one eyebrow, and Rhiannon realised that she had an appalled look on her face. 'What is it?'

She tried to relax her face into a smile. 'I'm sorry for your family,' she said after a moment. 'There has been a great deal of sorrow.'

'Needless sorrow,' he said, his tone hardening, and Rhiannon was reminded of the untold part of Lukas's story. His sisters might be desperate for love, but then, as a boy, surely Lukas had been too?

He'd learned to ignore it, to disregard it. No doubt his father had drilled into him the wastefulness of his mother's and sisters' lives, the importance of duty.

As he'd already said, he was still cleaning up their messes. No doubt running interference with the press, paying debts, trying to keep the Petrakides name untarnished.

All by himself.

Her heart ached—ached for the boy he had been, watching his mother leave him at only five years old, and for the man he'd become. A man who couldn't love, couldn't trust, because he was afraid.

The idea of Lukas being afraid of anything seemed ridiculous, laughable, and yet in her heart Rhiannon knew it was true. He was afraid to love, afraid to be vulnerable, afraid it would lead to ruin.

'Enough of this sad talk,' Lukas said. He reached for the hamper Adeia had packed. 'I didn't come here to talk about the past, but the future. First we eat.'

Rhiannon was glad for the reprieve. The sea air had whetted her appetite, and she wasn't quite ready to jump into a talk about the future—especially when their discussion of the past had brought so many uncomfortable memories churning to the fore.

Lukas brought out a dish of black olives, a tomato and feta salad, and some crusty bread. They both dug in with gusto.

'There isn't anything nicer than this,' Rhiannon said after a moment. 'Sitting in the sun, in the middle of the sea, eating delicious food.' With a delicious man. She kept that last thought to herself, although she felt her cheeks warming.

'Paradise,' Lukas agreed.

They finished their bread and salad in silence, and then Lukas brought out another covered dish.

'I saved the best for last.' He opened it, revealing a heavenly slice of baklava.

Rhiannon stared at the sticky sweet, her cheeks flaming. She couldn't quite meet Lukas's eyes.

'Adeia packed forks,' he said with wry humour, and an unwilling laugh escaped her.

'Good. Much easier that way.'

Lukas's gaze was thoughtful as he handed her a plate. 'It certainly is…although less enjoyable, perhaps.' And she knew they were not just talking about eating dessert. The memory of that intimacy was heavy and expectant between them.

They finished their baklava in silence. Afterwards Lukas put away the dishes and turned the sail for home.

The wind had quietened down, and the boat drifted slowly, lazily, along the water. Rhiannon trailed a hand through the foamy wake.

'Now,' Lukas said gently, settling himself beside her once more, 'we talk.'

She looked up through her lashes, took a breath. 'You sound like you have plan.'

'I do.'

Her heart began a heavy bumping against her ribs. 'I have a plan too,' she said. 'I've been thinking…' She hesitated at Lukas's carefully blank look.

'Tell me about it,' he said, after a long moment.

Rhiannon took a breath. 'I realise Annabel needs to grow up as a Petrakides. If I can be in her life, I'm willing to take a smaller role.'

'Are you?' Lukas asked, and she didn't like the dangerous neutrality of his tone.

'Yes. I could live in Athens—transfer my qualifications, learn Greek. If I could visit Annabel a few times a week…'

'You'd be willing to completely rearrange your life for a few hours a week?' Lukas asked, and there was both disbelief and condemnation in his tone.

'Why not? You're not willing to have me be *more* involved, are you?' Rhiannon lifted her chin. 'Over and over you've made it clear *you* will decide Annabel's future, and there's been more than a suggestion that I'm not involved! But you can't stop me from moving to Athens, Lukas.'

Lukas shook his head. 'This is not how I wanted to talk. Rhiannon, there need not be enmity between us. I've come to realise you care for Annabel. I do not doubt your sincerity…'

'But…?' Rhiannon prompted, a bitter edge to her voice. Lukas was silent. When she looked at him, his gaze was grey and steady, his face calm and yet filled with determination.

'There is another solution—one that I believe will be amenable to both of us.'

'What is that?'

'Marry me.'

CHAPTER SEVEN

Rhiannon could only stare, those two tempting, unbelievable words echoing in her mind.

'Marry you?' she finally choked out.

Lukas replied, steady as ever, 'It would be good between us.'

She shook her head, and spoke the only word, the only question, clamouring in her mind. Her heart. 'Why?'

'Because it makes sense. Because it's the right thing to do.' He spoke so calmly, so sensibly—and every instinct in her rebelled. If she'd had a moment's heady temptation—a moment's weakness—it was gone.

'Those are not good reasons to marry you, Lukas.' She drew her knees up to her chest, hugged them.

'They're very good reasons,' he replied evenly. 'Although perhaps not the ones you want.'

'You know what I want?'

He shrugged. 'No doubt you want some fairy tale fantasy. You want me to admit that I've fallen in love with you, that I can't live without you, that I must have you as my bride.' Each declaration was a sneer. A wound.

His smile was twisted, tinged with bitterness. 'You want me to act as a lovesick swain, a foolish, foppish boy, and that is not who I am.'

'There is a difference between being in love and

being lovesick,' Rhiannon said. 'But this isn't about what you want or what I want, is it? It's about your wretched duty.'

'And yours,' Lukas countered. 'Something I've noticed about you, Rhiannon—you don't want to be anyone else's responsibility, but you're quick to assume your own. I thought at first you were trying to palm Annabel off—' he held up both hands to ward off her furious denial— 'but now I know you weren't. You were trying to do your duty, just like you did with your parents. I can't imagine it was pleasant, nursing people who'd never loved you. I doubt they even gave you a thank-you.'

Rhiannon stiffened. She hated his perceptiveness, hated the way he gazed at her so calmly, as if he had not peeled away her secrets mercilessly, one by one. As if he hadn't just asked her to spend the rest of her life with him! He wasn't the least bit unnerved, and yet she felt positively unhinged.

'I did what I needed to do,' she agreed after a moment, 'because it was my responsibility. I was their daughter.' She drew in a breath, met the force of his magnetic penetrating gaze. 'But it is not my responsibility to marry you, Lukas. We don't even know if Christos is Annabel's father—'

Lukas waved her protestation aside. 'He admitted it, and Leanne named him as the father, even if she thought he was me. A paternity test will only confirm what everyone already knows—what we can see with our own eyes.'

Rhiannon shook her head. 'We can provide for Annabel another way. A better way. A loveless marriage can hardly benefit her.'

'Would it be so loveless?' Lukas's eyes glinted, and

the breath was momentarily robbed from Rhiannon's lungs.

'What are you saying?' she demanded, and he shrugged, unapologetic.

'I'm not saying I love you, or you love me. But there is a passion between us, Rhiannon. You cannot deny that.' To prove his point he leaned forward, ran his fingers along her bare shoulder.

Rhiannon shivered. She wished she could control it, wished he didn't affect her so damn much. But she couldn't, and he did.

'Agreed,' she said, her voice shaking only a little bit. 'But that's not enough. For me.'

Lukas was silent for a moment. 'Sometimes you need to accept what's given and realise it's the most you can have. Rhiannon, there is desire between us. In time affection, friendship. It is more than most people have. It is a strong basis for marriage. Can't it be enough for you?'

She shook her head, unable to deny, to confess. She wanted more. She wanted to be Annabel's mother, or as good as, and she wanted to be loved.

By Lukas.

The realisation hurt. It made her weak, vulnerable, needy. All the things Lukas believed love did to you.

And it did.

'I won't.' It came out in a wretched whisper. 'I won't *settle*. I've settled my whole life, accepted what little I was given, and I admit it now—I want more. More.' She lifted her head, met his cool gaze with blazing eyes. 'I want to be loved, Lukas. For who I am. I want to be with someone who can't imagine life without me, who needs me, who *knows* he needs me. Someone who accepts me and cherishes me.' She saw something flicker in his eyes—disgust? Pity?—and lifted her chin. 'I suppose that seems pathetic to someone like you, who gets by with cold duty as your companion.'

Lukas didn't reply for a moment, his expression shuttered and distant. 'No,' he finally said, and she was surprised at the regret and sorrow lacing his words. 'It's not pathetic. Just unrealistic.' He shook his head and shrugged, forcing a smile to his lips. 'There is time. We do not need to decide anything now.'

Alarm fluttered in her middle, and Rhiannon realised it was mixed with anticipation. It would be all too easy for Lukas to chip away at her resolve. She might say she wanted more, but she knew she was already falling for him, for the careless and calculated crumbs of affection he tossed her way. She wanted more, but she might accept little. For Annabel's sake. For her own.

'Enough talk for now,' Lukas said. 'Let's swim.'

Lukas directed the boat to a secluded cove on the island, out of view of the main house. He dropped anchor, took off his shirt, and dived into the water.

As he surfaced Rhiannon found her heart thumping far too loudly at the sight of his chest, bare and brown, with sparkling rivulets of water streaming down that lean, tanned flesh.

He slicked his hair back with his hands and raised one arrogant eyebrow. 'Coming in?'

It was a challenge, and one Rhiannon wouldn't refuse. 'All right.' She slipped off her sundress, conscious of how her bikini emphasised the slightness of her curves. There was only admiration in Lukas's gaze as he watched from the water and, emboldened, Rhiannon stepped onto the side of the ship and neatly dived in.

When she surfaced, Lukas was smiling. 'I didn't even ask if you could swim.'

She laughed, treading water. 'I wouldn't have dived in if I couldn't! That was one happy aspect of my child-hood...living near the sea.'

'Your parents took you?'

'School trips mostly,' Rhiannon admitted. 'Some-times they took me, though.'

He nodded in understanding, and then began to swim with long, even strokes to the shore. 'Let me show you the beach,' he called over his shoulder.

Rhiannon followed him, swimming to the shore. Lukas helped her out of the shallows, kept hold of her hand as he led her onto the beach.

'There's a legend,' he said, his fingers twined with hers, 'that pirates took a mother from this island about a thousand years ago. She was forced to leave her child, but as they passed the church where she used to light a candle, she prayed for salvation.'

'What happened?'

'The ship stopped. The pirates were amazed—and, naturally, frightened. When they realised why the vessel had stopped moving—because of a mother's prayer—they brought her back to the shore, back to her baby. It's considered a miracle.'

Rhiannon wondered why he'd told her that particular legend. Did he see parallels between that mother and her own desperate situation?

Would she be forced to leave the island? Leave An-nabel?

But Lukas had given her an option to stay. Marry him.

Why? she wondered. Why did he want to marry her?

Was it simply for desire's sake? Or was there another reason? One she couldn't begin to guess?

They'd walked the length of the beach, and now stopped before a rocky outcropping. 'The house is just over these rocks,' Lukas said. 'When I was a boy we spent our summers here. I used to clamber over those rocks and come here.' His smile was rueful, but Rhiannon thought she saw a hidden sadness in his eyes. 'No one could find me here.'

'You didn't want to be found?'

'Sometimes, no.'

Rhiannon could just imagine it. A boy without the love of his mother, saddled with more weight and responsibility than any grown man should have, already learning the futility and weakness of love, hardening his heart and his soul.

No wonder he'd occasionally wanted to escape it all.

For a moment her heart ached for that boy, the boy underneath the tough exterior now, and she wondered if Lukas could learn to love again. Learn to trust.

If he could…if that boy truly did still exist under the man…could he love? Could he love *her*?

Rhiannon swallowed. Already she was wondering, weakening.

Wanting.

'We should go back,' she said after a moment, when the only sound was the whisper of the waves on the sand and their own soft breathing. 'It's getting dark.' And her thoughts were twisting away from her, turning into impossible hopes, ridiculous dreams.

She couldn't afford to let that happen.

The sun was starting to sink in the horizon, turning the surface of the sea to shimmering gold, and, still holding her hand, Lukas tugged her back towards the sailboat.

'Are you up for another swim?' he asked, indicating the distance to the boat.

Rhiannon shrugged. 'Why not?'

She plunged into the sea after Lukas, watched as he cut through the water ahead of her and lifted himself easily onto the boat.

He'd let a rope ladder down the side, but trying to get her balance in the water, with the ladder jerking under her hands, was more difficult than she'd anticipated, and she began to fall helplessly back.

'Here…let me.' Lukas reached down, put his hands under her arms and hauled her up.

Tumbling forward, Rhiannon found herself pressed against the wet length of him—with very little material between them.

'I'm…I'm sorry,' she stammered, and his eyes glinted with humour as he held her to him.

'I'm not.'

Rhiannon's breath leaked from her lungs as that knowing glint turned from humour to desire. Lukas smoothed a damp tendril of hair from her forehead, caressed her cheek.

'Rhiannon…'

She knew what was going to happen—knew it in her bones, in the melting liquid core of her, in her heart.

The moment's silence was a question, and Rhiannon answered it by reaching up, letting her hands curl around his bare slick shoulders.

Lukas bent his head, kissed the salt from the hollow of her throat. Rhiannon moaned her acceptance, her need.

Her desire.

He kissed her lips softly. A tender promise. Rhiannon let her hands slide through his hair, damp and curling, let herself be laid down on the padded bench, with Lukas sliding his hands down her sleek, wet body.

'You are so beautiful.' His voice was ragged, uneven. 'I want you so much.'

She knew what a confession it was—for him to admit it, and to do so without shame. Without regret. Right now she felt only desire, want, need. It felt good. It felt right.

Smiling, she brought his face to hers, let their tongues tangle as he explored every soft hollow, every slender curve.

His hand cupped her breast, his thumb stroking her nipple through the fabric of her bikini to an aching peak. She slid her own hands down his chest, loving the hard, lean feel of him, yet not quite daring to let her hands slide further down to the pulsing heat at her middle. She was too naive, too nervous.

He smiled against her mouth. 'Touch me.'

Emboldened, she did, her hand skimming across the top of his swimming trunks before darting back at the feel of his hardness.

She felt every inch the shy virgin, but wished she didn't. Wished she was confident in her desire of him, his desire of her. Yet she wasn't, she knew. She was caught up in the moment, afraid to think. Almost afraid to feel.

Yet wanting it so much.

He chuckled. 'Let me show you.'

She didn't know quite what he meant until she felt the scrap of her bikini bottom being nudged away, his fingers brushing between her legs. She gasped as he stroked her knowingly, tenderly, and then gasped again—louder—as his finger slid inside her warm heat.

She'd never felt so consumed, so known, so much a part of something bigger and more wonderful than herself.

So loved.

His fingers moved with deft assurance, knowing her secret spot, the sensitive nub, and stroking it with tender purpose.

Lukas's lips curved in a knowing smile as Rhiannon arched helplessly against him, craving his touch, craving more.

His finger began to slide and stroke in rhythm, and, still in thrall, Rhiannon moved against him, gasping out loud.

'Lukas…'

'Let yourself feel, Rhiannon. Let yourself go.'

She shook her head, as if to deny the feelings—deep, wonderful, molten—spiralling within her to a crescendo she could not even name.

'Lukas…'

'Let yourself,' he commanded gently, brushing her lips in a kiss.

And she did. She cried out loud, a choking sob of pleasure as he brought her to that glorious crescendo, more heartbreaking and real and vibrant than anything she'd ever experienced before. Her muscles convulsed around his finger and her head fell back against the arm that cradled her head.

'I never…'

'I know.'

She laughed shakily. 'I suppose you do.'

She should have felt vulnerable, exposed. Shamed. She'd expected to—because she knew he didn't love her. She knew this was just sex.

Yet she wouldn't let herself think that way. Wouldn't allow her mind to wander down that treacherous path to its shameful destination.

She just wanted to feel…wanted. She wanted to enjoy it.

Still, she was conscious of the chill in the air, of the water cooling on her skin, her swimming costume still in disarray.

Lukas was staring at her with a teasing smile, a smile that reached deep inside her and grabbed hold of her soul. Her heart.

She *wanted* this man. She thought of his offer of marriage and realised she was tempted…far too tempted.

Lukas replaced her bikini bottoms, his smile turning knowing. 'You'll marry me now,' he said with smug satisfaction, and Rhiannon stiffened.

The feelings she'd denied rushed over her in an icy wave…vulnerable, exposed, ashamed.

She struggled to a sitting position, tugged hopelessly at her swimming costume.

'Are you telling me you planned that little scene to convince me to marry you?' Her voice came out on a shaky waver.

Lukas shrugged, his expression hooded. 'You can't deny what's between us.'

Rhiannon shook her head. 'Don't manipulate me, Lukas.'

'Is that what I was doing?' His eyebrows rose; his expression was cool. 'You seemed to enjoy it.'

'That's not fair.' She struggled to keep her tone calm,

reasonable. 'Don't use sex as a way of getting what you want.'

'Don't call something you agreed to with every fibre of your being manipulation!' Lukas replied, with a dangerous chill in his tone. 'You want me, Rhiannon, and I want you. It's that simple. Want.'

'You don't want anything,' Rhiannon flashed, and his smile was bitter.

'No, I don't. And, damn it, I didn't want to want you. But I do, and I admit it. I want you,' he continued with cold precision, 'and I will have you.'

'Don't order me around!'

'You want me too,' Lukas said flatly. 'Even if you think you're holding out for some absurd notion of what love is.'

'You don't know what love is!' Rhiannon cried, and Lukas's smile was bitter.

'Oh, yes, I do. And that's why I'll never love you, or anyone, again. We can have something much better than love, Rhiannon. We can have trust, affection, desire. Something real. Something to build on. We don't need love. Love makes a fool of you, a weakling, a slave.'

She shook her head wearily, then laid it on her knees. She couldn't continue this conversation. Couldn't explain to Lukas how it might make sense now, this marriage, but what about in a year? Five years? Ten?

How long would it take for resentment to lodge in his soul, in his heart? For any affection and desire they might have shared to turn into anger and bitterness because they'd really only married for the sake of a child, and not even one they could call their own?

She wanted more for Annabel. More for herself.

'Who made a fool of you?' she asked quietly, when the silence had gone on too long.

Lukas's face closed in on itself like a fan. He shook his head. 'Let's go home.'

Silently, every movement terse and controlled, he set sail for home. Rhiannon watched the first stars shimmer on the water and willed the tears back.

Tears she could keep from coming. She always had. The heartache she could not.

Back at home, Lukas wordlessly helped her from the boat. They walked up the dock, stiff and distant. It was hard to believe that less than an hour ago they'd been as intimate as lovers.

'I must check on my father,' Lukas said when they came to the door. 'I've been gone too long as it is.' He gave a brusque nod of dismissal. 'I'll see you at dinner.'

'I'll eat in my room,' Rhiannon said, on an impulse born out of self-preservation. 'It's been a long day.'

'Hasn't it?' Lukas's smile was ironic. He touched the tip of his finger to her chin. 'You can't run from me for ever, Rhiannon. Remember what I said. I *will* have you.'

'We'll see about that,' she replied stiffly, and went to find Adeia and Annabel.

Annabel crowed with glee when she saw Rhiannon, her chubby arms outstretched. Rhiannon took her as a matter of course, smiled as she lay her downy head against her chest, arms curling around her neck.

'See how she loves you!' Adeia said with chuckling admiration. 'No baby could love her mama better.'

Rhiannon looked up in surprise. She hadn't realised how Annabel had begun to bond with her, or she with the baby. Her decision to stay had been one of the heart, yet it had been because of her own past rather than anything to do with Annabel.

She simply hadn't wanted any child to experience what she had.

Now, as Annabel snuggled against her, she realised she didn't want *this* child to experience it. This child—only this child—whom she loved.

She would do anything to keep her safe, secure. Loved.

Even marry Lukas?

Her thoughts were in a restless ferment as she fed Annabel in the kitchen, eating there as well, to make less work for Adeia.

Upstairs, she bathed the baby and gave her a bottle, her mind still whirling hopelessly.

Marrying Lukas would provide Annabel with a secure future. Lukas might not love her—might never love her—but he would certainly provide for her. She could trust him with her life, if not with her heart.

And a part of her, she knew, wanted to marry Lukas. Wanted to be with him…wanted to accept what little he gave because it was more than she'd ever had before.

Wanted to discover if that boy still existed underneath the man—if she could find him again, make him fall in love.

With her.

It was a recipe, Rhiannon thought, for disaster. For heartache.

LUKAS STOOD QUIETLY in the doorway, watching his father sleep. Regret and anger churned within him and he raked a hand through his hair in sheer annoyance.

He'd handled the outing with Rhiannon completely

wrong. Worse, he'd put the proposal to her in exactly the way she would be sure to despise: as a matter of responsibility for both of them.

He should have played the besotted fool, pretended to be falling in love with her. She would have accepted that. He'd planned to take on the role when he'd put her on the boat, to set the stage for romance…seduction. Then his own sense of honour—not to mention dignity—had kept him from pretending to be something he wasn't. Something he never could be.

Yet to have put it so plainly, so coldly… Even he realised a woman like Rhiannon would rebel. Reject. He hadn't expected the swift, sudden stabbing pain when he'd heard her flat refusal. His pride had been hurt, but something else had as well. Something deeper.

He didn't like that realisation. Didn't like the thought that Rhiannon might be becoming important to him. Caring for someone was weakness. He knew that. He'd seen it.

He'd felt it.

Shaking his head, as if the brisk movement could banish the memories, the ghosts, the mocking laughter, Lukas turned his attention back to his father and saw the old man's eyes were open, watching him shrewdly.

'You look unhappy.'

'A bit annoyed, perhaps,' Lukas admitted in a clipped voice. 'Nothing that can't be set to rights. How are you, Papa?' He came into the room, his iron gaze sweeping the pitiful length of his father's diminished frame.

'I am as well as is to be expected,' Theo replied after a moment. His words were still slow, rasping. 'We knew this was going to happen.'

Lukas nodded—a choppy movement. Theo smiled.

His eyes were tired. They'd lost a bit of their sharpness, their hardness, and now they looked at his son with a sorrow that thoroughly discomfited Lukas.

'You asked her to marry you?' Theo said finally. 'And she refused?'

'Yes.' Lukas didn't know how the old man knew so much, so well, but he accepted it with a shrug. 'As I told you.'

'Perhaps I should have told you how to go about wooing a woman,' Theo retorted, then shook his head, lying back against the pillows. 'You don't present it as a business contract, Lukas.'

'That's essentially what it is.'

'What you want it to be.' Theo lifted his head, looked at his son. 'Why can't you admit you care for her?'

'I've known her for less than a week,' Lukas snapped. 'I don't know why you've suddenly taken a fancy to believing life is like one of the old myths, but it is not. There are hard facts in place, and Rhiannon knows them as well as I do.'

Theo shook his head. 'No wonder she refused you.'

Again Lukas felt that stabbing pain, and hated it. He would not care. He would not. Yet he had told her he would have her, and he would.

'I expected as much,' he said irritably, and, swivelling on his heel, left the room.

THE NEXT MORNING, after a troubled, dreamless sleep, Rhiannon decided to check on Theo. He didn't need much care yet, as he spent most of his time sleeping or resting, but she took her responsibility seriously, light as it currently was.

She peeked into his bedroom after breakfast, and saw him looking alert and well rested.

'You look well.'

He smiled briefly. 'I feel well. For however long it lasts.'

'The doctor is coming back this afternoon to check on you.'

Theo shrugged. 'I don't need a doctor. We all know I'm going to die.'

'Yes,' Rhiannon agreed quietly, 'but there are still ways to go about it. To manage pain, increase comfort and dignity.'

Theo nodded, looking away. Understanding his need for a moment's silence, Rhiannon busied herself with re-filling his water pitcher and straightening the bedcovers.

'Lukas cares for you,' Theo said after a moment. 'Though he'd descend to hell before admitting it.'

Rhiannon stiffened, straightened. 'Why are you telling me this?' she asked.

'Because I know he asked you to marry him, and I think it's the right thing to do.' It had taken Theo a while to say it, but his tone was still blunt.

'For Annabel?' Rhiannon stated flatly, and he nodded.

'Yes. And for you.'

'I won't be someone's responsibility.' Rhiannon shook his head. 'I'm sorry, Theo, because for whatever reasons you seem to want us to marry. Although I could've sworn you didn't like me when I arrived!'

Theo's smile glimmered briefly. 'I didn't, but then I saw how Lukas acted towards you. He has always told me he will never marry, and of course I want him to. I want grandsons even if I never see them. Heirs. And if he has in his heart chosen you—'

'He hasn't.' Rhiannon cut him off. 'And you already have a great-granddaughter who needs your love and affection. Lukas marrying me doesn't change that.'

Theo was silent for a moment. 'No,' he agreed, 'perhaps not.'

'I should go.' Her throat was tight, her mind seething once again.

Despite her firm refusals, there was a seed of hope, a spark of need, that had lodged itself under her ribs. She wanted to believe Lukas cared for her. She wanted to accept what little love she was given.

It was more than she'd ever had before, perhaps more than she'd ever be given.

A little.

Yet, Rhiannon wondered, could it ever be enough?

CHAPTER EIGHT

'THINGS HAVE CHANGED.'

Rhiannon looked up from where she was playing with Annabel on the sun-dappled floor of her bedroom. A shiver like an icy finger ran down her spine, despite the warmth of the room, the gurgle of Annabel's laughter.

'What are you talking about?' she asked, scooting off the floor so she could at least be almost at eye level with Lukas.

He stood before her, dressed in charcoal-grey trousers, belted narrowly at his hips, and a crisp white shirt open at the throat. His hair was newly washed and slicked back from his forehead, and his expression held foreboding. Anger. Resolution.

Nothing Rhiannon liked.

'Things have changed,' Lukas repeated, 'since we spoke yesterday. There are fewer choices.'

'Oh, really?' Rhiannon arched one eyebrow. 'Because it didn't seem like there were too many choices yesterday.'

'My lovely sister Antonia has got wind of what's going on. She wants Annabel.' He spoke flatly, harshly, and Rhiannon shook her head in confusion.

'Christos's mother? Annabel's grandmother?'

'Yes.'

'But…' Loss and fear were sweeping through her in empty consuming waves, yet she forced them back. 'Surely that's a good thing? You said Christos wasn't interested in Annabel, but if his mother is…'

'You don't know his mother.'

'But surely Annabel needs all the family she can have—' Rhiannon protested.

'Why? So you can make a quick escape? Changed your mind, Rhiannon?' Lukas jeered. 'Decided it's all too much for you? You want your life back? At least you can walk away.'

There was so much bitterness in his voice that Rhiannon could only shake her head in confusion. 'I'm not walking away,' she said finally. 'Even though at one point you wanted me to! But I'm not her mother, Lukas, even if I wanted to be, and I recognise who has the rights here.' She took a deep breath. 'I love Annabel. I realise that now. But she's not mine.' It hurt to say it—carved great, jagged pieces out of her soul—but she had to speak the truth. It was only what every newspaper, every judge, would say if it came to that.

'I thought you were different,' Lukas said after a moment, his voice flat. 'I thought you cared about Annabel and your responsibility to her.'

'And what *is* my responsibility?' Rhiannon flashed. 'To deny a child her family, her inheritance? Or to keep her all to myself simply because I want to? Because I want her? That's not duty, Lukas. It's desire. Sometimes,' she added icily, 'I think you confuse the two. It must make you feel better, to insist something you want is actually your responsibility. Does it relieve your guilt?'

There was a moment of silence so charged and appalling that Rhiannon felt as if she'd slapped him…hurt him. Lukas blinked, shook his head slowly.

'There may be some truth in what you say about a child's right to her family,' he said in a hard voice, 'but there's simply too much at stake. Antonia has rung me to say she wants custody—complete custody of Annabel. That means you wouldn't see her, I wouldn't see her, and she would grow up the plaything of a woman who's been a drug addict and a social parasite.'

His flat recitation of facts left Rhiannon chilled to the marrow. 'A judge would never grant custody to a woman like that,' she said after a moment, but her voice wavered.

'Wouldn't he? Antonia is the misunderstood darling of the newspapers. They report her antics and then spend pages explaining and forgiving her abominable behaviour. I blame myself; they need at least one Petrakides to give them news, and I don't. I never have.' He paused, and Rhiannon saw the guilt chase clearly across his features, reflected in the shadowy grey of his eyes, before it was replaced by the more familiar resolve.

'Antonia is Annabel's grandmother. I am only her great-uncle,' he continued tonelessly. 'In a court the judge is almost always going to side with a woman in custody cases—especially with one who bats her eyelashes and lets her lip tremble.' His own lip curled in a sneer. 'Antonia knows how to play people, and she'll play the judge. She'll parade witnesses to prove how she's changed her life, what a devoted mother she is.'

Rhiannon shook her head. 'But why? Surely she would only go to such lengths if she loved Annabel?'

'She's desperate.' Lukas cut across her. 'Antonia is unhappy, bored, and she's managed to convince her-

self that this is what she needs. If she can smear the Petrakides name while she's at it, all the better.'

Rhiannon shook her head, unable to take in the rapid
change of circumstances.

'Surely she'd be willing to negotiate?' she said, a desperate edge entering her voice. 'Compromise…'

'Perhaps with me,' Lukas agreed coolly. 'But certainly not with you.'

Rhiannon blinked. It was the Petrakides family that
had all the money, the power, the highly placed connec-
tions; she had to remember that.

'So what are you suggesting?' she finally asked, her
voice a scratchy whisper.

'We get married. I know you didn't see the necessity
of it before, but surely you do now? If we're married,
providing Annabel with a stable home, and the judge
knows that you've already forged a bond with her, Antonia's case will be weakened…perhaps so much that
she'd be willing to drop the whole thing. She doesn't
actually want Annabel. She just thinks she does. If she
got custody she'd have Annabel kitted out with nannies
and boarding schools and never see her. No one would.'
He paused, his mouth twisting in a bitter grimace. 'Or,
worse, she'd spoil her like a pet poodle—the way she
did with Christos. You see how *he's* turned out.'

'I haven't actually met him,' Rhiannon reminded
him, a touch of acid in her tone, and Lukas shrugged.

'You don't want to. So, what is it to be? Give Annabel up or marry me?'

Rhiannon opened her mouth, but only a soundless
laugh came out. She couldn't quite believe this was happening—that Lukas had given her such a drastic ulti-
matum so quickly.

'What about the paternity test? We should at least wait till then. A judge wouldn't even look at the case without one…'

Lukas tensed, then shrugged. 'Such a test will only confirm what we already know. Meanwhile Antonia will have gathered evidence, splashed tawdry headlines in the press. My family can do without those.'

'But—'

'Annabel has the look of a Petrakides,' Lukas continued in a final tone. 'And we know that Christos was with your friend Leanne, that he used my name. The dates match up. There's no escape.'

Escape. It made Rhiannon feel as if they were both being trapped…trapped into a marriage neither of them wanted.

But I want this.

The thought, the realisation, frightened her with its potency and its truth. She wanted to be with Lukas. She was halfway to falling in love with him, with the man she hoped—prayed—was underneath.

She just didn't want it to be like this.

'Surely there are other alternatives…?'

'Wait and see? By that time it will be too late. Rhiannon, I won't lie to you.' His tone softened, and he reached out to touch her, stroke her shoulders. 'I want to marry you for Annabel's sake—because I know my duty to a child of my blood. I won't let her be raised by a vain, selfish brat of a woman—I won't. And you shouldn't either. I know Annabel isn't yours, but she is yours in your heart, and she will grow to love you as a mother if she doesn't already—which I think she does.' He pulled her gently towards him, and Rhiannon found herself moving closer with reluctant, hesitant steps. 'As for us, we could have a good marriage. Children of our own, perhaps.' Her eyes widened, and he smiled. 'Why not? Why can there not be a little happiness for us?'

'But you don't love me,' Rhiannon said flatly.

'No, but I want you. You know I do.'

'And you'll have me?' She repeated his earlier words with a dry smile.

Lukas's eyes flashed silver as he acknowledged this truth. 'Yes. I desire you, and I will die before I hurt you. I will protect you, care for you, give you everything in my power.' He dropped his hands from her shoulders to spread them briefly in appeal. 'What more can you honestly ask for?'

Love. Need. Him needing her. It was so simple, so obvious, but so impossible to explain to a man like Lukas, who only saw what should be done, not what he wanted to be done. Or what she wanted.

Or even what she really needed.

She glanced down at Annabel. The baby met her gaze and reached up chubby arms in helpless demand. Up. Up into arms where she would be safe and cuddled and loved.

Choking back a nameless sound of despair, Rhiannon bent down and scooped the solid, warm bundle of baby into her arms. She pressed a kiss onto the top of Annabel's silky curls, dark and soft just like Lukas's.

She couldn't abandon this baby. She'd already made that decision, even though she had doubted herself at every turn, every twist in the strange path of fate that had brought her here.

Yet now she wondered if this opportunity was heaven-sent—given to her as a second chance. A chance to show a little girl how she could be loved.

Loved by someone who had not given birth to her but who had chosen to be her mother. A mother who would never shirk her responsibility because that duty was not dreaded but desired, joyfully carried out.

She looked up, saw the flickering of warmth in Lukas's steady gaze—and saw something deeper as well.

I want him.

She would take a little. Even if it wasn't what she'd once dreamed of. Even if he didn't love her. Even if that knowledge seared her, stabbed her, hurt her more than she wanted to acknowledge, more than she wanted to feel.

She'd do it for Annabel and, she knew, because she wanted to.

No matter how much it hurt.

She'd do it because this was Lukas.

'All right,' she whispered, and trembled inwardly at Lukas's smile of pure, primal victory.

THE NEXT FEW days passed in a blur of activity. Lukas was everywhere—on the telephone, on the internet, in the helicopter—arranging the small wedding that would be held on the island. Theo was exultant, and although his health was still failing there was a bloom in his cheeks, a sparkle in his eyes. He was a happy and triumphant man.

Rhiannon was numb. She cared for Annabel, she listened to the plans and conversations whirling around and above her, but found she could not consider what she'd done, what was happening.

What her future looked like.

When Lukas asked if there was anyone from Wales she'd like to invite to the wedding she merely shook her head. She found she wanted to be alone, away from the hive of expectant enterprise the villa had become.

Leaving Adeia in charge of Annabel, she escaped to the beach, walked along the silken sands, let the warm Aegean waters lap over her feet and soothe her soul.

What have I done?

She pressed her cold hands to her cheeks, closed her eyes.

Only what I needed to.

Only what I wanted to.

She could be happy with Lukas. She could let herself be happy. She knew he was only marrying her for Annabel, knew he didn't love her, no matter the desire— the lust—that pulsed between them.

It was still more than she'd ever had before.

She came to the rocky outcropping that separated the villa's beach from the private one she and Lukas had visited, and after a moment's pause she scrambled over the sharp rocks, picking her way carefully along the top till the hidden beach—Lukas's beach—their beach— came into view. As she made her way down she slipped, slicing her shin open on a jagged rock.

Muttering a curse under her breath, Rhiannon slid to the sand, covered the scrape with her hand. Blood trickled out between her fingers. She drew her knees up to her chest, laid her head against them, and wept.

The tears she'd held in since this whole crazy episode had begun came out in a hot, furious rush, a desperately needed release. There was no one to hear, no one to censure, no one to tell her to stop the theatrics, as her parents always had.

She hadn't cried like this in years, a numb, detached part of her brain acknowledged, even as the sobs came out—noisy, gulping ones, inelegant, ugly. Her face was wet, splotched, flushed.

She wiped her cheeks with the backs of her hands, thinking she was done, but the tears kept coming.

She had so many tears. Tears for the girl she'd been, lost and confused and begging for love, and tears for the woman she'd become, alone, afraid, seeking to love and be loved. She wouldn't beg any more, but she still wanted the happy ending.

The fairy tale that Lukas now demanded she relinquish for real life, hard facts.

'Rhiannon!'

Rhiannon looked up, saw Lukas towering above her on the rocks like a dark angel. He climbed nimbly down, his face drawn in lines of tender anxiety.

'Rhiannon, I've been looking for you. I heard the noises—I thought it was a hurt animal. What is wrong?'

'Nothing,' she denied, and he looked incredulous.

'You are crying as if your heart has been broken and you tell me nothing is wrong? I'm to be your husband. You must confide in me.'

'I must?' she repeated with a broken little laugh. She found she didn't care how ridiculous or pathetic she looked. It had felt good to cry.

'Rhiannon. Please. I want to know.' He took her hands in his, glanced down and exclaimed at the bloody cut on her leg. 'What happened? Is this why you are crying?' He looked up at her face, assessing, swift. 'But, no. It is something else. Still…' He withdrew a handkerchief from his pocket and pressed it to the cut. 'You must let Adeia see to it when you return to the villa.'

'I'll see to it myself,' Rhiannon protested, and he shrugged.

'As you wish. It is a nasty cut. Now...' He let his fingers cup her cheek, but Rhiannon didn't lean into that gentle caress—wouldn't let herself. Lukas noticed; she saw the flash of acknowledgement in his eyes. 'What is wrong?'

'Everything. Nothing.'

He shook his head, curbing his impatience. 'Tell me.'

She jerked her chin from his hand and looked out at the flat, calm surface of the sea. 'Lukas, my whole life has changed in a matter of days. I've agreed to marry a man I barely know, a man who has told me quite clearly he doesn't love me and won't ever love me. I know you think this is only what I should be doing, what it's my responsibility to do, and perhaps you're right. God knows, I've lived my whole life doing what I should do, what people expected me to do, no matter how much it hurt. But I thought...' She drew in a shaky breath, let it out in a rush. 'I thought, when my parents died, that part of my life was over. I thought that maybe, just maybe, I could start living for myself. That sounds terribly selfish, doesn't it? But I didn't mean it that way. I just wanted a little pleasure, a little fun...a little love.'

'And you think you're sacrificing all those by marrying me?' Lukas asked quietly.

'The love—certainly. You've said as much. Pleasure?' She glanced at him, managed a wry smile. 'I'm sure we'll find some pleasure. As for fun... You don't seem like a fun guy.'

'No?' He sat next to her, trailed his fingers thoughtfully in the sand. 'No, I don't suppose there's been much time for fun in my life. I always do what I'm supposed to as well. What is expected...what I expect of myself.'

'And now—this marriage—isn't it just more of the

same?' Rhiannon asked, knowing the answer and yet wanting it to be different. Wanting Lukas to tell her that, no, this was not about duty. This was about what he wanted. Wanting to believe the fairy tale even now.

'It is a duty,' Lukas said after a moment. 'But that doesn't mean it has to become a burden. We can be a family for Annabel, for each other. It can be good.'

Rhiannon nodded. Good. She'd wanted something great. Something big and magical and wonderful. But she'd settle for good. She'd make herself.

'Come back to the house,' Lukas urged gently. 'See to your cut and have dinner. The arrangements have been made. I was coming to tell you. We can marry tomorrow.'

Rhiannon's head jerked up. 'Tomorrow?'

'I thought the sooner the better,' Lukas admitted. 'Selfish, perhaps. But I want you, Rhiannon. Soon. I want you tomorrow.'

'Who is coming?'

'No one who isn't already here. We can have a reception in Athens later, if you like. You can meet my colleagues, as well as other members of the family. Invite friends from Wales.'

'I told you, there is no one.'

'No one?'

Rhiannon shrugged. Her handful of casual friends had never become more than acquaintances. She'd spent so long on her own, nursing her parents, that she'd forgotten how to socialise, how to be fun and light and chatty. If she'd ever known how.

She'd dated a few men—co-workers who had dropped her when she hadn't been bubbly, engaging, or free enough with her favours, and Rhiannon hadn't even minded.

That life had been small, cold. Hopeless. It had been hers, yet she hadn't realised until now just how pathetically empty it had been.

Perhaps that was in part why it had been so easy in the end to agree.

'Theo and Adeia will be witnesses,' Lukas said, 'and the priest from Naxos will fly in to marry us. I didn't think you'd mind something small.'

'I don't,' Rhiannon admitted. 'It's just all so sudden.'

'Let yourself go,' Lukas urged, and the warm caress of his words reminded her of a far more intimate encounter they'd shared not too far from here. She could almost feel his fingers on her, in her.

'I suppose I have no choice,' she said, trying to sound light and sounding brittle instead. She shrugged and stood up, brushing the damp sand from her shorts.

Lukas watched her for a moment, eyes dark, guarded, thoughtful.

'You have choices,' he said after a moment. He was still sitting, looking up at her with knowing eyes. 'You could walk away. Walk away from me now. I'd let you.'

Rhiannon stared at him, saw the dark hunger in his eyes. He was testing her, and perhaps himself. He sat completely still. Tense, watching.

'I'm not walking away from anyone now,' she said quietly. 'I've made my decision, Lukas. I'll stand by it.'

She was surprised at the naked relief on his face before it was masked. 'Good.'

He stood up, took her hand, and led her carefully back over the rocks.

THE DAY OF her wedding dawned pearly and fresh, with a warm, promising breeze rolling off the sea. Rhiannon stood at the window, breathing in the fresh, salty air, letting it fill her. Fill her with hope.

She didn't want to start her wedding day—her marriage—with bitterness and recrimination. She'd cried all her tears yesterday. There would be none today.

Today was for beginnings, for beauty. For the possibility of what could be, limited as it sometimes seemed.

She looked through her clothes for an appropriate wedding dress—Lukas hadn't seemed to remember that little detail in all of his planning. There was nothing remotely bridal, and she was choosing between the little yellow sundress and the loose silk trousers when a knock sounded at the door.

'Come in.'

It was Adeia, smiling shyly and holding a hanger swathed in plastic. 'Master Lukas—he doesn't think of everything,' she said in careful English. 'Not as much as he thinks he does. He forgot your dress, no?'

'He did,' Rhiannon admitted with a rueful laugh, and Adeia thrust the swathed hanger forward.

'For you.'

Rhiannon took it in surprise. 'But how…?'

Adeia pointed to her chest. 'Mine.'

'Your dress?' Rhiannon asked, hoping her scepticism did not show on her face. Adeia had to be sixty years old at least, and she was stout and round. Never mind the style or condition of the dress, Rhiannon couldn't imagine it would fit her.

'I make some changes,' Adeia said with a little grin. 'You see.'

Carefully Rhiannon took the plastic off, and gasped

at the dress that lay beneath. It was a traditional Greek outfit, with a white linen under-dress, and sleeves decorated with brightly coloured embroidered bands. A scarlet apron sewn with gold coins was there to go over the dress.

'It's beautiful, Adeia,' Rhiannon said. 'Like something out of a story!'

'You'll wear it?'

'Absolutely. Thank you for lending it to me.'

Adeia beamed, and Rhiannon kissed her weathered cheek.

It didn't take long to slip on the dress and apron, and Rhiannon was amazed at the transformation. With her olive colouring and dark, curly hair she could pass for Greek anyway, and now, with the dress, she felt as wild and free as a peasant girl.

She didn't look like someone who was afraid or desperate—someone who cared what people thought of her. In this dress she could be anyone she wanted to be. She could be a woman who laughed and grabbed at life with both hands...who took what was offered and enjoyed it.

That was who she wanted to be.

That was who she *would* be.

She kept her feet and head bare, and went in search of the wedding party...and her groom.

The wedding was to be held on the beach, and as tradition demanded Lukas was waiting with her bouquet at the front door.

'Everyone is ready and waiting outside,' he said softly as she came down the stairs. 'The priest is here.' He let out a low, delighted chuckle as he surveyed her costume. 'Who is this Greek princess coming to visit me?'

Rhiannon smiled. 'Do you like it?'

'Very much.' He handed her the flowers, a simple bouquet of wild orchids tied with ribbon.

Rhiannon knew the wedding ceremony would be traditional Greek Orthodox, as Lukas had requested, and now she found herself wondering just what it would be like.

Lukas took her arm and they walked together down to the beach. The sun was high and bright in the sky, the only sound the gentle lapping of the sea on sand.

Theo, Adeia with Annabel in her arms, her husband Athos, and the priest, a smiling, bearded man in his thirties, all waited at the beach. Everyone beamed when they saw her, delighted by her dress, and perhaps by the simple fact that a wedding was taking place.

Lukas Petrakides was getting married. Without pomp or paparazzi, or any fuss at all.

It amazed her, stunned her that this was happening—that she was entering this world...Lukas's world.

Rhiannon didn't understand much of the Greek that was spoken, although she understood the symbolism. The priest blessed the two rings Lukas had procured, and placed them in their hands.

Rhiannon watched the burnished gold band slide onto her finger, felt the strange, heavy weight of it.

Theo swapped the rings between Lukas and Rhiannon three times, much to her bemusement. Lukas grinned and whispered, 'It's tradition. You'll find we do many things three times.'

Was she imagining the lascivious intent in those words?

The priest joined their hands, and Rhiannon felt a bolt of awareness travel from her fingers to her toes, straight through her heart, at the feel of Lukas's warm, dry hand encasing hers.

After some prayers, the priest brandished two flowered crowns and laid them on her and Lukas's heads.

'The *stefana*,' Lukas explained in a murmur. 'They symbolise the glory and honour we have received.'

Glory. Honour. Lofty words for a marriage that was simply a matter of necessity.

Rhiannon smiled in understanding, but she wasn't sure she really understood.

Everything felt so special, so romantic. So sacred. And yet it wasn't exactly real...was it?

Theo exchanged the crowns between them three times, and Rhiannon met Lukas's laughing gaze with a smile of her own.

Then the priest proffered a cup of wine, and Lukas told her they must each drink from it three times.

The priest took their hands and led them around the makeshift altar. Rhiannon followed, bemused when he broke the ribbon that had joined their crowns and, with a wide smile, pronounced them man and wife.

'Married,' Lukas murmured, and there was blatant satisfaction—possession—in his voice.

Married. For better, for worse. For ever.

She just hoped they'd done the right thing. For Annabel...and for themselves.

Adeia had prepared a wedding breakfast in the villa, and they all retired there for the celebration.

Rhiannon found she enjoyed the simple food and conversation. Simple pleasures. Easy. Enjoyment that postponed what she knew would come—what she both dreaded and desired.

'You should go,' Theo chided when the meal was

long-finished and they were still sitting among the scattered remains. 'The boat ride is at least an hour.'

'Boat ride?'

Theo pretended to look abashed, and Lukas rolled his eyes. 'Yes, boat ride. We have to go somewhere for our honeymoon, don't we?'

Rhiannon shrugged. 'Do we?' They were already on a magnificent island—where else could they go?

'We do,' he replied firmly. 'Adeia has seen to your bags. All you need do is change, and we will be off.'

Rhiannon felt the first stirrings of genuine excitement. She hadn't been off the island in over a week, and the quarters, although luxurious, could sometimes be cramped. She realised she was looking forward to going somewhere new…with Lukas.

It was late afternoon before they were actually aboard Lukas's boat, with baggage stowed, ready to sail.

Theo and Adeia saw them off, and even Annabel waved from the housekeeper's comfortable embrace.

'She'll be all right,' Lukas said quietly, clearly reading Rhiannon's thoughts. 'It's only for one night.'

She nodded agreement, though she was reluctant to relinquish her care of Annabel even for so short a time. The little girl had barely been out of her sight since Leanne had died.

'So, where are we going?'

Lukas, dressed in faded chinos and a blue cotton shirt open at the neck, smiled mischievously over one shoulder as he hoisted the sail. 'You've been on a private and secluded island already, so I thought to myself, What else can I give you? And then the answer came.' He paused, eyes dancing, and Rhiannon laughed.

'What?'

'Company.'

Still mystified, she shook her head, and Lukas smiled. 'You'll see.'

The sun had started to sink towards the waves when the boat finally approached land. There was a neat cove, twinkling with lights, framed by whitewashed buildings with brightly painted doors and shutters.

'Amorgos—the nearest island,' Lukas explained. 'A small place, as yet mostly undiscovered by tourists.'

'You don't want to build the next Petra Resort here?' Rhiannon teased, and he pretended to shudder.

'No, never.' He moored the boat by one of the docks, and helped her out onto the weathered wood.

'You look beautiful,' he murmured as she took his hand. 'I bought that dress hoping I'd one day see you in it.'

'You saw me in it the other day,' Rhiannon protested. She looked down at the short, flirty sundress, its simple fabric skimming over her body, hinting at the curves underneath.

'Yes…but this is how I imagined it. You, here, belonging to me.' His hands touched her waist gently, and he brushed her mouth in the lightest of kisses—a promise, Rhiannon knew, of what was ahead.

Fear and anticipation unfurled in equal amounts in her middle, spread grasping tendrils throughout her limbs, so her only response was a slight shake of her head.

'Lukas…'

'We can talk later,' he promised softly. 'Now we eat. And dance. And sing!'

Laughing, Rhiannon let him pull her along, down the dock, into the music and lights of the village.

They walked down a cobbled street to a taverna whose tables stretched right to the water. There was little more than a lapping sound as fishing boats gently nudged each other in the darkness.

The taverna was crowded with people, most of whom seemed to know Lukas and called to him with joyful, unaffected greetings. Lukas responded in kind, with laughter and slaps on the back, while Rhiannon watched, bemused. She felt as if she were seeing a different Lukas—one she hadn't believed existed.

No one here cared that Lukas ran a real estate empire. No one bowed and scraped. Here they were all friends, and the older men treated him like a younger brother, or a son, despite the fact that he could most likely buy the entire island twice over with his pocket change.

Lukas, his arm around her shoulders, drew Rhiannon into the crowd and lights. Rhiannon heard him speak Greek, and knew he was introducing her as his wife simply by the way jaws dropped and eyes widened— before the night descended into a cacophony of congratulations.

When they were seated at a table, with large glasses of rich red wine set in front of them, as well as a dish of olives, Rhiannon raised her eyebrows.

'You're known here?'

Lukas shrugged, smiled. 'I'm known everywhere.'

Rhiannon shook her head slightly at the inherent arrogance in the simple statement. That was the Lukas she knew, understood. Yet she also knew she was seeing a different Lukas now—a man who was more human and perhaps more like her than she'd ever dared imagine.

'Yes,' she said, 'but everywhere you're known as

Lukas Petrakides, reclusive real estate tycoon. Here you're known simply as yourself…aren't you?'

He gazed at her, his eyes turning silver in the moonlight, a thoughtful expression on his face. 'Yes…perhaps you're right. Here I am myself. My grandmother was from Amorgos before she moved to Athens in search of work. When my father bought our island I spent many of my boyhood days here. Happy days.'

In an otherwise unhappy existence? Rhiannon wanted to ask, but didn't. Slowly she was gaining a picture of Lukas's life…of a childhood torn apart by a mother who followed her lover rather than her family, a father who instilled in him an unshakable, crippling sense of his own responsibility.

'What made you happy?' she asked, and Lukas shrugged.

'Simple boyhood things. Fishing, swimming, learning to sail.'

'With people who loved you?' It slipped out before she could help it, and Rhiannon bit her lip. She didn't want to start an argument. She didn't want to hear his cold denial.

There was a moment of silence, and in the flickering lights Rhiannon couldn't see the expression on Lukas's face as he toyed with his wine glass.

'Yes,' he said at last. 'There is something in that.'

Her heart bumped against her ribs as she realised what he was saying.

The boy underneath the man. Still there.

'Our childhoods were similar in some ways,' she said, 'despite the obvious differences.'

He raised his eyebrows in silent question.

'You had a lot more money,' Rhiannon hastened to

explain, 'yet at the same time we were both—' She stopped, unsure if she should continue with the bleak picture she was painting.

'Both...?' Lukas prompted.

'Unhappy,' she finished softly, and looked down at her drink.

'Good thing we have both learned to be happy,' Lukas finally said, and there was a flat neutrality to his voice that told Rhiannon the moment of intimacy—of connection—was over.

'They didn't know you were married,' she observed after a moment, and Lukas chuckled.

'No one does. Right now it's a well-kept secret.'

'The press will go wild, I suppose,' she said gloomily, and Lukas covered her hand with his own.

'That is why I married you—to shield you from such speculation. They *will* go wild, but it will die down. If you hadn't married me, Rhiannon, they would have written that you were my mistress, or worse.' He shook his head. 'I did not want that.'

'No.' Rhiannon tried to ignore the leaden feeling his words had caused. *That is why I married you.* One of the many cool, practical reasons. 'How did you know all these friends would be here if you didn't tell them?' she asked.

'I have my ways.' Lukas's smile was a flash of white in the oncoming twilight. 'I told them I had a surprise to show them tonight. But they never would have thought of a wife!'

'It seems that no one ever thought you'd get married at all.'

'I always said I wouldn't,' Lukas admitted with a tiny shrug.

'Why not? Surely your responsibility includes providing a Petrakides heir?'

Lukas was silent for a moment, his face hard, and Rhiannon wondered if she'd pressed, pushed, too hard. It was a simple question, yet she was aware of the subtle jibe underneath.

'I have three sisters to provide heirs,' Lukas finally dismissed. 'And my sense of responsibility only extends so far.'

Rhiannon's eyes widened. Was Lukas actually saying that there was something he *wouldn't* do out of duty? Marry? Yet that was exactly what he'd done.

'I've really slipped the noose around your neck, haven't I?' she joked feebly, hearing the horrible, hollow sound of her voice.

'No. It was my idea, my choice. And it is no noose, Rhiannon, unless we choose to make it so.'

Rhiannon heard the warning and heeded it. It would take two to make this marriage work. She understood that. She only hoped they would both be able to hold up their end of this awkward bargain.

A red-faced man with a curly beard approached the table, clapping his hands and urging Lukas and Rhiannon to rise.

'They want us to dance,' Lukas explained with a little smile. 'The Syrtos—a traditional Greek wedding dance.'

'I don't know the steps,' she protested, even as he pulled her to her feet.

'You'll figure it out.' He wrapped his arm around her shoulder, pressing her to his side. Rhiannon could feel the warm, steady heat of him all along her body, felt her own blood pulse and heat in response.

Musicians were playing a merry if somewhat dis-
cordant tune, and everyone had gathered into a circle,
arms around each other's shoulders, stamping their feet
and shouting.

Rhiannon was pulled into the circle, pressed next to
Lukas, and then they began to move.

It was a simple rotation of steps—right foot, back,
left foot—but Rhiannon soon found it hardly mattered
what foot she put where. Everyone was moving as they
wanted to, stamping and leaping and roaring with laughter.

Somehow, somewhere, she let her inhibitions slip
away and reminded herself of that wild peasant girl
who'd looked back from the mirror that morning. A girl
who didn't cling or beg for love. A girl who was wild
and free. For a few moments, with the music and the
laughter and the lights, she became that girl.

The night passed in a whirl of colour and sound, of
food and drink, and embraces and smacking kisses on
both cheeks. Rhiannon barely understood most of what
was said, but it didn't matter. She certainly got the gist.

The moonlight was turning the sea to silver by the
time Lukas finally said they had to depart—news which
was greeted with cheers and ribald laughter.

Shaking his finger warningly at the crowd, yet chuckling a bit too, he led Rhiannon down the cobbled street.

'Some of them have had too much to drink,' Lukas
said in half-apology, but Rhiannon, who was feeling
pleasantly dozy from three glasses of wine, just giggled.

'I don't mind.'

'They mean well.'

'I gathered that…though I barely understood a word
that was said!' She laughed, and it turned into a hiccup.

Lukas stopped, his hands on her shoulders, and turned her to face him.

'Rhiannon, you're not drunk, are you?' His lips were twitching, eyes sparkling, yet he still managed to look serious.

Rhiannon looked indignant. 'Drunk? Hardly! I had a few glasses of wine!'

'It's strong stuff.'

'I'm fine.' She tried to shrug away, but Lukas steadied her with one finger on her chin.

'Good,' he breathed, drawing her lips closer to his own, 'because I don't want you out of your head on our wedding night...in our wedding bed.'

'I'm—' His lips touched her own. A brief caress, nothing more. Yet it flickered awareness straight to Rhiannon's soul, acted like a bucket of icy water drenching her nerves, making her stone-cold sober and yet gloriously alive. 'Not,' she finished in a whisper, hearing the breathiness of her voice, seeing Lukas's knowing smile.

'Good. Our hotel is just this way.' He led her down the street, past quaint shops shuttered for the night, to a simple courtyard with high white walls and an iron gate, its interior filled with pots of geraniums and bougainvillaea. 'It's a simple place,' Lukas warned her. 'There are no luxurious resorts on Amorgos. But I think it will suit our needs.'

Rhiannon merely nodded. For the reality of their situation was becoming very much present, and her heart was beginning to thrum in heady response.

Lukas fished a key out of his pocket and opened the door. Their bags had already been placed inside the room, which was simple, yet clean and welcoming.

A wide pine bed with white linen sheets dominated

the space. A large window above it looked out onto the harbour, its sashes thrown wide open. A slightly battered dresser was across from the bed, and a door led to a bathroom.

Rhiannon loved it. She didn't want luxury, didn't want more examples of Lukas's wealth and power. She wanted this…a simple, clean room and the two of them.

Lukas cleared his throat, and Rhiannon wondered if he felt some of the awkwardness she was experiencing.

'Would you like a bath?'

'I'll clean up a bit,' she said, brushing back her tangled curls with a self-conscious hand.

Lukas gestured to the bathroom, and Rhiannon spent a few awkward seconds scrambling in her bag for her nightgown while he stretched out on the bed, calm and relaxed.

Her fist closed around the filmy scrap of material, the nightgown he'd purchased for her only a week ago—although he could have hardly had *this* scenario in mind. Could he?

'I'll be right back,' she mumbled, and bolted into the bathroom.

She didn't want a bath. Only a few moments to calm her racing heart and figure out a way to approach this… situation.

Rhiannon's mouth twisted in a wry smile. The situation, she acknowledged, was sex, pure and simple. Something she'd never done before. She didn't know if Lukas knew that, or had simply guessed it. Wasn't sure she should say.

Twenty-six-year-old women were rarely virgins these days, she knew. Although she suspected Lukas would have an irritatingly arrogant satisfaction in learning that he was her first, her only lover, Rhiannon felt encumbered by her lack of experience.

She glanced in the mirror, saw her flushed face, bright eyes, the wild tangle of hair. She still looked like that peasant girl.

If only she could be like that now...confident, in control. For so much of her life she'd let other people dictate who she was, what she did—and all to get the smallest scrap of affection. Of love.

She didn't want to be that way with Lukas. She refused to live in his shadow, to beg for love she knew he wasn't willing to give. Yet she also recognised her own helpless, hopeless tendency to do just that.

She slipped off the sundress, reached for the virginal white nightgown—something that spoke of bridal sacrifice. Then she stopped.

She wouldn't be that girl. She would be a woman— full, free. That was how she wanted to start this marriage. That was how she would go on.

Taking a deep breath, she opened the bathroom door.

Lukas glanced up when she opened the door, his eyes flaring in admiring surprise when he saw what she wore: nothing.

Rhiannon stood there, shoulders thrown back proudly, eyes blazing challenge. 'I'm ready.'

'I'd say so,' Lukas murmured, swinging his legs off the bed. His hands went to the buttons of his shirt. 'I think *I* need to be ready...'

'No.' Rhiannon strode forward, stilled his hands with her own. 'Let me.'

Lukas hesitated, his gaze sweeping the naked length of her, and part of Rhiannon—a large part—wanted to cover herself. Hide.

Yet she didn't. Lukas acquiesced, leaned back against the pillow. Smiling a little at this victory, Rhiannon began unbuttoning his shirt.

Her fingers trembled a tiny bit as she worked the buttons through the cloth, exposing a broad expanse of perfect bronzed flesh. She smoothed her hands across his bare chest, smiling as Lukas shuddered slightly in response.

She pulled the shirt off his shoulders and he helped her by shrugging it to the floor. Then her hands went to his belt buckle—and stopped.

Lukas was still, silent, waiting for her lead.

After a moment Rhiannon undid the belt, slipped it through the loops and tossed it to the floor. She unbuttoned his trousers, tugged at the zip while her knuckles brushed his straining hardness.

She began to pull off his trousers, her hands skimming down his legs, while Lukas suppressed an oath and kicked them off.

'I'm finding it hard to wait,' he muttered thickly, and at the blatant look of desire hazing his eyes Rhiannon felt her own response leap to life, race through her veins, fill her with heady power.

'You'll have to wait a little longer,' she said, an ancient, womanly smile curving her lips.

Lukas groaned and leaned back against the pillows. An offering to her. Hers.

He still wore his boxer briefs, yet Rhiannon didn't hesitate as she reached for them—for him. Now she wanted to see him. She felt her own power, felt the excitement and passion coursing between them, and it urged her on.

The briefs fell to the floor and Lukas lay there,

naked, magnificent. Rhiannon's breath caught in her lungs at the sight of him.

She reached a hand out, curled it around him, heard his choked moan as she stroked him softly.

'Rhiannon…let me touch you…'

'Soon,' she promised, and laughed deep in her throat at Lukas's moan of pleasure. 'I've never been touched before, you know,' she said softly. 'Did you know that? Did you know I've never had a lover?'

'I wondered,' he choked out as her hand continued its bold stroking. 'Although it's rather difficult to believe right now…'

'Is it?' she murmured. Her fingers drifted up his chest, teased his nipples. She leaned over him, her breasts skimming his chest, and kissed him deeply.

Lukas returned the kiss, his hands coming to her shoulders. 'Let me touch you,' he whispered, and she did.

She took his hands, drew them to her breasts. Now she was the one giving in to pleasure, moaning in delight and awe as his hands caressed her, his fingers teasing her with knowing assurance, before he bent his head and applied his mouth to where his hands had been.

Her own hands fisted in his hair, pulled her to him in silent demand.

He stretched out beside her, his hands skimming her skin, teasing the juncture of her thighs. 'It's been a long time for me,' he admitted, his voice hoarse, 'but I don't want to rush you.' He paused. 'I don't want to hurt you.'

'You won't,' Rhiannon said, amazed at her own confidence, her audacity. She drew his hand back to her legs. 'Touch me.'

And he did, his fingers slipping inside, his eyes burning into hers.

'You're beautiful…' he whispered, and she *felt* beautiful.

She'd shed her fear like a tired skin. She felt new and strong and powerful. She gasped as his fingers continued to stroke her into flames, a whirling torrent of need and pleasure that overwhelmed her, caused her to gasp and cry out.

'Lukas…'

'Let yourself go,' he commanded, and she laughed shakily, pulling him towards her in an urgent kiss.

'I *am*…'

'Good.'

She was so close to the edge, to explosion. Her hips moved restlessly, rhythmically, seeking the release she knew would come.

Yet she didn't want it to be like this, with Lukas in control, his eyes glazed with desire.

'*You* let yourself go,' she demanded, and his eyes widened as she rolled on top of him and began to draw him into her own warmth.

It was a strange new feeling, this filling inside her, yet it was welcome. She laughed aloud as Lukas gasped and began to move, clasping her hips to his.

'Am I hurting you?' he asked raggedly, and she laughed again. The twinge of pain had been lost in the haze of feeling—wonderful, glorious, hot.

'No,' she said, 'you're not hurting me.'

Then they were both lost to the rhythmic movement, this ancient dance. Rhiannon didn't need to be taught, didn't need to be shown.

She knew. She felt him deep inside her, could see how their bodies were joined as one.

It was wondrous. It was beautiful.

It was love.

She gave herself up to the exquisite sensation, allowed herself to be fully possessed. Consumed. She heard Lukas cry out, heard their voices joining as their bodies were joined, and knew she loved him.

Loved him.

She also knew—realised it with an intense, wonderful rush—that love didn't make you weak. It made you vulnerable, but it also made you strong.

She loved him.

The thought didn't humble her, didn't frighten her. It only made her smile. It made her cry out when release came, hot and joyous and fast, and she smoothed Lukas's hair back with gentle fingers as he buried his face in her neck, his own breath choked and ragged.

I love you. She wanted to say it. Opened her mouth to. Yet breathed the words back in before they were more than a whisper of sound.

He didn't want to hear that. Would be appalled, horrified. Perhaps even angry.

Lukas didn't understand about love, Rhiannon realised with a rush of sweet sorrow. He only saw it as weakness, causing hurt, pain, problems.

Yet once he'd loved. Needed love, wanted it. The boy underneath. She would find him. She could.

She would have to.

CHAPTER NINE

'WHAT SHALL WE do today?'

Lukas was lying next to her, his head propped on one hand, as the early-morning sun dappled the floor in dusty beams and the sea sparkled outside like a jewel.

Rhiannon felt a warm glow spread through her, as if she'd swallowed sunshine, and the sum of her lonely, loveless years melted to nothing as she basked in the easy affection of Lukas's gaze.

She smiled up at him, shrugging. 'Anything.'

'Anything?' Lukas repeated, trailing one tempting finger along her bare ribcage.

'Anything,' Rhiannon agreed, even as desire began to flow through her, turning her both weak and strong. She wanted his touch, and was unafraid to show it.

Lukas kissed her, his hands stroking her body to flame, and Rhiannon gave herself up to the glorious sensation of being loved.

Loved.

She wanted to believe it—wanted to believe that Lukas could love her. That perhaps he did love her, even if he refused to acknowledge it.

Was she completely naive? She pushed the thought away.

Afterwards as they lay together, Lukas's fingers absently stroking circles on her midriff, Rhiannon felt compelled to say, 'I don't want to leave Annabel for too long.'

'No,' Lukas agreed. 'We can sail back this afternoon. But this morning...'

'Is half gone,' Rhiannon finished ruefully, for the sun that shone on them now was hot and high in the sky.

'We can have breakfast in Katapola,' Lukas decided, 'and perhaps visit the ruins. There's an ancient village near here, but everyone was forced to flee when a fire destroyed most of the trees and livestock. It turned Amorgos to a barren, lifeless island for hundreds of years.'

'But it's come back to life now?' Rhiannon said with a little smile, and she couldn't ignore the similar question unfurling in her own heart: could it happen to Lukas?

Could she breathe life into his loveless existence? Resurrect his faith in love?

She didn't know. Hers had been, but she'd been hungry for it. Ready to believe. Ready to love.

Lukas wasn't.

Still, she wanted to believe it could happen—and that she could be the one to do it.

After they'd dressed, they breakfasted at a café by the harbour, eating yoghurt and honey and drinking strong coffee.

At a market stall Lukas bought bottled water and a straw hat for Rhiannon, for their dusty walk into the hills.

They left the lively village streets behind them for a dirt track that wound its way through rocky fields, up into the hills that Rhiannon saw were scattered with ruined stone—the crumbling foundations of an ancient town, an ancient life.

The only sound was a distant goat's bell, and the rustle of grass as they walked. She could smell the clean, dry scent of wild rosemary and thyme, mingled with the tang of salt from the sea.

'Have no archaeologists come to investigate all this?' she asked, as Lukas showed her the half-standing walls of what looked to be a potter's house.

He shrugged. 'Amorgos likes to keep things the way they are. There are so many ruins in Greece—a few untouched ones will hardly go amiss.'

'It's nice that it's left like this,' Rhiannon agreed, and he nodded.

'No one to spoil it.'

He linked his hand with hers—a careless, affectionate gesture that still managed to go straight to her heart.

'You're like a different man here,' she said impulsively. 'Not the real estate tycoon.'

'Tycoon?' He laughed dryly. 'Is that how you see me?'

'That's how the world sees you. Intimidating, remote, powerful. Do you know how scared I was when I first sought you out in that bar?'

'Were you?' Lukas murmured, and suddenly Rhiannon remembered that sizzling moment of connection, the way she'd been drawn to him as if pulled by a wire.

'I want us to be like this,' she confessed softly.

Lukas turned to her, his eyes dark, questioning. 'Like what, Rhiannon?'

If there was a challenge in his voice, she didn't heed it. Didn't want to. 'Happy.'

He nodded. 'I would like us to be happy too,' he said,

his face averted, and already Rhiannon felt as if she were losing him, as if he were pulling away.

They were both silent. The dry grass tickled Rhiannon's bare legs as she sat on an old block of stone, the last remnant of someone's house, someone's life.

The sun beat down hotly and the sky was a bright, hard blue, without a cloud in sight. The sea was a flat mirror, reflecting the brilliant sunshine.

The moment, the easy intimacy, was slipping away, and Rhiannon didn't want it to go. Wouldn't let it.

'What if things change?' she asked, quietly enough that Lukas might not have heard her. Her heart was pounding and her mouth was dry, but she had to know.

Lukas heard, and he swivelled to face her, eyes alert with wary challenge. 'What might change?'

'What if...?' She licked her lips, continued. 'What if we fell in love...with each other?'

The silence was awful, terrifying in its blank rejection. Rhiannon stared down at her feet, her toes curling inwards as her whole body wanted to hide from the question she'd put out there so baldly, so boldly, when she didn't really have the courage to see it through.

She saw Lukas's feet move, felt him crouch next to her.

'Rhiannon.'

His fingers were on her chin, lifting her face to meet his own unyielding gaze.

'Rhiannon,' he repeated, in a voice that despite its softness took nothing away from its lethal intent. 'I am not going to fall in love with you. I made that clear from the beginning. I've seen what loving someone does to you. It makes you weak, selfish and stupid. I'm not going to do that. Ever. And if you think it might happen by accident, if you think you can change me or make me love you, you are wrong. Wrong.' He paused, his gaze steady on her, making sure she understood.

Rhiannon felt the colour drain from her face. She was too horrified, too stricken to speak or even to blush. The terrible finality of his tone seemed to reverberate through her bones, through her soul, making a mockery of every fragile hope she'd just begun to cherish.

'I'm sorry,' Lukas said, more gently now. 'I thought you understood that. I thought I'd made it clear.'

Rhiannon gave a slight, self-protective shake of her head. When she spoke, it was through stiff, numb lips. 'You did.' She struggled up from the stone, shrugged away Lukas's hand and began the long, stony walk back to the village.

They returned to the hotel in silence, the easy and enjoyable banter of only a few hours ago now replaced with a taut tension. They packed up their few things stiffly, jerkily, before heading back to the boat.

Once on board, Rhiannon curled in a seat as far away from Lukas as she could. She didn't want to watch him, to see the long, rippling muscles of his shoulders and back while he hauled on the sails. Didn't want to replay the words that he'd spoken so flatly, so mercilessly, on the hill.

Yet they kept replaying anyway, a remorseless echo in her brain, reminding her that once again, as always, she'd begged for love and been refused.

Love made you strong.

She'd felt strong last night. In Lukas's arms she'd revelled in the power of their joined bodies, joined hearts. Except it had to have been false. Because there was no power, no strength, no joy in her current agony, in Lukas's flat rejection, in knowing once again she was where she'd been her whole life: living as someone's burden.

LUKAS WATCHED RHIANNON out of the corner of his eye, his hand resting on the jib. She was curled up like a whipped puppy, her face closed in on itself, her eyes gazing unseeingly at the stretch of sea before them.

Guilt assailed him, stabbed him with tiny needles. He didn't need this. Hadn't wanted it.

Yet he deserved it.

He'd acted selfishly, wanting Rhiannon's body without her heart. Wanting her to enter a loveless marriage when she'd admitted she wanted love more than anything else.

He'd pushed aside her objections, her desires, in preference of his own. He wanted her. He recognised that—admitted that it hadn't been responsibility for anyone that had driven him to marry her. It had been need. Desire.

He just didn't want to love her, and he certainly didn't want her to love him.

She would learn, Lukas told himself. She would realise that desire and affection were better than love. She would come round.

And if she didn't...? Lukas smiled savagely, his face averted from his bride.

There were no other options. Not for either of them. He wouldn't let there be.

WHEN THE BOAT came in sight of the Petrakides island, Adeia was already coming from the villa towards the dock, her apron blowing in the breeze.

Anxiety clutched at Rhiannon's heart, tightened around it like a vice. 'Is something wrong?'

'I don't know.' Lukas's face was filled with foreboding, and Rhiannon realised that the problem—if there was one—might just as easily concern Theo as Annabel.

'Master Lukas,' Adeia called breathlessly as Lukas tied up the boat. 'I've been looking for your boat all morning—"

'What's happened, Adeia?' Rhiannon cut in. 'Is it Annabel? Theo?'

'Neither. Master Lukas, your sister arrived last night. She is insistent that she take the baby with her.'

Lukas swore under his breath before jumping nimbly from the boat. He turned to help Rhiannon down, then excused himself.

'I must go and see Antonia.'

'I'm coming too.'

He shook his head in swift denial. 'This does not concern you, Rhiannon—'

'It absolutely concerns me,' she retorted. 'That's why we married, remember? I'm as involved as you are, Lukas, so *don't* shut me out now.'

Lukas gave a terse nod. 'So be it.'

Antonia was in the lounge when they entered the villa. She was a tall, thin woman, expertly made up, but with a sharpened hardness to her that came from years of dissolute and disappointed living.

'Hello, Antonia.' Lukas spoke with a calm cordiality that Rhiannon doubted anyone in the room was close to feeling.

Antonia put her hands on her bony hips. She wore an expensive suit in a glaring shade of pink—something chic and completely unsuitable for either island living or life with a baby.

'Christos told me everything, Lukas. I want her.' Her eyes flashed, and Rhiannon felt her own blaze at the woman's tone, wheedling and greedy, as if she were demanding a sweet.

'I'm afraid,' Lukas said mildly, 'that it's not going to be that simple.'

'Why not? I'm her grandmother, her closest living relative besides Christos, and he supports me taking her. You'll find he'll stand with me in court.'

'Antonia, do you really want to drag us all—and the Petrakides name—into court?'

'I don't give a damn about the Petrakides name,' Antonia spat. 'That's just you and Father. Both of you care more about the idea of our wretched family than the people in it—no wonder Mama left when she could, grabbed happiness when she found it.'

Unmoved, a muscle ticking in his jaw, Lukas raised one eyebrow. 'As you have? With drugs, drink, and far too many lovers?'

Colour blazed in Antonia's cheeks and she shot Rhiannon an angry, furtive glance before shrugging. 'I've put such ways behind me now, Lukas. You'll find I have quite a collection of witnesses to testify to that fact. And any judge will understand how I was driven to what I did because my own home life was so appalling!'

'Spare me the theatrics, please, Antonia. No one cares about your poor little rich girl story.'

Antonia thrust her chin out. 'Don't you think, Lukas, that a judge will be more sympathetic to a close relative who is willing to love this child than to someone who takes it because he doesn't want scandal to stain his precious name?'

The jibe hit home, for Lukas's face went white and he spoke stiffly. 'We'll just to have see… Unless you are willing to see sense and drop this farce right now. I know you don't really care about Christos's child. You haven't even met her.'

'I do care!' Antonia shrieked. She looked near tears, and Rhiannon felt a stab of sympathy for the woman, distraught as she clearly was. 'I *will* care. You might not need anyone to love, but I do. I *do!*'

This last ended on a wail of desperation. Rhiannon's heart was tugged in spite of her intentions to remain unmoved. Antonia was so obviously unhappy—needy enough to convince herself that a baby would provide her with purpose and pleasure.

Antonia took a deep breath, composed herself. 'A judge will rule—'

'Against a stable married couple with the child's best interests at heart? I don't think so.'

Antonia's mouth opened, closed. 'Married?' she repeated. 'But who…?' Things clicked into place and she turned a furious, disbelieving stare on Rhiannon. 'You married this English nobody? For the sake of a child you don't even care about? You do take your duty seriously, Lukas, don't you?'

'Yes,' he replied in a tight, controlled voice. 'I do.'

She flung her head back, her face bright with hectic colour. 'We'll see what the judge says.'

'I hope it doesn't come to that, for all our sakes, Antonia.'

'You mean for *your* sake,' she threw back, and Lukas gave a tiny shrug.

'You're welcome to stay, of course, but perhaps it might be prudent for you to return to London.'

'You want me gone already?' Antonia jeered. 'I don't want to stay anyway. But I'll return to Athens, Lukas. As you know this case will be tried in a Greek court. And then we'll see…won't we?' She turned her vitriolic gaze on Rhiannon. 'I don't know if you married him for the kid or the money, but I promise you, you will be unhappy.'

Then, with an angry click of heels, she was gone.

Rhiannon was silent, recovering from the violence of the encounter, the words still pouring through her like acid.

You will be unhappy.

It had almost sounded like a curse.

In the distance, she heard the sound of a helicopter lifting off, and sagged slightly in relief. She was gone.

'I'm sorry about that.' Lukas finally spoke into the silence. 'I told you what she was like, but I had no idea she'd be so vicious.'

'Desperate,' Rhiannon corrected quietly. 'She's unhappy, Lukas.'

He shook his head. 'By her own hand. She makes more trouble for herself than anyone else possibly could.'

Rhiannon lifted her head, met his cold, steely gaze. 'Can't you find it in your heart to feel sorry for her?'

'Sorry?' Lukas raised his eyebrows in incredulity. 'Rhiannon, this is the woman who wants to take Annabel away from you—from us! And she'll lie, cheat and steal to do it. Why should you feel sorry for her?'

Rhiannon shrugged. 'I don't applaud her methods, but she's obviously desperate for love. She thinks a baby will somehow provide meaning in her life. At one time I wasn't that different, you know.'

'You were willing to give Annabel up,' Lukas objected. 'You can hardly compare yourself to Antonia!'

'I was willing to marry a stranger,' Rhiannon snapped, 'to stay with her! Don't think you know me so well, Lukas.'

He gazed at her for a moment. 'Is that what I am? A stranger?'

'Sometimes you feel like one,' Rhiannon admitted, trying to keep her voice steady and cool. 'Even if I don't want it to be that way.'

'I told you what this marriage would be like,' he said, an angry, impatient edge turning his voice sharp. 'I warned you that I wouldn't love you. I don't have that to give, Rhiannon. Full stop.'

'I know, Lukas.' She felt quite suddenly unbearably weary, tired of this argument that went in endless circles because they wanted different things and couldn't understand how the other could want what they didn't.

Or, in Lukas's case, want anything at all.

He wanted nothing...except maybe her body.

'I need to check on Annabel,' she said, her voice toneless and flat.

Reluctantly Lukas let her go.

'I'll need to go to Athens tomorrow morning,' he said. 'I've left my business too long, and if Antonia is going to make trouble I need to be on hand.'

Rhiannon shrugged her acceptance.

'I want you to come with me.'

She turned in surprise. She'd expected to remain on the island, not to interfere with Lukas's business, with his life. 'You do?'

'We're *married,* Rhiannon.' Lukas spoke patiently. 'I want you with me. I want you in my bed, by my side.'

In his bed. He made it so wonderfully clear. 'Fine. Annabel comes too.'

'Of course.'

She turned away, walked up the stairs, and felt Lukas's restless gaze burning into her back.

Annabel was delighted to see her. With the baby chortling on her hip, Rhiannon went to check on Theo.

He was propped up in bed, his cheeks still sunken, his hair lank and dry, but his eyes glinted brightly and he smiled when he saw her.

'How was the honeymoon? Short, I fear?'

'Long enough,' Rhiannon replied, and Theo frowned. 'What is wrong?'

'Nothing.' She smiled, setting Annabel on the floor so she could check his vitals. 'Has the doctor been?'

'Yes. I'm stable for the moment. Don't fuss over me. What is wrong? What has happened?'

Rhiannon smiled down at him. Somehow, in some strange way, she'd become fond of Theo—and, even more oddly, he'd become fond of her. She didn't know why—didn't know if it was just because she was the female Lukas had been willing to marry, or if the affection was based on something deeper.

She knew Theo wanted them to be happy, just as she did. But she couldn't make Lukas love her.

She'd learned that lesson a long time ago, when she'd been the sweetest, most polite, most obedient little girl in the world, and it hadn't made her parents soften at all. They hadn't wanted her; they'd done their duty and, like a canker, it had festered slowly into resentment until everything she'd done had become an irritation, an annoyance. A burden.

Did you ever love me?

I tried.

She'd begun to believe things could change, that she could change Lukas. She'd begun to believe in love again. In someone loving her.

But it wasn't going to happen, Rhiannon thought sadly. And, like her parents, Lukas would start to resent her when the desire faded, when he'd had enough of her body. There'd be nothing left but the burden.

'Well?' Theo demanded, and she managed a smile.

'Theo, you know our marriage wasn't a love match. We're doing as well as we can.'

'But you care for each other?' Theo insisted, and Rhiannon wondered how to answer that.

Care for each other? She loved Lukas—loved his strength, the way he made her feel safe, the feel of his arms around her. Loved the little boy he'd been, the boy she hoped he still was underneath, determined to guard his heart so damn carefully.

'Rhiannon…' Theo reached for her hand. 'You must give him time. He's spent thirty-one years of his life trying not to love anyone.' Theo smiled sadly. 'I taught him that. After Paulina—my wife—left I hardened my heart. I hardened Lukas's too.'

Rhiannon's heart ached at the regret in Theo's voice. 'What about your daughters?' she asked, thinking of Antonia, her desperation and her bitterness.

Theo shrugged. 'They were older, and more like their mother. They understood why she left but I refused to. I made sure Lukas refused to, as well.'

'Why did she leave, do you think?' Rhiannon asked

quietly, and Theo's eyes hardened briefly before he shrugged.

'I thought we had the same dream...to build the Petrakides business, to establish a name for ourselves and our children. That wasn't enough for her. She found what she wanted with a racing car driver—a fool who gave her false promises. But she believed them, and they made her happy...for a little while.'

The long speech had exhausted him, and he lay back against the pillows, his face haggard and grey.

'You should rest now,' Rhiannon said. She tucked the covers around his gaunt frame before picking up Annabel and slipping quietly from the room.

Sighing, she returned to her bedroom to settle Annabel for her afternoon nap.

She laid the baby on her back on the bed, tickling her tummy and smiling as Annabel kicked her feet and waved her starfish hands enthusiastically.

'You seem to have done all right without me,' she said, and she blew a raspberry on Annabel's tummy. 'Miss me much, sweetheart?'

Annabel gurgled in response, and Rhiannon heard a quiet voice from the door.

'She obviously adores you.'

She froze, then turned to see Lukas leaning against the doorframe, a look of tender wistfulness on his face. The breath caught and dried in Rhiannon's throat at that look...the look of a man who desperately wanted something.

Wanted love.

She gave herself a mental shake—because, no matter how much her heart wanted to believe that was true, Lukas had given her his opinion on the subject, and she wasn't quite naive enough to believe she could change him.

Was she?

'Do you want to hold her?' She scooped Annabel up. 'She's just been changed, so this is a good time.'

'All right.' Gingerly Lukas took hold of her, his arms going around her awkwardly but with increasing confidence. Annabel laughed and reached up to pat both of his cheeks.

This is our family, Rhiannon thought with a strange sweet pang. *Our family.* Her throat suddenly felt tight, and her eyes stung. Because that seemed like a lot just then.

She'd never had a proper family before—and neither, it seemed, had Lukas.

'She has the Petrakides look,' Lukas said as he smoothed Annabel's dusky curls back from her forehead. 'It's in the eyes.'

Annabel tugged hard on Lukas's ear and he captured her little hand in his. 'Easy, *thisavre mou,*' he said with a little laugh.

At his gentle rebuke, Annabel screwed up her face and burst into noisy tears.

Lukas looked stricken.

Rhiannon smothered a laugh. 'She's just tired. I was about to put her down for a nap.'

'It will take some time for her to get used to me,' Lukas admitted ruefully as he handed her back to Rhiannon. 'For us all to get used to each other.'

Rhiannon nodded, accepting the peace offering. 'Yes,' she agreed, 'it's all very strange.'

Lukas glanced around the room. 'I'll have your

things moved into my bedroom this afternoon. Annabel can be in the room adjoining.'

'I thought we were going to Athens tomorrow,' Rhiannon protested. 'It's hardly neces—'

'It is,' Lukas said firmly. 'Because I want it to be so.'

'I thought,' she retorted acerbically, 'you didn't want anything.'

'I want you, and I'll have you,' Lukas replied. 'Tonight.'

Rhiannon glared. 'Do you have to be so base?'

'What is base about us loving each other as husband and wife?'

'Because it's not about love, Lukas. Remember?'

Annabel cried again, and Rhiannon turned away. 'I need to put her down for a nap.'

Lukas nodded tersely before turning on his heel. Rhiannon heard rather than saw the door click shut.

She put the baby to bed, doing her best to suppress the fury that boiled through her.

He'd have her, would he? Did he have to make it so appallingly clear that it was simply sex for him?

Desire. Lust.

LATER THAT NIGHT, after Annabel was settled in her new room and Theo had been seen to, Rhiannon knew there was no putting it off.

She'd busied herself away from Lukas for most of the day, unable to see him without hurting, without wanting. More. Yet she knew this was the bargain he'd offered—a bargain she'd accepted. One she'd thought she could live with.

It was her own fault—her own problem—if now she found she couldn't.

When she finally approached the bedroom to where he'd had all her things moved—*his* bedroom—she found it empty.

An irritating disappointment settled over her as she surveyed the wide, empty bed—the cream-coloured duvet smooth and untouched, the pillows plumped.

The room was furnished in dark wood and light colours. A masculine room. When Rhiannon took a breath, she inhaled Lukas's scent, that achingly familiar mixture of soap and pine, pure male.

She paused on the threshold, uncertain what to do. Go to bed by herself? Wait for Lukas?

Everything was so new, so strange.

After a moment's indecision she went back downstairs, following her instinct, her heart, to the lounge.

The door was closed, just as before, and she couldn't hear a sound, but somehow she knew.

She pushed it open with her fingertips, saw him at the piano. His head was bowed over the instrument, his fingers poised on the keys without touching them.

He looked, Rhiannon thought, anguished.

'Lukas…?'

He looked up when he saw her, his expression turning guarded, blank.

'I thought you'd be asleep.'

'I was waiting for you,' Rhiannon confessed, and he raised an eyebrow.

'Why? You made it clear earlier that you did not want me with you tonight.'

'I…' She stopped, licked her lips. 'I do want you with me,' she admitted. 'I just don't like it to sound so…base.'

'But to you,' Lukas replied, his tone almost musing, his fingers rippling discordantly over the keys, 'it *is* base. Because I don't love you. I'll never satisfy you, will I, Rhiannon? I'll never please you because I can't give you what you most want.'

The raw truth of it made her blink, stare. She'd expected him to admit it, she supposed. She just hadn't expected him to sound as if it made him sad.

As if it hurt.

'We can try to be happy,' she said after a moment, but she heard the hollow ring of her words. 'For Annabel's sake.'

'And for our own?'

'Yes...' she said.

He nodded slowly. 'I've done the right thing all my life. The responsible thing, the thing everyone told me was my duty. I've lived by it. And I convinced myself I'd done that with you. But maybe I just wanted you. Maybe I made a mistake.'

'If you did, it's already done,' Rhiannon replied. 'Unless you want a divorce?' Why did that thought make her nearly nauseous? She didn't want to leave Lukas.

She just didn't know if she could stay with him.

'No,' Lukas said quietly, 'I don't want a divorce. I'll never want a divorce.'

Even if they were both miserable, Rhiannon thought. Lukas would never shirk his responsibility in such a way. He would never bring a single blemish to the family name.

Yet the strangely lost look on his face reminded her of the boy he'd been—the boy whose mother had walked out on him when he was only five, the boy who'd been told not to love anyone.

This was the man she loved.

She moved closer to him, knelt by his side. Lukas

looked down at her, smiling slightly sadly at her in a way that made Rhiannon ache. Want.

She reached up to place her hands on either side of his face, to draw him to her for a kiss. A kiss that was meant to be tender, gentle. Healing.

Lukas broke the kiss first, leaning his forehead against hers. He sighed softly.

'Let's go to bed,' Rhiannon whispered, and she led him by the hand, upstairs, to the room they now shared.

He stood by the window, still and silent, watching her with that same sweet sorrow.

'You don't have to—' he began.

Rhiannon shook her head. 'I want to.' She slipped out of her clothes before turning to him, unbuttoning his shirt, sliding off his trousers.

Lukas pulled her to him. 'I want you,' he groaned against her mouth. 'I need you.'

As he laid her gently on the bed, his hands stroking and caressing her with an urgency Rhiannon felt kindle in her own soul, she knew that would have to be enough.

It was all Lukas had to give.

THE NEXT MORNING Lukas was gone from the bedroom when Rhiannon awoke, tangled in the sheets and feeling bereft by his absence.

He soon appeared with a tray of coffee and rolls, which he set on the table by the bed. 'Annabel's still sleeping, but we need to leave for Athens within the hour.'

'So soon?' Rhiannon said in concern, for the deep frown between Lukas's dark brow told its own story.

'Yes. I've just had word that Christos joined his mother in Athens yesterday. With the two of them determined to cause trouble together, we need to sort this out as soon as possible. I'm quite sure Antonia will drop this ridiculous custody case when she sees its futility, but I'd prefer the press not to get wind of it. Then we can start adoption proceedings for Annabel.'

Rhiannon nodded. There were so many obstacles to overcome, yet at least they would do it together. Lukas had said 'we'.

The flight to Athens was brief, and Rhiannon spent most of her time settling Annabel.

A limousine met them at the airport, whisking them to Lukas's villa in Drosia, a suburb to the north of Athens, in the pine forests at the foot of the Penteli mountains.

'I'm sorry to leave you here,' Lukas said when Rhiannon and the baby had been unloaded from the car. 'but I must go directly to the office. The staff will make you comfortable in the meantime.'

'All right,' Rhiannon said, accepting the reality, yet feeling a bit hesitant about the sudden rapid changes.

Lukas pressed a hard kiss on her mouth. 'Tonight.'

Rhiannon could only nod. 'I hope it all goes well.'

She watched the car disappear down the long, twisting drive, swallowed up by the dense pine forests flanking the narrow lane.

She turned towards the house, an impressive villa that looked as if it had been built into the mountainside, or had sprung from the very stone.

She opened the front door, stepped into the tiled foyer.

'Hello...?' Her voice echoed into the empty space.

Then she heard the tapping of feet, and a man appeared in the doorway. He was dark, slim, handsome in a laconic way, and he smiled at her in a manner Rhiannon didn't like.

'You must be the English nobody,' he said pleasantly. 'I doubt you were expecting me—nor was my dear uncle, for that matter. I'm Christos.'

CHAPTER TEN

RHIANNON'S ARMS TIGHTENED around Annabel as a matter of instinct. This was Annabel's father. The man she'd come to Greece to find.

Yet now she wanted him gone.

'Lukas has just left,' she said when she finally found her voice. 'If you wanted to speak to him.'

'I did,' Christos agreed, 'but I suppose I can speak to you instead.'

'All right,' Rhiannon agreed evenly. 'If this is about your mother and her custody case—'

'Oh, that.' Christos laughed—an unkind trill. 'She's dropped that. She's halfway back to London by now, I should think.'

'But...' Rhiannon's head spun as hope and suspicion clashed and tangled. 'Are you serious? I spoke to her only yesterday—'

'My mother is—as I am—capricious.' Christos smiled. 'I asked for a drink from that slouch of a house-keeper, but she hasn't brought it yet. Would you care for anything?'

'No,' Rhiannon said stiffly. 'I'm fine.'

'Are you?' Christos laughed again and led the way into the lounge.

Rhiannon followed him on wooden legs. She had a

growing sense of dread, an icy pooling in her middle, and she wasn't even sure why.

The lounge was an airy, spacious room, and Christos sat on one sofa, indicating that Rhiannon should take the other. She did, and though Annabel squirmed to get down, Rhiannon kept her firmly on her lap.

'So why did you marry Lukas?' Christos asked in a musing way. 'Or should I ask why did he marry you?'

'To provide a stable home for Annabel,' Rhiannon replied. 'A child should have two parents.'

'More than I had,' Christos agreed. 'More than Lukas had, for that matter.'

'What do you know about that?'

He shrugged. 'My grandmother left when he was five. But you've been told that, I suppose? Apparently Lukas didn't speak for nearly a month after she was gone.' He laughed. 'He was that shaken up! Then, when he finally did speak, he sounded like a parrot of my sainted grandfather.' His mouth twisted in a cruel smile. 'My mother has never had time for him, and neither do I.'

Rhiannon pressed her lips together. 'Do you know your grandfather is very ill?' she asked, and Christos shrugged.

'My mother mentioned it, but nobody really cares. Why should we? He's hardly done right by us.'

'I suppose that's why no one has visited,' Rhiannon said stiffly, and he laughed.

'I'll see that old bastard at his funeral, with his money in my fist.'

She shook her head, unable to quite believe his callousness, or his clear delight in shocking her. 'Why are you here, Christos?'

'Well...' He leaned forward. 'I wanted to tell Uncle Lukas the news. See the look on his face. The horror! He's always done his damn duty, and hated us for it, and now he's done it again and he didn't even have to.' He chuckled. 'Won't that just kill him?'

The cold, the dread, were intensifying. Rhiannon's hands tightened around Annabel, and she squawked in protest.

'What are you talking about?'

'I wonder why Lukas married you,' Christos continued, ignoring her question. 'He clearly didn't have to. It was a drastic measure, even for him. But I can't really believe he wanted to, either.' The once-over he gave her was both blatant and dismissive, and had Rhiannon gritting her teeth.

'Maybe you should just leave.'

'Oh, I will. This place is out in the sticks. I much prefer the family flat in Athens. But I'll tell you my news—before I stop by and tell Lukas too.' He jerked a contemptuous thumb towards Annabel. 'She's not mine.'

'What?' Rhiannon stared blankly. It was the last thing she'd been expecting.

'She's not mine,' Christos repeated. 'I finally got around to taking the paternity test, and the results came back today. There's ninety-nine per cent chance we're not related.' His smile widened. 'So I don't know who that brat belongs to, but it's not me...or anyone in the Petrakides family.'

'But you spent the weekend with Leanne,' Rhiannon said numbly.

'I did. But she obviously found someone else as well. We didn't spend every moment together, you know. By the time we'd got on the plane I was already a bit bored.'

Rhiannon shook her head, refusing to believe. To accept. 'She spoke so warmly of you...'

'Did she? We had a good time, I suppose. It seems she had a good time with someone else too.'

Was it possible? Rhiannon wondered. It had to be. Yet why would Leanne...?

She'd been desperate to believe, Rhiannon supposed. Leanne had thought Christos was a good man, a rich man. One who could provide for her daughter. Perhaps she'd wanted Rhiannon to find him. When you were unhappy and desperate, you could convince yourself of almost anything.

As she nearly had...like Lukas being able to love. *Her.* So who on earth was Annabel's father? Rhiannon wondered. Another man Leanne had met in Naxos—or someone before or after?

She would never know.

Christos rose elegantly from the sofa. 'Sorry to be the bearer of bad news,' he said, without even a breath of regret. 'I wonder what will happen now? A quickie divorce? Or will Lukas stand by you, no matter how much it hurts? That should be interesting to see.'

Rhiannon couldn't form a reply. Her mind was too numb, too frozen. Annabel squirmed again, and with unsteady hands she set her on the floor.

The front door clicked shut.

She was alone in a strange house, in a strange city, with a stranger's child.

She looked down at Annabel. She loved her, no matter who her father was—or wasn't.

She doubted Lukas would feel the same.

How many times had he told her he would do his duty to a child *of his blood?*

Not some changeling he had no connection to!

A bubble of hysterical laughter rose to her lips. She pressed a fist to her mouth, willing it down. Willing herself to be calm.

Annabel was not a Petrakides. Yet they were still married. Lukas would never agree to a divorce; he'd said as much. She was tied to him—tied to him for no reason but his own inflated sense of responsibility. For her.

A burden.

There was no reason for them to be married now.

No reason at all.

Had there ever been?

Rhiannon stilled even as her mind whirled. Christos had expressed surprise that Lukas had been willing to marry her, to go so far to protect Annabel's future.

Even Rhiannon hadn't seen the necessity for such drastic measures, and yet she'd accepted them. She'd agreed.

Why?

Because I loved him, she acknowledged, *even then.*

Because she'd believed he could change. That she could change him.

Why had Lukas agreed? Was it just responsibility... or something more? Could she hope? Could she challenge him, confront him?

How could she not? Her heart began a steady thud.

Love made you strong.

She leaned her head against the back of the sofa, closing her eyes. It was such a risk...

It was worth it. It had to be.

A tentative knock sounded at the door.

'Master Christos...?' The housekeeper, a slight

woman, with grey hair scraped back in a bun, holding a drink on a tray, stood in the doorway.

'He's left,' Rhiannon explained, then smiled wearily. 'But I'll take that drink.'

THE VILLA WAS cloaked in darkness when Rhiannon finally heard Lukas's car come up the drive. It had been a long, painful afternoon; she'd endured hours of wondering, questioning, fearing, hoping.

After a fretful afternoon Annabel had fallen asleep in her car seat, as there was no travel cot in the villa.

It was just as well, Rhiannon thought, considering what she might have to do. What she was willing to do.

Her life and her heart were on the line.

The front door opened, and she heard his soft, steady tread.

'Rhiannon…?' He came into the lounge, saw her standing in the middle of the room, and his face turned to stone.

'What are those?'

'My bags,' Rhiannon said flatly. She nudged a suitcase at her foot. 'I trust Christos found you?'

'Yes, he did.' Lukas raked a hand through his hair. 'So you know?'

'If you mean about Annabel—'

'You said she looked like a Petrakides!' Rhiannon couldn't keep the note of accusation, of hurt, out of her voice.

'I suppose,' Lukas said heavily, 'I wanted it to be true.' He looked at the suitcases by Rhiannon's feet. 'But why—?'

'If Annabel isn't Christos's baby, Lukas, then she's not related to you. She's not…' Rhiannon took a breath, dragging it desperately into her lungs. 'Your responsibility.'

Lukas was silent for a moment, studying her. 'She is now,' he finally said. 'As you are.'

'That's where you're wrong. I've never wanted to be your responsibility. You tried to make me into some wretched duty, but I won't accept it, Lukas. I have my own life, and you're not responsible for it.'

'You're my wife,' Lukas said flatly, as if that ended the discussion.

'We can get divorced.' Rhiannon forced herself to ignore the look of furious incredulity that slashed across his features. 'Or have the marriage annulled.'

'Annulled? On what grounds?'

She shrugged. 'A fancy solicitor could find some reason, I'm sure.'

He shook his head slowly. 'No.'

'No? Just like that? You can't order me—'

'There will be no divorce.' His voice was so flat, his expression so cold, that Rhiannon felt her nerve begin to desert her.

What on earth was she doing?

'Then I'll leave.'

He paused, raised one eyebrow. 'In the middle of the night? With Annabel?'

'She's asleep in her car seat. I can call a taxi.'

'You don't speak Greek.'

Rhiannon's smile was brittle. 'I've found an English-speaking service already.' She held up the mobile he'd given her. 'It's on speed dial.'

Lukas shook his head slowly. 'You won't leave.'

'Try me.' Her heart was pounding, her face flushed,

her mouth dry. She didn't *want* to leave, but she would if it came to it. If Lukas forced her.

'Let me make myself clear,' Lukas said, and his voice was ominously calm. 'You are not *allowed* to leave.'

'I don't care how powerful you are, Lukas, you can't keep me here. And I'll tell you right now—the only way I'd stay is if you loved me.'

He froze, stared at her in incredulity. 'Love? That's what this is about? I have already told you, Rhiannon—'

'I know what you said. I know what we agreed. But things have changed, Lukas. *I've* changed. And this is the way it is now.'

'You ask too much!'

'Do I?' Her smile was sad. 'There's no reason for us to be married, Lukas, except for love. Don't you see that? We can't use Annabel as a reason or as an excuse.'

'Excuse?' he repeated furiously, and she lifted her chin.

'I'm not going to stay married to you simply because you can't have a blemish on your family name. My life—my love—is worth more than that.'

Lukas's face was white, his eyes blazing silver. 'You will not divorce me, Rhiannon.'

The quiet warning in his voice made her only more determined. 'Tell me why not, then, Lukas.'

'Because we're married, and I honour my vows,' he said through gritted teeth. 'Now, I've had quite enough of this discussion…' He turned to leave the room.

'I haven't.' Rhiannon grabbed his arm, pulled him towards her. He froze, swivelled slowly.

'What do you want from me?' His voice was stony, cold, yet she heard—felt—the frayed edges, and knew he was losing control of that remote, icy demeanour. She wanted it stripped away. She wanted him bare, as bare as she was, with her emotions, her heart splayed open.

'Your love. I love you, Lukas.'

He looked at her, nonplussed and silent. Rhiannon felt the humiliation, the pain, the rejection, and forced herself not to give in. She took a breath.

'I won't stay in a marriage without love.'

'You should have thought of that before you took your vows,' Lukas replied coldly. 'Now I'm going to bed.'

Rhiannon watched him stalk out of the room, her heart thudding dully against her ribs, her pulse rushing in her ears. She was going about this all wrong. She'd wanted to draw a confession from him, a declaration, but it wasn't happening.

She was just making him angry.

With leaden steps she walked upstairs, found Lukas in the bedroom, tugging off his tie. She watched him sadly, feeling so far away from him, so distant from his emotions, his thoughts, his heart.

And she wanted to be close. She wanted to be so close.

Lukas glanced up and saw her. 'Coming to bed?' he queried sardonically, and Rhiannon shrugged.

'Is that where you want me?'

His eyes glinted. 'It's a start.'

Rhiannon swallowed. 'Fine.' She strode to the foot of the bed and began to undress. It was a deliberate, brutal striptease, designed not to seduce but to shame. Shame them both.

She unbuttoned her blouse, slipped it off her shoulders, shrugged off her jeans.

Lukas watched, a muscle ticking in his jaw, his face impassive.

She hesitated for a second before slipping off her underwear. She stood there naked while Lukas watched, arms crossed.

'Is this what you want?' she demanded. 'My body? Sex? Nothing else? Is that enough for you?' She lay on the bed, spread her thighs. 'Then take it, Lukas. And maybe you'll see how empty it is without love.'

Distaste flickered in his eyes. 'You're acting like a whore.'

'No,' she retorted, 'you're treating me like one.'

She lay there naked, exposed, open. Knowing this was how it must be. She couldn't demand that Lukas share his weakness, his truth, if she didn't share hers.

'It was good between us,' he told her, and with calculated tenderness he moved his hand up her calf, towards her thigh. 'I could make you want me even now.'

'Yes, you could.' Her voice trembled as his hand slid further, teased her. She saw the desire dilating his pupils, making his breath come quicker, as hers was.

He dropped his hand and turned away. His tie was loosened, his shirt half unbuttoned as he raked a hand through his hair. 'Why can't that be enough for you?'

'Because I want you to love me.' She sat up, still naked, unashamed. 'And I think you do. You may have been pretending otherwise—'

Her voice trembled, and Lukas shook his head in disbelief. 'If anyone is pretending, Rhiannon, it's you.'

She hoped that wasn't true. She desperately wanted it not to be true.

Now she needed to be bold. She needed to beg.

'Lukas, I love you.'

He shook his head—a violent movement of instinctive denial. 'No—'

'And you love me.'

The silence was terrifying. He stared at her. His face was cold, as if carved from ice, from stone, his eyes hard. Dead. 'No.' He spoke so flatly, so finally, that Rhiannon almost considered giving up.

Almost.

'Christos wondered why you married me,' she said, her voice a thread. A thread of steel. 'Why you felt you needed to—'

'For Annabel,' Lukas cut across her. 'Let's not rehash this, Rhiannon. It will only become painful...for you.'

'Too late.' She tried to smile, felt the tears. 'The thing is, Lukas, Christos got me thinking. Thinking things I'd already begun to wonder about. To hope for. You didn't need to marry me to secure Annabel's future. You said yourself that Antonia was fickle, that she might drop the custody case simply because she was bored. A judge would not even have considered her suit seriously, despite any witnesses she brought forward. Marriage was an extreme reaction—even for you.'

'Was it?' He stood still, his arms hanging by his sides, his hands loose, yet Rhiannon could feel the tension in him, knew he wanted to clench his fists.

'Yes. And I went along with it. I let you convince me because I wanted to marry you. I loved you even then—even though I was afraid you'd end up hurting me because you wouldn't love me back.'

'As I am now?' He hissed. 'Rhiannon, if you're trying to convince yourself—'

'Maybe I am.' Her voice wavered, broke. 'Look at me, Lukas. Look at me here, naked, on my knees, doing the one thing I swore I would never do again. Begging for love.' She shook her head, tears rolling slowly down her cheeks. 'You know why I'm doing it? Why I'm letting myself? Because love is *strong*, Lukas. Love makes you strong. Even here, begging as I am, I feel strong. I *am* strong. Because I love you. And I know that's a good thing, a beautiful thing, that will never weaken or destroy me.'

He began to shake his head. Stopped. There was an anguished, arrested look in his eyes, as if he wanted to stop listening, to deny what she said, what he felt.

There would be no stopping now.

'Christos told me about your mother. How she left and you didn't speak for a month.'

'Don't—' It came out as a harsh cry, and yet still she continued.

'She hurt you—more than anyone else could—and you've never wanted it to happen again. Don't let her win, Lukas. Don't let her keep you from loving.'

He strode towards her, grabbed her arms and hauled her to her feet. 'You know nothing! *Nothing!*' he said savagely and then kissed her, hard. It was a demand, a punishment. 'This is all we'll have. All we'll ever have. It's all I have to give, Rhiannon, so stop doing this!' His voice broke, surprising them both, and he pushed her away. *'Stop.'* It came out as a plea, his shoulders hunched, his face averted.

'I'll stop,' Rhiannon said quietly. She didn't bother to wipe the tears that streaked silently down her cheeks, didn't hide the ache of longing and sorrow in her voice. 'I'll stop when you look at me and tell me you don't love me. Look me in the face—in my eyes—and say those words.'

'Fine!' He turned towards her, his face filled with fury, with despair. He opened his mouth and Rhiannon's

heart began to break. 'I don't—' He stopped, snapped his mouth closed, and strode to the window. His back was to her, and she could see tension, anguish, in every taut line of his body.

She held her breath, her cheeks still damp, and waited. The silence stretched between them, aching and expectant.

'When my mother was going to leave,' Lukas began, in a strange, distant voice, 'I heard her talking to my father.'

He stopped, his face still averted, his body still thrumming with tension. Rhiannon took a shallow breath and kept on waiting.

'She told him that she loved Milo. Her lover. She said she hadn't known what love was till she met him. That he made her feel happy and alive.' He shook his head slowly. 'I didn't understand what she was talking about, of course. I was only five. But I thought that *I* loved her as much as this Milo did.' He paused, raking a hand through his hair before dropping it. 'My father pleaded with her to stay. He was...pitiful. Even as a five-year-old I realised that, and I was embarrassed for him. Of course I didn't realise my mother was leaving me at that point. I never thought she would leave *me*.'

His voice choked slightly, and he kept his face turned away from her. After a long, ragged moment, he continued.

'I saw her go down the stairs. Milo was waiting outside. My father said she would lose us—the children—and after only a second she said, "I don't care."' He laughed—a short, sharp sound. 'I couldn't believe it. I ran up to her, told her to take me with her. I couldn't believe she'd be willing to leave me...that she'd want to. Of course now I realise Milo wouldn't have wanted the encumbrance of four children. My mother was very beautiful, but she was still ten years older than he was, and she needed to do everything she could to keep him.'

'What happened then?' Rhiannon asked in a whisper, when it seemed as if Lukas wouldn't continue.

'I was every bit as pitiful as my father.' His voice was flat, toneless. 'I begged, I pleaded, I sobbed. I clung to her legs, her shoes. She kicked me off. She said, "Take him."'

Rhiannon closed her eyes briefly, pain slashing through her as she thought of what Lukas had gone through. What he was going through now, remembering.

'I don't remember how they got me off her. I don't even remember her leaving. But I never saw her again.'

'Lukas…'

He shook his head, flinging up one hand to keep her from speaking. 'My three sisters were in school or out on their own at that point. I'd been a late and unexpected addition. It was just my father and me, and he shaped me in the pattern of his own deep bitterness. I don't blame him, because I was already bitter…even as a child. I vowed to never let that happen to me again.'

He turned to face her, and Rhiannon's heart twisted, expanded at the bleak honesty on his face.

'So, you see, Rhiannon, I've lied to you. I lied in telling you that I wouldn't love anyone because I'd seen how it weakened and cheapened others. It isn't *others* that have kept me from giving my heart, it's been myself. *I* was weakened…cheapened. I wanted to protect myself from that happening again.' He smiled—a painful twisting of his lips. 'The trouble is, I haven't been able to keep myself from falling in love. I've fought it every step of the way—lied to myself about why I wanted to be with you, even why I needed to marry you. I insisted to myself it was a matter of responsibility—yes, wretched duty—but it wasn't. It was a matter of love.'

'Lukas…'

'I love you, Rhiannon. Perhaps from the moment I saw you. Not at the reception, but the night before, on the beach. You were alone and I watched you. I felt like I knew you, like I'd finally met someone who might understand me.'

'You have,' Rhiannon said in an aching whisper, her voice raw with unshed tears.

Lukas walked slowly towards her, defenceless, open. Weak, vulnerable.

Strong.

'Will you forgive me? I've been a fool, a reluctant fool, and I'm so thankful you've stayed with me… You made me see myself.'

Rhiannon nodded, relief and joy rushing through her in a sweet, sweet wave as Lukas's arms came around her, drawing her close to him, drawing her home.

'You weren't really going to leave, were you? You scared the hell out of me, you know, with those bags.'

'I didn't want to leave,' Rhiannon admitted in a muffled voice, her head against his shoulder. 'But I was prepared to…I would have done anything to make you realise you loved me.'

'You were so sure?' Lukas teased, and Rhiannon gave a wavery laugh.

'No—and that was the worst part. Knowing it might all be for nothing…again.'

'But it isn't,' Lukas assured her, 'and it never will

be.' He chuckled softly. 'Wait till my father hears this. He won't believe it.'

'He might,' Rhiannon replied with a smile. 'I think he is wiser than either of us.'

'We'll return to the island as soon as business is taken care of. If you don't mind...?'

She shook her head. 'And you don't mind that Annabel isn't a Petrakides?' Rhiannon knew in her heart that he didn't, but she still had to make sure.

'What I care about,' he told her, 'is that we're a family. And we are. Perhaps the first real one for both of us.'

Rhiannon nodded, and Lukas kissed a tear from her cheek. 'No more tears,' he whispered. 'For either of us.'

Only love...good, pure, wonderful.

Strong.

* * * * *

BOUND TO THE GREEK

CHAPTER ONE

'COME RIGHT THIS WAY, Mr Zervas. You're going to meet with Eleanor, our top planner.'

Jace Zervas stilled his stride for no more than a second as the word reverberated through him. *Eleanor.* He hadn't heard that name in ten years, hadn't let himself think it.

Of course, it had to be a coincidence. There were certainly more Eleanors in the United States—in New York City—than the one who had broken his heart.

The assistant who had led him through the elegantly sparse lobby with its designer sofas and modern art now stopped in front of a door of tinted glass, gave a perfunctory knock, then pushed it open.

'Eleanor? I'd like to introduce you to—'

Jace didn't hear the rest. For as the woman in the office swung round to face him, his mind buzzed, blanked. It *was* Eleanor.

His Eleanor. Ellie.

He knew she was as surprised as he was that he was here, that *they* were here, face to face. Although her expression didn't really change, he was aware of the slight widening of her eyes, the parting of her lips.

Then she drew herself up, gave him a professional smile that managed to irritate him with its coolness, and said, 'Thank you, Jill. That will be all.'

The assistant, surely aware of the current that crackled through the air, glanced speculatively between them. Jace ignored her, his gaze fixed on Eleanor Langley, so utterly, appallingly different from the Ellie he'd once known. 'Shall I bring coffee?'

A tiny pause. 'Certainly. Thank you.'

The assistant left, the door clicked shut, and Jace's mind kicked back into gear.

Of course he should have expected this might happen. He'd known Ellie was from New York, and her mother was an event planner. Why shouldn't she have followed the same career path?

Because the Ellie you knew hated her mother's career, her mother's world. The Ellie you knew—or at least thought you knew—wanted to open a bakery.

Clearly much had happened in the last ten years.

'You've changed.' He didn't mean to say it, yet it was impossible not to notice it. The Ellie he'd known ten years ago had looked nothing like the shiny, polished woman in front of him.

His Ellie had been relaxed, natural, *fun,* so different from this woman with her tailored black power suit, her highlighted hair barely brushing her cheekbones in an elegant chestnut bob. Her hazel eyes, once warm and golden, now seemed darker, sharper, and were narrowed into assessing slits. As she moved back around to her desk Jace saw her shoes: black three-inch stilettos. His Ellie had never worn heels. His Ellie had never worn black.

Yet why was he even thinking this way? *His* Ellie hadn't been his at all. He'd realised that all too terribly when he'd last seen her…when she'd lied to him in the worst way possible. When he'd walked away without another word.

ELEANOR LANGLEY STARED down at the burnished surface of her desk and took a deep breath. She needed the moment to regain her poise and control. She'd never expected this moment to happen, although she'd fantasised about it many times over the last decade. Coming face to face with Jace Zervas. Telling him just what she thought of him and his cowardly creeping away.

She'd envisioned herself slapping his face, telling him to go to hell, or, in her more dignified moments, sweeping him with one simple, disdainful glance.

She had not pictured herself trembling, both inside and out, unable to think of a single thing to say.

Stop. She'd worked too hard for too long to let this moment defeat her. Taking another breath, Eleanor lifted her head and settled her gaze coolly on the man in front of her.

'Of course I've changed. It's been ten years.' She paused, letting her gaze sweep over him, although she had a feeling it wasn't as disdainful as she might have wished. 'You've changed too, Jace.' It felt strange to have his name on her lips. She never spoke of him. She tried not to think of him.

He *had* changed; his ink-black hair was now streaked with grey at the temples and his face looked leaner, longer. Harder. Eleanor noticed new lines from nose to mouth, and the faint fanning of crow's feet by his eyes. Somehow those lines didn't age him so much as give him an air of dignity and experience. They even emphasised the steely grey of his eyes with their silvery glints. And his body hadn't changed at all, it seemed: still long, lithe, and powerful. The grey silk suit he wore only emphasised his muscular shoulders and trim hips; he wore it, as he had the cashmere sweatshirts and faded jeans of his college days, with ease and grace.

He looked, she thought a bit resentfully, great. But then, she reminded herself, so did she. She spent a lot of time and effort making sure she looked great; in her job a professional and even glamorous appearance was a must. She was grateful for it now. The last thing she wanted was to be at a disadvantage. She straightened, smiled even, and flicked her hair back from her face in one quick movement. 'So you're my two o'clock.'

Jace smiled back, faintly, but his eyes were hard. He looked almost angry. Eleanor had no idea what *he* had to be angry about; he was the one who had left. If any-one should be angry— She stopped that thought before her resentful mind gave it wings. She wasn't angry. She was over it. Over him. She no longer cared any more, at all, about Jace Zervas.

She turned to her planner, still open on her desk, and trailed one glossily manicured finger down the day's appointments. 'You're here on behalf of Atrikides Holdings?' she asked. 'It says Leandro Atrikides was supposed to have been coming.' She looked up, eye-brows arched. 'Change of plans?'

'Something like that,' Jace agreed, his voice taut. He sat down in one of the leather armchairs in front of her desk and crossed one leg over the other.

'Well.' She made herself smile and sat down behind her desk, hands neatly folded. 'How can I help?'

Jace's lips tightened, and Eleanor wondered if that was going to be it. Ten years of anger, bitterness, and overwhelming heartache reduced to nothing in a single sentence. *How can I help?* Yet what other choice was there? She didn't want to rake over the past; it would be messy and uncomfortable and far too painful. She wanted to pretend the past didn't exist, and so she would. She'd treat Jace Zervas like a regular client, even though he was far from one, and she hardly wanted to help him. She didn't even want to talk to the man for another second.

The sane thing, of course, would be to respectfully request a colleague to take Jace as her client, and step away from what could only be an explosive situation. Or if not explosive, then at least angrily simmering. She could see it in the hard steel of his eyes. She could feel it bubbling in herself.

Yet Eleanor knew she wouldn't do that. Her boss wouldn't be pleased; Lily Stevens didn't like changes. Messes. And Eleanor could certainly do without the gossip. Besides, there was another, greater reason why she'd face Jace down in her own office. She didn't want to give him the satisfaction of making her run away. As he had.

'Well,' Jace replied after a moment, 'obviously I'm here because I need you to plan an event.'

'Obviously,' Eleanor agreed, and heard the answering sharpness in her tone. This was not going well. Every little exchange was going to be pointed under the politeness, and she didn't think she could take the tension. The trouble was, she didn't know what else to do. Talking about the past was akin to ripping the bandages off old wounds, inflaming the scars that still remained on her heart. Her body. Even remembering it hurt.

She clamped her mind down on that thought. Jace

Zervas was just another client, she told herself again. Just a regular client. She let her breath out slowly and tried to smile.

'What I meant,' she said evenly, 'was what kind of event are you hosting?' She gritted her teeth as she added, 'Some details would help.'

'Isn't there some form that's been filled out? I'm quite sure my assistant did this all on the telephone.'

Eleanor glanced through the slim file she had on Atrikides Holdings. 'A Christmas party,' she read from the memo one of the secretaries had taken. 'That's all I have, I'm afraid.'

A knock sounded on the door, and Jill came in with a tray of coffee. Eleanor rose to take it from her. She didn't want her assistant picking up on the tension that thrummed angrily through the room. God knew how she'd try to use it; Jill had been jockeying for her position since she arrived, fresh from college, two years ago.

'Thanks, Jill. I'll take it from here.'

Surprised, Jill backed off, the door closing once more, and Eleanor set the tray on her desk, her back to Jace. She still heard his lazy murmur.

'You didn't used to drink coffee. I always thought it was so funny, a girl who wanted to open a coffee shop and yet didn't drink coffee herself.'

Eleanor tensed. So he was going to go there. She'd been hoping they could get through this awkward meeting without referencing the past at all, but now Jace was going to talk about these silly, student memories, as if they shared some happy past.

As if they shared anything at all.

A single streak of anger, white-hot, blazed through her. Her hands shook as she poured the coffee. How

dared he? How dared he act as if he hadn't walked—
run—away from her, the minute things got too much?
How dared he pretend they'd parted amicably, or even
parted at all?

Instead of her going to his apartment building, only
to find he'd left. Left the building, left the city, left the
country. All without telling her.

Coward.

'Actually, I think it was enterprising,' she told him
coolly, her back still to him. Her hands no longer trembled. 'I saw the market, and I wanted to meet it.' She
handed him his coffee: black, two sugars, the way he'd
always taken it. She still remembered. Still remembered brewing him a single-serve cafétière in her student apartment while she plied him with the pastries and
cakes she was going to sell in her little bakery. While
she told him her dreams.

He'd said everything was delicious. But of course he
would. He'd lied about so many things, like when he'd
said he loved her. If he'd loved her, he wouldn't have left.

Eleanor poured her own coffee. She took it black
now, and drank at least three cups a day. Her best friend
Allie said so much caffeine wasn't good for her, but Eleanor needed the kick. Especially now.

She turned back to Jace. He still held his mug, his
long, brown fingers wrapped around the handle, his
expression brooding and a little dark. 'That's not how
I remember it.'

Disconcerted, Eleanor took too large a sip of coffee
and burned her tongue. 'What?'

Jace leaned forward. 'You weren't interested in meeting a market. You weren't even interested in business.
Don't you remember, Ellie?' His voice came out in a

soft hiss. 'You just wanted to have a place where people could relax and be happy.' He spoke it like a sneer, and Eleanor could only think of when—and where—she had said that. In Jace's bed, after they'd made love for the first time. She'd shared so many pitiful, pathetic secrets with him. Poured out her life and heart and every schoolgirl dream she'd ever cherished, and he'd given her—what? Nothing. Less than nothing.

'I'm sure we remember quite a few things differently, Jace,' she said coolly. 'And I go by Eleanor now.'

'You told me you hated your name.'

She let out an impatient breath. 'It's been ten years, Jace. Ten years. I've changed. You've changed. Get over it.'

His eyes narrowed, the colour flaring to silver. 'Oh, I'm over it, Eleanor,' he said softly. 'I'm definitely over it.'

But he didn't sound over it. He sounded angry, and that made Eleanor even angrier despite all her intentions to stay cool, not to care. He had no right, no right at all, even to be the tiniest bit furious. Yet here he was, acting as if she'd been the one to do something wrong. Of course she *had* done something wrong, in Jace's eyes. She'd made the classic, naive mistake of accidentally getting pregnant.

JACE STARED AT her, felt the fury rise up in him before he choked it all down again. There was no use in being angry. It was ten years too late. He didn't want to feel angry; the emotion shamed him now.

Yet even so he realised he wanted to know. He needed to know what had happened to Eleanor in the last ten years. Had she kept the baby? Had she married the father? Had she suffered even a moment's regret for trying to dupe him so damnably? Because she didn't look as if she had. She looked as if she was angry with him, which was ridiculous. She was the guilty one, the lying one. He'd simply found out.

'So.' She sat down again, behind the desk, so it served as a barrier between them. Not that they needed one. Time was enough. Putting her coffee carefully to one side, she pulled out a pen and pad of paper. Jace watched the way her hair swung down in a smooth, dark curtain as she bent her head. Everything about her was so different from the Ellie he had known, the Ellie he remembered. The woman in front of him was no more than a polished, empty shell. She gave nothing away. She looked up, her hazel eyes narrowing, her mouth curving into a false smile. 'Can you give me a few details about this party?'

Damn the party. Jace leaned forward. 'Did you have a boy or a girl?' God only knew why he wanted to ask that question. Why he even wanted to know. Surely there were a dozen—a hundred—more relevant questions he could have asked. *When did you cheat on me? Why? Who was he? Did he love you like I did?*

No, he wasn't about to ask any of those questions. They all revealed too much. He had no intention of letting Eleanor Langley ever know how much she'd hurt him.

His voice was no more than a predatory hiss, an accusation, yet Ellie's expression didn't change. If anything it became even more closed, more polished and professional. The woman was like ice. He could hardly credit it; the Ellie he'd known had reflected every emotion in her eyes. She'd cried at commercials. Now Ellie—Eleanor—simply pressed her lips together and gave her head a little shake.

'Let's not talk about the past, Jace. If we want to be professional—' Her voice caught, finally, and he was glad. He'd almost thought she didn't feel anything and God knew he felt too much. So this icy woman could thaw. A little. Underneath there was something, something true and maybe even broken, something *real*, and for now that was enough.

He leaned back, satisfied. 'Fine. Let's be professional. I want to hold a Christmas party for the remaining employees of Atrikides Holdings.'

'Remaining?' Ellie repeated a bit warily.

'Yes, remaining. I bought the company last week, and there has been some unrest because of it.'

'A corporate takeover.' She spoke the words distastefully.

'Yes, exactly,' Jace replied blandly. 'I had to let some of the employees go when I brought in my own people. Now that there is a new workforce, I'd like to create a feeling of goodwill. A Christmas party is a means to that end.'

'I see.'

Yet Jace could see from the flicker of contempt in her eyes, the tightening of her mouth, that she didn't see at all. She was summing him up and judging him up based on very little evidence—the evidence he'd given.

Yet why should he care what she thought of him? And why should she judge at all? She'd been just as ruthless as he was, as enterprising and economical with the truth.

And he'd judged her with far more damning information.

ELEANOR WROTE A few cursory notes on the pad of paper on her desk. She wasn't even aware of what she was writing. Her vision hazed, her mind blanked.

Was it a boy or a girl?

How could he ask such a question now, with such contempt? His *child.* He'd been asking about his child.

She closed her mind on the thought like a trap, refusing to free the memory and sorrow. She couldn't go there. Not now, not ever. She'd kept those emotions locked deep inside herself and even seeing Jace Zervas again wouldn't free them. She wouldn't let it. She drew in a deep breath and looked up.

'So what kind of Christmas party are we talking about here? Cocktails, sit-down dinner? How many people do you anticipate coming?'

'There are only about fifty employees, and I'd like to invite families.' Jace spoke tonelessly. 'Quite a few have small children, so something family-friendly but elegant.'

'Family-friendly,' Eleanor repeated woodenly. She felt her fingers clench around the pen she was holding. She could not do this. She could not pretend a moment longer, even though she'd been pretending for ten years—

Was that all her life had been? Pretending? Pretence? And she hadn't realised it until she'd come face to face with Jace Zervas.

Stop, she told herself yet again. *Stop thinking, feeling.* Another breath. Somehow she made herself nod as she wrote another note on the pad of paper. 'Very well. Now—'

'Look,' Jace exhaled impatiently, 'I don't really have

time to go over every detail. I came here as a favour, and I have a lot to do. I'm only in New York for a week.'

'A week—'

'I need the party to be this Friday,' Jace cut her off.

Eleanor's mouth dropped open before she quickly closed it. *That* hadn't been on the memo. 'I'm afraid that's impossible. Venues are booked, I have a complete client list—'

'Nothing is impossible if you throw enough money at it,' Jace replied flatly. 'And I chose your company because I was assured you could make it happen.' His gaze, cold and contemptuous, raked over her. 'I was told the top event planner would see to me personally. I suppose that's you?'

Eleanor merely nodded. She didn't trust herself to speak.

'Then email me a list of details to go over by tomorrow morning.' Jace rose from his chair. 'You've done very well for yourself, Ellie,' he said softly. 'I wonder how many people you had to climb over to get to this lovely little spot.' He glanced out of the window at her view of Madison Square Park, the leafless trees stark against a grey winter sky.

His comment was so blatantly unfair and unwarranted that Eleanor could only gasp. And fume. What right did he have to make such a judgment? If anyone should be judg*ing*—

Jace headed for the door. 'I don't think I'll need to see you before the party,' he said, and somehow this bored dismissal stung her more than anything else had.

He was going to leave, just like that, after raking up the old wounds, after asking about her baby— their baby—

'It was a girl,' she burst out, the words like staccato gunfire. Her chest burned, and so did her eyes. Her fingers clenched into a fist on her desk. Jace stilled, his hand on the door. 'A girl,' she repeated tonelessly. 'Since you asked.'

He turned around slowly, lip curled in an unpleasant sneer. 'So I did,' he replied. 'But actually I really don't care.'

And then he was gone.

CHAPTER TWO

'ELEANOR? DID JACE Zervas just leave the office?'

Eleanor jerked her head up to see her boss, Lily Stevens, standing in her office doorway. Under her glossy black helmet of hair her eyebrows were drawn together sharply, her mouth a thin red line. The elegantly disapproving look reminded Eleanor of her mother, which was unsurprising since Lily and her mother had been business partners until five years ago.

'Eleanor?' Lily repeated, more sharply, and Eleanor rose from her desk, trying to smile. How long had she been lost in her own miserable reverie? 'Yes. We just concluded our meeting.'

'That was fast.'

Eleanor moved around her desk to put Jace's coffee cup—barely touched—back on the tray. 'He's a busy man.'

'Jill said things seemed tense when she came in here.'

Of course Jill would run to her boss, Eleanor thought with resentment. What a frenemy! This business could be cut-throat, and everyone was trying to claw a way in or up. She gave a little shrug. 'Not really.'

'I don't think I need to tell you,' Lily said, her tone making it clear she thought she did, 'that Jace Zervas is a very important client? His holdings are worth over a billion—'

'You don't need to tell me.' She didn't need Lily telling her how rich and powerful Jace was. She'd known that already. When she'd met him as a twenty-two-year-old exchange student in Boston, he'd been from money. Rich, entitled, spoiled.

Except he'd never seemed spoiled to her...until he'd left. Then he'd seemed rotten right through.

'I want you to do everything in your power to make this party a success,' Lily told her. 'I'm releasing your other clients to Laura for the week.'

'What?' Eleanor heard the outrage in her voice, and strove to temper it. She had several clients she'd been working with for months, and she knew Laura—another frenemy—would be eager to scoop up the contacts and run with them. Eleanor gritted her teeth. This business could be brutal. She'd toughened up a lot in the last ten years, but it still made her weary. She also knew there was nothing she could do about it.

If Lily was going to make that kind of executive decision, so be it. He wasn't worth her jeopardising her career; he wasn't worth *anything*. She would work on Jace's damn party for a week. And then she would forget—again—that she'd ever met him.

Lily's eyes narrowed. 'Is that going to be a problem, Eleanor?'

Eleanor bit the inside of her cheek. She hated that tone, that silky, dangerous, warning tone that her mother had always taken with her as a child. Funny, how she'd ended up in a job just like her mother's, with a boss just like her mother.

Except there was nothing remotely funny about it, or even coincidental. Every choice, every decision had been intentional, a way of distancing herself from everything she'd been or believed in. A way of reinventing herself.

And it had worked.

Now she turned to smile sweetly at her boss. 'Of course not. I'm absolutely thrilled—and honoured, Lily—to be working with Mr Zervas. Getting his account is a coup for the agency.'

Lily nodded, seemingly satisfied. 'So it is. Are you meeting with Zervas again?'

'I'll email him the particulars tomorrow.' Eleanor shuddered inwardly to think what that meant. She'd be tied up in begging calls for the rest of the day, recalling favours and currying some more so she could make this thing happen.

The idea that she would have to slave away all for Jace burned in her gut, her heart. It was just *wrong*.

But she wasn't about to lose her job over this, or even her cool. And, Eleanor told herself, there could be some sweet, sweet satisfaction in showing Jace how he hadn't hurt her at all.

Even if he really had—and horribly at that.

She spent the rest of the day immersed in work, planning Jace's party while refusing to think of the man himself. A call to Atrikides Holdings yielded some interesting—and unsurprising—information.

'It all happened so fast,' gushed the staff member Eleanor had been connected to when she asked to speak to someone about details. Eleanor leaned back in her chair and prepared to hear some gossip. 'One minute everything was fine—it's a family business, you know—and the next he swooped in and took over. Fired half the people.' The woman—Peggy—lowered her voice to an awed hush. 'They had to leave that very day. Pack their stuff in boxes. Even Talos Atrikides—the CEO's *son!*'

'Well, hopefully this party will go some way to smoothing things over,' Eleanor replied. She could listen to the gossip, but she wouldn't indulge in it herself. She knew better.

Still, as she hung up the phone, the conversation left her a little shaken. She'd fallen in love with Jace Zervas when he'd been just twenty-two years old, charming, easy-going, carefree and careless. She hadn't realised just how cold—and cold-hearted—he'd been until he'd walked away.

And hearing about his actions with Atrikides Holdings today confirmed it. He really was that man.

The other one—the one she'd fallen in love with—had been nothing more than a mirage. A lie.

It was nearly midnight by the time Eleanor finally stumbled out of the office, exhausted and eyesore from scanning endless sheets of paper with their myriad details. Still, she had the basis of a party to propose to Jace—via email—tomorrow. Massaging her temples, she headed out into the street, the only cars visible a few off-duty cabs. It looked as if she would have to walk.

It was only a few blocks to her apartment in a high-rise condo on the Hudson River, a gleaming testament to glass and steel. Eleanor didn't particularly like the modern architecture, or the building's fussy, high-maintenance residents, but she'd bought it because her mother had said it was a good investment. And she didn't spend much time there anyway.

Sighing, Eleanor nodded hello to the doorman on duty and then headed in the high-speed lift up to the thirtieth floor.

Her apartment was, as always, dark and quiet. Eleanor dropped her keys on the hall table and flicked on the recessed lighting that bathed the living room with its modern sofa and teakwood coffee table in soft yellow light. Outside the Hudson River twinkled with lights.

Her stomach rumbled and she realised she had skipped dinner. Again. Kicking off her heels, she went to the galley kitchen and peered in her near-empty fridge. It held half a carton of moo shoo pork and a yogurt that was—Eleanor peered closer—two weeks past its sell-by date. Neither looked appetising.

Dispiritedly Eleanor closed the fridge. It was hard to believe she'd once baked cookies and muffins by the dozen, had dreamed of owning her own café. She'd been unbearably, determinedly domestic, and now she could barely feed herself.

She grabbed a handful of rather stale crackers from the cupboard and went back to the living room. Funny, she hadn't thought of her old café dream in years, yet when she'd known Jace she'd spent hours embroidering that daydream, how it would be a little bit of everything: coffee shop, bakery, bookstore, gallery. Warm, cosy, bright, and welcoming. The home she'd never felt she'd had. It—everything—had seemed so possible then, so bright and shiny.

And now having Jace back in her life so suddenly, so surprisingly, brought it all back. The dreams, the disappointments.

The despair.

Eleanor thrust the thought away as she munched another cracker. Her stomach rumbled again. Perhaps sleep was better. She was exhausted anyway, and at least when she was asleep she wouldn't feel hungry. Neither would she have to think—or remember.

Dropping her uneaten crackers in the bin, Eleanor turned towards her bedroom.

Yet as she lay in the darkness of her room, the duvet pulled up to her chest, sleep didn't come. She was exhausted yet her eyes were wide open and gritty. And despite her best effort for them not to, the memories came, slipping into her mind, winding around her heart.

Lying there in the dark, she could almost feel the late autumn sunshine slanting onto the wide-planked wooden floors of her college apartment. She saw herself, tousle-haired, young, laughing, holding out a cupcake to Jace. They weren't lovers then; they hadn't even kissed. Yet. He'd invited himself over to taste the treats she'd been telling him about when he'd come into the café where she worked for his morning latte. And high with anticipation, Eleanor had invited him in, revelling in the charged atmosphere as he took a bite of the cupcake right from her hand, and then, laughing, pulled her close for a kiss.

It had been so easy, so right, and she'd gone without even considering another option, a different choice. He'd tasted like chocolate.

She closed her eyes, her throat tight and aching. She didn't want to resurrect these memories. She worked hard never to remember them. Yet they came anyway, so sweet and yet so bitter for what came afterward.

The empty apartment. The disconnected cellphone. The bounced emails. The cold, cold despair when she'd realised just how alone she was.

Groaning alone, Eleanor turned on her side, tucking her knees up to her chest, and clenched her eyes shut as if that could keep the memories from coming and consuming her.

The blip of her baby on the monitor. The hard, sharp edge of the examining table, the cold slime of the gel on her tummy, and the endless silence of the technician, frowning, as she stared at the scan.

What's wrong?

Eleanor bolted up in bed and went to the bathroom for a herbal sleeping pill. She might have faced down Jace today, but she couldn't face the memories at night. They tormented her in a way even he never had. Their stark truth remained lodged in her gut, in her heart, like a stone. Nothing would remove it, or take away the bleak knowledge that she could never—

Eleanor closed her eyes again, tightly, and to her relief she finally slipped into a sleep made sweet by its absence of memories or dreams.

DESPITE HER BAD night, Eleanor was at her desk by eight o'clock in the morning. She saw Lily walk past her office door, nodding grimly, and she knew she'd been right to hurry to her desk that morning. She'd email the party plans to Jace, and then she'd put him out of her mind for ever. Or at least until he emailed back.

It took her nearly an hour to compose the email; it was aggravatingly difficult to strike the right tone, professional yet personable. She didn't want Jace to think for a second that she was affected by him. That she'd been hurt. Yet she hardly wanted to seem too friendly, either; that smacked of desperation.

Too tired to tweak the email any more, Eleanor just ended up sending a rather boring list of details, explaining in dry terms the choice of venue, the seating plan, the floral arrangements, the menu.

Then she determinedly pressed send.

Two minutes later her phone rang.

'This is completely unacceptable.'

Dumbly Eleanor stared at her computer screen, with its 'your message has been sent' confirmation still visible. It seemed impossible that in the approximately one hundred and twenty seconds since she'd pressed send, Jace had read her entire email and deemed it all unsuitable. Unacceptable, even.

'Excuse me?'

Over the phone Eleanor heard Jace exhale impatiently. 'This is all very standard, Ellie—'

'Don't call me that,' she said sharply. He ignored her.

'If I wanted a run-of-the-mill upscale do, I could have gone elsewhere. I came to Premier Planning because I was told you'd give me something extraordinary.'

Eleanor closed her eyes and prayed for patience. For mercy. She counted to ten, all the while listening to Jace's impatience, hearing it in those short little exhalations of breath, and then said coolly, 'I assure you there will be nothing run-of-the-mill about this party.'

Jace made a sound of disbelief that came close to a snort. 'Salmon pâté? Gardenias? Champagne? Standard luxuries.'

'That's an oxymoron, if ever I've heard one—'

'All of it is run-of-the-mill, Ellie.'

'I told you, don't call me that,' she snapped.

'Then impress me.'

That was the last thing she wanted to do. Why would she want to impress the man who had treated her like dirt, who had ground her heart into dust? Was her job really worth that much, worth her own dignity and pride?

Of course it was. It had to be. For the last ten years her job had been just about the only thing she had valued, the one thing she'd poured herself into. She wasn't risking it for Jace. He'd already done enough damage in her life.

'You gave me less than twenty-four hours to come up with an entire event,' she finally ground out. 'Of course I haven't worked out all the details yet—'

'I expected better than this.'

'Funny, I said that ten years ago,' Eleanor snapped. Then she closed her eyes. The last, the very last thing she wanted was to drag the past—their past—into this mess. And from the taut silence crackling along the phone lines, she had a feeling Jace felt the same.

'You have no idea,' he said coldly. 'Meet me at my office building for lunch, twelve o'clock sharp.' And then he hung up.

Eleanor cursed aloud, just as Lily poked her head in her office door and smiled narrowly.

'Everything all right, Eleanor?'

'Fine,' Eleanor replied thinly. 'I just got a paper cut, that's all.'

JACE HUNG UP the phone, massaging his knuckles as if he'd been in a fight. That terse conversation had not been a satisfactory outlet for his anger, for from the moment he'd walked into Eleanor Langley's office and seen her cool little smile that was what he'd been feeling. *Rage*.

He was furious that she seemed so unrepentant, that she'd attempted to foist another man's baby on him and didn't even possess the decency now to admit it or apologise. Yet what had he really expected of a woman who was willing to sink so low, to lie to someone she'd said she loved?

He didn't want to feel so angry, hated how it made the control he'd guarded carefully these last ten years slip away, so he hardly even knew what he was going to say or do. Or feel.

He'd never expected to feel so angry. He'd thought he'd got over Eleanor Langley and her betrayal, had put it far, far behind him. Now it felt fresh and raw and that made him even angrier. He didn't want Eleanor to affect him this much. He didn't want her to affect him at all.

Sighing impatiently, Jace turned back to the papers on his desk. Atrikides Holdings was a mess and he had plenty to occupy both his mind and his time. He didn't need to waste either on Eleanor Langley, not even for a second.

All he wanted from her was a party. That was the only reason he was inviting her to lunch, why he was even bothering to see her again. He'd make it clear just what kind of high standard of service he expected. He'd put her in her place. His lips curved in a humourless smile as his sense of calm return to cloak him in reassuring coldness. All he wanted from her was a party, and by God he'd get one.

THREE HOURS LATER Eleanor stood in front of the dark gleaming skyscraper that housed the offices of Atrikides Holdings. She took a deep breath and let it out slowly, and then resolutely headed for the door.

After she was cleared through security she took the lift to the building's top floor and stepped out into a room of elegant, old-style luxury with a stunning view of Central Park. She stared at the yawning rectangle of green, surrounded by concrete, the trees stark and bare above, as the elderly assistant pursed her lips before pressing a button on her telephone.

'Mr Zervas, I have Eleanor Langley for you.'

The reply was sharp, terse. 'Send her in.'

'You may go in,' the assistant said, nodding towards the wood-panelled double doors at the far end of the room.

Eleanor nodded back, swallowing down the sudden flutter of nerves that had risen to flurry wildly in her throat. She hated that she was nervous, almost as if Jace scared her. She would not let herself be cowed by him, not when he had been in the wrong ten years ago, not when *he* had been the coward then.

She certainly wouldn't be the coward now.

Squaring her shoulders, she knocked once, perfunctorily, before opening the doors and striding into the room.

The office was elegant, huge, and clearly not his. In one quick glance Eleanor saw the portraits of several Atrikides men on the walls, a side table cluttered with family photos. Children. She averted her eyes from the pictures. This had to be the office of the former CEO of Atrikides Holdings, Eleanor surmised, whom Jace had ousted along with half of the company's employees. A cold-blooded, corporate takeover. Should it really surprise her at all?

Jace stood behind the desk, his back to her. He didn't turn around even though he must have heard her come in.

Faintly annoyed, Eleanor cleared her throat. He turned,

and in that moment—a single second, no more—her breath dried and her heart beat fast and she remembered how good it had been between them, how she'd lain in his arms as the sun washed them in gold and he'd kissed her closed eyelids.

She forced the memory—so sweet and painful—away and smiled coolly. 'You've taken over the CEO's office, I see.'

Jace waved a hand in dismissal. 'For the time being. It's convenient.'

'And he was fired along with most of the employees, I suppose?'

'Most is an exaggeration,' Jace replied, his eyes narrowing, flashing steel.

Eleanor wondered why she was asking. It was almost as if she was trying to pick a fight—and perhaps she was, for the anger and resentment still simmered beneath her surface, threatening to bubble forth. She wanted to hurt him, and yet she knew she wouldn't succeed with these silly little jabs. She'd only hurt herself, by revealing her own vulnerability. The fact that she was making them at all spoke of how hurt she had been and still was. She drew in a steadying breath and managed a small smile. 'You'd like to talk about the plans?'

Jace didn't smile back. 'I'm not sure they're worth discussing.'

Eleanor bit the inside of her cheek. 'Fine,' she said when she could be sure her voice was level, 'let's discard them if you find them so unsuitable. But you could at least make an effort to be civil.'

To her surprise, Jace acknowledged the point with one terse nod. 'Very well. Let's have lunch.'

He led her to a table hidden in the alcove, a tiny

little table set intimately for two. Eleanor swallowed
hard. She didn't know if she could do this. Every second
she spent with Jace strained the composure she'd been
working at maintaining for the last ten years, the air of
professionalism that had become her armour. Just one
sardonic look from those steely eyes—she remembered
when they'd softened in pleasure, in love—made her
calm façade crack. It crumbled, and she was defenceless once more, the cracks in her armour letting in the
memories and pain.

She hated that she was so weak.

Jace drew her chair for her, the epitome of politeness, and with a murmured thanks Eleanor sat down.
Her hands trembled as she placed her napkin in her
lap. Jace sat in the chair opposite, his fingers steepled
under his chin, his dark eyebrows drawn together. He
looked so much the same, Eleanor thought with a lurch
of remembered feeling, and yet so different. His hair
was cut closer now, sprinkled with grey, and his skin
looked more weathered. That glint of laughter in his
eyes was gone, vanished completely. Yet he still possessed the same compelling aura, like a magnetic field
around him. He still drew her to him, even though she
hated the thought. Even now she could feel her body's
traitorous reaction to his—the shaft of pleasure deep in
her belly, the tingle of awareness as he reached for his
own napkin, his fingers scant inches from hers. Eleanor made herself look away and a staff member came
in to serve them.

'Would you care for a glass of wine?' Jace asked.

'I don't normally—'

'Half, then.' He held up the bottle, one eyebrow
arched in silent challenge, poised to pour. Jerkily Elea-

nor nodded. This felt like a battle of wills, a contest over who could be the most professional. And she'd win. She *had* to. If he was so unaffected, well, then, she could be too, or at least seem as if she were. *Pretend*.

She could pretend to Jace and perhaps even to herself that the room didn't seethe with memories, that her heart wasn't splintering along its sewn-up seams. She *could*. It was the only way of getting out of here alive.

'Thank you.' She stared down at her salad, the leaves arranged artfully on a porcelain plate with an elegant little drizzle of vinaigrette. She had no appetite at all. Finally she stabbed a lettuce leaf with her fork and looked up. 'So why don't you tell me what kind of party you'd prefer?' She strove to keep her voice reasonable. 'If I have a few more details, we can brainstorm some ideas—'

'I thought that was your job. I already gave you a list of requirements—'

'You gave me less than twenty-four hours to mock up a plan,' Eleanor returned, her voice edged with anger, 'and a week to put it all together. Those are impossible conditions.'

Jace smiled thinly, his voice smooth and yet still conveying contempt. 'Your boss assured me your company was up to the task.'

Eleanor looked away and silently counted to ten. Breathe. In. Out. In. Out. 'I assure you, I am up to the task. But since the original plans were so unsatisfactory, perhaps I need a little more information about what you're looking for.' She hated this, hated feeling as if she had to kowtow to Jace, hated knowing he was baiting her simply because he could. At this moment it was hard to believe that they'd ever felt anything for each other but bitterness and dislike.

Jace exhaled impatiently. 'I want something unique and elegant, that shows the employees of this company that they will be cared for.'

'Except for the ones who were fired, you mean,' Eleanor retorted, then wished she could have held her tongue. Why was she so hung up on that? Who cared how Jace did business? She certainly couldn't afford to.

He arched one eyebrow, coldly disdainful. 'Are you questioning my business practices?'

'No, I just object to the idea of a party that makes it look like you care about these people when you really don't.' Jace stilled, his face blanking, and too late Eleanor realised how she had betrayed herself. Who she'd really been talking about.

Me.

She let out a slow, shuddery breath and reached for her wine. 'Just give me some details, Jace.'

Jace's mouth tightened, his eyes narrowing. 'I believe I mentioned yesterday that many of the employees here have families. The party needs to be family-friendly. Children will be invited.'

Eleanor's hand tightened around the stem of her wine glass. She didn't expect it to hurt so much to hear Jace talk of children. She realised, with a sudden laser-like dart of pain, that he could be married. Maybe he had children of his own. Maybe he just hadn't wanted *her* children.

The children she'd never have.

She had to stop thinking like this. She'd got over Jace and his betrayal—unbearable as it had been—years ago. She *had*. She'd even accepted her own loss, the heartache that she'd always carry with her. She'd moved on with her life, had made plenty of friends, developed an exciting and successful career—

'Family-friendly,' she repeated, trying to keep her mind on track. She'd forgotten that rather crucial detail in her flurry of plans. Conveniently. She preferred not to think about families—children—at all. They no longer figured in her life. At all. They couldn't.

'Yes,' Jace confirmed, and his voice held an edge now. 'As I told you yesterday. Weren't you taking notes?'

Finally goaded past her emotional endurance, Eleanor set her wine glass down with an undignified clatter. 'Perhaps I just had trouble believing a man like you could be interested in anything family-friendly,' she snapped. 'The image doesn't really fit.'

'Image?' Jace repeated silkily. 'What are you talking about, Eleanor?'

'You, Jace.' The remembered pain and hurt was boiling up, seeping through the barely healed-over scars. She stood up from the table, surprised by this sudden, intense rush of feeling. Suddenly she didn't want to keep her composure any more. She wanted it to slip, wanted Jace to see the turbulent river of emotions underneath. Even to know how much he'd hurt her. Perhaps she'd regret the impulse later, but now it was too overwhelming a need to ignore. 'You're not "family-friendly".' She held up her hands to make inverted commas, her fingers curling into claws. 'You certainly weren't when I knew you.'

Jace stood up too, his hip bumping the table, sloshing wine onto the pristine white tablecloth. With a jolt Eleanor realised he was just as angry—and emotional— as she was. Maybe even more so.

'*I* wasn't family-friendly?' he repeated in a low voice that was nearly a growl. 'And just how and when did you draw that ridiculous conclusion?'

Eleanor nearly choked in her fury and disbelief. 'Maybe when you left your apartment, left the damn *country* when I told you I was pregnant!' There was a buzzing in her ears and distantly she realised she was shouting. Loudly.

Jace let out an ugly snarl of a laugh. 'Oh, I see. How interesting, Ellie.' On his lips her name was a sneer. 'So I'm some monster that doesn't like children simply because I didn't want to take on another man's bastard.'

Eleanor's mouth dropped open. The buzzing in her ears intensified so she couldn't hear anything. Surely she must have misheard him. 'What did you say?' she asked numbly, still slack-jawed.

Jace's lip curled in contempt. 'You heard me. I knew that baby wasn't mine.'

CHAPTER THREE

THE ROOM WAS silent save for the draw and tear of their own ragged breathing. Numbly Eleanor turned away from Jace, from the table with its jostled dishes and spilled wine, and walked on wooden legs to the window.

Outside the sky was the ominous grey-white that promised a storm, the world below a winter palette of browns and greys.

Another man's bastard. Jace's words echoed in his ears, over and over, so Eleanor could not frame another thought or even a word. *Another man's bastard. Bastard. Bastard. Bastard.*

She closed her eyes.

'So you have nothing to say,' Jace said coldly, and that too was an indictment.

Eleanor shook her head. Her heart was thudding sickly and her knees nearly buckled. She'd never had such a physical reaction to a single piece of information, except when—

Tell me what's wrong.

No. She wasn't going to open up that Pandora's box of memories. Not with Jace in the room, with his ugly words still reverberating through the air.

And she wasn't going to defend herself either. There was so clearly no point.

Slowly she turned around. 'No,' she said quietly. 'I have nothing to say.'

Jace nodded in grim acceptance, and Eleanor knew she'd just confirmed the worst he'd ever thought about her. Judged again. She hadn't even realised, ever known, that she'd been judged in the first place. All these years she'd had no idea Jace had been thinking that. Believing the worst. And why? What reason had she ever given him?

She walked back to the table and reached for the attaché case she'd propped against her chair.

'I'm going to go now,' she said steadily. She was grateful her voice didn't tremble or break. 'I'll make sure Lily assigns someone else to your party.'

'What are you talking about?' Jace demanded, and Eleanor almost laughed. Did he actually think she'd work with him now? Considering what had just happened—what he thought—

She shook her head again. 'Clearly, Jace, we can't move on from the past, and it's affecting our—our work relationship.' What a ridiculous idea, as though they could have any relationship at all. 'There's no point continuing this way. Someone else will serve you better.'

'So you expect me just to forgive and forget,' Jace surmised, his voice sharp with sarcasm.

Now Eleanor did laugh, a short, humourless bark. 'No. I'm the one who can't. Forgive *or* forget.' She hoisted her bag on her shoulder and gave him a grim little smile. 'Goodbye, Jace.'

And somehow, *somehow* she managed to walk from the room with steady legs, her head held high.

JACE WATCHED ELEANOR walk away from him in stunned disbelief. He heard the click of the door shutting, the surprised murmur of his PA, the whoosh of the lift doors. And he still didn't move.

I'm the one who can't forgive or forget.

What the hell had she been talking about?

Muttering an angry oath, Jace whirled towards the window. What could Eleanor Langley possibly have to forgive? All right, perhaps he'd been ruthless in the way he'd cut her out of his life, leaving Boston—leaving her—so abruptly and absolutely. But he'd done it because the realisation that she'd been deceiving him all along had been too terrible to bear. He'd felt quite literally gutted, empty and aching inside. And meanwhile she—*she* had been trying to foist another man's child on him. Living a lie all along. She'd never really loved him.

Yet apparently Eleanor did think she had something to forget. To forgive.

What?

Impatiently Jace turned away from the window where a few random snowflakes had begun to drift down onto the asphalt. He felt restless, angry, uncertain. The last was what bothered him the most; he'd never felt doubt before. How could he? He'd known since he was fifteen years old that he was infertile.

Sterile. Like a gelded bull, or a eunuch. As good as, according to his father. For what good was a son who couldn't carry on the family name? Who had been unmanned before he'd even reached his manhood?

What use was a son like that?

Jace already knew the answer, had known the answer since his test results had come back and his father's dreams of a dynasty had crumbled to dust. Nothing. A son like that—like him—was no use at all.

He'd lived with that grim knowledge for half of his life. Felt it in every quietly despairing stare, every veiled criticism. His own infertility had consumed him before he'd even been ready to think of children, had dominated him as a boy and become part of his identity as a man. Without the ability to have children, he was useless. Worthless.

And yet now, with Ellie's words, doubt, both treacherous and strangely hopeful, crept into his mind and wound its tendrils of dangerous possibility around his thoughts. His heart.

What did Ellie have to forget? To forgive? What had she been talking about?

Half of him wanted to ignore what she had said, just move on. He'd get a different event planner, forget Eleanor Langley even existed. Never question what she said.

Never wonder.

Yet even as these thoughts raced through his brain, Jace knew he couldn't do that. Didn't even want to. Yes, it was saner, safer, but it was also aggravating as hell. He didn't want to doubt. Couldn't let himself wonder.

He needed to know.

ELEANOR WALKED ALL the way back to Premier Planning's office near Madison Square Garden, oblivious to the cold wind buffeting her face and numbing her cheeks. She was oblivious to everything, every annoyed pedestrian, cellphone clamped to an ear, who was forced to move around her as she sleepwalked the twenty-three blocks to her office. She felt numb, too numb to think, to consider just what Jace had said. What he'd thought all these years.

She stood in front of the building, still numb, still reeling, and realised distantly that she couldn't return to work. Lily would be waiting, anxious for a report—or worse. Perhaps Jace had already rung. Perhaps her job was already in jeopardy.

Either way, she couldn't face it. She turned her back on ten years of professionalism and went home.

Back in the apartment she dropped her bag on the floor, kicked off her heels, and slumped into a chair, staring out into space. She didn't know how long she stayed like that for, without moving, without thinking, but the sky darkened to violet and then indigo, and her stomach rumbled. She hadn't eaten since breakfast, and that had been no more than half a bagel as she hurried to work. Yet she still couldn't summon the energy to eat. To feel. Anything. She hadn't felt this numb—the pain too consuming to allow herself to feel it—for a long time. For ten years.

Finally she stirred and went to the bathroom. She turned both taps on full and stripped off her clothes, leaving her savvy suit crumpled on the floor. Who knew if she'd need it any more?

Twenty minutes into a good soak she felt her mind start to thaw. So did her heart. So Jace assumed she'd been unfaithful, had been labouring under that unbelievable misapprehension for ten long years. No wonder he was so angry. Yet how could he be so *wrong*?

How could he have thought that of her, considering what they'd been to one another? Even the logistics of infidelity were virtually impossible; she'd spent nearly every waking moment working, at school, or with him.

Yet he'd believed it, and believed it so strongly that he'd judged her without trial, without even a conversation. He'd been so sure of her infidelity that he'd left her, left his entire life in the States, without even asking so much as a single question.

Somehow it was so much worse than what she'd thought all these years: that he'd developed a case of cold feet. In her more compassionate moments, she could understand how a twenty-two-year-old man— *boy*—with his whole life in front of him might get a little panicked at the thought of fathering a child. She understood that; what she didn't understand, had never understood, was the way he'd gone about it. Leaving so abruptly. Abandoning her without a word or even a way for him to contact him. Cellphone disconnected. No forwarding address.

It hadn't been merely a slap to the face, it had been a stab wound to the heart.

And he'd done it not because of his own inadequacy, but because of hers. Infidelity. He actually assumed she'd cheated on him.

The bathwater was getting cold, and Eleanor rose from the tub. There was no point letting herself dwell on the recriminations, the regrets. If Jace Zervas had been able to believe something so atrocious and impossible about her so easily, obviously they'd never had much of a relationship at all.

And *that* was a truth she'd lived with for ten years.

She'd just slipped on her comfort pyjamas—soft, nubby fleece—when her doorbell rang. Eleanor stilled. She lived on the thirtieth floor in a building with two security personnel at the front door at all times, so no one made it to her door without her being alerted. The only option, she supposed, was a neighbour, although she'd never really got to know her neighbours. It wasn't that kind of building, and she didn't have that kind of life.

Cautiously Eleanor went to the door. She peered through the eyehole and felt her heart stop for a second before beginning a new, frenetic beating. Jace stood there.

'Eleanor?'

He sounded impatient, and it was no wonder. Eleanor realised she was hesitating for far too long. Resolutely she drew a breath and opened the door.

'What are you doing here, Jace?'

'I need to talk to you.'

She folded her arms and didn't move. She didn't feel angry now so much as resigned. 'I told you in your office I had nothing to say.'

'You may not, but I do.' He arched an eyebrow. 'Are you going to let me in?'

'How did you get my address?'

'Your boss gave it to me.'

Eleanor gave an exasperated sigh. *Of course.* Lily would do just about anything for a client, especially a rich one like Jace. 'How did you get past security?'

'I sweet-talked him.'

Eleanor snorted. 'You?'

'Andreas is manning the door tonight. He has six grandchildren back in Greece.' Jace smiled thinly. 'He showed me pictures.'

Eleanor slowly shook her head. She'd been on the end of Jace's charm once; she knew how forceful it was. And how false.

Sighing in defeat, she turned away from the door. 'Fine. Come in.'

He entered, shutting the door carefully behind him. Eleanor moved to the window, her arms creeping around her body despite her effort to maintain a cool, composed air. She felt vulnerable, exposed somehow, as if from the stark modernity of her apartment Jace could somehow guess at the emotional barrenness of her life.

Stop. She couldn't think like that. She had a job, friends, a life—

She just didn't have what mattered.

Love.

Stop.

'What do you want?'

Jace stood in the centre of her living room, seeming too big, too *much* for the space. He glanced around, and Eleanor saw him take in all the telltale signs of a single life. No jumble of shoes or coats, no piles of magazines or books. Just a single pair of heels discarded by the door. In the galley kitchen she saw her lone coffee cup from this morning rinsed and set by the sink. 'You live here alone?'

She lifted one shoulder in a shrug that couldn't help but seem defensive. 'Yes.'

He shook his head slowly. 'What about—the baby?' He spoke awkwardly, the words sounding stilted. They felt stilted to Eleanor. She didn't want him to ask. She didn't want him to know.

She didn't want to tell.

'What about the baby?' she asked evenly.

'He—or she, rather—doesn't live with you?'

'No.'

'The father retained custody?'

She gave a short, abrupt laugh. The weariness was fading away and the anger was coming back. Along with the hurt. She was tired of feeling so much, so suddenly, after ten years of being comfortably numb. She dropped her arms to her sides. 'What do you really want to talk about, Jace?'

'You said you were the one who couldn't forgive or forget. And I want to know why.' He spoke flatly, yet she saw something in his eyes she hadn't seen in ten years, something that hadn't been there yesterday or this morning. Need.

Hunger.

Why did he want to know? Why did he care?

'Because you may have felt you had just cause, but the fact that you abandoned me the very day I told you I was pregnant was a hard thing to get over.' She smiled thinly. 'Surprisingly, it seems.'

Jace shook his head, the movement one of instinctive denial. 'Ellie, you know that baby isn't—wasn't—mine.'

Anger, white-hot, lanced through her. '*I* know?' she repeated, her voice rising in incredulity. '*I* know? I'll tell you what I know, Jace, and that is that the only bastard I've ever met is you. First-class, A-plus, for thinking that.'

He took a step towards her in an action both menacing and urgent, his features twisted with what looked like pain. 'Are you telling me,' he demanded in a low voice, 'that the baby was mine? Is that what you're actually saying, Ellie?'

She lifted her chin. 'That's exactly what I'm saying, Jace. And the very fact that you could think for a moment—'

'Don't.' He held up one hand, and Eleanor saw to her shock that it trembled. 'Don't,' he repeated rawly, 'lie to me. Not now. Not again. Not about this.'

For a second Eleanor's anger gave way to another powerful emotion: curiosity. Jace faced her, his expression open and hungry. She'd never see him look so… desperate. There was more going on here than she understood.

'I'm not lying,' she said quietly. 'What makes you think I ever was?'

Jace didn't speak for a moment. His gaze held hers, searching for a truth he seemed hell-bent on disbelieving. 'Because,' he finally said, his voice little more than a ragged whisper, 'I can't have children. I've known it since I was fifteen years old.' He let out a long, slow breath before stating flatly, 'I'm infertile. Sterile.'

Eleanor stared. *I can't have children.* Such a stark and sorrowful phrase; she knew just how much. And yet coming from *Jace*…the words didn't make sense. They couldn't. Then in a sudden flash of remembrance she recalled the moment she'd told Jace she was pregnant, and how he'd stared at her so blankly, his jaw slackening, his eyes turning flat and then hard. She'd thought he'd been surprised; she'd had no idea just how stunned he must have been. Infertile. *Impossible.* It had to be. 'You must be mistaken.'

'I assure you I'm not.'

Eleanor shook her head, speechless, disbelieving. 'Well, neither am I,' she finally said. 'Mistaken, that is. I was a virgin when we got together, Jace, and I didn't sleep with another man for—a long while.' She swallowed. Years, in fact, but she wasn't about to tell him that. 'You were the only candidate.'

Jace smiled, the curving of his mouth utterly without humour. 'The facts don't add up, Ellie. Someone's lying.'

'I've told you not to call me that.' She turned away

from him and stared blindly out at the Hudson River, its murky black surface just visible under the city lights. 'Why does someone have to be lying, Jace? What if you're mistaken?' She turned around. 'Did you ever—even once—think of that?'

'I'm not!' The words came out in a roar, and she stilled, surprised by the savagery.

'How can you be—?'

'Trust me,' he cut her off, the two words flat and brutal. 'I am. And if I can't have children, there must be another—' he paused, his mouth curving in an unpleasant smile '—candidate.'

Eleanor cocked her head, curiosity and anger warring within her. 'Is it easier for you to believe that?'

'What the hell do you mean?'

She shrugged, a little unnerved by Jace's anger but still refusing to be cowed. 'You prefer believing I was unfaithful to you rather than the idea that you could be wrong, that it's a mistake—'

'It's not a mistake!' Jace leaned forward, lowered his voice to a savage whisper. 'It's *impossible*.'

Eleanor blinked, discomfited by his intensity. 'How did you find out you were infertile at such a young age?' she asked slowly. 'Most men don't find out until they're married and run into trouble with conceiving, don't they—'

'I had mumps. A lingering infection, and it made me sterile.'

'And you were tested—?'

'Yes.' He bit off the word, his lips pressed together in a hard line.

'But...' Eleanor shook her head, genuinely bewildered. 'Why? Why would you be tested at such a young age?'

Jace turned away from her. He drove his hands into his pockets, his shoulders hunched, the position one of defensive misery. 'My father wanted to know,' he said gruffly, his back still to her. 'I'm an only son, as was he. The male line dies out with me.'

Eleanor didn't reply. She couldn't think of a single thing to say, for suddenly everything was making horrible sense. No wonder Jace was so sure he couldn't be the father. No wonder he'd been so hurt. No wonder the whole idea of a pregnancy—a baby—that wasn't his would be an affront, an abomination.

The male line dies out with me.

For a boy from a traditional Greek family, that had to be very hard indeed.

Regret replaced anger, and it hurt far more. She swallowed past the tightness in her throat. 'Well, perhaps you should get yourself tested again. Because I assure you, Jace, the baby was yours. Why would I lie now? What point would there be?'

Jace was silent for a long, tense moment. 'I don't know,' he finally said. 'God help me, I don't know.' Eleanor stared at him, his back to her, his head bowed, and she wondered what he must be feeling now. Could he accept he wasn't infertile, that he'd been living with an incorrect diagnosis for his entire adult life?

Would he?

It would be hope and tragedy mixed together, for what was lost, for what now could be—

But not for her. Eleanor swallowed past the tightness in her throat, closing her eyes as if that could blot out the pain. The memory. Never for her.

JACE DREW IN a ragged, desperate breath, his head still bowed, his back to Eleanor. He felt the rage course through him, consume him, and he didn't trust himself to speak.

The baby was his. *Could* be his. Except in his gut—perhaps even in his heart—Jace knew the truth. He saw it in Eleanor's eyes, dark with remembered pain. The baby was his.

He wasn't infertile.

And all he could feel was anger. All he could think of was the waste. His life, his family, his father. Everything had pointed to his failure as a son, as a man. He'd lived with it, let it cripple him, let it guide and restrain his choices, and for what?

For a lie? A *mistake?*

The realisation made him want to shout to the remorseless heavens, to hit something, to hurt something. Someone. *It wasn't fair.* The cry of a child, and yet it bellowed up inside him, the need so great he clamped his lips together and drew another shuddering breath.

Eleanor, he knew, would never understand. How could he explain how utterly sure he'd been of his own infertility, so that he'd been able to walk away without once considering that she'd been telling the truth? He'd always been so certain that even now he wondered. Doubted.

It can't be.

And yet if it was…

Too many repercussions, too many unspoken—unthought—hopes and fears crowded his mind, his heart. He pushed them down, unable to deal with them now, to consider what they meant, what changes to both the

present and future—and, God help him, the past—they
would require.

The baby was his.

The baby was his.

He had a child.

JACE WHIRLED AROUND again, the movement so sudden
and savage that Eleanor gasped aloud and took a step
towards the window.

He crossed the room in three long strides and grabbed
her by the shoulders, his face thrust near hers. 'Where
is the baby? If it *is* my child—'

Eleanor closed her eyes. She didn't want this. She
didn't want Jace here, stirring up memories, regrets,
pain, and for what? Yet she knew he had a right to
know. She swallowed again. Her throat was so very
tight. 'Was,' she whispered. 'It was.'

'What—what are you talking—?'

'It *was* your child,' she explained very quietly, and
the fierce light that had ignited in Jace's eyes winked
out, leaving them the colour of cold ash.

'You mean…' his hands tightened on her shoulders
'…you had an abortion.'

'No!' She jerked out of his grasp, glaring at him.
'Why don't you just leap to yet another offensive assumption, Jace? You're good at that.'

He folded his arms, his expression still hard. 'What
are you saying, then?'

'I had a…a miscarriage.' A bland, official-sounding
word for such a heart-rending, life-changing event. She
turned away from him so he wouldn't see the naked
pain on her face. She felt the thickness of tears in her

throat. 'I lost the baby.' She swallowed. *My little girl,* she thought, *my precious little girl.*

Jace was silent for a long moment. Eleanor stared blindly out of the window, trying not to remember. The screen, the silence, the emptiness within. 'I'm sorry,' he finally said, and she just shrugged. The silence ticked on, heavy, oppressive. 'I'm sorry,' Jace said again, the word raw, and Eleanor felt again the thickening of tears in her throat. She swallowed it down, reluctant to let Jace enter her sorrow. She didn't want to rake it up again; she didn't even want him sharing it. She was still angry. Still hurt.

'I'll still have to be tested,' he continued, 'to make sure—'

'That the baby was yours?' Eleanor filled in. 'You still don't believe me?' She shook her head in disbelief. 'Just when would I have had this other affair, Jace? I spent every waking—and sleeping—moment with you for six *months.*'

'You don't understand—' Jace began in a low voice, but Eleanor didn't want to hear.

'No, I don't. I don't understand how you could think for a moment that I was unfaithful to you. But even if you did, because I suppose you must have had some kind of *trust* issue, I don't understand how you could walk away without a word.' Her voice shook; so did her body. 'Without a single *word.*'

'Eleanor—'

'It doesn't matter. I don't want to hear your explanations now. They don't matter.' She took a deep, shuddering breath and forced herself to sound calm. To feel it. 'It's ten years ago, Jace. Ten years. It really is time we both moved on.'

He was silent, and when she looked at him she saw how drawn and tired and *sad* he looked. Well, too bad. She hardened her heart, because she didn't want to feel sorry for him. She didn't want to feel anything; it hurt too much. 'If only I'd known,' he murmured, and she shook her head.

'Don't.' She didn't want him to open up the painful possibilities of what if, if only… No, they were too dangerous. Too hard even to think about now. 'And it doesn't even matter anyway,' she continued, her voice sharp. 'You didn't trust me enough to tell me any of this, or give either of us a chance to explain. That's what this was really about.'

Jace's brows snapped together, his body tensing, and Eleanor knew he was poised to argue. Again. She couldn't take any more, didn't have the energy for another round. 'Go get tested or whatever it is you need to do,' she told him. 'Satisfy your own curiosity. You don't need to tell me about it.' She paused, her voice sharpening again in spite of her best efforts to sound reasonable. '*I* know who the father was.'

Jace stared at Ellie's hard face, derision in every line, her eyes dark with scorn. He felt a scalding sense of shame rush through him. This hard, polished woman, this glossy professional who lifted her chin and dared him to feel sympathy or compassion or dreaded pity, was a product of his own judgment. His own failure.

If he'd stayed with Ellie…if he'd seen her through the miscarriage…would she be a different woman? Would she have stayed the same?

It was a pointless question. As Eleanor herself had said, this was all ten years too late. They'd both moved on. They'd both changed. He certainly wasn't the same foolish boy who'd let himself be besotted, who had eagerly fallen in love because the experience had been so intoxicating, so vital, so different from what he'd known.

Who had a heart to be broken.

No, he wasn't that same man. He'd changed, hardened, and so had Ellie. *Eleanor.* They were different people now, and the only thing they had in common was loss.

The loss of their baby. A sudden, new grief threatened to swamp him, and to his shock he felt the sting of tears in his eyes, the ache in the back of his throat. He forced the feeling down, refusing to give into such an emotion. He never cried. In the fifteen or so years since his life had changed for ever—or at least until now—he'd developed a foolproof way of dealing with his father's disappointment. He never acted as if he cared. Whether it was a flat, emotionless response, or a carefree, laughing one, either way he kept his heart off-limits. He remained detached. He *had*, until Eleanor. Somehow Eleanor had slipped through the defences he'd erected—that charming, laughing exterior—and found the man underneath. He wondered if she even knew how much she'd affected him.

And how had he affected her? In a sudden, painful burst of insight he pictured her in his apartment building, twenty years old and pregnant, realising he'd gone. He'd abandoned her utterly, and she'd been innocent.

Innocent.

He'd never, for a moment or even a second, considered that the child—their child—might have been his. This infertility was so much a part of him, a weight that had been shackled to him for so long, he'd never considered existing without it. He'd never even hoped for such a possibility.

And yet now for it to be given to him, and taken away, virtually in the same breath was too much to consider. To accept. He was left speechless, his mind spinning in dizzying circles, his heart thudding as if he'd just finished a sprint.

He didn't know what to think. To feel. And he was afraid—yes, afraid—to open up the floodgates of his own heart and mind to all the possibilities, all the realisations, all the regret and guilt and hope and fear. They would consume him; he would have nothing left. Nothing he could count on or control. He couldn't do that. Not yet, maybe not ever.

He needed to get this situation back under control, Jace knew, and there was only one way to do that.

'So,' Jace said, and was glad to hear how even his voice sounded. 'Let's talk about this party.'

CHAPTER FOUR

'WHAT?' ELEANOR HEARD the screech of her own voice and briefly closed her eyes. She opened them and shook her head. 'No.'

Jace arched an eyebrow in challenge. 'Why not? You didn't seem to have a problem with planning the party before.'

'You can't be serious. After everything—'

'We're professionals, Eleanor.' Jace's voice was hard, and Eleanor saw a bleak darkness in his eyes. She felt its answer in herself, and she wondered if Jace was trying to prove something to himself, just as she was. *The past is finished. It doesn't matter. I'm not hurt.*

But she was. And she was so tired of pretending she wasn't. Yet even so she couldn't admit that to Jace. She felt exposed enough, considering all she'd already revealed. She wasn't about to say anything more. 'Of course we're professionals, Jace. But I simply think it would be sensible—not to mention more productive— to have a colleague plan your event.'

'I don't.'

Why was he doing this? She shook her head again. 'I told you at your office—'

'That you were quitting? Lucky for you I didn't communicate that to your boss. I don't think she would have been pleased. And somehow I had a feeling you might change your mind.' His mouth twisted sardonically, his eyes glinting.

Eleanor didn't answer. She knew just how displeased Lily would have been. She might have thrown her entire career away in a single, emotional moment, and Jace at least had had the presence of mind not to let her do it.

She supposed she should be grateful.

Eleanor walked slowly back to the window. It had become her place of retreat; either that or she was simply backed into a corner. 'I don't understand why you want to do this,' she said quietly. 'Or what can be gained—for either of us.'

Jace shrugged one powerful shoulder. 'You're the best planner. Or so I was told.'

'You didn't even like my ideas,' Eleanor protested numbly. What she really wanted to say was, *Why doesn't being with me hurt you?* She felt his presence like an agony, exquisitely painful. And he wanted her to plan his *party?*

'I just know you can do better.'

She shook her head, even as she acknowledged that he was right. She *could* do better. She'd fought long and hard to get to where she was in her business and stay there. And she wasn't about to throw it all away simply because Jace had come back into her life—however briefly—and stirred up some old memories. She could shove them down again. She could handle this party. She could handle Jace. Doing it would help her feel more in control, and God knew she needed to feel that again.

She felt as if she were spinning out of it, and she couldn't stand the sense of powerlessness. She'd felt that before, when Jace had walked out of her life. When the ultrasound technician had sorrowfully shaken her head, and the doctor had come in to give her lots of important-sounding words and clinical, medical terms.

She wasn't going to feel it now.

She turned around. Jace gazed at her, waiting, assessing. She had no idea why he still wanted her to plan his wretched party, what he hoped to gain or prove. Or was the past nothing more than a finished chapter of a sad story? Could he actually move on so quickly, *minutes* after she'd told him the truth? She made herself not care. She'd done that before, plenty of times, starting when she was a little girl and her mother had worked late again and again, missing plays and soccer matches and anything important. When Jace had walked away, when she'd lost her little girl, when life had seemed empty and endless and without hope—she'd survived by making herself not care. By blanking her mind to any thought—any possibility—that was too painful. Too hard. And she could keep doing it. Keep surviving. Keep not caring.

Eleanor smiled coolly. 'Fine, Jace. I'll plan your party. Satisfied?'

'Getting there.'

'And it's late. I'd like to go to bed.' Too late she realised how laced those words were with innuendo—and remembrance. And so did Jace. She saw it in the subtle flaring of his eyes, the way they turned to sleepy silver. And before she could stop herself, her mind flashed images from a lifetime ago—a lifetime with Jace. Lying in his arms, tracing circles on the bare, bronze skin of his chest. Laughing, stretching like a cat, sleepy and secure. Sated. Loving every moment of being with him, because she'd been young and naive enough to think it was real and that it would never end.

Eleanor swallowed. 'I'm tired,' she said as an explanation, but it came out in a whisper. Jace smiled.

'So am I.'

Was she imagining the current that suddenly seemed to run between them, alive and electric? She must be, because surely, *surely* there was nothing between them. After everything that had happened—after everything she had endured—there could be nothing between them now.

Yet that didn't stop her from remembering just how good it had once been.

'Goodnight, Jace,' Eleanor said, and her voice, to her relief, sounded flat and final and almost cold. Jace ignored her.

He took a step towards her. Eleanor held her breath. She didn't speak, didn't move. Didn't protest. Another step, and he was only inches away. He lifted his hand and she braced herself for his touch, welcomed it even, wondering what it would feel like after all these years. What he would feel like.

And even as she stood there, still and silent, *waiting* for him to touch her, he dropped his hand, smiling almost sadly. 'Goodnight, Ellie,' he said, and this time Eleanor didn't try to correct him.

She watched him leave, not realising until the door had shut that she was still holding her breath. She let it out in a long, shuddery rush.

She could do this. She had to.

JACE STRODE FROM Eleanor's apartment, his body filled with a restless energy, his mind teeming with both possibility and fury. He was angry at himself, at fate, at life itself.

So much waste. So much wrong.

Guilt rushed into the corners of his mind, the empty spaces in his heart. He could hardly bear to think what Eleanor must have felt, what she'd endured alone.

If only—

Two desperate and dangerous words.

If only he'd known. If only he'd waited and said something, asked her—

If only. If only.

There was no such thing as *if only*. There was only regret.

And hope.

Jace shook his head in silent disbelief. Hope had long since become an unfamiliar concept. What on earth could he hope for? Love, family, children—he'd turned his back on them all. Was he now actually thinking that he could change that? Change himself? It would not be so easy.

For years work had been his only respite, his only comfort. He'd come to New York as a favour to Leandro Atrikides, and as a favour to his father. He'd clean up the family mess and then he'd go home to Greece.

And forget about Eleanor Langley…just as he had once before.

Except he'd never forgotten her, not really. She'd always lurked on the fringes of his consciousness, memories drifting and dancing through his mind even when he tried to push them away. She lingered there now.

He recalled her scent, something young and girlish and flowery. He didn't think she used the same perfume now. And her hair had been wild and curly and artless, not her current glossy bob. He remembered the feel of those curls bouncing against his chest as she laughed in his arms.

Now Eleanor Langley looked totally different from the young woman he'd fallen in love with. He wondered if the changes were intentional. Had she transformed herself into this hardened career woman on purpose? Or had it happened gradually, without her even realising, the product of ten years' ceaseless striving in this heartless city?

And what about underneath?

Had her heart changed?

Ten years ago he'd judged her heart. He'd thought her cold and scheming and had walked away without ever finding out the truth. He'd thought he'd known it. He'd been so sure...

Now every certainty had been scattered, leaving him both hopeful and afraid. He didn't know what the future could hold, for him or Eleanor. He didn't even dare think, or question or wonder.

If only...

Jace left Eleanor's building, clamping his mind down on that thought as he walked down the dark, empty street.

ELEANOR WOKE SLOWLY, swimming upwards through consciousness from a deep and dreamless sleep. She blinked slowly; her room seemed to be obscured by a soft white haze.

As she sat up in bed, pushing her tangled mass of hair out of her eyes, she realised why. It was snowing. She scrambled out of bed and hurried to the window, pressing her hand against the cold glass. Outside the city's skyscrapers were lost in a snowstorm. Huge white flakes drifted down and the streets were already covered, the parked cars no more than white humps.

Snow. She smiled, suddenly feeling as excited and hopeful as a child when she'd had a rare snow day. There had been a blizzard once, when she was nine, and her mother had been forced to stay home from work. Eleanor still remembered that magical moment when her mother had decided to stay home for the day. The telephones hadn't been working, and, according to the television, no one was going anywhere. For a moment that pinched look had left her mother's face and she'd smiled and shrugged. 'I guess we'll have a snow day,' she'd said.

They'd trudged to Central Park through several feet of fluffy whiteness armed with a metal baking sheet— all the sledges had been sold out at the shop—and gone sledging on Cedar Hill near Seventy-Ninth Street. The feeling of flying down the hill, the world no more than a blur of muted colour, her mother's arms wrapped around her, was one Eleanor had never forgotten. She carried it with her like a treasure.

Snow. This sudden snowstorm felt like a treasure, a promise, a gift. Snow covered up all the grime and grit and hard concrete of the city, all the memories and regrets. It was a new beginning. A new hope. She didn't have to think about what had happened before, didn't have to carry the heavy, unbearable weight of ten years of memories or last night's conversation with Jace. She'd let the snow fall over it, cloaking it in whiteness, hiding it from herself.

Suddenly, certainly, Eleanor knew how to make this party just what Jace wanted. What she wanted. Smiling with a new determination, she turned away from the window.

She soon became immersed in organisation, making calls, checking facts and details, and arranging the most amazing party Jace Zervas could ever imagine. The party of her career.

She loved the buzz of creating something, seeing it emerge from her own imagination, and this party in particular was both a challenge and a dream. She had just days to conjure something spectacular.

The amount of work also kept her from thinking. Remembering. She was grateful for the activity that kept her from dwelling on the pain Jace had raked up, the regrets that still lingered on the fringes of her mind.

If only I'd known...

In her mind she never let Jace finish that sentence.

Every night she fell into bed, too exhausted to think or wonder, yet even so in that vulnerable moment before sleep overtook her she found herself picturing Jace's face, both as it had been ten years ago, young and smiling, and as it was now, determined and harsh. She remembered that shiver of electric awareness when he'd been in her apartment, when she had thought—perhaps even hoped—that he might touch her, and the memory carried her into the cocoon of sleep and insinuated itself into her dreams.

THE DAY BEFORE the party Eleanor spent the afternoon making sure everything was in place at the event site. So much of planning an event like this was simply getting on the phone, putting in orders, cajoling and commanding at turns. Now the real fun began: making the magic.

'It's so unusual to have a party here at this time of

year,' Laura, the woman who managed the boathouse in Central Park, remarked as Eleanor went over the party details with her. 'Especially with a request for the outside terrace. We're completely booked for spring and summer, but December...'

'I know,' Eleanor agreed. It was part of the reason she'd just chosen the park's boathouse as the venue; most other places had already been booked. And it was perfect for the kind of party she had planned. She surveyed the room, taking a mental count of the chairs and tables. 'My client is looking for unusual,' she explained, satisfied with the arrangements so far.

'It won't be too cold?' Laura asked dubiously. Although the boathouse had inside seating, its most spectacular feature was the pillared terrace overlooking the park's lake. Now the lake was frozen solid, and in the distance Eleanor could see the Angel of Bethesda fountain still shrouded in snow.

'I hope not,' she said cheerfully. 'Of course, we're working on that.' She'd ordered electric heaters to be placed on the terrace in strategic spots, to warm up cold little hands and feet.

'Well, all right,' Laura said, still sounding doubtful, and Eleanor pushed away the thought that perhaps she was in fact crazy. Ever since she'd first seen those few fat flakes drifting down, she'd been gripped by a vision, a *memory,* and she'd let it drive her through one of the most intense working weeks she'd ever experienced.

It left little time or room for doubt. Yet now as Laura went back to her office and Eleanor was left alone in the boathouse's Lake Room, she wondered if Jace would think this party was impressive enough. *Suitable.*

And she wondered why she should even care.

Sighing, Eleanor shook her head and walked over to the glass doors that led out onto the terrace. It was too late for doubts or regrets; the party was tomorrow night. Everything had been ordered, prepared, paid for. The invitations, in the shape of snowflakes, had been sent out to all the employees. All that was left was the doing.

Eleanor turned the door handle and pushed it open; a gust of freezing air hit her in the face. Drawing in a deep lungful of the cold, frosty air, she stepped out onto the terrace.

The sky was just darkening to violet, the sun disappearing behind the stark, bare branches that fringed the park. Eleanor stood by the railing, surveying the silent, frozen lake, the park empty of tourists or pedestrians on this cold evening. It never ceased to amaze her that she stood in nearly the exact centre of a city of eight million people, and the only sound was the creak and crack of shifting ice.

It's going to be okay.

She let herself relax, unloosen all the tensed, tightly held parts of herself. She didn't let herself relax too often; she knew from experience it was too hard once you let go to get it all back together again. Yet now, just for a moment, she let herself be still, serene—or as close to it as she could be.

It's going to be okay.

She wasn't even sure what was going to be okay: the party? The future? Something more nebulous that she couldn't yet name? Eleanor had no answers.

'They told me I'd find you here.'

Eleanor tensed, all the loosely held parts of herself coming together in a cold, hard ball. She turned slowly around to survey Jace.

He stood in the doorway, dressed in a navy suit and wool overcoat, a briefcase in one hand. His cheeks were reddened with cold, emphasising the silvery glint of his eyes and the inky blackness of his hair.

'On the terrace?' Eleanor said a bit stupidly, for despite her cool smile her mind seemed to have slowed down, only able to process how amazing he looked.

Jace smiled crookedly. It reminded her of the way he used to smile, back when they were students. Lovers. He hadn't smiled like that in the last week; all his smiles had been cold or calculated, a cruel curving of the lips. This one was real, lopsided, and yet somehow sad. The memories still lay between them, heavy and unspoken. Eleanor wondered if they would always be there. 'Actually, in the restaurant. But the door was open, so I figured you came out for a breath of fresh air.'

'Very fresh,' Eleanor agreed, and Jace smiled again. Her heart turned right over, a flip-flop that was both exciting and a little alarming. She didn't want to respond to him, not physically, not emotionally. She didn't want to feel anything at all. Yet somehow, even now, after everything they'd been through, after everything she'd endured, she still did.

He set his briefcase down by the door and joined her at the railing. 'How's it going?'

'Good.' She gave a quick little laugh; it sounded sharp. She knew what that laugh was: a defence mechanism. She inched away from him. 'You haven't been checking up on me all week. I expected an email or phone call to make sure the arrangements were *acceptable*.' Her emphasis on the word, Eleanor knew, sounded petty.

'I thought it best,' Jace said after a second's hesitation, and Eleanor saw his fingers tighten on the railing.

And before she could stop herself, Eleanor whispered, 'Why didn't you just get someone else, Jace?' Her voice sounded little and lost.

'I don't know.' He stared out at the frozen lake, his features harshening once more. 'I didn't want to walk away from you…like that.'

Like before. Her heart turned over again. It was, she thought ruefully, as desperate and flailing as a dying fish. She averted her face as she replied, 'It would have been easier.'

Jace turned away from the railing and the lake, and Eleanor knew that the conversation—*that* conversation—was over. 'It looks like you've done a fabulous job, at any rate,' he said, his voice brisk and light. Eleanor felt equal and infuriating amounts of disappointment and relief. She really didn't want to talk about the past, about *them,* yet here she was, ripping off scabs, opening wounds.

'It's cold out here.' The lake, she saw, was now cloaked in darkness. Above the trees lights winked on in the elegant apartment buildings lining Fifth Avenue. 'I should go back inside, check on the details before I return tomorrow.'

'All right,' Jace agreed, and he followed her back into the Lake Room. Eleanor didn't look at him as she consulted her list, mindlessly scanning the endless items she'd assembled for the party. She felt rather than saw Jace, still standing by the door, watching her. Even though he stood halfway across the room, she imagined she could feel the heat emanating from his body, winding around her own heart and warming her from the inside.

'There's still a lot to do,' she told him, her eyes fixed firmly on her list. She felt a strange new tension crackling between them, snapping inside her. A sexual tension, and she wasn't prepared for it. She'd spent ten years being angry at Jace Zervas; she wasn't ready to feel anything else. She didn't want to. 'I'll have to be back here early in the morning,' she told him brightly, at least half aware that she was starting to babble. 'Setting up. There's a lot of outside work—'

'Outside?' Jace asked, taking a step closer. 'What's outside?'

'Snow,' Eleanor said simply, and looked up.

Mistake. Jace was looking at her so intently, yet it was an intensity she felt rather than saw, as if his gaze reached right down into her soul and touched it. Held it, even. In that moment she remembered—she *felt*— the power he'd held over her ten years ago, when she'd given him everything. Her body, her dreams, her very life. Her happiness. And for a little while he'd kept them, treasured them, or seemed to. For such a short, sweet time life had seemed so wonderful.

Somehow she found a way to drag her gaze from his. She didn't want to feel that way again. It *was* wonderful, it was captivating, and it was also extremely dangerous. If you gave someone your happiness, you might never see or feel it again.

'Snow?' Jace repeated, the word a question. 'What does this party have to do with snow?'

'Everything.' Eleanor looked back at her list, although the words blurred in front of her. She was tired, exhausted, and she probably couldn't do much good

here. Yet the thought of going home made her feel a
little sad. A little lonely. She could call Allie, go out
for a drink—

'Eleanor?' Jace broke into her thoughts. 'You look a
million miles away.'

She looked up, distracted, discomfited, because she
knew why she didn't want to go home, or out, or anywhere but where Jace Zervas was.

He still held this awful, awful power over her; she
was still captive. The thought was utterly aggravating.

'Sorry.' She forced herself to give him her sunny, and
rather impersonal, smile, falling back on professional
ploys she knew well. 'Snow, yes. When it blizzarded the
other day, I thought how much fun snow is for children,
especially city children, who don't see all that much of
it. Winter for us—them—usually just means cold and
a lot of grey slush.'

'And?'

'So I thought a party centred around snow—building
snowmen, sledging, that sort of thing—would be fun.
Family-friendly,' she reminded him, the stress on the
word only slightly edged. Even now, it hurt. She summoned her professional smile. 'Some of my happiest
childhood memories have to do with snow.'

'Really.' Jace took a step towards her. Even though
he was still a good ten feet away, Eleanor felt he was
too close. She made herself not move. 'I never knew
that,' he said quietly.

'Well, snow days, you know. No school.'

'You didn't like school?'

She shrugged. 'What kid doesn't want a snow day?'

'Did you build snowmen? Go sledging?' He arched
an eyebrow. 'Somehow I can't see your mother doing

that.' He paused. 'Based on how you described her to me, of course.'

Did he remember, after all these years? Eleanor did. She remembered lying in Jace's arms, probably boring him with the silly little details of her life, her family. How she resented her mother for working so much, for being so hard and stern, for never giving her a father. She'd had an anonymous sperm donor instead, the easy, convenient way for a career woman to have a child. She'd even told Jace how she'd always insist on her own child knowing its father—

Ironic, that.

'Once she did—' She stopped. She wasn't ready to share that memory. 'Anyway, you don't know everything about me, Jace.'

'Once,' he repeated softly, moving towards her, 'I thought I did.' He took another step closer to her. She saw a dark urgency in his eyes, felt its desperate answer in herself.

Why was she thinking like this? Feeling like this? Breathless and buzzy and so achingly aware?

'No, you didn't,' Eleanor informed him, keeping her voice curt. *Focus.* Focus on what Jace was saying, rather than how wonderful he looked. How close he was. How she could take one step—maybe two—and be in his arms.

Eleanor turned away, busying herself with the already fastened clasp of her attaché case. 'Admittedly, I made a fool of myself,' she continued in that same curt voice, 'telling you every empty thing that came into my head, but there was plenty you didn't know about me.'

'Like what?' Jace challenged softly. He'd moved even closer and she could feel him again, his heat and his strength, the sheer power radiating from him, making her, absurdly, want to lean on it. Lean on him. Already she could imagine his arms enfolding her, his chin resting on her head as he used to do—

Eleanor straightened. 'Like the fact that I wouldn't lie,' she said shortly.

Jace stilled, and the room crackled with a new kind of tension. A chilling remoteness that made Eleanor feel as cold as she'd been on the terrace.

'Right,' Jace said, and his voice sounded distant. 'Of course.' Eleanor forced herself to say nothing. No apologies, no excuses. No regrets. 'You've changed,' he said after a moment, and she tensed.

'I've been saying that all along.'

'You're the kind of person you never wanted to be,' Jace told her quietly. Eleanor froze, her mind shocked into numbness, and then she whirled around.

'That's a rather arrogant statement,' she said, her voice coldly furious. 'Not to mention incredibly rude.'

'You told me,' Jace replied steadily, 'that you never wanted to be like your mother.'

'You've never even *met* my mother—'

'You told me she was an event planner, the best in her field. Never missed a day of work. Never made a softball practice.'

Eleanor's breath came out in a slow, surrendered hiss. *'Stop—'*

'Consumed by her career, hardened and weary and lonely,' Jace finished. Each word was an indictment, delivered in a terrible, matter-of-fact tone. 'I could be looking right at her.'

Eleanor felt her face drain of colour. Her fingers, clutching the strap of her attaché so tightly, were aching and numb. She hated that Jace had assessed her so thoroughly, so damningly. She hated that he was right.

'You don't know anything,' she said, the words forced out of a throat that had closed in on itself, tight with tears. She hated too that he'd made her so emotional, when for ten years she'd managed to be as cool and professional and feelingless as ice. As snow.

'Don't I?' Jace took a step closer. Eleanor saw compassion on his face, softening those taut lines, turning his eyes to a soft, sympathetic grey. 'What made you change so much, Ellie?'

A single stab of fury streaked through her, startling her out of numbness. 'Even now you don't know the answer to that question?' she demanded, her voice harsh with accusation. 'I'll tell you what changed me, Jace. You did.'

His eyes widened, his jaw slackening for the briefest of seconds. 'Ellie—'

'And I told you, don't call me that. I stopped being Ellie the day I went to your apartment building and nobody was there.' She saw him give a little shake of his head, and she wanted to scream at his arrogance. He had no idea what she'd been through. No idea at all. He'd chosen to damn her and miss it all. 'So don't call me that again,' she informed him brutally, 'because that Ellie? The one you think you knew so well? She no longer exists. She hasn't for ten years.'

And with that, leaving Jace still shocked and speechless, Eleanor turned and left the room.

CHAPTER FIVE

EVERYTHING WAS READY. Or, Eleanor amended silently, as ready as it ever would be. She glanced around the dining room; the first guests were scheduled to arrive in just ten minutes.

She'd spent the entire day at the boathouse, arranging centrepieces and party favours, checking to make sure the sound system worked and the band, who had arrived an hour ago, had everything they needed. She'd visited the kitchen several times to check on the food, and just fifteen minutes ago she'd finally retired to the Ladies to freshen up and change into her cocktail dress. She'd bypassed her standard LBD, classic but boring, in favour of a spangled silver sheath dress that glittered when she moved. By the time the party rolled round, event planners were meant to fade into the background, not take centre stage. Yet Eleanor hadn't been able to resist this dress. It made her feel like a snowflake. And she needed to feel good, craved that little pleasure because ever since she'd seen Jace last night she'd been out of sorts, emotionally edgy and drained at turns. He'd thrown her completely off balance, and she hated it. One minute she felt coldly furious, the next aggravatingly aware. She hated the flip-flop of her moods, her own body. She hated that Jace had caused this, that he was the source of her weakness.

She straightened a few napkins, moved a few of the freshly cut pussy-willow branches that made the stark yet elegant centrepieces for the table. The colour of the soft grey buds reminded her of Jace's eyes.

Forcing her mind away from that train of thought, she glanced outside at the terrace, where snow had been carted in to make playful mounds, ready to be turned into snowmen and igloos. A special kids' cocoa bar with four different kinds of hot chocolate and several flavours of marshmallows and whipped cream had been set out by the electric heater.

Family-friendly.

She didn't normally do parties with children, and she'd been surprised how much she had enjoyed it. Surprised and a little sad, for children surely were not in her future. She'd accepted that long ago, had had years to live with it, yet now, with Jace back in her life—for however short a time—the pain was fresh again. Did you ever *truly* heal?

She heard a sound at the door, and with both relief and a little anxiety she realised the first guests were arriving. The party had started.

JACE STOOD AT the threshold of the Lake Room, gazing in amazed wonder at the transformed space. The dining room was the epitome of understated elegance, strung with fairy lights, everything silver and white and crystalline. Like snow. He took in the long, graceful branches of pussy willows in their crystal vases, the snowflake ornaments at every child's place, and then glanced outside where children were delighting in playing with the mounds of snow, their faces already happily smeared with chocolate.

It was perfect.

He was only sorry to have missed the beginning, both for Eleanor's sake and that of Leandro Atrikides. Already he saw the speculative, sideways looks employees slid him, wary and uncertain. It had been Leandro's damn son Talos who had kept him from being prompt; the greedy bastard was still angling for a bigger payout.

Jace suppressed a sigh. Sometimes he wished he'd never involved himself in this unholy mess; Leandro's avaricious children had made a near ruin of his company. Jace's buyout had been little more than a mercy mission.

Yet if he hadn't come to New York, he wouldn't have seen Eleanor again...

And he was glad he had.

Wasn't he?

He realised he was searching for her through the crowds, had in fact been doing so since he'd arrived. He'd been thinking about her since he'd seen her last night, since she'd damned him with those words:

That Ellie? The one you think you knew so well? She no longer exists.

And it was all, utterly his fault. He was to blame for making Eleanor Langley the woman she was now.

You're the kind of person you never wanted to be.

Harsh words, and he knew he'd hurt her by saying them. But he couldn't take them back. He wouldn't. Yet what could he do about it? How could he help her?

And even if he did help her, somehow, wasn't he just doing it to make himself feel better? Still selfish.

Jace moved through the crowds, scanning the throng for a glimpse of Eleanor.

And then he saw her, and his head emptied of

thoughts. She stood by the window, surveying the party scene with a preoccupied air, and yet despite the tiny frown between her brows she looked lovely. Breathtaking in a shimmery dress that moved like liquid silver, encasing a slender body Jace remembered and knew so well. His palms suddenly itched to slide along that silky material and find the curve of her hip, the dip of her waist. To pull her towards him, to have her come to him, unresisting, unrepentant.

To feel Ellie in his arms again.

'ELEANOR!'

Eleanor turned, nerves fluttering low in her belly as she saw Jace coming towards her. It was a feeling that was both familiar and strange, for the nerves were not caused by anxiety, but anticipation. Even though they'd parted on such harsh terms last night, her body still leapt when she saw him. Almost as if she were *glad* to see him. Even though she shouldn't be.

He stopped in front of her, reaching out with both hands to clasp hers. Eleanor accepted his touch—his hands were warm, dry, and strong, his fingers folding over hers—without even thinking about what she was doing. Part of her brain knew she should step back, smile coolly, and remain safely distant. Yet that part of her had fallen silent and still. She did nothing.

He was smiling at her with warm admiration, his gaze sweeping her from the top of her elegant chignon to the tips of her rhinestone-encrusted stiletto sandals, and it did something rather pleasant and shivery to her insides. It also kept her from forming a single coherent thought.

'You look magnificent.'

'So do you,' Eleanor blurted, and then blushed. But he did, she couldn't deny it. He wore a dark grey silk suit, his crimson tie a festive splash of colour, the expensive material emphasising his powerful frame, a body she knew and remembered. A body she had once loved.

'And this party is wonderful,' Jace continued in that same warm voice, a voice she also remembered, low and honeyed, sliding over her senses.

'Thank you,' she murmured, and slipped her hands from his. Her brain was reminding her why this wasn't a good idea. Why she needed to remain poised, polished. Professional.

'Very unique.'

'That's what you wanted.' She realised she sounded a little sharp; she felt sharp, as if she were nothing but edges. She softened her words with a smile even as she took a step away. 'Everyone is about to sit down for dinner, so I should go see to a few things—'

Jace nodded his acceptance. 'I'm sorry I was late.'

'You can be late to your own party if you want.' Damn, she still sounded defensive. Why did Jace still affect her in so many ways? Her hands tingled from his touch. Her heart hurt. And the fact that he had been late hurt too. It shouldn't matter. She shouldn't care. She'd spent ten years making sure she didn't care.

Yet apparently she still did.

'I'd better go,' she said, and turned quickly away before Jace could say anything more.

A minor dilemma in the kitchen—a shortage of vegan meals—kept her occupied for the next while, and she managed to avoid Jace as she moved around the room, making sure everyone was happy and fed. Yet even so her gaze kept sliding to him of its own accord. He was seated at the head table, his head bent as he chatted and laughed with the guest on his right, a curvaceous brunette poured into an emerald-green cocktail dress. She was, Eleanor knew from the guest list, Leandro Atrikides's daughter, Kristina. She looked as if she wanted to gobble up Jace in one delicious bite.

And, Eleanor told herself, so what if she did? She was *not* jealous. Jealousy would be both pointless and absurd. She didn't *care* what Jace did, or with whom he did it. She couldn't. Eleanor turned away, smiled and chatted with a young couple five tables away from Jace and made sure not to look at him again.

At the end of the meal, just before Eleanor was about to cue the music for dancing, she heard the sharp, crystalline clang of a fork tapped against a wine glass and the room fell warily silent.

Jace rose from his seat.

Eleanor held her breath.

'Thank you all for coming,' Jace began in a melodious voice that flowed over her and the rest of his audience. 'It is a pleasure and an honour to be among you today.' He let his gaze rove over the room, warm and smiling. Eleanor stepped back away from the table, into the shadows. She wasn't sure why she didn't want Jace to see her—or if he even would—but she felt safer against the wall, away from the light. 'I'm very grateful for your presence,' Jace continued, 'especially in this difficult period of change.' Eleanor saw people shift in their seats, heard a few murmured whispers. Jace must have felt the sudden, palpable tension in the room, although he gave no sign of it. He smiled easily and kept talking.

'I want to assure you that I will do everything in my

power to ensure a smooth transition, and that it is my first concern to uphold the integrity of this company, which Leandro Atrikides instilled nearly half a century ago.' He paused, letting his gaze linger on a few faces, then looked up to scan the entire audience. Eleanor retreated even further, so her back came up against the wall. 'But this evening is a time for celebration, and I am delighted to see all of you—' here he smiled at a sleepy child lolling against her mother's arms '—enjoying yourselves. So let me take a moment to thank the person who made it all happen, and in the space of a single week. Eleanor?' Her name was a question, and Eleanor blinked, stunned, speechless.

She'd been thanked before, although not very often. Event planners were meant to be invisible, as if the party magically put itself together. That was the goal. Yet here was Jace, extending his hand, smiling warmly, and looking right at her.

Somehow, even though she was skulking in the shadows like some shamed wallflower, he'd found her. And under the admiring heat of his gaze, Eleanor felt as if she'd stepped straight into the spotlight.

She heard people shift and murmur yet again, and knew her silence was becoming ridiculous. And so unlike her. She was professional. This was professional.

Even if it didn't feel like it.

Clearing her throat, she stepped away from the wall as a patter of applause fell around her like rain. She gave a little nod of acceptance. 'Thank you, Mr Zervas.' His name stuck in her throat.

'And thank you,' Jace replied. 'This couldn't have happened without you.'

She nodded again, jerkily this time, and stepped

back into the shadows. To her relief the conversation resumed, and she was forgotten. Yet when she looked up she saw Jace was still gazing straight at her, and the look in his eyes—something both fierce and primal—made her legs so weak that she sagged helplessly against the wall once more.

She managed to avoid him for the next hour, although why she was avoiding him at all, Eleanor had no idea. What was she scared of? They'd parted so harshly last night, and while her mind reminded her of that painful conversation, her body tingled with awareness and memory. Desire, even.

Eleanor stopped in mid-stride on the way to the kitchen and blew out a long, slow breath as she acknowledged her attraction to Jace. Her aggravating and overwhelming attraction. It shouldn't even surprise her, really. Ten years ago she'd been overwhelmed by desire for him from the moment he'd entered the coffee shop where she'd been a barista and asked for a latte in that delicious Greek accent. Even after they'd been dating for several months, he'd still had the power to leave her speechless and desperate with longing in a matter of minutes. Why should that change?

As long as she reminded herself that her body's reaction to Jace was purely biological, chemical, nothing more than hormones or pheromones or whatever those things were—

'I'm almost starting to think you're hiding from me.'

Eleanor stiffened. Ahead of her the kitchen loomed, bustling, bright, safe. The hallway was narrow, dark, and empty. Except for her and Jace.

She turned around slowly, taking in his powerful frame, his immaculate suit. He smiled, that sleepy, suggestive smile she knew so well. She'd teased him that he knew it, and he always acted innocent and even affronted. Now she had no doubt: he knew. He knew the power of that smile, how it made her feel. What it had once made her do. And perhaps what it could make her do again. That was why she was avoiding him.

'Hiding from you?' she repeated, forcing a light little laugh. 'Hardly, Jace. Just busy.'

'Of course,' he murmured, still smiling, and Eleanor had a feeling he wasn't fooled. Even if it was true; she *was* busy. Although maybe not quite that busy. 'Still,' he continued, making Eleanor tense again, 'surely you have a few moments for me? For a dance?'

'A dance?' she repeated blankly, and his smile deepened, revealing a dimple in his cheek. She'd forgotten about that dimple; he hadn't smiled widely enough in the last week for her to see it.

Yet even though he was smiling now, even though he was looking at her with that seductive sleepiness she remembered so well, she sensed something underneath. Something deeper and darker, marred by sorrow. He hadn't forgotten. The past still loomed between them. No matter how light he kept his voice, Eleanor sensed he was pretending—hiding—perhaps as much as she was.

'Yes, you know? Dance?' He held out his arms as if he were leading an imaginary dance partner and did a quick box-step in the hallway. Eleanor folded her arms, trying to be resolute and regretful and failing. She was actually smiling, although perhaps not as widely as Jace. Yet it felt good to smile, felt right to leave the cares and regrets behind, if only for a night.

'I don't really dance.'

'Good thing I do. And I'm a good teacher.'

'Really?' She arched an eyebrow. 'We never danced before.'

He stopped mid-step and dropped his arms. 'We were too busy doing other things, I suppose.'

Eleanor's cheeks heated and she was grateful for the shadowy dimness of the hallway. Why had she mentioned the past? Why had she referred to anything about their old relationship, their old selves?

'One dance, Eleanor.'

He made it sound like a challenge. And it *was* a challenge; suddenly Eleanor wanted to show Jace Zervas that she could dance with him and remain unaffected. She could walk away. She was desperate to prove to him—and to herself—that he really didn't affect or matter to her at all. And she'd enjoy it at the same time. One dance.

'Fine.'

She walked past him, stiff with resolution, back out into the crowded light of the party. She heard Jace walk behind her, felt the heat of his hand on the small of her back. The band she'd chosen herself was playing a lively swing tune and all around her couples were happily cutting up the floor. Eleanor wasn't much of a dancer—she was usually working behind the scenes, not *in* them— but she thought she could manage a brisk shuffle.

Jace's hand pressed against her back, steering her through the crowd to a spare space on the dance floor. Eleanor turned to face him, firm smile in place. Jace smiled lazily back—as if he knew exactly what she was thinking, that she was simply trying to prove something. Just as he was.

'Shall we?' Eleanor asked brightly and Jace reached for her hand, his fingers threading through hers.

'Oh, yes.'

He pulled her to him, and when Eleanor resisted that sensual tug he murmured so only she could hear, 'Come on, Eleanor. We're dancing.'

'Right.' She let him draw her closer, knowing it was dangerous, feeling that awful desire leap in her belly as she inhaled the woodsy musk of his cologne.

'You're dancing like a twelve-year-old boy,' he chided as Eleanor started an awkward box-step. 'And you're leading.'

'I can't help it,' Eleanor said, laughing reluctantly.

Jace placed his hand on her waist, his fingers splayed across her hip, and drew her close enough so she could feel the heat of him. 'This is how you do it,' he said mock sternly, and began to move her around the dance floor in a lively jitterbug.

Eleanor wasn't sure how she did it. Somehow Jace put enough pressure on her waist to guide her along, twisting and whirling her with such a natural ease that Eleanor was left breathless, amazed at her own gracefulness.

The other dancers had cleared a space around them, and several couples had stopped to watch, clapping their hands in time to the music.

'You're making a scene,' Eleanor hissed when she came close enough to Jace to have him hear. His arm slid along the length of hers before he grabbed her hand and whirled her in a neat, fast circle so her dress spun out around her in a silver arc.

'Isn't that the point?' he challenged with a wicked smile, and Eleanor felt her insides melt.

This was so dangerous. This was the Jace she'd once known, the Jace she'd fallen in love with. The Jace who had broken her heart. She preferred the harsh, hard man she'd met in her office; there had been no danger of falling in love with *him*.

'Where did you learn to dance?' she asked breathlessly as Jace spun her around yet again.

'I have five older sisters. How could I not learn how to dance?'

'Five?' she repeated in surprise. She'd had no idea.

'Now for the finale,' Jace said and Eleanor stiffened in alarm.

'I can't—'

'Yes,' he told her as he pulled her closer, 'you can.'

And before Eleanor knew what he was doing he'd flipped her right over so her legs had gone over her head until she was on her feet again, dazed and incredulous. Around them people clapped and cheered.

'Jace!'

'Wasn't that fun?'

'That doesn't matter—' she blustered. How many people had seen her underwear?

'Don't worry,' he murmured, drawing her close again, 'no one saw anything.'

'How did you—' She didn't finish that question and shook her head. It *had* been fun, yet she couldn't quite keep herself from still acting annoyed and defensive; those postures were her armour. They kept her safe. She wasn't ready to unbend entirely.

The song had ended, replaced by a slow jazz number. Distantly Eleanor recognised the sexy, mournful wail of a single saxophone as Jace lazily pulled her even closer so their hips collided and his hands slid down to her lower back, his fingers splayed across the curve of her bottom.

'Jace—' Eleanor hissed, trying to move out of the

all-too-close contact. Around them couples swayed to the music.

'Relax. It's a slow dance.'

Relax? How on earth was she supposed to relax with her body pressed against Jace's, his hands moving lazily up and down her spine? She was conscious of how thin her dress was, how little separated their bodies—

Eleanor clamped down on that thought. Fine. She could endure this. She could still walk away with her head held high—except, there was no *enduring* about it. It was far, far too pleasant to let her body relax into Jace's, to enjoy the feel of his hand on her back, his fingers burning her through the thin material of her dress. Too wonderful to let him pull her closer, to lean her head against his chest so her lips hovered less than an inch from the warm skin of his neck.

They'd never danced before. There had been no opportunities. Their love affair had been conducted in the café where she'd worked, walks in the park, and the big double bed in Jace's apartment. Eleanor hadn't even known Jace could dance just as she hadn't known he had five older sisters. He'd never told her, just as he'd never told her so many things. She'd been in love with him, yet in some ways she'd barely known him. It made her wonder if you even could be in love with someone you hardly knew. Had it simply been infatuation?

'See how easy this is?' Jace murmured. His lips brushed her hair and his breath tickled her cheek. Eleanor closed her eyes.

Yes, it was easy. Far, far too easy. She'd wanted to cling to the knowledge that they were two different people now, that even if she could forgive and forget what had happened between them—which she didn't even know if she could—a relationship was impossible. Unwanted on both sides.

Yet in Jace's arms all those resolutions fell away, as insubstantial as smoke, or the snow that had already started to melt into slushy puddles. In Jace's arms, she was conscious only of how everything felt so wonderfully, painfully the same.

The song ended and they remained swaying for a heartbeat before Eleanor found the strength to break away. Her face was flushed and she could feel a rather large strand of hair against her cheek, falling down from her professional, sleek chignon. Her image was falling apart. *She* was falling apart.

'I need to go. There are things to do.'

'Okay.' She risked looking up, saw how shuttered Jace's eyes looked, his jaw taut. This dance had cost him something too. Why were they doing this? Flirting with the past? Flirting with each other? Surely it could only lead to heartache...for both of them.

'Thank you for the dance,' she said, and hurried away without waiting for Jace's reply.

JACE WATCHED ELEANOR weave her way through the crowd. His body tingled where he'd touched her. He felt alive, more alive than he had in years, and yet restless and edgy as well.

What was he doing? What was he trying to prove? Dancing with Eleanor was dangerous. There could be nothing for them now, not with the past still lying so heavily between them. Not when he was leaving in less than a week. He didn't even *want* there to be anything between them; he wasn't interested in love, and learning he might actually be fertile couldn't change that.

Could it?

The best thing—the wisest and safest—would be to leave Eleanor alone. To walk away right now, and let them both get on with their lives. Yet even as he made this resolution, Jace realised he was still looking for her. Waiting for her.

Wanting her.

ELEANOR AVOIDED JACE for the rest of the night, feeling ridiculous as she skulked in the corners of rooms, hurried down hallways, and kept an eagle eye out for his appearance. Yet avoiding Jace had become necessary for her sanity, her safety. That dance had broken down the barriers she'd erected between them, barriers between the past and the present. Barriers she needed. She didn't want to get close to Jace, couldn't let herself love him or be infatuated with him. Whatever it was— had been—she had no desire to feel it again. Not with a man she still couldn't trust. Not with Jace.

Still, she couldn't avoid him for ever. He found her after the party had finished, the last guests trickling out into the night, and the staff starting to clear the party's debris.

'Always busy,' he murmured.

Eleanor didn't turn around, though she could feel him behind her. 'I have a lot to do. It's a party to you, Jace, but for me it's work.'

He propped one shoulder against the wall of the Lake Room where she'd been going over her list of rented equipment on one of the cleared tables. 'It was a great party. And great work.'

'Thank you.' Needlessly she ticked an item off on her list. One of the staff hoisted a tray of dirty wine glasses and left the room, making Eleanor tinglingly aware of how alone she and Jace were. The last guests had gone into the park and the darkness, and, now that the room was cleared, all the staff seemed to have vanished. She ticked another item off on her list, eyes fixed firmly upon it.

'I'm leaving for Greece in three days,' he said quietly. He sounded sad. Eleanor tensed.

'I see.'

'I'd like to think...' He paused, clearing his throat. Eleanor looked up, surprised by the naked vulnerability in Jace's eyes. The list fell from her hand, forgotten. 'I'd like,' Jace started again, 'to return home knowing things are—resolved—between us.'

Resolved. The word echoed through her. What did that mean? How did you find resolution, that oft-touted closure? Eleanor wished she knew. 'Fine,' she said after a moment. 'Consider us resolved.' She picked up her list again and stared at it blindly.

'Eleanor—'

'I don't know what you want, Jace. Whatever it is, I don't think I can give it to you.' She swallowed, stared at her list. 'I'm sorry.' She might have danced with him, had even *wanted* to dance with him, but it meant nothing. She knew that, she felt it now. Her body might betray her again and again, but her mind and heart remembered just what Jace had done. Her mind and heart wouldn't forget. Couldn't forgive. She slipped her list into her bag and met Jace's troubled gaze. Even now her body reacted to his nearness, both with wanting and remembrance. Even now she remembered how she'd felt in his arms, both an hour ago and a lifetime ago. From somewhere she summoned the strength to move past him, making sure they didn't even brush shoulders. 'Goodnight, Jace.'

She walked out of the room without looking back, fumbling for her coat by the front door. She usually stayed for longer after a party, making absolutely sure everything was cleaned up and taken care of. But she couldn't tonight, couldn't handle another moment of being near Jace, of enduring the temptation of being near him.

She hated that her body was so weak, that she still desired the man who had betrayed her. At least she'd been strong enough to walk away.

JACE STOOD ALONE in the Lake Room, everything empty and silent around him. In the distance he heard the door click open and shut. Eleanor had gone.

He let out a long, slow breath. It was better this way. It really was. It had to be. Yet even so, the restlessness didn't leave him; the regret still weighed heavily on his heart.

It might be better this way, but it didn't feel like it. Too many things still lay between them, words unspoken that needed to be said.

Consider us resolved.

He didn't.

His body taut with grim purpose, Jace strode from the room.

OUTSIDE THE PARK was dark, the last guests already long gone. Eleanor dug her hands deep into the pockets of her coat and walked resolutely towards Fifth Avenue. There should be plenty of cabs there, even at this hour.

She'd only been walking a few minutes, skirting the

edge of the Sailboat Pond, afloat with model boats in the spring and summer but now drained and empty, when she heard footsteps behind her. Eleanor's heart stilled even as she quickened her pace. The park was generally safe at night these days, but this was New York and she knew to be careful.

'Eleanor, I'm sorry.'

It was Jace. Eleanor's heart resumed its normal thump for only a second before it began beating all the faster. It was *Jace*. She slowed her pace and turned around.

'What did you say?'

'I'm sorry.' She could barely see him in the darkness; the only light was from a high, thin crescent of moon just emerging from behind the clouds. She couldn't make out the expression on his face, but she could hear the contrition and regret tearing his voice and it startled her.

She hitched her bag higher up on her shoulder. 'What for?'

'For hurting you so badly.' Jace took a step closer to her, and now the moon cast a pale, silvery glow over his features, etched in regret. Eleanor's breath dried in her throat. 'For walking away so utterly. For not being there when you must have been going through a very difficult time.'

'Don't—' Eleanor whispered. He had no idea just how difficult a time she'd been through. He had no idea how much she'd needed to hear these words, and yet how afraid she was to hear them, because an apology required a response. It meant things would change. *She* would have to change.

'Don't say sorry?' Jace smiled, that wonderful crooked smile Eleanor knew and had once loved. 'But

I have to. For my sake, as well as your own. We can't be—resolved—until I say it. I know that.'

'I don't need—' Eleanor began, roughly, for her throat was already clogged and tight. Yet she couldn't even finish the sentence. It was a lie. She *did* need. She needed Jace to apologise. She needed to be able to forgive him. For ten years she'd managed to move on without it, but her heart had stayed in the same place. She hadn't realised just how much until Jace had come back into her life.

He was right in front of her now, so close she could reach out and touch him if she wanted to. She didn't move. 'Will you forgive me, Eleanor?' Jace asked softly. 'For hurting you so much?'

Eleanor wanted to shake her head. She wanted to cry. She wanted to tell him she wouldn't, because she was still angry and hurt and afraid, and yet she wanted to say she would because she needed the closure, the redemption. She nodded jerkily, unable to offer him more.

It didn't matter. Jace closed the small space between them, pulling her into his arms. She felt the soft wool of his coat against her cold cheek as she remained in the circle of his embrace, unresisting, unable to move or push away as she surely should do. 'I'm sorry,' he said again, his voice rough with emotion, and the shell around Eleanor's hardened heart finally cracked and broke.

'I forgive you,' she whispered, the words barely more than a breath of sound. Her throat was so tight. She tilted her head up to look at him, meaning only to offer absolution, yet there must have been too much yearning in her eyes—too much desire—for Jace's own expression darkened and after a second's hesitation—a second that seemed to last for ever—he lowered his mouth to hers.

The first brush of his lips against hers was a shock, electrifying her from the tips of her fingers to the very centre of her soul.

Then her senses sweetly sang to life as both body and mind and even heart remembered this, remembered Jace. How he felt. How he tasted. How right she'd always been in his arms and under his touch.

Her lips yielded to his, parting, inviting, and Jace took full advantage, deepening the kiss so Eleanor felt that plunging sensation of helpless desire deep in her belly, so she craved more, and *more,* her hands sliding over his coat, across his shoulders, down his back, bringing her closer to him.

She didn't know how long the kiss went on. And it was more than a kiss. Jace's hands had slipped under her coat, under her dress, cold against her skin and yet still enflaming her with his touch so that both their breathing was ragged and Eleanor's mind was as hazy and high as a cloud.

Her head dropped back, her back arching, a moan escaping her lips as his hands roved over her body and his mouth moved on hers. It had been so long. It had been ten years.

She couldn't think past this moment, couldn't register anything but the onslaught of her senses…until she heard two teenagers' raucous laughter from across the pond, the ugly sound jolting her out of that desire-induced haze and right out of Jace's arms. She jerked away, her chest rising and falling in shock, in shame, while she stared at him with dazed, disbelieving eyes.

He looked back at her, his expression just as stunned. Neither of them spoke.

Eleanor could hardly believe what she'd just allowed. What she'd done. He said sorry and she melted into his arms? She'd practically begged him to touch her, *take* her? Jace looked as if he hadn't even meant to kiss her, and maybe he hadn't. Maybe she'd kissed him without realising—

'Eleanor—'

'No.' She couldn't hear what he was going to say, no matter what it was. Anything Jace said now was sure to break her. 'This shouldn't have happened.'

'I know.' Those two sorry words almost made her cry. Somehow she didn't want him to admit it was a mistake, even though she knew it was. 'Even so—'

'No,' Eleanor said again. There was no *even so*. There couldn't be. She shook her head, backing away, and then with a stifled cry she fled into the night.

JACE WATCHED ELEANOR run through the darkness as if the very demons of hell were on her heels. Perhaps she felt they were. She had clearly been shocked by that kiss, and frankly so had he.

He'd meant only to say sorry, to make up for the past, and instead he'd reopened it, ripped the scabs off their scars. His heart ached with remembered pain. His body ached with unfulfilled desire.

What was he doing? Why couldn't he just leave Eleanor Langley alone? Jace realised he was still walking towards Fifth Avenue, following her fleeing footsteps. He slowed his stride.

Ever since Eleanor had come back into his life—ever since he'd discovered she'd been telling the truth—he hadn't been able to stop thinking of her. Thinking about the what ifs, wondering if life could give them a second chance.

Jace stopped in his tracks. A second chance at what? At *love?*

Did he really want that?

The last ten years he'd been hardening his heart against love, against any messy emotion. He'd focused on his business, building an empire instead of a dynasty.

And yet now…now he wanted more. He wanted Eleanor.

Ellie.

He wanted to reawaken the woman he'd lost when he'd walked out ten years ago. He wanted Ellie to find herself again, her true self, the self whom he'd loved and who had loved him. He wasn't even sure why; he didn't know what he even wanted with that woman. He'd lost her once, and he'd spent the intervening years making sure he never lost—anything or anyone—again.

Did he really want that change? That risk?

Did Ellie?

And how the hell could any of it happen, when he was leaving in a few days?

Jace stopped walking. The past was better buried. He knew that, felt it. No matter how these if onlys and what ifs might torment him, he knew they were only that. Possibilities, not realities. Not even hopes.

Distantly he heard the teenagers move off, still laughing raucously, and the laboured chug of the Fifth Avenue bus as it headed downtown. Letting out a long, slow breath, Jace slowly turned around and walked in the other direction.

CHAPTER SIX

ELEANOR DIDN'T GO back to her apartment. She didn't want to be alone, so she took a cab to the West Village, where her best friend Allie had a studio on the top floor of a brownstone. They'd both been interns at Premier Planning nine years ago. Allie had lasted two weeks. Eleanor had stayed for ever.

Even though it was now after midnight, she knew she could trust Allie to welcome her with open arms—and an open heart.

Still, she had to press the buzzer for a good thirty seconds before Allie came to the intercom.

'Who is it?' she demanded in a voice that sounded both sleepy and irritated.

Too emotional and fragile to explain, Eleanor just said, 'Me.'

Allie pressed the buzzer.

She was waiting outside the door in her pyjamas, hugging herself in the cold of the corridor, as Eleanor made her way up the six narrow flights of stairs.

'Eleanor, what on earth happened? You look terrible.'

'Thanks,' Eleanor managed wryly, and Allie shrugged this aside, taking in Eleanor's up-do and silvery dress.

'Actually, you look fantastic. You *sound* terrible. What's wrong?'

'Everything, it feels like,' Eleanor replied, her words wobbly. Now that she was finally here with Allie, safe, loved, the reality of her confrontation with Jace—and that wonderful, awful, confusing kiss—was slamming into her, leaving her more than shaken. Leaving her shattered.

Allie ushered her inside the cosy apartment, plonking the kettle on the stove before Eleanor had even asked.

'You want to talk about it? Didn't you have an event tonight?'

Eleanor sank onto the worn futon and kicked off her heels, nodding wearily. Allie's apartment was so different from her own modishly sterile condo; it was colourful and cluttered and shabby, and Eleanor loved it. Now it made her ache just a little bit for the kind of apartment she'd once had, the kind of life she'd once had. The kind of person she'd once been.

You're the kind of person you never wanted to be.

Eleanor pushed the thought away. Allie sank onto the futon across from Eleanor, flicked her long braid over one shoulder and propped her chin on her fist. 'So?'

'He came back.'

Allie's eyes widened, her breath coming out in a slow hiss. Eleanor knew she didn't need to explain who *he* was. One night long ago, when they'd both had too much wine, she'd told Allie her whole sordid story. Or most of it, anyway. She'd left out some of the heartache, the consuming loss that was too private to share.

'He did?' Allie finally said. 'How—?'

Eleanor didn't want to explain it. She didn't have the strength or will. 'Party,' she said simply, and Allie nodded. It was enough.

'What happened? Did the bastard finally apologise, I hope?'

Eleanor let out a choked laugh. 'Yes,' she managed, and covered her face with her hands.

'And isn't that a good thing?' Allie asked cautiously. Eleanor was prevented from answering by the shrill whistle of the kettle. Allie got up to make their tea, and Eleanor sagged against the futon. It *was* a good thing. At least, she'd always thought it would be. Yet when someone asked for forgiveness, you were meant to give it; you were meant to let go. And Eleanor wasn't sure she could. She might have told Jace she forgave him, but those were only words. *Could* she forgive him? What would happen if she did?

Allie returned, handing Eleanor a mug of tea before settling back onto the futon. 'So it doesn't seem like a good thing,' she remarked wryly. 'Why not?'

Eleanor let out a hiccuppy laugh. 'Well, I suppose it's not so much the apology, as the kiss that came after it.'

There was a second's silence and then Allie nodded. 'Ah.' She took a sip of tea. 'Was it nice?'

Eleanor burst out laughing, nearly spluttering her tea. It felt good to laugh, despite the pain and regret still tearing at her. 'That was the last thing I expected you to say.'

Allie shrugged. 'For all the apparent heartache it's causing you, I hope it was.'

'Very nice,' Eleanor admitted after a moment. She gazed down into the milky depths of her tea. 'Very nice,' she repeated quietly. Even now she could remember how good Jace had felt, how *right*, which was ridiculous because there had been nothing right about it all. It had been very, very wrong.

'So why exactly did he kiss you?' Allie asked after

a moment. She tucked her knees up to her chest and looked at Eleanor over the rim of her mug. 'Was he just caught up in the moment?'

'I don't know,' Eleanor said slowly. Why *had* Jace kissed her? Had it been a spontaneous gesture, as Allie had said? He had seemed so surprised, as stunned as she had...yet she could hardly believe that Jace would be so out of control. Had he been proving to her that she was still attracted to him? Had it been a mere amusement? Or worse—far worse—a *pity* kiss?

'Eleanor, stop whatever you're thinking. You're looking way too freaked out.'

Eleanor groaned. 'I'm feeling freaked out. You know I haven't had much time—or inclination—for relationships, Allie. I can't *do* this—'

'Does he want a relationship?'

Eleanor groaned again. 'No, of course not. That is—I don't think so. I shouldn't even care.'

'But you do,' Allie filled in quietly and Eleanor bit her lip, nipping hard.

'No,' she finally said, firmly. 'I don't. I can't. Ten years ago he broke my heart and—more than that.' She twisted the mug, her tea barely touched, around in her hands. 'My whole life collapsed, Allie. Everything. I never told you how—how bad it was, but it was. Bad.' She tried to smile wryly, but her lips trembled instead. 'Really bad.'

'Oh, Eleanor.' Allie reached over to place a hand on top of hers. 'I'm sorry.'

'So am I. And that's why this kiss—for whatever reason—was a bad idea. I'm not going to ever let myself feel that way again. Be used that way. And,' Eleanor finished, her voice turning hard and flinty, 'the simple fact is, I may have changed a lot in ten years, but Jace Zervas hasn't.' Not enough. Not in ways that mattered. She smiled grimly at her friend. 'I don't think he's changed at all.'

ELEANOR SPENT THE night on Allie's futon, and slept deeply and dreamlessly. By the time she swam to consciousness the next morning, the sun was high in the sky and Allie had already gone out for the coffee and croissants.

'I feel like I've been hit by a truck,' Eleanor muttered as she pushed her hair out of her face and blinked in the sunlight flooding the room. She hadn't even washed her face before going to bed, and her eyes felt sticky both with sleep and dried mascara.

'You basically were,' Allie replied cheerfully. 'The Jace Zervas Express.' She handed Eleanor a paper cup of coffee and a flaky croissant. 'Here. Sustenance.'

'You're amazing.'

Allie grinned. 'I know.'

Eleanor sat cross-legged on the sofa and ate the buttery croissant, licking the crumbs from her fingers, before she started on her coffee. She hadn't eaten much last night, as busy as she'd been with the details of the party, and she was starving.

Her cellphone beeped just as she took her first sip of coffee.

'My boss,' she explained when she'd located the phone and listened to Lily's brief message. She sounded her usual terse self, and simply asked her to call, which made Eleanor feel a flutter of panic. Had Jace talked to Lily? Had the party *not* been a success after all?

Had that kiss changed everything?

She ended the message and dropped her cellphone back into her bag. Leaning back against the sofa she took a sip of coffee, determined to forget Lily, forget Jace, forget everything, if just for a day. It was Saturday; she was with Allie. And she needed a break. She turned to Allie, smiling with bright determination. 'Let's go out. Do something fun. Go to the Greenmarket in Union Square and buy funky jewellery at St Mark's Place.'

'Funky jewellery?' Allie repeated, eyebrows arched. 'When have you ever worn funky jewellery?'

Eleanor bit her lip, her smile wobbling just a little bit. She used to wear funky jewellery. She used to look and feel and *be* so different.

She simply wasn't that person any more, and she didn't think she ever could be again. After she'd lost both Jace and their baby, she'd ruthlessly gone about becoming someone else...the person she was now.

The kind of person you never wanted to be.

Shrugging away the sorrow this thought caused, she smiled once more at Allie. 'Well, let's go to a museum, then. The Met or the MOMA.' She took her last sip of coffee, her voice taking on an edge. 'You're right, I'm really not a funky jewellery kind of person.'

MONDAY MORNING CAME soon enough, and as Eleanor walked through Premier Planning's office she was uncomfortably aware of the curious looks of everyone on the office floor, the sideways glances, the open speculation. Her skin prickled. What had happened? What had Jace done?

Then she stopped in the doorway of her office, for there in the centre of her desk was the most enormous, most outrageous bouquet of flowers she'd ever seen.

She dropped her bag on the floor and approached the arrangement of creamy white lilies and small, violet blooms that a card tucked in among the leaves told her was glory-of-the-snow.

Snow.

Her heart constricted. A little envelope had been taped to the crystal vase, and Eleanor took it with trembling fingers. She slipped the stiff white card out and read the two words printed on it: *Sorry. Again.*

Her fingers clenched on the card. Sorry for what? Sorry for the kiss? Sorry for—

'Well, well.'

Eleanor turned around, the card still clutched in her fingers. Lily stood in the doorway, as sharp and freshly pressed as ever, the expression on her thin face impossible to read.

'Good morning, Lily.'

'I'd say from those flowers that Zervas was pleased with the party.'

'I hope so.'

'I know he was pleased because he called me Saturday morning to tell me so. I knew we could do it,' Lily told her in a smug voice that made Eleanor wonder if her boss was taking credit for pulling off the event.

'That's…wonderful?' she said numbly.

Lily narrowed her eyes. 'It is, isn't it? You don't sound too thrilled, though. And you look terrible.'

Leave it to Lily not to sugarcoat it, Eleanor thought sourly. She moved the flowers to a side table. 'I'm just exhausted. Organising a party like that in just a week takes it out of even me.'

'You're right,' Lily conceded grudgingly. 'You can take a half-day, if you like.'

Eleanor shook her head. She didn't need more time to think, to dwell, to wonder. Nor did she need people like Jill or Laura eager to keep her clients or steal more while she was away. She needed to be here, at work, where she was needed and useful and busy. 'No, thanks. I'm fine. I need to catch up on all my other accounts anyway.'

Yet even as Eleanor worked solidly throughout the day, she found it still gave her mind plenty of time to wonder. To remember. She relived every second of that kiss with Jace, how unbearably good it had felt to be held by him again. How she realised her body had been waiting to be held again—by him—for ten long years.

How infuriated and frustrated and *scared* it made her feel. She didn't want to want him.

She was just about to leave for the day when her phone rang. Thinking it was a callback from a client, she reached for the phone quickly, her voice brisk and professional.

'Eleanor Langley.'

'Hello, Ellie.' A pause, and she heard a wry note of laughter in his voice as he corrected himself. 'Sorry. Eleanor.'

Her fingers clenched on the phone. Blood drained from her face, raced to other parts of her body. 'Hello, Jace.'

'I'm leaving for Greece tomorrow.' He spoke quietly, almost sadly. 'I just wanted to say I'm sorry. For the other night. I know me kissing you wasn't on either of our agendas.'

Agendas. She pictured herself pencilling in *kiss Jace*. No, that had definitely not been on her agenda. And obviously not on Jace's either, Eleanor acknowledged bleakly. 'The flowers did the job admirably,' she said after a moment, her voice sounding constricted.

'I'm glad you liked them.'

Eleanor didn't answer, couldn't, because her throat had tightened so terribly. The silence ticked on between them, punctuated only by the soft sound of their breathing.

Finally Jace spoke again. 'So I suppose this is goodbye. I don't intend to return to New York.'

'Not even to manage Atrikides Holdings?'

'I've appointed a CEO,' Jace said. 'Leandro Atrikides's nephew. That was the plan all along.'

'Whose plan?'

'Leandro's.' He sounded weary, and Eleanor realised with a jolt that the corporate takeover might not have been quite as ruthless as she'd thought. *Jace* wasn't as ruthless as she had thought.

But it didn't matter, because he was leaving New York. And there could be—would be—nothing between them anyway, which was how she wanted it. How it had to be. The past could be forgiven, maybe, but not forgotten. Not undone.

'I see,' she managed. Her voice sounded distant and polite despite the ache in her throat and even in her heart. 'Well, goodbye, then.'

Jace was silent, long enough for Eleanor to wonder what he was thinking. What he wanted to say. What *she* wanted him to say.

'Goodbye, Eleanor,' he said, and then he put down the phone.

Staring into space, Eleanor realised that Jace had just left her a second time. At least this time he'd said goodbye.

JACE STOOD UP and walked over to the floor-to-ceiling window of Leandro Atrikides's office, the view of Central Park now shrouded in shadows.

Tomorrow morning he'd take his private jet back to Athens. He had plenty of work to keep him busy, meetings to attend, companies to control, decisions to make. A life.

Yet right now it all felt empty, meaningless, and all he could think of was the woman he'd left, the woman he was leaving again. The life he'd lost a decade ago.

Irritated, Jace shook off his maudlin thoughts. They were not worthy of him. Regret was a useless emotion. The best option, the only option, was to move on. To forget. As they both surely should do.

And that was what he *wanted* to do, anyway. He wasn't interested in resurrecting some youthful affair that had most likely been doomed from the start. He wasn't interested in becoming that carefree young man again, the man with a heart to break, even if he grieved the loss of the woman he'd once known. He'd wanted to bring that woman back last night; he thought apologising would help. Kissing her wouldn't. Didn't.

That kiss, Jace knew, had been a mistake. Even if it hadn't felt like one at the time.

That kiss had unearthed memories, desire, regrets— all of which Jace wanted to keep buried, and he had no doubt that Eleanor did too.

Sighing, shrugging off these thoughts, he told himself he should return to his penthouse hotel suite. He'd order in and go to bed early, take a morning flight back to Athens. He was neither needed nor wanted here.

Yet still he remained, hands in his pockets, staring out at a darkening sky.

Three months later

'WHY DO YOU work so hard?'

Jace looked up from the financial newspaper he'd been scanning as he drank his morning coffee. 'Sorry,' he said, giving his sister Alecia a still-distracted smile. 'Habit.' He reached for one of the rolls on the table. They were sitting in one of the cafés off Kolonaki Square, in one of Athens's best neighborhoods.

Across from him Alecia made a face and reached for a roll herself. 'I don't mean reading your newspaper, Jace. It's everything. Ever since you came back from that trip you've been like a grumpy bear, growling at everyone who sees you. And you've missed three family dinners—that's at least two too many. I know you try to miss them anyway, but still...' She smiled teasingly as she said it, but even Jace could see the shadows of worry in her eyes.

He broke his roll in half. 'What trip do you mean?'

'The one to the States. New York, wasn't it?'

Jace shouldn't have asked. He already knew what trip, knew what lay behind his sister's concerned comments.

Eleanor. He couldn't get her out of his mind. He hadn't been the same since he'd seen her. Since he'd left her. Again.

Sighing, he reached for his cup and took a small sip of the strong, syrupy Greek coffee.

'I'm worried about you, you know.'

'Don't be.' The words came out harshly, too harshly, for he and Alecia had always enjoyed a close relationship. She was older than him by only eighteen months, and the only one of his sisters still to be unmarried. She understood him perhaps better than anyone else did, and she was the only person he'd told about Ellie. Yet he hadn't told her about Eleanor, or what had happened in New York three months ago.

'Jace? What's going on?'

'Nothing.' His throat constricted and his fingers tightened around the coffee cup. He wasn't ready to share everything he'd learned in New York: that he'd made a mistake, that he wasn't infertile, that he'd ruined what might have been his only chance at happiness and perhaps even love. He could barely voice those sentiments to himself. For the last three months he'd been working as hard as he could to keep from thinking about them. To keep from thinking about anything.

Yet it obviously hadn't worked, for Alecia had seen that something was amiss, and Eleanor never really left his thoughts. She invaded his dreams. He felt her like a constant presence, a mist over his mind, even though she was thousands of miles away.

'Is it a woman?' Alecia asked playfully, and Jace's head jerked up.

'What?'

'A woman.' Alecia smiled, her chin resting on her laced fingers. 'If I didn't know you better, I'd think it was a woman. You seem almost lovesick.'

Lovesick. What a terrible expression. Love. *Sick*. And he didn't love Eleanor; he didn't even know her any more.

'Alecia, that's ridiculous.'

'Is it?' Alecia cocked her head. 'I know you haven't given any women a chance since that conniving slut back in Boston—'

'Don't.' Jace bit the word off, heard the tension and

anger in his voice. Alecia blinked in surprise. 'I don't want to talk about her.'

'I know how much she hurt you, Jace. Even if you've never wanted to admit it.'

'Don't,' he said again, and barely managed to get the word out. He turned his head, not wanting Alecia to see the naked emotion and pain on his face. Not wanting to feel it himself. He missed her, he knew. He couldn't hide from it. He missed Ellie. *Eleanor*. Since seeing her in New York, he hadn't felt complete or whole or happy.

He *needed* her.

He just didn't want to.

'All right, then,' she said after a moment. 'Let's talk about something else. Papa is going to be seventy next month, and no one's done a thing about it.'

Jace tensed, as he always did when his father was mentioned, but then he made himself relax. 'And what,' he asked Alecia with a bland smile, 'are we supposed to do about it exactly?'

'A party, Jace! I know Elana usually organises such things, but she's busy with her four—Lukas is applying to university this year—and Tabitha is pregnant with her third—'

'Her third?' Jace murmured. 'Already?' He could never keep track of his sisters and their growing brood. Admittedly, he didn't try very hard. He sent expensive presents and occasionally he showed up. For so long he'd felt separate from all of them, with their busy lives and their bands of children. He'd felt so *other*.

Yet now he didn't need to; he'd gone to a fertility specialist as soon as he'd returned to Athens, and the results had come back two weeks ago. He had, the doctor told him, limited fertility. It would still be possible to have a child; it would have been possible ten years ago.

It had been. He thought of the daughter he'd had and never known, and then closed his mind off from the memory-that-wasn't.

He'd avoided thinking about the implications of the doctor's news because it hurt too much. It hurt to realise he had wasted so many years of his life; it hurt even to think how glad his father would be at the news now. His existence would finally be validated. Jace hadn't told him—or anyone—yet. It wasn't as if he were about to run off and make that oh-so needed heir. Unlike his father, he had no desperate urge to create a dynasty. He refused to be defined by either his inability or ability to have children.

'Jace, are you listening to a word I'm saying?' Alecia asked, good-natured impatience edging her voice, and Jace smiled in apology.

'Sorry. Go on. Tabitha's pregnant and Elana's busy.'

'And Kaitrona is hopeless at organising these things, and Parthenope isn't speaking to Papa—'

'Parthenope isn't? Why not?'

Alecia waved a hand in dismissal. 'Oh, who knows? Someone's always in an argument with him. He said something rude to Christos once—'

'Ah.' Christos was Parthenope's husband, a charming city type that his father didn't trust. And, Jace knew well, his father had always been a plain speaker.

You're sterile. You cannot have children. What use is it to me, to have no more Zervas men to follow me? What good are you?

'What about you, then?' he asked, pouring them both more coffee.

'I just started a new job and it has crazy hours,' Alecia replied. 'Which you'd know, if you listened to me for more than five minutes. Honestly, Jace, you're hopeless. Who is she?'

'*She* is no one,' Jace replied, an edge to his voice. 'Don't start assuming things and spreading rumours, Alecia.'

'Who, me?' She blinked innocently. 'Anyway, since none of us can do it, that only leaves one person.'

'Mother?' Jace guessed, and Alecia rolled her eyes.

'You, Jace, you! You can organise a party. I thought we could have it out on that island villa of yours. You hardly ever go there, and it's the most amazing place I've ever seen.'

Jace stilled, his face blanking. Give his father a party? A celebration thrown by the son who had been nothing but a disappointment? Such a party could only be an insult, a mockery, especially considering how strained and distant their relationship had been and still was. 'I don't think that's a good idea, Alecia.'

'I know you and Papa have your differences, Jace, but you're his son—'

'I'm not the right person to do this,' Jace cut her off flatly. He knew his sisters didn't understand the tension between him and his father; Aristo Zervas had wanted to keep his son's infertility—his family's shame—a secret.

'Fine, then hire someone to do it,' Alecia replied. A steely look that Jace knew well had entered her eye. She wasn't going to let go of this.

'Alecia—' He stopped as her suggestion sank in. *Hire someone to do it.* The words echoed in Jace's mind, reverberated in his heart. He felt, bizarrely, as if everything had just slid into place. As if everything suddenly made sense. It was as if he'd been waiting for this opportunity, and now that it had fallen into his lap he knew just what to do. What he wanted to do, what he needed to do.

'So?' Alecia asked, sipping her coffee, her smile turning just a little bit smug. 'What do you think?'

'I think,' Jace said slowly, 'that it's a good idea. And I know just the person to do it.'

ELEANOR PICKED UP another stone, worn silky smooth by the endless tide, and, aiming carefully, threw it into the Long Island Sound. Satisfied, she watched it skip four times before sinking beneath the waves. She heard the crunch of footsteps on the sand behind her.

'You've been doing that for hours.'

Eleanor reached for another stone, offering her mother a quick smile. 'It's therapeutic.'

'You need therapy?'

'I live in New York. Doesn't everyone there need it?'

'Probably.' Her mother sighed and sat down on the hard, cold sand. It was almost April, and, although the trees were starting to bud and daffodils lined the drive up to Heather Langley's beach cottage, the wind and waves were still cold. 'You want to tell me about it?' she asked eventually and Eleanor skipped another stone across the water. She'd arrived at her mother's place last night, and she'd leave tomorrow. They hadn't spoken much beyond pleasantries; her mother knew better than to press.

'Not particularly,' she replied lightly. She knew her mother—and her mother knew her—too well to dissemble or pretend there wasn't anything going on. Yet she didn't trust her mother with the truth.

Their relationship had always been a strained one, marred by ambition and yet marked with moments of intimacy and caring. Still, it wasn't enough to make her want now to unburden her heart and reveal her vulnerabilities.

'Lily says you're doing well at work. Amazing, really.'

'Thanks.' It seemed like the only thing in her life that *was* going right. Since Jace had left, she'd poured herself into work more than ever before. It grated on her nerves that her mother and her boss talked about her, checked up on her. It was ridiculous and even inappropriate, yet Eleanor knew she couldn't tell either of them that. They were best friends, competitors and colleagues until a minor heart attack had forced Heather into early retirement. She'd left her job and the city and taken this cottage out on Long Island. Once in a while she planned someone's beach party in the Hamptons, but her career was essentially finished, and Eleanor thought it was the best thing that had ever happened to her mother—and to their relationship.

She sighed, sinking onto the sand next to her mother, her elbows resting on her knees. 'It's nothing, really. I'm just restless.'

'You've been at Premier Planning for a long time,' Heather said after a moment. 'Maybe you should think about something else.'

Eleanor rounded her eyes in mock horror. 'Give up my job? That's the last thing I'd expect you to say.'

Heather shrugged. 'A job doesn't have to be everything. I know it seemed like it was for me, but—' She stopped, uncertain, and Eleanor smiled to help her out.

'I know.'

Her mother smiled in apology. There was still so much that hadn't been said between them. From her fatherless childhood and her mother's workaholic schedule, to the whole mess of Jace and her pregnancy—an entire language of loss and hurt that neither of them knew how to speak.

'Well,' Heather said finally, 'a sabbatical maybe.'

Eleanor shook her head. 'I'm okay.' She couldn't give up work; it was all she had. Yet she didn't know *what* she wanted to do. Ever since Jace had left New York— ever since he'd kissed her—she'd been feeling restless and edgy and uncertain. Wanting something different. Something more. Maybe even wanting Jace. Yet she wasn't about to abandon her senses or her job for some impossible dream, some distant fantasy that was never meant to be real.

Smiling, she stood up and stretched her hand out to her mother. Heather took it. 'Come on. It's pretty cold out here. I've got one more afternoon before I have to head back to the city, and I fully intend to beat you at Scrabble for once.'

Laughing, Heather let her change the subject. 'I'd like to see you try.'

MONDAY MORNING CAME soon enough, and Eleanor arrived at work a bit weary from her three-hour journey on the Hampton Jitney the night before.

Shelley, the receptionist, rose from her desk as Eleanor entered the office. 'I have your nine o'clock waiting in your office.'

'My nine o'clock?' Eleanor repeated. She'd gone through her schedule that morning while sipping coffee at the sink, and her first appointment was at ten.

'Yes, he said he'd like to wait there.' Shelley, all of twenty-two years old, made a swoony type of face that caused Eleanor a ripple of unease.

'All right,' she murmured, walking down the hallway. Her office door, she saw, was closed. Lily poked her head out of her own office.

'I pencilled him in,' she told Eleanor briskly. 'Apparently he was *very* impressed. Would only have you for this project, and this time there's no rush.'

Eleanor's unease increased to foreboding as she reached for the knob of her door and turned.

'Hello, Eleanor.'

Jace Zervas stood in the centre of her office.

CHAPTER SEVEN

'WHAT ARE YOU doing here?'

Eleanor closed the door quickly behind her before her boss could hear any more of the conversation. Her heart was thudding heavily and her palms felt slick. Even more alarming were the sudden nerves that fluttered through her, making her tingle in—what? Annoyance? Anticipation? *Excitement?*

She sidestepped Jace to move behind her desk, where she felt safer. Slipping off her coat, she felt a flicker of gratitude that she was wearing one of her smarter outfits: a cream silk blouse and a cherry-red pencil skirt, with nails freshly manicured to match. Her hair was pulled up in a sleek twist, and her appearance felt like both her armour and her ammunition. She used it; she hid behind it.

'A party, of course.' He smiled, but Eleanor thought she saw a shadow of something in his eyes—uncertainty? Fear? This was foreign territory for both of them. He'd shed his cashmere trench coat and wore a charcoal-grey suit that matched his eyes perfectly. His silver-grey silk tie emphasised their metallic glints, and Eleanor had trouble tearing her gaze away from him.

'A party?' she repeated, looking down to reshuffle a few random papers on her desk. 'I hardly think I'm an appropriate candidate for—'

'You're the best.'

She looked up. 'I'm not that good.'

Jace took a step closer, one finger to his lips. 'Shh. Don't let Lily hear you.' He smiled, teasingly, and Eleanor felt those wretched nerves flutter through her again, as flighty and feather-brained as the pigeons crowding Central Park, fighting over a few paltry crumbs. 'She's quite a dragon,' Jace continued. 'She was business partners with your mother?' At Eleanor's sharp intake of breath he looked up and smiled. 'We had a little chat while I was waiting for you.'

'I really think it's better, Jace, if someone else organises this party. Anyway, I didn't think you were even coming back to New York.'

'This party's not in New York.'

Eleanor's breath came out in a rush. 'Then I'm certainly not the right person to plan it. Everything I've done is New-York-based—'

'You organised a birthday party in the Hamptons.'

'Still city-based,' Eleanor countered firmly. 'The client lived year-round in Manhattan. Anyway, it's not worth arguing about. I don't care if your party is in Times Square, I don't want to organise it.' Brave words. Brave sentiments. She wished she sounded stronger. Felt surer. In truth she felt horribly uncertain. Half of her wanted to leap at the chance of spending more time with Jace; half of her wanted to run away.

The contradictory nature of her own emotions was ridiculous. And annoying.

'Actually,' Jace said, smiling faintly as he watched her, 'the party is in Greece. It's my father's seventieth birthday party.'

'What?' The word was more of a squawk. Jace's

smile deepened so Eleanor saw his dimple. She wished she didn't. That dimple made him look friendly, approachable. Desirable.

'Have you ever been to Greece?' he asked as he started to stroll round her office, gazing at the rather pedestrian artwork on her walls.

'No,' she replied flatly. 'In fact, I've tried to avoid the whole country.'

'I think you would enjoy it. It's beautiful this time of year. Not too hot.'

'I'd hardly be relaxing,' Eleanor countered, then wished she hadn't. She didn't even want to discuss this. She was not going to Greece.

'Well, I don't want to run you ragged like last time,' Jace replied. 'The party's not for nearly a month.'

'Doesn't matter. I can't organise a party like that from here, and I can hardly go to Greece for a month.'

Jace stopped strolling and turned around to face her. He was smiling, but his face still looked grave. 'Can't you?' he asked softly.

Suddenly the atmosphere in the room changed, a different kind of tension tautening the air between them. Suddenly Jace seemed very close, even though he hadn't moved. Eleanor drew in a deep, shuddery breath.

'Don't, Jace.'

'Don't?' he repeated, the word a question, and Eleanor shook her head. She didn't want to explain. She didn't even know what to explain. She just knew that seeing him again was both a joy and agony, the emotions tangled so closely that she could not separate one from the other, or from herself. She wished he hadn't come, yet she'd been waiting for him to come.

He must have sensed something of her turmoil, for he

took a step closer and said with a little smile, 'A couple of weeks in Greece. Can't you think of worse things?'

A couple of weeks in Greece *with you,* Eleanor amended silently. 'I can't leave my other clients for that long,' she began, trying to stay professional.

'Lily said someone else could take them. Laura or someone?'

Laura. Of course. She'd snagged her clients last time. Eleanor sagged into her chair as she felt the first flickers of defeat. 'You've already spoken to Lily,' she stated flatly and Jace shrugged.

'How could I not?'

She looked up, her eyes wide and meeting his own directly, daring him to be honest. 'Why me?'

'Why not you?' Jace countered quietly.

Eleanor swallowed, her gaze sliding away. 'You know why.'

Jace was silent for a moment, and when he spoke again his voice was light. 'I don't know any other event planners, and I think you're the best for the job.'

He didn't want to talk about the past. Fine, she didn't either, so she'd stick with the present. There was enough trouble with that. '*Me?* How about someone Greek for starters?' Eleanor drew in a breath, ready to launch into a tirade of how she couldn't go with Jace, she couldn't plan his party. She didn't want to. She was afraid to. She *wouldn't*.

'Actually, Eleanor, you'd be doing me a favour,' Jace cut her off, his voice quiet and a little sad. Eleanor closed her mouth with a surprised snap. 'My relationship with my father has never been—what it could be. What it should be.' He glanced away, his expression turning distant, shuttered. 'I'm afraid I've been a disappointment to my father, in many ways,' he confessed in a low voice. 'This party could help in healing our rift.'

This was more than Jace had ever shared with her before. About his life. About himself. She felt as if she'd been given a tiny glimpse into his mind, his heart, and it left her aching and curious and wanting to know more.

She cleared her throat, striving to keep her tone professional. 'I still don't know if I'm the right person for this, Jace...considering.' It occurred to her that perhaps he'd never told his family about her. Perhaps he'd walked right back into life in Greece without a single backward glance or thought at all. Strange—and stupid—that it hurt to think that, even now.

'You'd be helping me out,' Jace told her. 'Although I recognise that might not be a point in my favour.'

Eleanor flushed. 'I don't have some kind of—vendetta,' she told him. 'Really, Jace, the past is forgotten.' It was a lie, but she said it anyway.

'Do you really think so?' Jace queried softly. 'I know I can't forget that easily.'

Eleanor's flush deepened. She didn't know what Jace was talking about, but she knew there were plenty of things she couldn't forget. Like the first time he'd kissed her, after she'd given him a chocolate cupcake she'd baked, so that she couldn't eat chocolate even now without thinking of that wonderful, breathless moment. Like how wonderful it had been to lie in his arms, the sun bathing them in gold. How he was the only person who had ever made her cry with joy.

'I don't know,' she said slowly, yet as the words came out of her mouth she realised she already knew, she'd known from the moment she'd walked in and seen Jace in her office. She might have offered a few paltry protests for form's sake, but in her heart she'd already agreed to go to Greece.

The question she had no intention of answering or even asking herself was *why*. Was it simply pressure from work—Lily would undoubtedly insist she go—or a deeper, more dangerous reason? A reason that had nothing to do with business and all to do with pleasure?

With Jace.

'Two weeks,' Jace told her, his tone turning brisk and reasonable. 'Not that long, but long enough to plan a small family party. And the weather will be fabulous. I'm sure you could use a break.'

Eleanor nodded jerkily and pulled a fresh pad of paper towards her. 'Where exactly is this party going to be?'

She saw triumph gleam in Jace's eyes, turning them silver, and his mouth curled upwards in a smile of victory. 'At my villa. I own a small island in the Cyclades.'

Her head jerked up. 'Your private *island?*'

'It's very small.'

'Sure it is,' Eleanor muttered, and uselessly scribbled 'island' on her notepad. She could hardly believe she was agreeing to this so readily, so easily, and yet she knew how little choice she really had. If Lily wanted Jace's business, and Jace wanted her to plan the party, she was left with very few choices.

But why does he want me to plan the party? And why do I want to go?

Eleanor forced the questions aside and turned to smile with sunny professionalism at Jace. 'Can you give me a few details?'

'I don't think that's necessary,' Jace replied easily. He rose from his chair, and after a second's hesitation

Eleanor rose as well. 'I'm returning to Greece on Friday, and I'd like you to come with me. That should give you enough time to wrap up things here for a bit, and it will also leave enough time on the other end to plan the party.'

'Right,' she replied, her mind spinning. Friday. Greece. *Jace.*

'If you have any questions, don't hesitate to contact me,' Jace continued, matching her best, brisk and professional tone. 'Otherwise, I'll see you Friday morning. I'll send a car to pick you up at your apartment at nine o'clock?'

Eleanor nodded her acceptance, and, with an answering nod, Jace picked up his coat and was gone.

Eleanor sank back into her chair just as Lily poked her head round the door.

'Well?'

'I guess I'm going to Greece.'

'Good.' Lily nodded with smug satisfaction. 'I told him it wouldn't be a problem.' She paused, eyes narrowing. 'You did seem a little reluctant to work with Zervas before, Eleanor, which surprised me. I trust you've got over it?'

Eleanor nodded wearily, too overwhelmed to offer a defence. 'It's fine,' she said, and almost believed it.

THE DAYS BETWEEN Monday and Friday flew by and crept along at the same time. Eleanor immersed herself in work, transferring clients, wrapping up details, and yet it still left her with far too much to think about.

She alternated between wondering if she was making the biggest—or perhaps the second biggest—mistake of her life, and convincing herself that this was nothing more than a business trip. It wasn't like the *biggest* mistake she'd made, which had been to fall in love with Jace Zervas in the first place.

She had no intention of doing that again.

Neither her mother nor Allie were convinced.

'I just don't see why you're going,' Allie said for the third time as they shared a Chinese takeaway in her apartment on Wednesday night. 'Or, more importantly, why he's taking you.' She lowered her chopsticks to regard Eleanor severely. 'Do you think he's interested in you again?'

'No,' Eleanor said firmly. 'It's nothing like that.'

'How can you be so sure? He kissed you, didn't he?'

'Yes, but…' She shook her head, realising she couldn't answer the question. She didn't know why Jace had kissed her. She had no idea why he wanted her to go to Greece. 'We're different people,' she stated, rather uselessly, for Allie just narrowed her eyes.

'Not that different. I just don't want this jerk to hurt you again, Eleanor. That's all.'

'He's not a jerk,' Eleanor whispered. She felt herself flush as Allie stared at her in disbelief. 'At least, not as much of one as I once thought,' she amended, and Allie snorted.

'Well, that's reassuring.'

'I suppose I'm realising that I never really knew him,' Eleanor explained slowly. 'I know we were supposedly infatuated with one another, but Jace never really talked about himself. I only realised that later—when I saw him again, and he said things…' She paused, helpless to explain. 'I never knew he had five sisters. Or he didn't get along with his father. Or—'

'Oh, help,' Allie cut her off, her eyes widening in horror. 'You're in love with him already, aren't you?'

'No!' The word was a yelp. Eleanor scrambled off the sofa and stood there, chest heaving in denial. 'No,' she said more calmly. 'Of course not. But I suppose seeing him again—for real—is important to me. Necessary. I need the closure.'

'But didn't you get that when he apologised?'

She took a breath and let it out slowly. 'Not really. I need to know that I can't fall in love with him again. That there really is nothing between us, and that we're just too different. Too changed.' She sighed, the truth coming to her as she spoke it. 'Then I'll finally be able to move on.' Why did that idea make her feel sad rather than hopeful? Was she *still* fooling herself?

'Maybe,' Allie allowed, her voice laden with doubt. 'What if you find out you can fall in love with him, Eleanor? What if you *do?*'

That was another question Eleanor couldn't answer, and didn't even dare ask.

Her mother was just as doubtful of the wisdom of Eleanor's decision, but they didn't discuss love or anything close to it. They never had.

'I wouldn't get within a hundred feet of that man,' Heather said darkly when Eleanor called her to tell her she'd be out of town, 'but if it really is just business…'

'Of course it is.' She sounded far more certain than she felt.

'I'm sure you know what you're doing,' Heather said briskly. 'And in any case, it's wonderful that Lily thinks so highly of you.'

Eleanor didn't want to argue that it was actually Jace—and his money—that Lily thought highly of. She was too tired and she had too much to do to argue the semantics. 'I'll talk to you when I get back,' she said, and after exchanging a few more pleasantries she hung up the phone.

Surveying the mess of her bedroom, the contents of her wardrobe spilled across her bed, she wondered just what to pack—and what to wear when she saw Jace tomorrow.

She settled on a pair of tailored tan trousers and a petal-pink cashmere sweater set that would have made her feel like a granny save for its hugging fit. Paired with a pair of kitten-heeled open-toed sandals, they made her feel professional and just a little bit sexy, which gave her confidence a needed boost as she waited in her building's lobby for the car Jace had sent.

The limo came promptly at nine. As the driver opened the door and Eleanor slid into the car's luxurious interior, Eleanor felt a flicker of disappointment that it was empty. Jace wasn't there.

'Mr Zervas will meet you at the airport,' the driver told her as he pulled away from the kerb. Eleanor did not reply, although she wondered what kept Jace in the city so that he couldn't share the journey to the airport with her. Not, she told herself sternly, that it mattered. Determined to focus on business—which was what this whole trip *was*—she reached for a file folder and began jotting down preliminary ideas for the party.

This activity kept her busy all the way to the airport, mainly because she wanted it to. She didn't want or need time to think, to question just why the *hell* she'd agreed to come to Greece with Jace, on the pretext of some party. She'd told her mother it was business; she'd told Allie more of the truth—that she needed closure.

Yet the nerves exploding inside her, her clammy hands and growing panic all made Eleanor realise that there might be more to it than that. A lot more.

She clamped down on the train of thought before it could go anywhere, and as they arrived at the terminal she gratefully slid out of the car as the driver opened the door.

'Hello, Eleanor.'

Nearly yelping in surprise, Eleanor looked up to see Jace smiling at her. He was dressed, as she'd nearly always seen him dressed, for business, and he looked, as he always did, magnificent. Eleanor swallowed rather dryly.

'I thought you'd be late,' she said, trying not to sound flustered. 'Since you didn't come in the limo—'

'I didn't have time to drive to your apartment in Chelsea,' Jace explained, 'so I grabbed a cab. I hope it didn't inconvenience you?'

How could a limo to her front door inconvenience her? Eleanor wondered. Or was Jace obliquely referring to the fact that she'd been disappointed? How did he *know?* 'No, of course not,' she said briskly, and Jace touched her elbow to guide her inside.

They bypassed the endless queues at the ticket counters for a discreet security checkpoint for private airline passengers.

'We're travelling on your private jet?' Eleanor practically squeaked when she realised this. 'To your private island?'

'I like my privacy.' Jace smiled, a flash of white. 'And I confess I find it more convenient. No need to book tickets or schedule flights, or be at the mercy of an airline and its asinine whims.'

The security guard waved them through, and easily, naturally, Jace put his arm around Eleanor's shoulders as he shepherded her towards the boarding area. 'Come.'

Moments later they were boarding a small, sleek, and utterly luxurious aeroplane. Eleanor took in the leather sofas and teakwood coffee tables with a sense of disbelief. She'd experienced her fair share of first class service as an event planner, yet in those cases she was arranging the luxury for her clients; *she* was the service. Here she was the one being served, and it felt amazing.

'Stretch out,' Jace said with a smile as she sat on one of the sofas. 'Enjoy yourself.'

Eleanor smiled a bit uncertainly. She was torn between enjoying herself—which this jet cried out for her to do—and keeping things businesslike. Professional. Safe.

'There will be plenty of time to plan the party later,' Jace told her with a little smile, making Eleanor wonder yet again how he knew her so well.

Because, she reminded herself as reached for the seat buckle, he didn't know her well. At all. He hadn't known her well enough ten years ago to trust her with the truth, and he certainly didn't know her now.

Moodily she stared out of the window as the plane began to taxi down the runway. Within minutes they were lifting off, leaving the dank grey March skies for the vast blue above.

One of Jace's staff came to offer drinks, and Eleanor accepted a glass of orange juice. She took a sip and set it down, too restless and uneasy to drink more. She fidgeted with the clasp on her seat belt, crossed and recrossed her legs, and stared blindly out at the endless blue sky.

'You can undo your seat belt now if you like,' Jace said, and Eleanor jerked her head around. He sat stretched out on the sofa opposite her.

'Oh, yes,' she mumbled, flicking again at the clasp. 'All right.' She undid the belt and stretched her legs out, feeling as if she were participating in a charade. She didn't feel remotely relaxed, and she doubted she was giving a good impression of it either.

'Why are you so tense, Eleanor?' Jace asked. 'You look drawn tighter than a bow.'

'I feel tense,' Eleanor admitted. 'And why shouldn't I be?' she added with a note of challenge. 'I don't even know why I'm here.'

Something dark—a shadow of pain, or perhaps even uncertainty—flickered in Jace's eyes. 'To plan my father's birthday party.'

'I know, but—' Eleanor let out a long, exasperated breath. 'I don't understand why you chose me to plan this party. It makes no sense. Someone local, with Greek contacts, would have been—'

'I didn't want someone local,' Jace cut across her quietly. 'Even if it made sense.'

His words sounded like a confession, and they created a sudden awareness in the air; it crackled like a current between them. 'Well, you should have,' Eleanor replied robustly in a desperate bid to ignore the current that practically pulled her out of her seat towards Jace.

Could she *ever* resist him?

'I didn't want someone local,' Jace repeated softly. 'I wanted you.'

Eleanor felt as if all the breath had been robbed from her body; her mind spun emptily and her chest hurt. She stared at Jace, pulled by the magnetic silver of his eyes, the faint smile curling his mouth—how she remembered that mouth, how it felt, how it tasted—

Don't. Don't remember, don't want—

Somehow she managed to draw a breath in, and the desperate dizziness receded. She reached for her orange juice and took a much-needed sip. 'Don't, Jace.'

'And,' Jace continued, leaning forward, 'you want me.'

'What?' The word was a yelp, a squeal, and it didn't hold the disdain Eleanor wanted it to, nor even the outrage. She sounded like a kicked puppy. She drew herself up, replacing her juice on the table with a decisive clink. 'Don't do this, Jace.'

'I didn't want to,' Jace replied. His voice was low even though his smile remained wry, light. 'Why do you think you didn't hear from me for three months? I've been trying to forget you, Eleanor, and the damnable truth is I can't.'

He almost sounded annoyed, and that made Eleanor smile faintly. She knew just how he felt. Then reality came crashing in. 'Is that why you hired me, Jace? To—to—have some kind of—' She sputtered uselessly, unable to say the word. *Affair*.

Meaningless. Sordid.

What else could he possibly want?

'I'm talking about more than just physical attraction,' Jace said, his voice soft and yet steely, and Eleanor stiffened.

What could he possibly mean? And why did his words terrify her so much? She couldn't untangle the sudden fierce emotion within her: surprise, alarm, fear, *hope*.

'What do you mean?' she asked. She tried to sound

dismissive but came off as demanding instead. She *wanted* to know, yet she was still afraid to hear his answer.

Jace didn't reply for a long moment. He looked pensive, guarded, as if he were hiding his heart as much as she was. 'I'm not sure.'

Eleanor sank back against the soft leather cushions. 'Okay...'

'I don't know what can be between us,' Jace continued. His tone was matter-of-fact, almost flat, yet his words raced right to Eleanor's nerve endings and made her whole self tingle with both longing and fear. 'All I know is I haven't been able to put you from my mind these last three months.' He turned back to her, his expression hard and determined. 'I said goodbye to you in New York, Eleanor, and I meant it. I wanted to walk away. God knows it's easier.'

Eleanor couldn't speak. Her throat was too tight, so she just nodded—jerkily—instead. It *was* easier. Or at least it was supposed to be.

'But it hasn't been easier,' Jace continued, his voice roughening with emotion. 'It's been hell. And so I decided to invite you to Greece—and forget the party, frankly—because I want to figure out what this is between us, and the only way I know of doing that is seeing you. Being with you. Knowing you, this new you, and you knowing me. And whatever *this* is, maybe it will go somewhere, and maybe it won't.' He let out a short, sharp laugh that ended on a ragged sigh. 'That's quite an appealing proposition, isn't it?' He shook his head and glanced away, rubbing his jaw with one hand. 'I must be crazy.'

Eleanor blinked and swallowed, trying to ease the

tightness in her throat. She'd expected Jace to offer her some kind of smooth suggestion of seduction; if she was honest, yes, she'd expected it from the beginning, no matter what she'd managed to convince herself about this trip being business.

But this? This was real. Honesty. Vulnerability. It sent her spinning into a void of unknowing, uncertainty, because she couldn't scoff or sneer or pretend. Jace had been honest, and he deserved an honest answer. 'No,' she finally managed, her voice scratchy, 'you're not.' Jace turned to look at her sharply, and Eleanor smiled weakly. 'Crazy, that is.'

A corner of his mouth quirked up, although his gaze remained intently, intensely fastened on hers, filled with a wary hope she both felt and understood. 'I'm not?'

She shook her head. She didn't trust herself to say anything; she didn't even know what she would say, or what she felt. Like Jace, she knew there was still something between them. She just didn't know what it was. A remnant of their youthful infatuation? Or something new? And if it was something new, it was far too tender and fragile to test it, to trust it.

She had no idea what to do, and the thought of spending two weeks in Jace's company—with him—frightened and exhilarated her more than anything ever had before. She'd been nervous before; now she was terrified.

Thankfully Jace must have sensed this, or maybe he was feeling it himself, for he leaned forward to touch her hand—lightly, so lightly—and, smiling, said, 'It's a long flight, and you look exhausted. You should get some rest.'

Eleanor nodded, grateful for the escape sleep would provide…if only she could will it to come.

JACE WATCHED ELEANOR out of the corner of his eye as she shifted and fidgeted on the sofa, trying to get comfortable. Her eyes were closed, clenched shut really, and she didn't look remotely relaxed.

Yet why should she be? He certainly wasn't. Jace stared down at the papers he'd spread out on his table tray, notes on the latest business meeting regarding an acquisition of a plastics company in Germany. Important information, yet he couldn't process a single detail. His mind was spinning from what he'd just told Eleanor…hell, what he'd just told himself. He'd never intended to say any of that. He'd never meant even to think it.

He still didn't know what it meant, what it could mean for the next few weeks, or even longer than that— who knew how long? What was he thinking? Wanting? He'd known he wanted—needed, even—to see Eleanor again, to get her out of his system, or maybe back into it… He didn't know which, didn't know which he even wanted. He felt as if the course he'd set for himself, the life he'd planned on, had been shipwrecked and he were left tossed on a sea of new possibilities…possibilities that were bewildering and strange and perhaps unwelcome. Perhaps exciting. He didn't know what he wanted any more, what shape he hoped his life would take.

Annoyed with himself, Jace let out a frustrated breath and turned determinedly back to his papers. Enough wondering. Enough thinking. Eleanor was here with him, and he would be satisfied with that for now.

CHAPTER EIGHT

SHE MUST HAVE dozed, for when Eleanor woke up, blinking groggily, she could tell some time had passed. How much she had no idea, but Jace was no longer sitting next to her, and her hair, when she patted it experimentally, was sticking up in several different directions.

Great. So much for her poised, polished, *professional* appearance. Yet hadn't that been a charade anyway?

I want to figure out what this is between us, and the only way I know of doing that is seeing you. Being with you.

Jace's words echoed through Eleanor's mind, still surprising her with their honesty. Her reaction, fizzing with excitement and uncertainty, surprised her too. She'd been so careful to be professional with Jace, and her ever-captive heart had betrayed her. She still wanted him. Maybe she even loved him. Yet how could you love someone you didn't even know, weren't sure you ever really knew? And if she didn't love him, then this whole thing was nothing but immature infatuation, and she needed to get it out of her system. Return to New York a freed woman. Maybe that was what Jace wanted as well. Freedom, not love.

'You're awake.'

Eleanor turned around in her seat to see Jace standing in the aisle. He'd exchanged his business suit for a casual polo shirt and khakis, and he looked wonderful. Relaxed and confident and approachable, like the old Jace. Not the harsh, hardened, businessman she'd already become accustomed to.

'Sorry to conk out like that. How long did I sleep?'

'Nearly four hours. We'll be there in another couple of hours. Do you want something to eat?'

In answer Eleanor's stomach rumbled audibly, and Jace grinned. 'I remember how loudly your stomach growls when you're hungry. I always knew it was feeding time.'

'I am hungry,' Eleanor admitted. It still made her feel uneasy—vulnerable—for Jace to recall those sweet, forbidden memories. Little things, silly things, and yet so achingly precious.

Jace raised a hand, and within seconds a staff member arrived with a tray of food. Eleanor took in the fresh fruit, the plates of salad and sandwiches, and realised she wasn't just hungry, she was starving.

'Dig in,' Jace said, and she did.

'So where exactly are we going?' Eleanor asked after she'd finished most of her sandwich and salad. She toyed with a bit of pineapple on her plate, shredding the succulent fruit with the tines of her fork.

'My island. It's near Naxos. Like I said, very small.'

Eleanor looked up, her eyes narrowing speculatively. 'How small?'

Jace waved a hand in dismissal. 'A couple of kilometers, no more.'

'And there's nothing on it but your villa?'

'A few staff houses, an airstrip.'

'Really.' She let out a reluctant laugh. 'I always knew

you were rich, but I didn't know you were *Fantasy-Island*-type rich.'

Jace arched his eyebrows. 'What does that mean exactly?'

'Private jet, private island.' Eleanor shrugged. 'It's like a soap opera.'

'They are conveniences as well as luxuries. And I have worked hard to earn them, I must admit.'

'You have?' Why did this surprise her? She supposed it was because after Jace had left, she'd painted him in her mind as the spoiled son of a shipping magnate. It was easier to accept his abandonment that way. Over the years she'd embroidered that image, yet now she realised—of course—that might not be who Jace was—or ever had been—at all.

She really didn't know him.

She popped the piece of pineapple in her mouth. 'So what did you do to earn it?'

'Investments. Financial management.'

'I thought your father was in shipping.'

'He is. But I did not go into my father's business.' A new, steely note had entered Jace's voice although his posture and expression were both still easy and relaxed. 'He wanted a dynasty, and neither of us believed that to be a possibility.'

Eleanor straightened in her seat. She cleared her throat, wanting to ask the question that remained unspoken between them yet knowing there was so much more to Jace's alleged infertility than the condition itself; years of heartache and family strife seemed to accompany it. 'Did you…get tested again?' she finally asked. Jace's expression didn't change. 'For fertility?'

'Yes.' He gave a little shrug, as though the matter

was of no consequence. Perhaps it wasn't. 'I have limited fertility, the doctor says.'

Eleanor's heart twisted, a little wrench she should have long become used to when the topic turned to children. 'That's pretty good, isn't it?' It was possibility, hope. More than she would ever have. Limited was better than nothing.

Jace shrugged again. 'Whether or not I can have children has not been a pressing issue for me as of late.' The news should have reassured her, especially considering her own situation, yet somehow it just made her sad. So much lost. So much gone…for both of them.

Jace gave her the ghost of a smile, no more than a shadow passing across his face. 'Apparently, after childhood mumps, limited fertility can return in later years.' He shook his head and laughed softly, although the sound held little humour. 'Amazing, a simple Internet search could have saved us both so much heartache.'

'I don't know about that,' Eleanor said, and Jace stilled, his expression becoming alert and a little wary.

'What do you mean, Eleanor?'

She shrugged. 'Even if you knew the baby was yours, Jace, would you have stayed?' The question seemed to drop into the stillness, tautening the very air between them.

Jace tensed, and Eleanor saw in the steely silver glint in his eyes, the thinning of his mouth, that he was angry. She'd made him angry with her question. 'Of course I would have. I would never walk away from my own child.'

She didn't want to have this fight. She didn't want to feel this hurt. Shrugging again, Eleanor turned to look out of the window, sunlight shimmering on the faint wisps of cloud. 'You didn't trust me enough to give me a chance to trust you,' she said quietly. 'No matter what might be between us now, Jace, there will always be that.'

'Then you can't forgive?'

'I'm not saying that. I'm just saying that we've never had a chance to trust each other.' She turned back to look at him directly, compelled to honesty even though she'd wanted to avoid this conversation. 'It's not something that ever comes easily, and it certainly won't now, with our history.' *Not,* she added silently, *when I'm scared to trust you. To love you.*

Jace was silent for a long moment, and Eleanor waited and watched. It was only when he spoke again that she realised she'd been holding her breath. 'Then I suppose we'll just have to see what happens,' he finally said, a faint smile curving his lips even though his eyes looked shadowed and sad. 'And what we allow to happen.'

They steered clear of such intense topics for the rest of the flight, chatting about the weather and films and other innocuous things, until Jace excused himself to finish his work before they landed on Naxos to transfer to a smaller plane that would take them on the short flight to his island.

Eleanor didn't bother to pretend to work; her nerves were leaping and jumping inside her too much to make sense of anything. She felt an unsettling mix of anticipation and alarm. The sun had set and the sky was a deep and endless black, the pinpoints of a million stars reflected in the sea below. As the island came into view, Eleanor saw the lights of Naxos's main village shimmer along the harbour.

The plane taxied to a stop and Eleanor reached for her things. Jace shepherded her out of the plane, and she barely had a chance to view the huddled whitewashed buildings of Naxos in the distance as she walked across the tarmac to a much smaller plane.

The flight to Jace's island took all of ten minutes, and when the plane landed there were no friendly village lights to welcome them. The island was dark, lost on a sea of night, and despite the balmy air Eleanor couldn't quite keep from shivering.

She tilted her head up to take in the endless sky, spangled with stars. 'I don't think I've ever seen so many stars.'

'I don't think you can see a single star in New York,' Jace agreed. 'Come. My staff will see to our bags.'

Eleanor followed him into an open-topped Jeep. She was conscious of so many things: the emptiness all around them of sea and sky, the deep darkness of the night, and the fact that, despite the discreet staff moving their luggage into another waiting Jeep, she felt as if they were the only two people left on earth.

Jace started the Jeep, flicking on the headlights, which barely pierced the darkness, unrelieved by the flicker of a single street lamp or house light. They were alone. On an island. In the middle of the sea.

Eleanor swallowed and glanced sideways at Jace. As she did she became conscious of yet another thing: how different he was here, in his casual clothes, navigating the rocky, rutted road that skirted the sea as it wound round an outcropping of rock. Here he wasn't the college student or the businessman; he was someone else entirely.

She wondered just who that was.

'It's after eleven o'clock at night,' Jace told her, 'but it's still early in East Coast time. Would you like something to eat?'

'Maybe,' Eleanor allowed. She felt tired and yet inexorably, impossibly alive, thrilled and alarmed and wary of all these new sights, sounds, and changes. 'Something small would be nice,' she decided, and Jace flashed her a quick smile.

'I'll have my cook prepare something. You can freshen up and change if you like. The luggage is right behind us.'

Jace drove the Jeep around another curve and the villa came into view: a huge, sprawling whitewashed structure, every window and doorframe spilling a riot of bougainvillea, lights glimmering from inside. Jace killed the engine on the Jeep and turned to Eleanor.

'Welcome.'

A smiling, red-cheeked woman with her hair caught up in a headscarf met them on the doorstep.

She spoke rapidly in Greek, and Jace nodded and smiled his approval. Then, in halting English, she spoke to Eleanor. 'Welcome, Miss Langley. We are happy to see you here.'

'Thank you,' Eleanor murmured. Jace touched her shoulder.

'This is Agathe. She takes care of just about everything for me.' He smiled again at Agathe and then Eleanor followed her upstairs.

Agathe led her to a spacious suite of rooms overlooking the gardens at the back of the villa, bathed in moonlight; Eleanor could only make out the twisted trunks of olive trees and the glint of the sea at their edge.

Her luggage arrived moments later, and she took the

opportunity to change her clothes and wash her face. Even though it was now nearing midnight, she felt energised and awake and alive.

Agathe had gone to see to their dinner preparations, and, dressed in a pair of cotton capris and a loose, flowing top in pale green, Eleanor stepped out to explore the villa…and to find Jace.

The air was dry and smelled faintly of lavender and thyme; through the open windows Eleanor could hear the gentle shooshing of the waves on the sand. She walked down the tiled hallway to the front stairs, her hand skimming the wrought-iron bannister. The foyer below was empty, and once downstairs she peeked into a large, comfortable-looking living room and a dining room with a table that looked to seat at least twenty. Both were dark and empty.

She wandered towards the back of the house, drawn by the light spilling from an open doorway and the tempting aroma of lemon and garlic.

She stepped into the kitchen to see Agathe busy at the stove, and, to her surprise, Jace setting the table in the alcove that overlooked the water. He'd changed as well, and showered if the damp hair curling at his nape were anything to go by. Eleanor swallowed. He looked wonderful.

Jace glanced up as she stood in the doorway, and smiled easily. 'Come in! Agathe has made a feast, as always.'

Agathe protested even as she placed dish upon dish on the table. Eleanor took in the Greek salad bursting with plump tomatoes and cucumber, a thick wedge of feta cheese resting on top, and the freshly grilled souvlaki, still on its skewer. There was a lentil soup garnished with olives and crusty bread, and several traditional Greek dips to accompany it.

'I can never eat all this,' Eleanor produced, laughing a little.

'You must try,' Jace replied as he pulled out her chair. 'After all, food is love.'

Love. Eleanor swallowed again. That was a word they'd never talked about, not ten years ago and certainly not now. Oh, she'd thought it plenty of times; she'd certainly believed it before Jace had walked away. Yet now just the idea of love—the mere mention of it— made her palms slick and nerves flutter from her belly to her throat.

'Thank you for this, Agathe.'

Agathe made more protesting noises before discreetly disappearing into another room. A candle flickered on the table between them, and the room was silent save for the sound of the sea coming from the open window.

'This is lovely,' Eleanor said. 'Thank you.'

Jace gave a little shrug. 'I'm afraid I'm spoiled by Agathe. She was my childhood nurse growing up, and I employed her here when she had no more charges at my family home.'

'She loves you very much.' The words popped out inadvertently, even though Eleanor didn't want to mention that dreaded L-word. Jace just smiled and spooned some tzatziki onto her plate.

'She is a good woman.'

Eleanor took a spoonful of the hearty bean soup; it was delicious. 'So do you live here most of the year?'

'When I can. I have a flat in Athens for business, but this is really my home. Or at least my escape. I've had to travel so much for work, I don't know if I could call any place my home.'

'Those corporate takeovers,' Eleanor murmured. She took another sip of soup. 'What's the real story behind you taking over Atrikides Holdings?'

Jace looked up, surprised. 'The real story?'

'I don't think it was the heartless takeover you made it out to be.'

'I try not to have any takeover be heartless.'

Eleanor raised her eyebrows. 'I had no idea you were so sensitive.'

Jace only looked amused. 'Sensitive? No. It's simply good business. Unhappy workers are never very productive.' He gave her the glimmer of a smile. 'I don't like to lose money.'

'Ah.' She reached for a piece of bread. 'And Atrikides?'

Jace shrugged. 'It was a favour to Leandro. His son was embezzling from him and he didn't have the strength to deal with it himself. He's an old man, and he doesn't have much longer to live.'

'So it was a mercy mission.'

Jace just shrugged again, and Eleanor glanced down at her plate. 'There's so much I don't know about you.'

A tiny, telling hesitation. 'Then ask.'

She didn't know what questions to ask. Where to begin. She didn't even know enough for that. 'Were you always interested in finance?' she finally asked. 'Starting your own company?'

'Yes,' Jace answered, then added, 'but it became more important to me.'

'When?'

He paused. 'Ten years ago.'

Eleanor nodded slowly in acceptance. Ten years ago.

Of course. The same time her work had become more important to her; it had filled the empty spaces in her heart, her womb. Jace, in his own way, had suffered a similar loss.

'Well,' Jace said when she didn't reply, 'if you won't ask questions, I will. What made you decide to become an event planner?'

'I needed to do something, and my mother suggested the internship. Premier Planning was her company before she retired.'

'So you're the boss's daughter?'

Eleanor shrugged. 'She certainly didn't give me any handouts. I had to apply for the internship like anyone else, and work my way up.'

'And what about your degree in restaurant management?'

Eleanor gave him a small smile even though his question—his ignorance—hurt. 'I never finished my degree.'

'You didn't? Why not?'

She shook her head, exasperated now. Jet lag must have caught up with her, for she suddenly felt unbearably weary. 'I was pregnant, and I intended to keep the baby. I dropped out.'

Jace looked startled, a streak of something like pain flashing in his eyes, and Eleanor knew he was realising how much he didn't know. Didn't understand. Just as she felt with him. They really did need to begin all over again—if they could.

'But after?' he persisted after a moment. 'Couldn't you have gone back?'

'I didn't want to,' Eleanor said flatly. 'Everything had changed.' She didn't want to talk about it with Jace, even though at least part of her acknowledged they would have to talk about it some time…if they wanted to have any hope of—anything—in the future. 'My turn for questions,' she said. 'What's your favourite colour?'

Jace looked startled again, but then his face relaxed in an easy smile and Eleanor knew he was as glad as she was for a safer topic of conversation. 'Purple.'

'No way.'

He arched an eyebrow. 'What? Not manly enough?'

Eleanor let out a reluctant laugh. 'There's no way purple is your favourite colour. I may not know you that well, but I know that.'

He sighed in mock defeat. 'All right, you win. It's blue.'

'Light blue or dark blue?'

'Dark. And you?'

'Orange.'

'Really?'

Eleanor smiled. 'Yes, but I picked it as my favourite colour in first grade because no one else liked it. I guess I wanted to be different.'

'You always were stubborn.'

'Determined, I call it.' Sometimes it had been the only thing that had kept her going. Another wave of fatigue crashed over her and she pushed her plate away. 'This was delicious, but I think the flight is finally catching up with me. I'm about to fall asleep in my chair.'

'Then we'd better get you to bed.'

His words, given with such lazy amusement, made awareness race through Eleanor's veins so she suddenly felt rather unbearably awake. She stood up awkwardly. 'Thank you for the meal—'

'Let me show you to your room.'

'I remember—'

'I'm a gentleman.'

Wordlessly Eleanor let him lead her from the kitchen. Her heart had begun thudding hard against her chest, and she wondered what might happen. What she wanted to happen.

Upstairs the hallway was dark, lit only by a wash of moonlight from the windows at its end. Jace led her to her door and she placed her hand on its knob, turning around so her back was pressed against the wood. 'Thank you…' The word ended in a whisper of breath for Jace was close. Very close. And she had a feeling he was going to kiss her.

She wanted him to kiss her.

He smiled at her and brushed a strand of hair away from her face, tucking it behind her ear so his thumb skimmed her cheek. Eleanor closed her eyes. The moment before his lips brushed hers seemed endless, agonising, because she wasn't sure he was even going to do it and she didn't want to open her eyes to find out.

Finally, *finally* his lips touched hers in a feather-light kiss that seemed to be more of a promise than a possession, because before Eleanor could part her lips or respond in any way—it was so sweet—he had stepped away.

Her eyes flew open and she stared at him. He gazed back at her with a rueful, almost sad smile. 'Goodnight, Eleanor.'

Before she could respond—or even think—he was already disappearing down the hallway, lost in the shadows.

Jace strode out of the villa, frustration and fury and even fear all warring within him. What had he done? And why had he done it?

He made his way down the track to the beach, awash in silver in the moonlight. A few metres away the waves crashed blackly onto the shore. Jace yanked his shirt over his head and kicked his trousers off and then, with one deep breath, he dived into the surf.

The water was cold—it was still early spring—and it made his head ache as he swam through the waves, breaking to the surface only when his lungs hurt and his head pounded.

He treaded water as he gazed up at the ink-black sky scattered with stars and wondered just why he'd brought Eleanor to Greece.

It had seemed like such a good idea when he'd spoken to Alecia. It had made sense when he'd flown to New York on the pretence of needing to visit Atrikides Holdings, which was managing just fine under Leandro's nephew. He'd justified it to himself because he'd needed to see her, because his body was hungry and his soul restless knowing she was there, knowing she'd never lied to him, thinking that maybe there could have been something between them all these years. Maybe there still could be.

Yet what he hadn't counted on was how risky it was. Eleanor wasn't interested in an emotionless affair. He'd *known* that, and yet he'd still brought her here as if they could have something else. Something more. As if he wanted that, which, God help him, maybe he did.

Even though he'd determined for ten years—and longer than that, *for ever*—never to lose his heart to anyone. Never to even have a heart to lose.

Jace cursed out loud, to the sky, the words lost in the rush of the waves. His body ached with fatigue and cold and, after another second of useless treading water— going nowhere—he headed back towards the shore.

Everything had changed when he'd kissed Eleanor— such a nothing little kiss, barely a brush of their lips. Yet in that fragile moment he'd realised just what he'd done by bringing Eleanor here. Not only had he opened himself up to possible pain and loss, but he'd exposed Eleanor to it as well. He could hurt her. Again.

Back on the beach Jace towelled himself off with his shirt and then sat on the cold, hard sand to dry off. He wasn't ready to go back into the villa, to a lonely bed just two doors from where Eleanor slept. Or maybe she wasn't sleeping. Maybe she was tossing restlessly just as he surely would, letting the memories wash over her like the surf over the sand.

The first time they'd kissed. He'd been determined to kiss her, and she'd been skittish and nervous, flitting around her apartment, plying him with cupcakes. He'd eaten them, laughing as he did so, because they'd both known what was better than any dessert. That first kiss had been so, so sweet; it had been innocence and longing entangled together.

The first time they'd made love, one Saturday afternoon, the room mellow with sunlight. He'd traced circles on her skin with his fingers and lips and she'd laughed and told him she was ticklish.

Ticklish! He'd been a little offended, because he'd been so breathless and aching with desire, and he'd set upon a course of making her want him as much as he wanted her.

He'd succeeded admirably.

But it hadn't been just sex. She'd opened up such a life to him, a sweet, simple life, and he'd let himself fall, had willingly entered into the dream she shared of a bakery and bookshop, let it all wash over him and pull him into a fantasy world that he'd never thought to inhabit because it was all so far from his life, from his father. With Eleanor he hadn't been a useless failure. He hadn't had his shortcomings tossed back at him again and again.

With Eleanor he'd just been himself. And yet he'd still run. Jace shook his head, the memories both hurting and humiliating him.

Even if you knew the baby was yours, Jace, would you have stayed?

The question, and the fact that Eleanor could ask it, damned him. And even now Jace was shamed by her lack of trust in him. Yet why should she trust him? He hadn't proved himself or his trustworthiness in any way. He'd only failed.

And he was afraid of failing again—failing Eleanor, failing himself—by opening this Pandora's box of possibility between them.

Staying away would have been easier. Safer. He just wished he'd had the strength to do it.

Suppressing a shiver as a chilly wind blew off the water, Jace slung his damp shirt around his neck and headed back to the villa, now no more than a darkened hulk under the sky. Inside all was quiet, the only sound the whisper of the waves. Jace peeled off his damp clothes and fell into bed naked, clenching his eyes shut as if he could keep the doubts from assailing him, the memories from claiming him.

Yet as he finally drifted off to sleep he could see Eleanor as she once was, relaxed and laughing as she held out a chocolate cupcake, and he heard her laughter as she tempted him to taste it.

He woke up craving chocolate. Craving Eleanor.

CHAPTER NINE

ELEANOR WOKE UP to the distant, mournful clanging of bells. She scrambled from her bed and peeked out the window; the sun was already high in the sky, glinting off the water, and on a rocky hill in the distance she saw the source of the sound: goats. The bells around their necks clanged and clanked as a boy shepherded them out of sight.

She quickly showered and dressed, slipping into a pair of tailored black trousers and a crisp white button-down shirt. Work clothes. Armour. After Jace's barely there kiss last night, she needed it. She felt entirely too fragile, too fearful.

Further armed with a pad of paper and the notes she'd taken earlier, she came downstairs to the kitchen, where Agathe was setting out breakfast.

'Dinner last night was delicious,' Eleanor said, wishing she spoke Greek. Agathe smiled widely, clearly understanding enough.

She waved towards the table. 'Eat. Eat.'

Eleanor sat down and, still smiling, Agathe poured her a cup of thick Greek coffee. Eleanor helped herself to yogurt, honey, and fresh slices of melon. 'Do you know where Jace is?' she asked hesitantly, and Agathe shrugged, spreading her hands. It took her a moment to finally find the word, but when she did, it caused double shafts of disappointment and relief to slice through Eleanor.

'Work. He work.'

'Ah. Right.' Nodding her thanks, Eleanor took a sip of the coffee. That was good, she decided. Jace was working, and so would she. That was why they were here, after all. To work.

Except yesterday, on the plane, Jace had told her to forget the party. The real reason she was here was because he wanted her to be. And *she* wanted to be, which was why she had agreed in the first place. God only knew what could happen, what they would allow to happen, as Jace had said yesterday.

Moodily Eleanor speared a slice of melon. If she were a less cautious person, she'd seize this opportunity with both hands and a lot more besides. She'd let herself enjoy Greece—enjoy *Jace*—and just see what happened. Such an easy thing to do. Just *see*.

Yet she wasn't that kind of person, although perhaps she once had been. Now she was careful and cautious and kept everything close, especially her emotions. Most definitely her heart. There was nothing easy about *just seeing* at all. It was impossibly difficult, incredibly dangerous, and she wasn't sure she could do it at all. She wasn't even sure she wanted to, despite the nameless longing that swelled up inside her, spilling out.

After breakfast, since Jace had not put in an appearance, Eleanor decided to explore the villa. She'd get a sense of what would work for the party, and present Jace with some kind of initial plan. She'd need to ask him about services too; Agathe certainly couldn't do all the cooking, and supplies would have to be either flown or ferried in.

Hugging her clipboard to her chest, Eleanor strolled through the villa's front rooms that she'd glimpsed last night. Both were spacious and comfortable, the scattered sofas and rugs giving a sense of casual elegance. They'd certainly suit for a party, but as she left them for the wraparound terrace, she decided the party should be held outside.

The air was dry and fragrant, the sun warm on her face, the sea shimmering with its light. Terracotta pots of trailing bougainvillea and herbs lined the terrace and in the distance Eleanor could still hear the goats' bells clanging. She stood for a moment on the terrace, lifting her face to the sun, and let herself simply enjoy the day.

'There you are.'

Slowly Eleanor opened her eyes. She turned around to see Jace standing in the double doors that led to the kitchen.

'Do you have *goats* on this island?'

Surprised, he raised his eyebrows. 'As a matter of fact I do.'

'Why?'

'You don't like goats?'

Eleanor suppressed a smile. 'I don't really have an opinion of them, actually.'

'Well, I find them very calming,' Jace replied, straight-faced, 'as well as incredibly cute.'

She'd forgotten what a silly sense of humour he had, how much he'd made her laugh, helplessly, holding her sides. How *happy* he'd made her feel. Now a reluctant bubble burst through her lips and she shook her head, smiling.

'Seriously.'

'We have to be serious?' Jace's face fell comically.

'Very well. When I bought this island, it was inhabited by a single farmer. He'd lived here all his life, was ferrying his poor goats and their milk and cheese to Naxos. I let him stay and he supplies the villa more than adequately.'

'And when you aren't here?'

'He uses my motorboat. He had a leaky rowboat that looked likely to capsize in a breath of wind, and he'd put a goat in it. The poor animal was terrified.'

Eleanor shook her head, not sure if she should believe him. He looked utterly sincere, yet she saw laughter lurking in his eyes, glinting in their depths, and it made her smile again, from the heart. 'Why would he take his goat to Naxos? I thought you said he sold the milk and cheese.'

'The creature was sick.' Jace took her arm, his fingers warm on her skin. 'Terribly so. Really quite nasty. You don't want to get too close to a sick goat. They're bad-tempered creatures as it is. Now come. I have a surprise for you.'

As Jace led her from the terrace all thoughts of goats, sick or otherwise, fled from her mind. She struggled to keep her tone businesslike and brisk. 'Actually I wanted to talk about the party—'

Jace waved a hand in airy dismissal. 'Plenty of time for that. Now come into the kitchen—'

'Is Agathe—?'

'She went to Naxos right after breakfast for supplies.'

'Then what—?' Eleanor stopped in the doorway of the kitchen and stared at the pile of supplies laid out on the granite worktop. Muffin pans and parchment paper, cake tins and cookie cutters. Sacks of flour, sugar, at least three dozen eggs.

Everything needed for baking. A bakery.

Eleanor swallowed. 'You got this all for me?'

'I thought you'd have some time to do what you always wanted to do,' Jace said.

'Thank you,' she said after a moment. 'It's very thoughtful.'

'There are recipe books,' Jace continued, 'although I know you liked to make your own. I remember that coffee-bean cupcake—'

Eleanor smiled wryly. That, actually, had been one of her less successful attempts. She left Jace's side to move to the worktop, letting her fingers run over the gleaming, pristine surface of a never-used cast-iron pan.

'I got everything I thought you'd need.'

'Very thorough.' He must have spent several hundred dollars, Eleanor thought. Pennies to a millionaire like him, and yet...

'So I'll leave you to it, then?' Jace asked, clearly not expecting an answer. 'Enjoy yourself, Eleanor. Go to town.'

Town, Eleanor wondered ruefully as Jace left the kitchen. Where was that? And was she supposed to enjoy herself baking? She hadn't baked so much as a single cookie in ten years.

And that had been a *decision*. One she'd made with purposeful determination.

Sighing, she pulled a cookbook towards her and flipped through its glossy pages. It reminded her of the little leather notebook she'd kept to write her own creative concoctions in. It had been well loved, covered in splotches of batter and dollops of dough, filled with excited scribbles and dreams. She didn't even know where it was now.

As she perused the tantalising items detailed in the cookbook, each with its own coloured photo, she realised none of them appealed. Baking no longer appealed. The dream of opening her own bakery had died long ago, and she had no desire to resurrect it now. She had no desire to be the woman she once was: carefree, naive, *stupid*.

Eleanor pushed the cookbook away, and then, finding herself annoyed, angry and unable to articulate why, she left the kitchen with all of its ingredients and utensils and walked back outside.

The terrace was deserted and she took the stairs down to the path that led to the beach. She kicked off her sandals—the sexy little kitten heels were ridiculous beachwear—and walked towards the water. The sand was silky-soft under her feet, the salty breeze blowing her hair into tangles as she let the waves lap her feet, the water as warm and salty as tears.

She wasn't sure how long she stood there, her hair blowing around her face, the bottoms of her dry-clean-only trousers getting wet and ruined, but she knew the exact moment that Jace came onto the beach.

She didn't have to turn to know he was there, to *feel* him. She also felt his confusion, his uncertainty, perhaps even his sorrow. Sighing, she sat down hard on the sand and drew her knees up to her chest.

'Eleanor?' Jace came closer, standing a few feet away. Eleanor could see his bare, sandy feet in her peripheral vision; he'd rolled his trousers up so his ankles were bare as well. 'Is everything—?'

'I didn't feel like baking,' she said rather flatly. 'To tell you the truth, I haven't felt like baking in—in a long time.'

Jace was silent. He sat down next to her, resting his forearms on his knees. 'For about ten years?' he guessed quietly and Eleanor let out a little laugh that sounded far too bitter.

'I told you I was a different person.'

Jace nodded slowly. 'Why did you stop baking?'

'I'm not sure,' Eleanor answered. She gazed out at the waves, glittering in the sunlight. 'I haven't really stopped to analyse it, but I suppose I wanted to separate myself from the person I was because—' she let out her breath slowly '—that person didn't work.'

Next to her she felt Jace stiffen. 'What do you mean?'

Eleanor shrugged. Every conversation kept leading to this, to what had happened between them, and all the things Jace still didn't know. She wasn't ready to talk about it. She didn't want to tell Jace just how desperate, how destroyed she'd truly been after his departure. She didn't want to feel so vulnerable. Couldn't.

'After—everything,' she began hesitantly, choosing her words with care, 'I decided to change myself. Be—someone new. It just felt like something I needed to do. And like I said, I didn't feel like baking.' Baking had reminded her of Jace. Even chocolate, supposedly a woman's dearest comfort, had reminded her of Jace. She didn't eat it even now. She turned to face him. 'I know you meant well, Jace, but—but doesn't this just show how different we are? How little we know each other any more, if we ever did?' Her voice had turned ragged, edged with desperation, and she realised she didn't know what she wanted him to say. Agree or disagree? Either would bring both disappointment and relief. Both had the capacity for heartache.

'Only if baking defined you,' Jace said slowly. 'Was it who you were, or simply something you enjoyed doing?'

Eleanor scooped up a handful of sand and let it trickle through her fingers. 'Both, in a way. And neither. I think the bakery idea was a reaction to the way I grew up. I wanted to create a place that was like home, or at least the home I'd always wanted.' She gave a little laugh. 'I think I was trying to be like the mother I'd always wanted, but I'm not sure that's really who I ever was.' She turned to look at him. 'You said I've become the person I never wanted to be, Jace, and perhaps that's true. But maybe that's the person I really *am*.'

She didn't add what she was really thinking: that that was a person Jace could never want or love. She understood why she was angry now, why she was afraid. Jace might have loved the woman she once was, but he didn't love her now. Everything he'd done was to try to turn her back into that young woman—girl—and Eleanor knew she could never be her again. She didn't even want to.

'I think you're overestimating how much you've changed,' Jace said carefully. Eleanor shook her head.

'Don't, Jace—'

'I'm not talking about opening a bakery or having a high-flying career,' Jace cut her off. 'Your job isn't who you are. I'm talking about something deeper. And I think I've come to know you enough to see that hasn't changed—not as much as you think. I don't want to change you, Eleanor. I want to know you.' Jace stood up before she could reply—she didn't even know what she would say—and held out his hand. 'Come on. I can see I made a mistake buying you all those ridiculous pans. Let's do something different.'

'Okay,' Eleanor said after a moment, and, accepting his hand, she came to her feet. She glanced down at her damp, sandy trousers with a grimace. 'Whatever it is, I should probably change—'

'Definitely.' Jace scooped up one of her sandals and dangled it by a finger. 'These may do in New York, or maybe even Mykonos, but not where we're going.'

To her surprise, Eleanor felt she was smiling. She'd been dreading that conversation, yet it hadn't been as hard as she'd thought. She knew there was still more to say, but now was not the time, and she felt relieved. 'Where are we going?'

'Hiking.' Jace pulled on her hand, a smile tugging the corner of his mouth. 'It's an adventure. You must have something suitable.'

'Maybe,' Eleanor allowed, and followed him back into the house.

Ten minutes later she'd exchanged her uniform—her armour—for more casual jeans, sneakers—she had no boots—and a plain tee shirt she'd intended only to wear to bed. She hadn't dressed like this in years; in New York she'd always had to look tailored and turned out, even when off duty. Her image was part of her profession.

Now she felt both a little self-conscious and refreshingly relaxed, the sun warm on her face, her hair curling in the heat. She had not blow-dried it that morning into her usual sleek, glossy bob.

'So where are we going?' she asked Jace as he struck out down the dirt track that led in the opposite direction they'd come the night before. 'Where *is* there to go on this island?'

'I thought I'd show you the sights,' Jace replied easily. 'As few of them as they are.'

They walked in companionable silence for a quarter of an hour, the only sound the rustle of wind in the olive trees that lined the track and the shoosh of the surf on the rocks below them. Then they rounded a curve and came face to face with a goat.

Eleanor skidded to a halt, an uneasy alarm creeping over her that was a step or two down from pure panic. Jace, who had kept walking, stopped when he realised she hadn't kept up. He glanced behind him, his eyebrows arching as he saw her frozen stance.

'Eleanor...you're not scared of a *goat?*'

'Not scared precisely,' she corrected him stiffly. 'I'm a city kid, Jace. Most animals I see are safely behind cages.'

'These goats are harmless,' Jace assured her. 'I promise.' As if to contradict him, the goat bleated loudly. Eleanor jumped. She'd never thought a bleat could sound so menacing. 'Just walk past her,' Jace assured her. 'She won't even care.'

'How do you know it's a she?'

'Her name is on the bell.' He pointed to the tarnished bell hanging around the goat's scruffy neck. 'See? Tisiphone.'

'Tisiphone? Isn't that one of the Furies?'

'Spiro likes Greek mythology,' Jace said quickly. He sounded earnest, but Eleanor could see he was trying not to smile. 'Honestly, it's no more than that.'

'And not the fact that these goats might be bad-tempered?' Eleanor countered. 'Like you told me this morning?'

'Only when on boats.'

Eleanor laughed, the sound rising from within her, freeing her somehow, loosening all those tightly held parts of herself. She wasn't *really* afraid. Well, maybe only a little. But with Jace standing just a few feet away, smiling, relaxed, his eyes warm and steady on her, she felt as if she could do anything. She could certainly walk past a goat.

Taking a deep breath, Eleanor marched rather quickly past the animal, her head held high. She let out her breath in a long shaky shudder as Jace put his arm around her shoulder.

'See? Not so bad.'

'Not so cute, either,' she muttered, and he gave out a shout of laughter, pulling her close to his side.

The contact, the intimacy, both physical and emotional, stole the breath from her lungs. She had missed this so much. This closeness, this connection. This was what being known was all about: letting another person see all the silly and stupid and sick parts of yourself, as well as all the wonderful and beautiful things. All of it, everything, out there, exposed, accepted. She craved it, and yet still it scared her.

'We need to climb now,' Jace told her, sparing her sneakers a single, dubious glance before he led her off the dirt road and straight into the scrubby hills dotted with lavender bushes and the twisted, gnarled trunks of olive trees. 'Careful. You can sprain your ankle on one of these loose rocks.'

Nodding, Eleanor picked her way carefully across the tumbled boulders. She stumbled once, and Jace was there in an instant, his hand holding hers with firm tenderness. Even when she'd righted herself he didn't let go.

They walked through the hills for another quarter

of an hour before Jace stopped in what appeared to be nothing more than a rock-strewn meadow and nodded in approval. 'Here we are.'

'What—?'

'Look,' he said softly. 'Do you see?'

Eleanor looked around, taking in the scrubby bushes and twisted trees, the rocks lying in neat rows…and then she saw. Out of the wilderness there was order, the crumbling foundations of a house—many houses—hidden among the scrub.

'It was a village,' Jace said quietly. 'Two thousand years ago.' He walked over to a low wall and touched one of the ancient stones. 'I've done a little amateur archaeology, and found a few bits. Clay pots, a broken pipe. Fascinating stuff.'

Eleanor walked between two rows of walls, realising after a moment she was actually walking down a street. It was beautiful, eerie, and a little sad. 'What happened?' she asked as she stepped in the gap between two walls: a doorway. 'Why did it all fall to ruin?'

Jace shrugged. 'A flood, a famine, plague or pirates? Who knows? Something happened that forced them to flee—but I did a little research to find out where they all went.'

Eleanor turned around. 'They went somewhere?'

He nodded, smiling. 'Yes, there's an archaeological dig on Naxos that shows some of the same pieces of pottery and sculpture that were here. Historians think it's likely that they took a boat over there and started again.'

'Just like the goat.'

'Exactly.'

They lapsed into silence and Eleanor gazed at all the ruined houses, now no more than lines of stone in the dirt. She could make out an entire village now, a whole society, and she felt a strange pang of sorrow. 'And they never came back?' she asked, hearing a wistful note in her voice.

Jace glanced around at the ruins, bemused. 'So it would appear.'

'I suppose they learned you can never go back,' Eleanor said. Her words sounded heavy, too heavy, and she wondered what she was really talking about.

Jace glanced at her sharply, clearly aware of the double entendre. 'No, you can't,' he agreed. 'But you can always go forward. Like they did.' He reached for her hand, lacing his fingers through hers. Eleanor let him, let him lead her back down the hillside. 'And forward is better,' he continued lightly. 'You should see the ruins at Naxos. Now those are amazing.'

Eleanor laughed, glad the moment had been defused. She didn't want to feel sad or worried or afraid. She just wanted to enjoy being with Jace.

And she *was*. That was the wonderful thing, she thought as they walked back down the dusty road. Somehow Jace had managed to dispel her fears and her worries, and she felt carefree and relaxed as she let the wind blow her tangled hair away from her face, her hand still held in Jace's.

By the time they reached the villa, Eleanor was hot and sweaty, and when Jace suggested a swim she accepted with alacrity.

Yet as she slipped into the relatively modest one-piece she'd brought she found herself conscious of all the bare skin she was showing…all the bare skin *Jace* would be showing, and her temperature soared higher.

He was already at the beach when she arrived, a towel

wrapped firmly around her waist. Eleanor couldn't tear her gaze away from him; his chest gleamed bronze and he walked with a loose-limbed elegance, every muscle rippling with easy power. He looked wonderful, amazing, and her body kicked into gear, her heart thudding and a lazy warmth spiralling upwards inside her. He turned and smiled at her, his warm gaze sweeping over her with obvious appreciation. Eleanor's whole body tingled.

Jace stretched out his hand. 'Come on in. The water's fine this time of year.'

Despite the warmth of the sun, Eleanor thought the churning waves looked decidedly chilly. 'It's quite early to swim, isn't it?' she asked, chewing her lower lip. 'It's still only March.'

'End of March,' Jace replied and dived neatly into the water.

Emboldened, Eleanor followed suit. Seconds later she felt as if her entire body had been encased in ice. 'Aargh!' She came up gasping and choking on a mouthful of salt water. Finding her footing on the sandy bottom, she glared at Jace. 'It's freezing!'

'Bracing, we call it,' Jace replied with a grin. 'And didn't you grow up spending your summers on Long Island? You should be used to this!'

'We never swam in March,' Eleanor grumbled, but she was laughing inside, and she couldn't contain her grin as she struck out through the water to be near Jace.

They swam for nearly an hour, laughing and playing in the water, until Jace informed Eleanor that her lips were blue. Before she could form a protest, he'd scooped her up in his arms, holding her against his chest as he strode from the sea. Eleanor's laughter died in her throat as she pressed her cheek against Jace's bare, dripping chest—she just couldn't help herself—and let him take her into the villa.

He carried her all the way upstairs, to her bedroom door, and there he set her down, her body sliding sinuously against his before he steadied her on her feet. Their faces were inches apart and Eleanor didn't speak, couldn't speak. All she could do was wait, breathless, for Jace to kiss her.

He didn't. Smiling, he touched her cheek with his cold fingers and said, 'I'll see you at dinner. Seven o'clock. And don't wear another black business suit. I want it to be special.' Pressing one finger against her lips—which parted instinctively—he left.

Shivering, aching with desire, Eleanor sagged against her door. What did Jace mean by special? And why hadn't he kissed her again? It must have been glaringly obvious that she wanted him to, that she'd been waiting for him to.

Sighing, Eleanor turned inside to her bedroom. Dinner seemed ages away.

JACE STRODE FROM the villa, whistling. He felt good, relaxed, *happy*. It made him aware of how long it had been since he'd felt that way, how Eleanor made him feel that way. He'd come to Boston all those years ago looking for a new beginning, a new life away from his father and his disappointment. He'd thought he'd found it with Eleanor. And maybe he hadn't then—but maybe he could now.

This afternoon had surprised him with its simple pleasures. He'd loved being with Eleanor, loved seeing her relaxed and happy as he had been. And, he realised, he'd loved being with *this* Eleanor, the one who had grown and changed yet still had glimmers of the woman she'd once been, the one he'd known. The youthful naiveté might be gone, but it had been replaced with something better and deeper: strength, as well as courage. He admired Eleanor for both what she'd endured and achieved. And more than admired, Jace acknowledged, which made him think of a dusty trophy or distant celebrity

Yet what did he feel for Eleanor? What was he doing here? What were *they* doing?

The tuneless whistle died on his lips as he considered the question. He'd loved spending time with Eleanor, but did he love her? Was he taking her heart in his hands, only to be poised to break it?

To hurt her—destroy her, even? Again.

Or as he'd said before, could they go forward, which was so much better than going back, and build something new? Something amazing?

Jace closed his eyes. He hated that he was afraid. He wanted her so much—he'd nearly accepted her silent invitation back at her bedroom door—but he didn't want to hurt her. Yet hurt and love came hand in hand, because when someone trusted you—cared for you—you were bound, at some point, to let them down.

Or was *he* the one afraid of getting hurt?

Jace opened his eyes. He knew there were no answers. He wouldn't let his own questions—his own doubts—stop him from what was surely the sweetest time of his life. These days with Eleanor were precious, and he wouldn't waste them. He would treasure and savour them.

He hadn't kissed Eleanor this afternoon because he'd

wanted to wait, he wanted to be sure she was ready in both her heart and her body.

As his own body made the insistent ache of its unsatisfied desire known Jace hoped Eleanor would be ready tonight.

He certainly was.

THE SUN WAS just starting to sink below the sea, causing its placid surface to shimmer with golden light, as Eleanor slipped on the cocktail dress she'd brought. She glanced at her reflection, lips pursed as she wondered if she was trying too hard.

The dress was sexy, probably the sexiest thing she owned. The stretchy material crossed in front, the plunging neckline accentuating the curve of her breasts. She wore a sparkly snowflake pendant she'd found at a market stall in Greenwich Village, and it nestled snugly between her breasts. The dress's skirt ended above her knees and swirled out as she walked, the silky material caressing her bare legs. She left her hair loose and her face free of make-up; the dress, she decided, was enough.

Slipping on a pair of high-heeled black sandals, she headed downstairs to meet Jace. From the top of the stairway she saw a spill of light coming from the living room, and her heart began to beat so fiercely she was sure Jace would be able to see it through the thin fabric of her dress.

Taking a deep breath, she entered the room. Jace turned as soon as he heard her, a smile lightening and softening his features. He wore a crisp white shirt and a pair of dark trousers, both exquisitely tailored and speaking of casual elegance. His admiring gaze swept her from head to toe, a grin tugging at the corner of his mouth.

'I thought I said no black.'

Eleanor pretended to pout. 'This is hardly a business suit.'

'No, indeed it is not.' Wicked humour glinted in his eyes and Eleanor's heart picked up its pace so it felt as if it were struggling right out of her throat. She felt so nervous, and yet so alive, so happy. It was scary, feeling this much. Feeling this happy.

'I thought we'd eat on the terrace. It's a warm night.'

'Sounds good.'

'May I get you a drink beforehand?' Jace gestured to the array of drinks displayed on an antique table.

'Um, no. Just wine with dinner.' She smiled, resisting the urge to wipe her palms down the sides of her dress. Her voice sounded strained, shaky, and, seeing that Jace noticed, she let out a little laugh. 'It's strange, but I feel nervous.'

He arched an eyebrow. 'Why?'

'I don't know,' Eleanor admitted. 'I suppose…because…this all feels so new. Like we're starting over.'

'We are.' His smile warmed her straight through, and she felt her body tingle with awareness and longing and something deeper…hope. Faith. Maybe it would be all right. Maybe this could work. Maybe they *could* start over. She smiled back.

Jace reached for her hand. 'Come. Let's go out to the terrace.'

She let him lead her just as she had that afternoon. Hazily Eleanor thought she'd probably like Jace to hold her hand for ever. She loved how easily his fingers laced through hers, how protected and cherished she felt from such a small and simple gesture.

Outside a candlelit table had been elegantly laid for two; Agathe was nowhere in sight. Jace pulled out her chair and laid the heavy damask napkin in her lap, then poured her a glass of wine, the rich red liquid glinting in the candlelight. After filling his own glass, he raised it, and Eleanor did likewise. *'Opa,'* he said, and Eleanor murmured it back before they both drank.

'So what does *opa* mean?' she asked once she'd set her wine glass back down.

'I don't know if there is a direct translation, but something close to cheers or—what is it you say in English?' He pursed his lips. 'Hooray.' Jace grinned. 'But if we were going to be truly traditional, we'd throw our plates on the ground.'

Eleanor widened her eyes in mock horror. 'And waste good food?' She speared a plump olive resting on top of her Greek salad. 'I don't think so.'

'My sentiments exactly.'

The meal passed quickly as Agathe slipped in and out with dish after delectable dish, and Jace kept her wine glass amply filled. Eleanor's nerves seemed to have evaporated in the warmth of his smile, the heat of his gaze. By dessert, rich, honey-soaked baklava, Eleanor felt entirely at ease and utterly relaxed.

She propped her chin on her hands and gazed at Jace speculatively, enjoying the way the candlelight glinted on his hair and caught the silvery depths of his eyes. He lounged back in his chair, a smile curving the mouth Eleanor had spent a good part of the evening gazing at, remembering how it felt on hers.

'What are you thinking?' Jace asked, and Eleanor gave a little shrug.

'Lots of things.'

'Such as?'

She wasn't quite relaxed enough to admit the true direction of her thoughts. 'That I like olives. I never did as a child.'

'They're an acquired taste. And?'

'And what?' She was teasing, flirting, and loving it. She hadn't acted this way for so long, hadn't been this relaxed since—for ever.

'And what other things are you thinking?' Jace asked softly.

'What you're thinking,' Eleanor returned, and Jace smiled.

'I'm thinking how lovely you look tonight,' he said. 'And how jealous I am of that necklace.'

Eleanor touched the snowflake pendant that nestled between her breasts and blushed.

'So tell me what you've been doing these last ten years besides work,' Jace said, dispelling the sudden tautening moment, and, a little disappointed, Eleanor picked up her fork.

'Not much, really,' she said, spearing her last bite of baklava. 'Work has been my life, more or less.'

'And are you happy like that?' Jace asked quietly.

'Are you?' Eleanor returned. 'Because, based on your private jet and island and who knows what else, I'm guessing that work has pretty much been your life too.'

She heard the challenge in her voice, felt it in her soul, and yet it rushed out of her when Jace replied softly, 'No. I don't think I am.'

'Oh.' Eleanor sat back in her chair. 'Well, neither am

I, I suppose,' she admitted. It was the first time she'd ever said it aloud. It was the first time she'd even let herself *think* it.

'So what would you like to do, if you could do anything?' Jace asked as he took a sip of wine. 'Not open a bakery, I guess.'

'Well…' Eleanor glanced down at her plate, suddenly shy. She hadn't expected Jace to ask so many questions; she hadn't expected to tell him so much. Yet somehow, strangely, it was easy. 'I had this dream—a daydream, really—about opening a non-profit foundation. I do love planning parties, and I've—dreamed—about doing it for charity. For sick kids or poor kids who can't afford or arrange a party of their own.' She looked up, smiling wryly. 'I don't know if it's even possible, but I like the thought of providing something fun—frivolous, even— for children who can never experience that.' And then, even though it had been easy to tell him, Eleanor suddenly found her throat becoming tight and her vision blurred. She looked back down at her plate and swallowed hard. She couldn't tell Jace more than that, or just why that dream was so precious. She'd told him enough already.

She felt the warmth of Jace's hand as he covered her own. 'That sounds like a very worthwhile dream.'

'Thanks.' She cleared her throat and risked looking up. 'What about you? What would you like to do with your life, if you could do anything?'

Jace sat back in his chair; Eleanor missed the warmth and security of his touch. 'I don't know. I've been so focused on building my business—making money—that I've never thought of doing anything else.'

'And it's not as if money is a concern,' Eleanor said lightly. 'You could do anything you wanted to, Jace.'

His lips twitched and from the warm gleam in his eyes Eleanor was suddenly quite sure he wasn't thinking about business. And neither was she. 'Mmm. That's an intriguing thought.'

'It is, isn't it?' she agreed shakily. Jace's gaze didn't leave hers as he drew his napkin from his lap and tossed it on the table. 'I think we're done with dinner.'

'Yes...' Eleanor whispered. Waiting.

Slowly, silently, Jace took her hand and drew her up from the table. Still without speaking he led her back into the villa, now washed in moonlight. Eleanor's heart hammered and her throat turned dry but still she followed him without a protest. Without a word.

When she saw he was leading her to his bedroom—not hers—she gave an involuntary little gasp, no more than a breath of sound, but Jace turned around to look at her, his face a question. 'Eleanor?' he asked, and she simply nodded.

Yes.

CHAPTER TEN

JACE OPENED THE door. His bedroom was cloaked in darkness, but in the glimmer of moonlight Eleanor made out the huge shape of a king-sized bed, the sheen of a satin duvet. Jace turned to face her, and her breath caught. He looked so intent, so intense, so…reverent. And so beautiful.

She realised then just how much she wanted this. Had been waiting for this. Even so, a flutter of fear forced her to admit, 'It's been a long time…for me.'

'Me too, actually,' Jace replied, and Eleanor heard the smile in his voice.

'Really?' She couldn't keep the disbelief from her own voice. Somehow she'd imagined that Jace had been enjoying countless easy and meaningless love affairs in the last ten years while she'd had only a handful of failed relationships.

'Really,' he confirmed, one eyebrow lifting in irony. 'And just why would you think otherwise?'

She shrugged, unable to admit that when he'd left her she'd painted him as a womaniser, a user. It had made her own loss more bearable. She was still holding onto what she'd once believed—assumed—about him, rather than what she really knew. What she was beginning to believe.

'I don't know,' she admitted softly. 'Maybe it's because I can't imagine any woman resisting you.'

'I only care about one woman,' Jace replied, his voice as soft as hers, 'and she's been quite accomplished at resisting me.' His voice caught, and Eleanor heard the vulnerability. 'I only hope she doesn't resist me now.'

'She won't,' she whispered, and Jace drew her to him, cupping her face in his hands as he kissed her with a sweetness that left Eleanor fulfilled and aching at the same time.

He pulled away, and she saw the glimmer of his smile, the flash of his teeth in the darkness, as he led her to the bed. Nerves fluttered through her once more. She was ten years older and probably ten pounds heavier than the last time they'd been together. She might look killer in a business suit, but naked? She had *stretch marks*.

And Jace looked just amazing. That belief was confirmed as he shrugged out of his shirt, his chest gleaming in the moonlight. He reached for the zip of her dress, and in one simple, sensual tug he pulled it all the way down to her waist. Eleanor shrugged, instinctively, and the dress slithered to the floor. She caught her breath, waiting as Jace gazed at her; she wore only her bra and underwear.

'You are beautiful,' he whispered. 'And I've waited a long time for this.'

'So have I,' Eleanor whispered back, a laugh lurking in her voice. Smiling, Jace slipped her bra straps from her shoulders. Within seconds she was naked, struggling between self-consciousness and a confidence she wasn't sure she really felt. Yet when Jace reached out one hand and with his fingertips gently traced a path down her body from her collarbone to her hip she felt as if he were memorising the map of her body, as if he were treasuring it. And she relaxed.

Even better, Jace shrugged out of the rest of his own clothes so he stood there, magnificent and naked, before leading her to the bed. The satin duvet was slippery on her skin until Jace peeled it back, stretching out beside her so their bodies just barely touched. The only sound was their breathing. Carefully, cautiously, Eleanor laid a hand on Jace's chest. His skin was warm. God help her, she was so nervous. So afraid. And yet still so happy. It was a strange, unsettling mix of emotions.

'Don't be afraid,' Jace whispered. He brushed a strand of hair away from her face, dipping his head so his lips were inches from her. 'We don't have to do this.'

Eleanor felt the plunging sensation of deep disappointment. 'Oh yes, we do. You're not running away now.'

'I'm not moving,' Jace assured her. His lips grazed her ear, her jaw, and Eleanor shuddered. 'I'm not going anywhere,' he promised.

Eleanor closed her eyes as his lips moved from her jaw to her neck to her breast, and she added silently, *Not ever*.

Conversation became improbable after that, and then impossible. The exquisite sensation of being, not only cherished, but also possessed forbade all speech or even thought. Jace moved over her, teasing, treasuring as Eleanor's slick fists bunched on his back, her nails digging into his skin as he kissed his way up and down her body, taking his time in the most sensitive places.

Then, when Eleanor thought she could bear it no more, he rolled over so she was on top of him, his erection pressing insistently against her stomach as he looked up at her and smiled. 'Your turn.'

'My—turn?' Now she was shy. Now she had control. Slowly Eleanor lowered her head and kissed his chest. She remembered this, remembered how good it had once been between them. It had been so long, but she remembered. She moved lower, gaining confidence as she heard Jace's moan of pleasure.

Then, before she could move to the very heat and heart of him, he flipped her over and with a low growl said, 'All right. Now it's *both* of our turns.'

He entered her in one sweet, smooth stroke, and Eleanor closed her eyes, felt the surprising sting of tears behind her lids. This was so good. So right. To know and be known. To be as one.

One. One *person*.

That was how it felt in this moment of sweet union, the connection between them more intense and powerful than it had ever been, wiping away ten years of history, ten years of memories and sorrow and pain. This was more. This was better.

This really was starting over. Something new, something new and good and pure.

AFTERWARDS THEY LAY silently, Eleanor in the circle of Jace's arm, her head on his shoulder. She drifted her hand across the taut skin of his abdomen, half amazed at how comfortable she already was with his body.

'You know,' Jace said quietly, 'we didn't use protection.' Instinctively Eleanor stiffened, and Jace felt it, his arms tightening around her. 'I've never thought I had to ask this before, but is there any chance you could become pregnant?'

Such a simple question. So honest, so blunt, so basic. Eleanor swallowed. 'No,' she said quietly, her throat tight, 'there isn't. It's—taken care of. I'm on the pill.'

Jace nodded, saying nothing, and Eleanor was too afraid to ask. Did he *want* a baby, now he thought it might be a possibility? He'd implied before that his fertility wasn't a concern, yet how could it not be? How could it not be a consuming desire?

Her throat was tight, too tight, and the sleepy, sated feeling that had been stealing through her now seemed to evaporate completely, leaving her tense and wide awake. She should say something, start explaining, yet she couldn't. She was too afraid to ruin this moment, to ruin everything.

She closed her eyes, her throat still tight, the emotion too near the surface, seeping through.

'Eleanor?' Jace queried softly. She knew he could sense her sorrow. She just shook her head, unwilling to speak. In response Jace pulled away a little, but it was still too much. Her eyes were still closed, but she knew he was looking at her. Examining her. Then, with one gentle finger, he traced the silvery line of one of the stretch marks that ran along the inside of her hip. His voice, when it came, was no more than a husky murmur. 'Tell me about our daughter.'

Eleanor let out a choked sob of surprise. *'Jace—'*

He bent his head and kissed that silver streak of skin, the badge of her motherhood that never was. 'Tell me,' he whispered, but Eleanor knew it was a command. She knew he deserved to know. And, surprisingly, amazingly, she realised she wanted to tell him.

In actuality it was easy. She'd been dreading this conversation for days, weeks, *years,* but now that it was here, that Jace had asked, the words spilled from her lips. No one else knew. No one else had been there.

'She was beautiful,' she whispered. *'Beautiful.'* Jace didn't speak, but she felt the welling of his own emotional response, the swell of sorrow he must now feel that she had been living with for ever. 'Perfect,' she added. 'And I don't just mean the usual ten fingers, ten toes. Her face was like a little rosebud. A folded up, unfurled rosebud.' Eleanor could still see the closed eyes, the pursed lips. God, it hurt.

Jace's hand found hers. He squeezed her fingers tight, hard, almost hurting, and Eleanor welcomed the touch. *Touch me,* she silently commanded. *Hold me. Don't ever let me go. Not now, especially not now.*

'What happened?' he finally whispered. Eleanor shook her head, her eyes still clenched shut.

'It was her heart. It had a defect and it just—stopped. Like a clock winding down. Nothing else was wrong. She was perfect in every way. But when I went for my six-month check-up, there was no heartbeat.' She drew in a ragged breath. 'They said it happens sometimes with the Dopplers, they can't find the heartbeat. They told me not to worry—yet.' Jace squeezed her hand harder, and Eleanor squeezed back, holding on, needing him now as her anchor. 'So I had an ultrasound. I saw her there on the screen, all curled up, unmoving. Silence.' The room had echoed with it. She drew in another breath, the sound a desperate gasp. 'So I had to be induced. Like labour. Like birth—only, it wasn't. It was the hardest, loneliest thing I've ever done.'

'Was your mother there? Or a friend?'

'No. My mother was in California on a business trip

and couldn't get back. And my friends were in college. This was totally out of their realm.'

'So you went through it alone? Eleanor, I'm sorry.' His voice was rough, his hand still clenched over hers.

'The thing that kept me going was knowing I would at least see her. Hold her in my arms. That would have to be enough.' She turned to him, her hand slipping from his to rest on his chest in an act of supplication. 'And I did, and she was beautiful, Jace, oh, God, she *was*—' And then the tears she'd been holding back for far too long finally fell, streaming down her cheeks in hot, healing rivers as Jace held her and rocked her silently.

Finally, after an eternity, she drew in a gulping breath and tried, if not to smile, at least to seem calm. And she did feel calm, now. 'I've never told anyone that before.'

'No one?'

She shook her head. 'It was easier not to. But you—you deserve to know.'

'Do I?' Eleanor heard the bitter note of recrimination in his voice. 'What a bastard I was. You never—never should have had to go through that on your own.'

'It's okay—'

'No,' Jace said savagely, 'it's not okay. I'll never accept that it was.' He clasped her hands, still resting on his chest, in his, and gazed at her with tear-bright eyes. 'Forgive me, Eleanor, for what I did. For what I assumed. And most of all for how I failed you…in so many ways. I don't ever want to fail you again.'

Eleanor nodded jerkily. 'I forgive you,' she whispered, and this time she meant it and believed in it with all of her heart. When he'd asked in the park it had been too soon. She hadn't been able to let go, and Jace hadn't known enough. Now it was real. Now it was true.

Now it was good.

She rested her head against his chest, exhausted, emotionally drained, yet still sated and, surprisingly, happy. She knew there was more to say, and she felt then she had the strength to say it. Just not now. Not yet.

Jace gathered her in his arms, resting his chin on top of her head, and Eleanor felt as if she could happily stay like that all night or, even better, for ever.

HE'D HAD NO idea. No true idea of all the pain and heartache and grief he'd caused. Still holding Eleanor in his arms, Jace closed his eyes in bitter and desperate regret. He'd known he'd hurt her, but he'd had no idea of how much. No wonder she couldn't trust him.

Except now he thought she did, and the realisation terrified him. He wasn't ready for that kind of trust. He didn't know what to do with it.

He was afraid of failing.

What good are you? What use?

Jace closed his eyes. Gently he stroked Eleanor's tear-dampened hair, awed by the courage she'd shown in so many amazing and unbearable ways. She still had the sweetness of the woman he'd known ten years ago, but now with it she possessed a strength that humbled him.

Jace's heart contracted and he felt a tightness in his throat as Eleanor curled her body into his in an act more intimate than what they'd just done. She rested her head on his shoulder, her hair tickling his nose, and with a satisfied little sigh she slept.

WHEN ELEANOR AWOKE Jace was gone. She stretched sleepily before feeling the empty space next to her in the bed, feeling it in her heart. Her whole body went rigid. Where had he gone? Did he regret last night? She thought of all the things she'd done—*said*—and closed her eyes. She couldn't bear it if he regretted it.

'Good morning.'

She bolted upright, the sheet falling from her naked body. Jace sat in a chair across from the bed, his laptop opened on the coffee table next to him. He wore only a pair of jeans and his hair was a little mussed.

'Good morning,' Eleanor answered. She slipped back down under the sheet.

'I didn't want to disturb your sleep,' Jace told her, giving her that wonderful crooked smile, 'but I couldn't leave you either.'

'You couldn't?'

'No.' The word was a confession, and it was enough. Eleanor didn't want to test or examine anything; she just wanted to trust. Finally. She smiled, shyly, and Jace stood up, stretching out one hand towards her.

'Let's get some breakfast. I'm starving.'

'So am I,' she admitted and slipped from the bed.

The morning was touched by magic. When they came into the kitchen breakfast had already been laid and the aroma of fresh coffee filled the room, although Agathe was nowhere in sight. She had, it seemed, anticipated their every need and then tiptoed quietly away.

After a lazy hour or two of eating and talking—Eleanor couldn't believe how relaxed she felt—she decided she needed to do a little work at least.

She stretched and regretfully pushed away from the table. 'I should start planning this party.'

'We have time.'

'Jace, your father's party is in ten days. It takes time to order things, food—'

He shrugged, reaching for her hand. 'We still have time—'

'I need to think of a theme,' she insisted even as she let him slide his fingers along hers, his thumb finding her palm and brushing against it in a way that made her whole body faint with longing. 'I was wondering,' she continued, still determined to do some work, 'if you have any photos or things from your childhood. We could put them around—'

Jace's fingers tightened on hers for a tiny second. 'Why? This isn't my party.'

'No, but we're celebrating your father's life. Memories are important—'

'Are they?' he asked with a strange little smile and withdrew his hand.

Eleanor frowned. She knew Jace's relationship with his father must have been difficult at times; he'd indicated as much, especially in regards to his alleged infertility. Yet this was his *father,* and he was throwing a party for him. Would a photo or two really be unwanted? Resented, even?

Jace's face had gone strangely still, even blank, and Eleanor was left with the feeling that he was wearing a mask, just as she'd felt when he'd danced with her at the party. Except this was a different mask, a colder, crueller one, and she had no idea what emotion—what person—hid underneath. Even after last night and everything she had shared, she suddenly wondered if she still knew Jace…at all.

She pushed the thought away, not liking it. 'Do you have any better ideas?' she asked, lightly, and Jace shrugged.

'There is a box of old photographs up in one of the

spare bedrooms. My sister Alecia had them and she didn't have room in her new flat, so she brought them here one visit. You can take a look through them, if you like.' He rose from the table, his face still ominously blank. 'If you're going to do some work, so should I. I'll see you at lunch?' Although it was a question, Jace didn't give her time to answer. Eleanor watched him stride from the room without a backward glance, and she felt his withdrawal—emotional and physical—like a coldness creeping into her bones and stealing over her soul.

She sat in the kitchen for a few minutes, listening as a door in the distance clicked firmly shut. She thought of all the things she'd said last night. What had Jace said? What had *he* shared?

Uncomfortably, painfully, she became aware of how one-sided last night had really been…how one-sided everything had been. It seemed *she* was the only one starting over.

Sighing, trying to push away her growing sense of discouragement, she decided to find the photographs. She was used to immersing herself in work to stop the hurt. The fear. She could do it again, even if she was tired of it. Even if she didn't want to.

Upstairs she walked along the silent corridor, poking her head in empty bedrooms, peering in darkened cupboards until she finally came across a wardrobe filled with cardboard boxes. Hesitantly she pulled one out; a faded photograph fluttered to the ground and Eleanor stooped to get it. She studied the picture: five darling, dark-eyed girls, and a laughing little boy who had the same crooked smile she knew—and loved.

Loved. The word caught her by surprise. Did she

love Jace? Did she know enough about him to love him? Eleanor tried to study the question from an objective, analytical standpoint, and failed. How could you be objective about love? She knew her heart raced when she saw him. She knew how treasured and cherished she felt in his arms. She knew how happy he made her feel, and how he always could make her laugh, even when she didn't want to.

Was that love? Was it real? Could it be enough?

There were so many things she didn't know about him. His secrets. His hopes. His fears. His favorite colour.

Purple.

Her lips twitched and a smile bloomed on her face, stirred in her heart. Perhaps she did know him enough. Perhaps you didn't need to know someone's whole history to love him. And, Eleanor thought as she opened the box she pulled out, perhaps she could find out some of the things she didn't know. Yet.

She spent the rest of the morning and a good part of the afternoon gazing at a lifetime of photos. Birthday parties, Christmas dinners, lazy summer days on the beach, from round-cheeked babies to curly-haired toddlers, the scraped knees of early childhood to the gangly insecurity of adolescence. She saw Jace's early life documented in snapshots, from a laughing little boy to a solemn-eyed youth whose expression looked…haunted. Gazing at those photos, Eleanor guessed Jace must have been about fifteen. He would have already had mumps. He would have learned of his own infertility. She could see the struggle and the sorrow in every taut line of his adolescent face.

And yet the man she'd known in Boston, the student

she'd fallen in love with, had been young and laughing and seemingly carefree. Had that been a façade, just as it had been the night of the party? A pretence, to cover the pain? She knew all about that.

'I see you've found them.'

Eleanor's head jerked up and she saw Jace lounging in the doorway. From the long shadows slanting across the floor, she figured she must have been in this room for hours. 'Yes,' she said. She glanced down at the photo of Jace she was still holding: a snap of him as a teen, his father standing behind him, his hand heavy on Jace's shoulder. Neither were smiling. 'Yes, I did.'

Jace ambled into the room. 'Let me see,' he drawled, reaching for the photograph. Eleanor gave it to him wordlessly. As Jace took it his face tightened, his eyes narrowing, and Eleanor's heart ached. She thought of how much that photo revealed, and yet how much it didn't say. How much she still didn't understand. 'Ah, yes,' he said as his gaze flicked over the photo before he handed it back to Eleanor. 'You might not want to put that one on display.'

Eleanor put it back in the box. 'Jace…tell me about it.'

'It?' he repeated, the single word not inviting questions.

Still Eleanor persevered. 'Your family. Your past. Your father.'

Jace hesitated, and Eleanor held her breath. *Tell me,* she implored silently. *Open up to me like I opened up to you.* That was what love was. To know and be known. Then he gave her a cool little smile and turned back to the door. 'There's nothing really to tell. Agathe's made dinner. You haven't eaten all day. You must be hungry.'

And leaving her with more questions—and more disappointment—than ever before, he left the room.

JACE WALKED QUICKLY from the bedroom, from Eleanor. He felt restless, edgy, even angry. He didn't like the thought of her thumbing through those photos; he didn't like what they revealed. He didn't like Eleanor asking questions, wanting answers. What answers could he give? How could he tell her the truth? He didn't want her to know about his father's disappointment, how *he* had been such a disappointment.

He didn't want to be a disappointment to Eleanor.

Sighing, Jace raked a hand through his hair. Everything had been going so well. They'd both been so relaxed, so happy. Why did a few meaningless snaps have to ruin it? Why did these old feelings of fear and inadequacy have to swamp him, rushing through him in an unrelenting river as he looked through those photos, as he remembered every tiny sigh and little remark his father made, each one wounding the boy he'd been so deeply?

He wasn't that boy any more. He wasn't even infertile any more. Yet here he was, still mired by feelings of fear and inadequacy. It came to him then in a startling flash of insight that he wasn't just afraid of hurting Eleanor; he was afraid of being hurt himself.

That was what caring—love—did to you. It opened you up, it left you open and exposed, raw and wounded.

And yet it was—it could be—the best thing to ever happen to him…if he let it.

He just didn't know if he could.

As he retreated to his office, burying his thoughts and his fears with paperwork and business deals, he wondered if perhaps the past couldn't truly be forgotten. Perhaps you could never escape the old memories, fears, failures. Perhaps you couldn't start over after all.

BY THE TIME Eleanor had cleaned herself up and arrived downstairs for dinner, any remnant of the darkness and anger she'd felt from Jace upstairs had vanished. Instead he was his usual relaxed, carefree self, smiling readily, chatting easily, pouring her wine—yet Eleanor didn't trust any of it.

Now her mind seethed with questions, and they made her heart hungry and restless. Why was Jace holding back now, when she'd given him nearly everything? Was he regretting the night they'd shared, the secrets *she'd* shared? She still felt painfully conscious that he hadn't shared anything, that he was keeping himself distant and remote and *safe,* and it scared her.

Yet after dinner, when Jace led her upstairs, she didn't have the strength or even the desire to protest. Eleanor's heart bumped against her ribs and her fingers tingled where he'd laced them through his, pulling her along gently.

'Jace—'

'Is something wrong?' he murmured, lifting his free hand to brush it against her cheek. Eleanor leaned her face into the cup of his palm as a matter of instinct, a decision of need. She didn't just want him any more; she needed him. She couldn't fight this, and she didn't even want to, not for something so nebulous as a few haunted memories. Didn't she have those too?

You told them to Jace. He's keeping them from you.

She pushed the thoughts—and the fears—away and, smiling softly, followed him into the bedroom.

CHAPTER ELEVEN

THE NEXT WEEK followed the same pattern. When they weren't working—Jace on his business and Eleanor on the party—they were enjoying each other's company, in bed as well as out of it, but Jace still seemed distant to Eleanor, withdrawing more each day. His heart felt hidden, and she didn't know how to find the true him, the man she thought she loved.

Every question she asked that would make him talk about himself he deflected with a joke or a question back at her, and Eleanor realised how, in all the time she'd known him, he'd never really talked about himself. He'd never been vulnerable, or emotional, or even real, the way she had.

The inequality of it made her feel even more exposed, and terribly uncertain. Perhaps, when these two weeks were over, she would go back to New York and Jace would return to Athens. Perhaps these two weeks were all they were ever meant to have. What had Jace said? *And whatever* this *is, maybe it will go somewhere, and maybe it won't.* It was so little, Eleanor thought now. So very little, and yet she'd accepted it, fallen into his hand with the ease of a ripe peach. And that was what she felt like: something to be plucked, enjoyed, and then discarded.

With the party only a week away, Eleanor was forced

to push aside her own personal concerns for the far more pressing one of the upcoming event. She'd made preliminary orders for food, and booked a band from Naxos, but she still felt she lacked the key idea that would bring this party together, that would give it both a theme and a heart.

And Jace wasn't helping at all.

'Does your father have any favourite foods?' she asked one afternoon. She'd sought Jace out in his office, and now he barely looked up from his laptop as she waited for his answer. Last night they'd made love—at least it had felt like love—but now Eleanor thought they seemed like strangers.

'I really don't know.'

Eleanor sighed impatiently. 'What about music? Games? Activities? Help me out here, Jace. This is your father's party.'

Jace looked up, his lips pressed together, his eyes flashing. 'And, as you can probably see for yourself, I never knew my father very well. We've barely talked in fifteen years.'

Eleanor's mouth dropped open as shock raced icily through her. She'd guessed their relationship was strained, but this? Utterly estranged?

'Why, Jace? And why on earth are you having the party here if that's—'

He shrugged, the gesture one of dismissal. 'If you need details, you can ring my sister Alecia. The party was her idea—she can tell you what you need to know.'

Eleanor bit back the retort that he might have volunteered this information several days ago; she didn't want to argue. And even though they hadn't had an argument, precisely, she left the room feeling disgruntled and unhappy and heartsore.

Up in her room she reached for the phone and dialled the number Jace had given her. After a few rings a bright, cheerful voice answered.

'*Kalomesimeri.*'

Eleanor scrambled for the basic Greek phrases she'd learned in the last week. Fortunately, most people she'd dealt with had spoken English. She hoped Jace's sister was the same. '*Kalomesimeri... Mi la te Anglika?*'

'Yes, I certainly do,' Alecia replied, her voice warm with laughter. 'And you sound American.'

'Yes. My name is Eleanor Langley, and I'm planning your father's birthday party.'

'An American planning the party! How original of Jace. And I suppose he's not being helpful at all, and sent you to me?'

'That's it exactly,' Eleanor said in relief, and Alecia gave a gurgle of laughter.

'Typical Jace. So busy with his precious work. He wasn't always like this, you know.'

'No,' Eleanor agreed, then realised Alecia would have no idea she had a history with Jace. She didn't particularly want to share that information, either. 'No?' she said again, this time a question.

'No, he was quite fun in his youth,' Alecia replied dryly. 'But I suppose everyone must grow up. What is it you want to know?'

'I'd love some details about his—your—father. I found some photographs, but—'

'Oh, yes, I dropped those off ages ago.'

'Well, what is your father like?' Eleanor asked.

'And what kind of party would he like? I've been trying and—'

'Oh, you don't need anything fancy,' Alecia assured her. 'My father grew up on the docks of Piraeus. He was a street rat, and he worked his way up to what he is now. He can't stand anything ostentatious or ornate... he likes things plain. And he speaks plainly too. He can be a grumpy old bear sometimes, to tell the truth, but I know he loves us all.'

Silently Eleanor wondered if Jace knew that as well. From everything she'd witnessed so far, she doubted it. 'All right,' she said slowly, still wondering just what kind of party she could put together.

'He loves old rembetika music,' Alecia told her. 'You know the street music with guitars? He grew up on it, and he's not ashamed of his past.'

'Rembetika,' Eleanor repeated. She reached for her notebook.

'But, you know, the main reason for the party is for us to be all together as a family,' Alecia continued, her voice turning serious. 'We haven't been together properly in years—one of my sisters is usually off having a baby, or Jace can't make it because of work. Having everyone together will be the most important thing about the party—that's what really matters.'

'I see,' Eleanor said. She wondered how Alecia could speak about her father in such a warm, loving way when Jace's experience was obviously so different.

'Of course, you must have tarama salata—fish-roe salad—and loukomia, a kind of jellied sweet. They are his favourites.'

'Tarama, loukomia,' Eleanor repeated, scribbling madly. 'Thank you.'

ARMED WITH THIS new information, she set about arranging orders, finding a provider of the aforementioned food, and ringing up the band in Naxos to ask if they played rembetika. She still felt utterly out of her depth, and, combined with the sudden alienation she felt from Jace, it made her feel more like a lonely stranger than ever.

'How's it going?' Jace asked that evening as Eleanor pored over her notes spread across the kitchen table. Jace had skipped dinner, claiming work, and Eleanor had eaten with Agathe. She'd barely seen him all day, and now the moon was high in the sky, casting its lambent light across the smooth surface of the sea.

'Fine,' Eleanor replied a bit shortly. 'Your sister had some good information.'

'Good.' They both fell silent, the tension tautening between them. Eleanor turned back to her notes. 'Come to bed,' Jace said finally, his voice a lazy murmur.

She looked up, saw Jace's sleepy smile, and knew he wanted to solve everything with sex. And it would be so easy to say yes; God only knew, her body wanted to. She felt longing uncoil sinuously within her as Jace stretched out his hand.

'No, Jace.' He stilled, wary, and Eleanor shook her head. 'I...I need to work for a little while longer. The party is in just a few days.'

'Fine.' He dropped his hand, and Eleanor saw a new coolness creep into his eyes, harden the planes and angles of his face. Without another word he turned and left the room.

An hour later she came to her own bed, not Jace's, and crept into it alone. Half of her wanted to find Jace, or have him find her, yet she knew neither would solve what was—and wasn't—between them. She needed more than what they found together in bed, good as that was. She needed honesty, yet she was too much of a coward to ask for it.

THE NEXT MORNING when Eleanor came into the kitchen Jace was already there. In a business suit. His briefcase rested against the leg of his chair. Eleanor's stomach plunged icily, right down to her toes. Jace looked up from the newspaper he'd been scanning.

'Good morning.'

'Are you leaving?' Eleanor blurted, hating how afraid she sounded.

'I need to go to Athens for a short business trip,' Jace replied smoothly. 'I'll be back for the party.'

'For the *party?* You're leaving me here until the party?' She hadn't expected *that*. She hadn't expected Jace to run away again.

'I'll be back before the party,' Jace explained, and Eleanor heard a bite of impatience in his voice. 'Surely you don't need me to help plan it? I wasn't being much help, as far as I could tell.'

'No, you weren't,' Eleanor agreed, sitting opposite him. She reached for the coffee pot, then pulled her hand back. Her fingers were trembling, and she didn't trust herself to hold it. She didn't trust herself at all. 'But I didn't expect you to *leave*—' Her voice caught, and she swallowed. 'What's going on, Jace?'

He didn't answer for a moment. Eleanor looked up at him, saw his expression was guarded, wary. 'Nothing,' he finally said. 'I told you, I have some business to attend to. I'll try to wrap it up as quickly as I can.' He turned back to his newspaper, conversation clearly over.

Frustration, disappointment, and fear all warred within her, bubbling up. 'And when you come back?' Eleanor asked evenly. 'What's going to happen then, Jace? Just what is between us?'

He looked up from his paper. 'I know there are things that need explaining between us,' he said slowly. 'We're both still figuring out what's going on—and what we want.'

Eleanor nodded jerkily. It all sounded so nebulous, so nothing. 'And?'

'And I think we can have that conversation when I return,' Jace finished. 'When the party is over, and we're both more relaxed.' He glanced at his watch. 'I have an eleven o'clock meeting this morning. I should go.' He rose from the table, and Eleanor just watched him numbly. She could hardly believe he was going, that he was leaving her here alone.

'Eleanor,' Jace said quietly. He reached out and gently—so gently—touched her cheek. 'This isn't the end.' Before Eleanor could respond or even process that statement, he'd picked up his briefcase and was gone.

As she heard the front door open and then click softly but firmly shut she realised she didn't believe what Jace had said. This certainly *felt* like the end.

THERE HAD BEEN no real reason to go to Athens. Jace knew that, and the knowledge ate at him as he flew across the Aegean Sea, azure blue flooding his senses from both above and below. He was running away... again.

Yet he couldn't stay with Eleanor, couldn't bring himself to give her what she needed—honesty, trust, *love*—until he had figured out what he was going to do. If anything was possible.

If *they* were possible.

Yet if he'd thought he might clear his head away from the island and Eleanor, he was completely mistaken. The doubts and fear seethed through his mind, tormenting him here just as they had at the villa.

I'll disappoint her. I won't be enough. She'll hurt me.

Wasn't that what he was afraid of? Hurt? Opening himself up to the pain and beauty of love? He was a coward, a frightened little boy. *Life* was pain. Life was hope.

And, burying himself in work, he'd avoided truly living for far too long.

His intercom buzzed, startling him from his thoughts.

'Alecia is here,' his assistant said, and Jace sighed wearily.

'Send her up.'

'I heard you were in Athens,' Alecia said as she breezed into the room, airily trailing shopping bags. Jace stifled a groan. He loved his sister, but he didn't particularly feel like seeing her now. Alecia was far too astute.

'How did you hear that?'

'I rang that American party planner of yours and she told me,' Alecia said as she sprawled in the chair across from Jace's desk. 'She sounded terribly gloomy, Jace. Are you sure she can pull off this party?'

'Absolutely.'

Alecia's eyes narrowed and she leaned forward. 'You have quite a lot of faith in her, don't you? Where did you meet this paragon?'

'She planned a party for me in New York,' Jace replied, shuffling some papers on his desk. He could feel his cheeks warm, damn it.

'New York…' Alecia repeated thoughtfully. 'And I *did* say you've been so grumpy since you came back from there…'

'Whatever it is you're thinking, Alecia—'

'It is a woman, isn't it? It's this—Eleanor. Another American.' She shook her head, even though she was smiling gleefully. 'Well, I hope she treats you better than—'

'Don't.'

'Oh, Jace.' Alecia leaned forward. 'You know we're the last holdouts for marriage and babies and all that. I'd love to find Mr Right, of course I would, but sometimes I think I'd rather you found your Princess Charming.'

Jace's mouth twitched. 'I didn't know there was such a person.'

'You know what I mean. It's not good to be alone. And I'd love to see you settled with a wife and babies— a little girl with your eyes—'

Pain pierced Jace's shell, the armour he'd been building around his heart. He'd had a daughter. Maybe she'd had his eyes. He'd never know. 'I don't know if that's in store for me, Alecia,' he said quietly. Even if it was possible.

'Why not? Why shouldn't you have a family of your own, a family to love?'

A family. The word caught Jace by surprise, on the raw. He felt his thoughts tumble and slide, for ever shift. A family. Not a child, an heir, a dynasty. Not a thing to be obtained, a possession, a means to an end, the way his father had seen a son, a grandson.

A *family*.

In that moment he could picture it so clearly, so beautifully. He saw himself, he saw a baby, he saw *Eleanor,* and all the fear fell away.

This was what he wanted. What he needed.

He loved Eleanor. It was suddenly so obvious, so overwhelming. It wasn't a possibility or a fear or a hope. It was *real*. His love. His family.

'Yes,' he said slowly, starting to smile. 'A family.'

FOR THE NEXT few days Eleanor immersed herself in work. She was good at that, good at using it to push her thoughts and fears away. Yet overseeing food deliveries and arranging catering still left her with far too much time to remember how good it had been between her and Jace, and wonder whether it really was over. He didn't call, and although she had his mobile number she wasn't quite desperate enough—yet—to ring him, when he obviously had no interest in speaking with her.

The afternoon before the party Eleanor was in the kitchen, going over sleeping arrangements of all the guests with Agathe, when her mobile phone finally trilled tinnily. Eleanor reached for it with a sense of relief; she'd been waiting for Jace to call all this time, even if she'd pretended—to herself—that she wasn't.

'Jace?'

'Hello, Eleanor.' His voice sounded warm, and even happy, and Eleanor felt it reverberate all through her body. She closed her eyes in relief. It was going to be okay. She hoped. 'How's the party planning going?'

'Good, I think. The party is tomorrow, you know,' she added, trying to sound light but not quite able to keep the edge from her voice. 'Your family is arriving all throughout the day. When are you coming home?'

Home. She should have said *back*. Maybe this wasn't home; maybe *she* wasn't home.

'I'll be back tonight. I'm sorry I was delayed. I was waiting on something.'

'Waiting on something?' Eleanor repeated, wishing she had just a little bit more information, a little bit more insight into Jace's mind.

'I'll tell you everything tomorrow,' Jace said. 'I promise.'

Yet as Eleanor hung up the phone she knew she had no idea what *everything* was. What he'd been doing for the last few days, or the secrets of his heart that he'd been keeping from her.

Disconsolately she turned back to the to-do list she'd left on the table.

JACE HUNG UP the phone, smiling. He knew Eleanor felt uncertain and confused and perhaps even afraid, but if she could hold on for one more day—if he could—then he knew everything would work out. Everything would be perfect.

Amazing, how his doubts and fears had fallen away in light of that one word, that one great truth: family.

For years he'd simply seen his infertility as his inability to sire a child, to please his own father. He hadn't considered—hadn't let himself consider—what it really meant. What he'd really been missing. And now that it could be a reality, now that the floodgates of his heart had finally opened, he knew exactly what he wanted. A family, with the woman he loved. Eleanor.

Love had been such a scary word, a terrifying idea. Love meant you let people in, and once you did they held the power to hurt you. Hurt him the way his father had, the way Eleanor had—or he'd thought she had. He hadn't ever wanted to experience that again, and so for ten years he hadn't let anyone in. He hadn't let anyone even close.

Yet now he was ready; he was more than ready. He was eager, excited, as giddy as a child. Tomorrow he would tell Eleanor he loved her. He would ask her to marry him and they would start their future together. He could see it all perfectly bright, shining and pure.

THE DAY OF the party dawned bright, hot, and clear. Eleanor gazed out at the flat, endless blue sky, devoid of a wisp of cloud, or the telltale streak of a jet. She hadn't heard Jace come back last night, even though she'd stayed up past midnight. She wondered if he'd returned at all.

Resolutely Eleanor turned away from the window. She still had a lot to do.

Yet when she came down into the kitchen, Jace sat at the table, drinking coffee and scanning the newspaper, looking wonderful. Eleanor's heart seemed to clamber right up into her throat.

'Jace—' she managed. She felt a smile spread across her face.

'Good morning.' He turned, his eyes warm as his gaze swept over her. 'I came in so late last night, I didn't want to disturb you.'

She nodded, swallowing. 'I'm just glad you're here.'

'As am I.' He paused, and Eleanor suddenly had the feeling that he was going to say something important, maybe even something wonderful, and her heart began to beat with a fast, unsteady rhythm. Then he smiled and said, 'I just heard that my sister Parthenope will be arriving with her brood in just a few minutes. But…we need to talk. There are things I want to tell you.'

Eleanor nodded mechanically. 'Okay.' What things? she wanted to ask. Demand. Good things? Jace rose from the table and came towards her. He brushed an unruly strand of hair from her face and then bent to kiss her. His lips were cool and soft.

'I have so much to say to you,' he said, and it felt like a promise. Eleanor made herself believe it was.

Jace's family arrived throughout the day, throngs of children and five glamorous sisters who possessed the same ink-black hair and grey eyes that he did. Eleanor greeted them all, trying to keep their names straight, smiling politely and nodding her head, all too aware that to them—to anyone—she was nothing but a stranger to fade into the background. The party planner. As far as they were concerned, she had no importance or relationship with Jace at all. And Jace was kept busy with the demands of his family so that Eleanor wondered if that was indeed all she had become. The very fact that she didn't know, that she might have handed Jace Zervas her heart again only for him to break it, was more than aggravating. It was agonising.

By mid-afternoon the party was in full swing, although Jace's parents hadn't arrived. Children played on the beach and climbed on the deckchairs while their parents lounged around, talking and laughing. Eleanor went from room to room, making sure there was enough food and drink, that everyone was happy. Jace was surrounded by his sisters, although Eleanor saw him beckon her over several times. She ignored it out of some perverse sense of duty, and also because she wasn't sure she wanted to hear how Jace introduced her.

This is my indispensable party planner...

'You've done such a wonderful job.' Alecia found her in the foyer, straightening the collection of photos she'd retrieved from upstairs and arranged in a display that highlighted what looked like the happiest moments of the Zervas family. Eleanor turned from the photos. 'Thank you.'

'My father will be so pleased, when he arrives.'

'Do you know when that will be?'

Alecia gave a little laugh. 'Who knows? Soon, I hope. He's like Jace, works all the time. Those two are really far too alike.'

'Are they?' Eleanor murmured, and Alecia cocked her head.

'How did Jace hire you?' she asked, and Eleanor heard suspicion. 'An American is really an unusual choice.'

'We're—acquaintances,' Eleanor prevaricated, and a feline smile curled Alecia's mouth.

'Acquaintances? Because I was quite sure when I saw Jace a few weeks ago that he'd met a woman. And when I suggested he hire someone to plan this party, he brightened considerably.' She pursed her lips, gazing at Eleanor with open speculation. 'I wonder if you know anything about that?'

Eleanor flushed. She was not about to reveal the intimacies of her relationship with Jace, not when she still had no idea what the future could possibly hold. 'I'm not sure,' she hedged.

The front doors of the villa were suddenly flung open, freeing her from a more detailed reply.

Aristo Zervas stood in the doorway, tall and imposing, the same steely eyes as Jace's sweeping over the room—and his family—with a cold assessment. His wife, Kalandra, her dark hair streaked with grey and her face wreathed in a welcoming smile, held onto his arm.

'Papa!' Alecia hurried towards her father, enveloping him in a hug, which he returned stiffly. Two of Jace's other sisters, Parthenope and Elana, followed suit. Jace, having entered the hallway upon his father's arrival, didn't move. Eleanor could feel the tension thrumming through him; she felt it in herself. It was as if they were waiting for a storm to break.

'Jace.'

Jace inclined his head. 'Father.' He drew himself up. 'There's someone I want you to meet.'

It felt unreal when Jace reached for her, a dream, as his arm curved around her waist. 'Father, this is Eleanor Langley.'

Aristo moved towards them. His silver gaze turned on Eleanor, took her in from her toes to the top of her head in one arctic sweep. Jace's arm tightened around her protectively. 'She is very important to me, Father.'

'Is she?' The corner of Aristo's mouth twitched up in what could be a smile or a sneer. Still spinning in shock, Eleanor managed to find her voice.

'It's nice to meet you, sir.'

Aristo nodded gruffly, then turned back to his son. 'So you were able to come to my party. Not working for once.' He paused, meaningfully. 'I don't know why you work so hard. Who are you going to pass it all on to?'

Eleanor flinched, the barb hurting her as well as Jace, although his face remained expressionless. He'd lived for years with remarks like that, she supposed. She felt nerves dance low in her stomach, a reminder that she hadn't told him everything. Yet when could she confess? What if it changed things? How could she *still* be such a coward, even now with Jace's arm around her, when he'd told his own father how he felt?

She is very important to me.

'The work is its own reward, Father,' Jace replied evenly. 'Now I'm sure you want to greet everyone else.' With a stiff nod, he drew Eleanor away from Aristo and everyone else crowding the foyer. Eleanor was barely aware of where he was going until they were on the terrace, and Jace tugged her towards the beach.

'Jace—the party—'

'They can do without us for a while. I've been trying to talk to you all day. I'd almost think you were avoiding me.'

'No—' Eleanor protested, half-heartedly, for she knew she had been avoiding him. Even now she was afraid, and it wasn't just because of what Jace might say, but what she *hadn't* said.

The sky was lavender, darkening to violet, the first stars visible on the horizon. Despite the lingering warmth of the sun, the wind that blew off the water was chilly. Eleanor kicked off her sandals as Jace led her across the beach; the sand under her feet was silky and cool.

'I'm sorry I didn't speak to you sooner.'

'It's all right.'

Jace turned back to her. The wind ruffled his hair and in the growing darkness Eleanor couldn't quite make out his expression. 'I'm sorry about my father as well. As you can see, we don't have a very close relationship.'

'Has it always been that way?' Eleanor asked.

'Ever since the mumps made me infertile.'

'Why would that affect your relationship so much?' Eleanor burst out. 'It wasn't your fault—you're still his son—'

He sighed and raked a hand through his hair. 'After five girls, my father's every hope was realised when I was born. I was the apple of his eye for the first fifteen years of my life—I still have those memories to hold onto.' He paused, and Eleanor thought he might stop, he might distance himself again as he'd done in the past. Then he continued more quietly, 'And my father's every hope dashed when I contracted mumps, and the doctor told him I would be infertile. All his life he'd worked hard building up an empire to pass onto his son, his son's sons. The Zervas dynasty.' He gave a short, humourless laugh. 'His dreams of a legacy—a dynasty—were destroyed that day. I was as good as useless. And he never let me forget it. And the damnable thing is, the doctor was *wrong*.'

Eleanor swallowed, her throat tight. 'Oh, Jace—'

'It doesn't matter any more.'

'But it does, of course it does—'

'No,' Jace corrected softly, 'it doesn't. I don't care what my father thinks of me, Eleanor. I'm not living my life to gain his approval, although perhaps I was doing that subconsciously by working so hard. Who knows?' He spread his hands wide. 'But when I went to Athens I realised what I wanted out of life.'

Her breath dried in her throat. 'What do you want?'

'You. I love you.'

Eleanor blinked back tears. She hadn't expected this; even now, when everything seemed so good, she hadn't expected so much. Honesty and love. Everything. 'I love you too,' she whispered.

'I went to Athens because I was scared,' Jace said. 'Everything was happening so fast, and I didn't know if I could handle it. I told myself I was afraid of hurting you, but I think I was really afraid of being hurt myself.'

'I know what that feels like,' Eleanor whispered.

'Ever since my father learned I was infertile, I felt like a failure to him, and in a way to everyone. I wasn't good enough on my own, just as a person. So I had ways of keeping people out. To keep from letting them in.' He gave her a crooked smile. 'I'd play the clown or just act like I didn't care. If you act like you don't care, perhaps you really won't.' Eleanor nodded, understanding, recognising those self-protective tendencies in herself, and Jace continued, his voice roughening with emotion, 'But that changed when I met you all those years ago. I let *you* in. With your kindness and your laughter and even your chocolate cupcakes. I couldn't help myself. And when I thought you'd lied to me—it hurt. So much. I was wrong, and yet I let that hurt fester inside me for years.' He shook his head in sorrowful acknowledgement of the years they'd lost. 'Then I found myself letting you in again, here on the island, and it scared me. I didn't want to be scared, but I was, and that's why I went to Athens. I needed to sort things out in my own mind—'

'And you did?' Eleanor broke in. 'You seem different now. More…sure.'

'I am.' Jace drew her to him, his hands smoothing the hair away from her face. 'I'm so sure, Eleanor. It was hell without you, even for just a few days, and it made me realise—actually my sister made me realise—'

He paused, laughing a little, and Eleanor prompted, 'Your sister?'

'Funny, the power of just one word. Family.' Eleanor

shook her head, not understanding, and Jace reached for her hands. 'She told me she'd always wanted me to have a family, and I'd never thought of children that way before. I haven't thought of children at all for so long—I've even avoided my own nieces and nephews. But when I thought of my own inability to have children, it was simply as a failure. A disappointment to my father, to myself to provide an heir. To continue the dynasty. I never thought of it—of them—as a *family*.'

Jace was smiling, yet each word was a hammer blow to Eleanor's heart. Her throat was too tight to speak, so she just shook her head. She should have told him. Of course she should have told him. Why hadn't she? How could she have allowed it to come to this?

'But in that moment,' Jace continued, squeezing her hands, 'I realised what I wanted. What I've wanted all along, even though I've been fighting it. Love is scary, Eleanor. You know it as well as I do. Hope is dangerous.'

Oh, God help her, Eleanor thought numbly. So scary. *So* dangerous. She just shook her head, helplessly, as a tear slid down her cheek. In the darkness she didn't think Jace saw it.

'I want us to be a family, Eleanor,' Jace said softly. 'More than anything. And more than just that—I want us to spend the rest of our lives loving each other. I want to see you hold my son—or daughter, I don't care which. I never thought I could have it, I didn't even dare dream—but now I know it can be, and I want it all with you.' The moon slid from behind the clouds and in its silver rays Eleanor saw the tender, triumphant smile on Jace's face. She felt him slip his hands from hers as he dropped to his knee and fumbled in his pocket for what could only be a jewellery box.

'This is what delayed me an extra day in Athens. I wanted it to be perfect. It was my grandmother's, but I had the stone reset.' With a growing sense of unreality Eleanor watched as Jace stretched out his hand, flicking open the box. The moonlight glinted off the most amazing, enormous antique diamond she'd ever seen. 'Eleanor Langley, will you marry me?'

CHAPTER TWELVE

ELEANOR GAZED AT the ring, gazed at Jace and all the love shining in his eyes, and shook her head helplessly. 'Oh, Jace.'

'Is that a yes?'

'I never expected this,' she began, helplessly, for her mind was seething with disappointments and fears. She really *hadn't* expected this. She'd been living in the moment, enjoying Jace, loving him, yet her stupid, stubborn mind had pushed away any real thoughts of the future. Conveniently ignored the realities—the truths Jace had given her tonight. She'd wanted his honesty, yet now that she had it she realised it changed everything. For the worse.

'Eleanor?' Jace asked softly. 'What's wrong?' He stood up, reaching out to brush her damp cheek with one thumb. 'You're crying.'

'I'm overwhelmed.'

'That's okay.'

She nodded, jerkily, because it wasn't okay. It wasn't remotely okay. Of course Jace wanted children. A family. She'd been a blind fool, a willingly blind fool, not to see it—think it—before now. She hadn't wanted to think it. Hadn't wanted to be completely honest with Jace. She'd lacked—still lacked—the courage.

Jace wanted children—a family—and there was no

way she could fit into that happy picture. Just as there was no way she could take that dream away from him now.

'Jace!' One of his sisters—Eleanor thought it was Parthenope—called from the terrace. She didn't understand the Greek, but the gist was all too apparent. They needed Jace back at the party.

'Photographs,' he explained tersely. 'I don't—'

'No. Go.' She shook her head, wiping her wet cheeks, and tried to smile. 'This is a party, Jace. We can talk—later.'

'Come with me. You should be in the photos—'

'No, no one even knows me yet. Besides, I need to check on the food. I'll see you later.' Already Eleanor was walking away from him, reaching for her sandals, not looking back.

'Eleanor,' Jace called, and she heard the frustration and confusion in his voice, sharpening her name. 'Whatever this is, it can be solved.'

Two more tears slid down her cheeks. Jace knew her, understood her so well. But he didn't know the most important thing, the thing she'd kept hidden. Shame roiled through her. All this time she'd been berating Jace for hiding his heart from her, yet now he'd been as honest and vulnerable as he could be, and she was the one who was still hiding. Who had been hiding all along, and who was still afraid. And some things couldn't be solved.

JACE SMILED FOR photo after photo, his cheeks aching, as his gaze swept through the foyer. Where was Eleanor? She'd disappeared from the beach after his proposal—and that hadn't gone nearly as well as he'd expected.

In the moment when he'd shared that precious dream, Eleanor had looked devastated. And Jace had no idea why.

Frustration gnawed at him and as the photographer readied for yet another snap he broke away from the gathered crowd of his family.

'Jace,' Alecia protested, but he just shrugged as he strode away.

'I need to find Eleanor.' A feeling of foreboding stole over him as he walked through the empty rooms of the villa. He shouldn't have waited for so long.

HALFWAY TO THE kitchen the answer had presented itself, so apparent, so appalling. She needed to leave. She needed to leave *now*. If she stayed, she'd tell Jace the truth; he'd wrestle or coax it from her, and she didn't have the strength to resist. Then she would have to face the unbearable pain of his rejection, or, perhaps worse, the stoic acceptance of her own inadequacy. She couldn't do that to herself. She couldn't do it to Jace.

Yet she was on an island, and the only way off was Jace's private jet. Where could she hide? How could she escape? The questions pounded inside Eleanor's mind; she forced all other, more rational thoughts away.

Then Eleanor saw the lights of a farmhouse glimmering in the distance, heard the clank of a bell, and the answer came to her. *Of course.*

Hurrying upstairs to change into more serviceable clothes, she grabbed her purse and her passport—leaving everything else—and desperate, despairing, headed out into the night.

The track winding through the hills was lit only by a pale wash of moonlight, and Eleanor stumbled on the rocks and twisted tree roots. Even as she ran she knew she was being foolish. Yet she also knew she couldn't stay and watch Jace's dream be destroyed—or hers. She couldn't face him. She couldn't face the truth because it hurt too much.

Love hurt. Why had she risked it again after all these years? Why had she risked it with *Jace?*

After a quarter of an hour she found the farmhouse, huddled among the hills, and knocked on the door. Behind her somewhere a goat bleated.

The man who answered the door was grey-haired and a bit scruffy, a mug of coffee held in one hand. He stared at her blankly.

'Yassas...parikalo...' Every Greek word evaporated from her frazzled mind as she gazed at him helplessly.

'I speak English,' he told her, the words flat and a bit rough.

'Oh, thank God. I need to go to Naxos—on your boat—'

'At this hour?' He looked appalled.

'It's important—*please.*'

Something must have convinced him—the wildness in her eyes, or perhaps the ragged edge fraying her voice, or the wad of crumpled twenties she thrust at him. In any case, he shrugged, nodded, and said, 'I get my boots. It take twenty minute in the boat.'

Eleanor sagged against the doorway in relief.

A few minutes later they were on the beach, the sea no more than a sound in the darkness, the waves crashing onto the shore. The wind whipped Eleanor's hair into tangles, and she stared at the forlorn little rowboat dubiously. It really was small.

Good Lord, what was she *doing?*

'Is this the only boat?'

The farmer shrugged. 'The motorboat, it belong to Zervas.' He gazed at her speculatively, and Eleanor wondered how much he knew. How much he'd seen over the last few weeks.

For a moment—a second—she hesitated, wondering if she could go back to the villa and explain everything to Jace. Maybe he would understand. Maybe it would be okay. *Maybe.* She couldn't trust a maybe, she couldn't act on it. The fear that had taken root in her heart was too pervasive, twining its poisonous tendrils around every thought, every dashed hope.

She couldn't go back. She couldn't tell Jace the truth. She couldn't bear to see him disappointed, the dream he'd shared with her dashed, destroyed—

I want to see you hold my son—or daughter, I don't care which. I never thought I could have it, I didn't even dare dream—but now I know it can be, and I want it all with you.

Eleanor closed her eyes, a tiny sob escaping her. Her shoulders shook.

'You get in the boat?' The farmer held onto the edge of the boat with one work-roughened hand as the waves churned around him. Eleanor could hardly believe what she was doing, yet she was too afraid to face the other choices.

Coward. You're more of a coward than Jace ever was.

'Miss?'

'What the *hell* do you think you're doing?'

Eleanor froze. She felt a hand clamp down hard on her shoulder and whirl her around. Her purse slipped onto the sand. 'Jace—' She was glad to see him, even now, after everything. Glad and relieved, even though Jace looked livid. His angry gaze travelled from her to the man waiting with the boat. He spoke a few terse phrases of Greek and numbly Eleanor watched the man give a philosophical shrug before hauling his boat back onto the beach. Within seconds he was gone, swallowed up by the darkness.

Jace's gaze snapped back to her; his eyes were the colour of cold iron. 'So what is this?' he growled, his voice low and savage. 'Some kind of *revenge?*'

'Revenge?' Eleanor repeated blankly. Then her eyes widened and her heart squeezed painfully, robbing her of the ability to talk or even think—

'So I can see how it feels,' he sneered. 'Is that what this was all about, Eleanor? Coming to Greece, being with me, everything—' His voice tore and he pressed his lips together, his eyes flashing furiously.

He was *hurt*. She'd hurt him with her disappearance, of course she had. She'd hurt him more than the truth ever could.

She really was a coward.

'It's nothing like that, Jace,' she whispered, but he didn't look as if he'd even heard her. 'I swear to you, this wasn't revenge!' Her voice rose in a yelp as he pulled her along the beach, driven by his own fury and pain. 'Where are we—?' She stopped talking when she realised Jace was not in a mood to listen.

He led her away from the beach, back towards the villa, its lights twinkling in the distance. Eleanor thought of facing all his family there and closed her eyes. She couldn't. 'Please,' she managed. 'Can't we just talk—alone?'

'Oh, yes,' Jace growled back at her. 'We are most certainly going to talk.'

Yet he didn't speak again until they'd reached the villa; he stalked past it, with Eleanor having no choice but to follow, her arm still in his strong grip.

'Where are we—?'

'Where do you think?' he snarled. 'Where you want to go.'

Eleanor didn't understand what he meant until she saw the dull gleam of his private jet under the moonlight.

'Jace—'

'Now.' He let go of her and she stumbled at the sudden release. The jet loomed in front of her, large and silent. 'I rang the pilot—he lives on Naxos. He should be here in a few minutes.'

Eleanor gazed at him, his face hard and implacable, his eyes two narrowed slits. 'Why—?'

'He can take you wherever you want to go. Back to New York, I presume.' He drew a breath, and it hitched. 'You didn't have to take a leaky rowboat in the middle of the night if you wanted to leave me, Eleanor. All you had to do was say.'

The look of naked pain on his face was too much for Eleanor to bear. She wrapped her arms around herself even though the wind wasn't that cold. What a mess everything was. What a mess *she'd* made. 'I don't want to leave you, Jace,' she whispered.

'Considering I found you trying to board a boat to Naxos without a single word of explanation, I find that hard to believe.'

'It's true.'

'So did it feel good? To leave me hanging, just as I

did you? No word, no warning? Had you been waiting for this?' Each question was a laceration on her soul.

'*Stop*. I wasn't—I didn't mean—'

'Excuses!' Jace slashed a hand through the air. 'Well, get on the plane, Eleanor. Nothing is stopping you now.'

Anger made her straighten her shoulders and cross the tarmac to poke a finger in the hard wall of his chest. 'I'm not getting on that plane, Jace. Not yet, anyway. Yes, I ran away. But I didn't mean to leave you—it wasn't some kind of revenge—' Her voice broke on that horrible word, but she forced herself to go on. To confess the truth. 'It was fear. I was *scared,* Jace. I still am.' She dropped her hand and bowed her head, felt the sting of tears in her eyes.

Jace was silent for a long moment. 'What are you afraid of, Eleanor?' He didn't sound angry any more. He didn't sound particularly forgiving, either. Eleanor looked up. This was the hard part. This was why she'd run away in the first place.

'Afraid of disappointing you. Of you leaving me or staying with me for the wrong reasons—I'm not sure which would be worse.'

Jace's expression didn't change, didn't soften. 'Now it sounds like *you* don't trust *me*. Why would you disappoint me? Why would you think you could?'

She drew a breath and met his gaze directly. It hurt. 'Children, Jace,' she said rawly. 'I should have told you before. I meant to tell you—when we—that first night—' She swallowed, her throat so very tight. 'But I couldn't. I was too scared. And then everything was going so well, and I just stopped thinking about it because I wanted to be happy—for a little while—and you said you didn't even think about children very much—'

She let out a hiccuppy sob, knowing she wasn't making sense yet unable to speak the bald, bare truth.

Jace's face darkened, his mouth thinning. 'What are you saying?'

'I can't have children.' She saw the shock slice across his features, his mouth dropping open before he snapped it shut.

'What—how—?'

'It's not a fertility issue. I mean, I can *have* children, but—' She closed her eyes. In her mind she saw the ominous, silent screen of the ultrasound. Saw her baby's heart stilled for ever. 'Our daughter had a heart defect. She was never going to develop properly, never going to live. After—afterwards I had some testing done.' She opened her eyes. 'It's genetic, Jace. A genetic defect. A fluke, inexplicable, but there it is. And the doctors said it's seventy-five per cent likely that the same thing will happen again—with any pregnancy of mine.' She swallowed past the aching tightness in her throat. She couldn't bear to look at Jace now, so she gazed into the distance, in the darkness. 'I can't live with those odds. I can't—I can't go through it again. Not ever.'

Jace was silent for a long moment. Too long. Eleanor had no idea what he was thinking, feeling. She didn't think she could bear to know. She stared down at her feet, her vision blurring. Somewhere she found her voice. 'I should have told you, I know. I felt like you weren't being honest with me, but I was the one who was hiding something. I'm sorry.' Jace still didn't say anything, and it was the second time in her life that silence had been such an endless agony. She drew a long, shuddering breath and turned towards the plane. 'I...I guess I'll go now.'

'*Eleanor.*' Before she could even move, Eleanor found herself surrounded by Jace, his arms around her, pulling her towards his chest. She was enveloped so her cheek rested against the warmth of his neck, her body tucked wonderfully into his. 'I'm sorry,' he whispered. 'I'm so sorry that you had to go through that.'

'I'm sorry I can't—'

'I'm sorry too,' Jace whispered against her hair. 'I won't pretend that I'm not, or that it doesn't hurt.' Eleanor swallowed a sob, and she felt Jace's fingers brush at the tears that were sliding coldly down her cheeks. 'But, Eleanor, *Ellie,* when I told you I wanted us to be a family... I wasn't—it's more to me than just having a biological child. Yes, I expected that, because I didn't know it was any different for you. But do I want a biological child—an *heir*—more than I want you? No. Never.' His arms tightened around her, drawing her closer to himself. 'God knows, my father drilled into me the utter importance of an heir, and it wrecked a good part of my life. Do you think I want to make that mistake again?'

Stunned, Eleanor couldn't answer. Couldn't think. She only hoped. Jace brushed the tangled curls away and cupped her face in his hands in a gesture so tender and achingly sweet that she couldn't keep the tears from slipping down her cheeks. He brushed at them with his thumbs.

'I was telling you I love you, Eleanor. *You.* All of you. Neither of us is perfect or even whole. We have scars. Memories. Regrets. But that's what love is. What it *does.* It takes everything—good and bad—and lives with it. Accepts it. Do you accept me with all *my* failings and mistakes?' He smiled crookedly, and Eleanor let out a sound that was half-laugh, half-sob.

'Yes.'

'And I accept you. I'm not walking away because of this. I'm not walking away at all.' He brushed his lips softly across hers. 'Not this time, and not ever.'

'But I don't want you to be disappointed,' Eleanor whispered, her throat still so very tight.

'Disappointed?' Jace's face seemed to crumple for a moment. He shook his head. 'I always felt my father was disappointed in me for not giving him what he wanted, the ability to continue our precious bloodline. I lived with that shame for years, and I don't think I ever escaped it until I met you. You made me feel whole. Happy. Like the man I was supposed to be, the man I wanted to be.'

'But if you want—'

'I want *you*. And I could never make any person— and especially you—feel that way. And I could never be disappointed in *you*. Yes, I'm disappointed that we won't have a child that is part of both of us, but that's something we can deal with together. I love you, Eleanor. I love your strength and your courage and your humour and your smile—everything. I love that you have drawn out the best in me, made me the man I want to be. No matter what, you couldn't disappoint me.'

Eleanor could hardly believe what he was saying. She wanted to trust it—with all her heart, she wanted to trust it—yet even so she still felt the lingering traces of fear.

'You told me—you wanted children. That's a big thing, Jace.'

'I want a family. Our family. And there are more ways than one to have children. We could adopt—do you want children, Eleanor?'

'I never—' She swallowed, nodded. 'Yes.'

'Then we'll work it out. We'll face it together. And whatever disappointments come our way, we'll face *them* together.' He drew her to his chest once more. 'That's what I want more than anything. No more running away, for either of us.'

Eleanor slipped her arms around Jace's waist, felt the warmth and strength of him and knew she had it—him—to lean on for now, for ever. The thought was amazing. Humbling too. 'No running away,' she repeated softly. She leaned back so she could look up at Jace and see the love and tenderness turn his eyes to soft grey. 'I love you, Jace. I'm sorry I panicked. I shouldn't have run away. I just couldn't think—'

'I know how that feels. But from now on we think. We talk. And we do it together.'

She nodded, unbelievably happy, incredibly grateful.

Jace turned back to the track that led to the villa. 'I'll have to ring the pilot and tell him the flight is cancelled.' He nodded to the house, glimmering with lights ahead. 'I'm afraid we have a good deal of explaining to do. My sisters are going to be seething with questions.'

'That's okay.'

There was a lot ahead, Eleanor knew. A lot to figure out. Work, children, family—even what continent they were going to live on. Yet as Jace led her back to his home she realised she wasn't afraid any more. She was excited. Whatever lay ahead, they would face it—together.

* * * * *

We hope you enjoyed the
THE BILLIONAIRES
COLLECTION!

If you liked reading these stories, then you
will love **Harlequin® Presents®**.

You want alpha males, decadent glamour and
jet-set lifestyles. Step into the sensational,
sophisticated world of **Harlequin® Presents®**,
where sinfully tempting heroes ignite a fierce and
wickedly irresistible passion!

Enjoy eight new stories from
Harlequin Presents every month!

Available wherever books and ebooks are sold.

SPECIAL EXCERPT FROM

 HARLEQUIN®

Presents

*Harlequin Presents welcomes you to the world of
The Chatsfield—synonymous with style, spectacle…
and scandal! Read on for an exclusive extract from
Lucy Monroe's stunning story SHEIKH'S SCANDAL.
The first in an exciting new eight-book series:*
THE CHATSFIELD.

* * *

THE guest elevators at The Chatsfield hotel in London were spacious by any definition, but the confined area *felt* small to Aaliyah Amari.

"You're not very Western in your outlook," she said, trying to ignore the unfamiliar desires and emotions roiling through her.

"I am the heart of Zeena Sahra—should my people and their ways not be the center of mine?"

She didn't like how much his answer touched her. To cover her reaction she waved her hand between the two of them and said, "This isn't the way of Zeena Sahra."

"You are so sure?" he asked.

"Yes."

He laughed, the honest sound of genuine amusement more compelling than even the uninterrupted regard of the extremely handsome man. "You are not like other women."

"You're the emir."

"You are saying other women are awed by me."

She gave him a wry look and said drily, "You're not conceited at all, are you?"

"Is it conceit to recognize the truth?"

She shook her head. Even arrogant, she found this man irresistible, and she had the terrible suspicion he knew it, too.

Unsure how she'd got there, she felt the wall of the elevator at her back. Sayed's body was so close his outer robes brushed her. Her breath came out on a shocked gasp.

He brushed her lower lip with his fingertip. "Your mouth is luscious."

"This is a bad idea."

"Is it?" he asked, his head dipping toward hers.

"Yes. I'm not part of the amenities."

"I know." His tone rang with sincerity.

"I don't do elevator romps," she clarified, just in case he didn't get it.

Something flared in his dark gaze and Sayed stepped back, shaking his head. "I apologize, Miss Amari. I do not know what came over me."

"I'm sure you're used to women falling all over you," she offered by way of an explanation.

He frowned. "Is that meant to be a sop to my ego or a slam against it?"

"Neither?"

He shook his head again, as if trying to clear it.

She wondered if it worked. She would be grateful for a technique that brought back her own usual way of thinking, unobscured by this unwelcome and unfamiliar desire.

* * *

Step into the gilded world of THE CHATSFIELD!
Where secrets and scandal lurk behind every door...

Reserve your room in May 2014!